We Shall Be Monsters

We Shall Be Monsters

A Novel

Alyssa Wees

 New York

For Kara, my sister and best friend
(Sorry, no centaurs in this one either)

PART ONE

1

Gemma

MAMA BRUSHED MY HAIR AS I SAT ON A WOODEN stool in front of the mirror, my little television on mute in the corner, flickers of color and light. The hairbrush was old—a century old at least—and one of her most prized antiques: sterling silver, with thick yellow bristles like discolored teeth. I knew from experience that the handle was always icy cold, like it had just been plucked up from the snow, but Mama wielded it as if it didn't bother her at all. It was the only item she ever refused to sell, even though she kept it in the display case at the back of the shop when she wasn't using it on me. Like a secret, except it wasn't a very good one. It was dull in the light, even after a polish.

Outside, the clouds gathered like blackbirds on a branch, peeking through the window. Staying very still, I told Mama about the boy I'd seen at the edge of the woods. But she said never mind, it was only a shadow. And I said no, too pale to be a shadow, and she said well, a rabbit then. Bigger than a rabbit I said, and she said hush. She always said that. *Hush.* So all I was left with was the sound of my pulse in my ears and the bristles of the brush scraping my scalp and my big eyes blinking back at me. I sat very straight and pressed my knees together, waiting for it to be over.

Hush.

I was not allowed to go into the woods because of the mon-sters there. I did not know what a monster was, only that it would eat you. I did not want to be eaten, but I did so long to see a monster. Mama would not describe them to me. *Night-mares,* she said. *You will have nightmares if I tell you. You will never sleep soundly again.*

I tried to tell her that I had nightmares anyway—sometimes before I went to sleep—even though I had never encountered a monster. I would be lying there in the dark and all of a sudden my heart would begin to beat very fast, like a fox's in an open field. I would sweat a little and my breath would come in gasps. And I was so afraid, only I didn't know what I was afraid of. And that fear was worse than the fear of any monster, because I could see nothing, hear nothing, feel nothing there to frighten me. At least, if I saw a monster, I would have a reason to be afraid.

Hush.

I did see a boy in the woods, though. He was a fairy prince.

I knew he was a fairy because his voice was like the leaves curling in autumn, and I knew he was a prince because of the crown he wore in his thick brown hair, laurel and berries as red as fresh blood. Also, he told me so.

He told me lots of things.

Like how to tell a poisoned apple from a sweet one, and how to call the sun to come out after the rain. How to listen to the trees when they are telling you that an enemy is approaching, and how to waltz in the high fairy fashion: swept up on the wind, gliding a foot or more above the earth. He taught me the proper way to curtsy before his mothers—the queen and queen consort of the fairies—for when he brought me before them one day, after he had vanquished the dreadful Hunting Beast who was known for snatching fairies from their beds and eating them up. With his silver sword and scabbard, with his shield blessed by the Great Ensorceller of the Hidden Moon, he would slay the monster that came hunting every few years and free his people from its chilling shadow. And once he had completed this most noble quest—*One cannot become a hero without a quest,* he told me—there would be a feast that lasted days and weeks held in his honor, and there would be song and dance and revelry that would light up the night sky as if it were noon.

He told me I was invited.

But—he was still very young, and still in training, hardly older or stronger than me, a girl of only twelve. And a half.

"We must be patient," said the fairy prince to me, "because I will have one chance to kill the Hunting Beast, and only a fairy full grown can do it."

Only a man and not a boy, even if he was a prince.

"And why must *you* be the one to slay the creature?" I asked, my heart tangling with fear for him. "Why can't the queen do it, or the queen consort? Or some other soldier so you don't have to be in such danger?"

The fairy prince smiled in that way that made me blush down to the bones in my cheeks, and he leaned very close. "Because it was foretold, my Gemma Belle, that the very bravest of knights would vanquish the Beast once and for all, and the stars are never wrong."

(He called me that, his Gemma Belle, and it was like a song.)

I didn't tell Mama any of what he told me, because I wanted these things for only the two of us to share, the fairy prince and me. But I didn't like keeping secrets from her. It made my throat feel raw. So that night while she brushed my hair, I told her just a little: just about the fairy feast we'd have after he slayed the Hunting Beast, about the music and the dancing. I longed to show her how I would curtsy before the queen and her wife but she would not stop brushing my hair.

"And why must the prince murder this Hunting Beast?" she

said when I was done, in a tone like anger but under glass, and I didn't like that, that one word she'd said: *murder*. The fairy prince never said murder, only slay or kill or defeat—a noble act, heroic. Murder, though; it made me shiver and made my heart spin, dizzy.

"It is for glory," I said, and that was a word I liked: *glory*. Glorious. It had a melody. I let myself get wrapped up in the fantasy—fairy lights and vining waltz, the prince's hands in mine. Mama watched me in the mirror, watched me with her wide, dark eyes that could see things about me that even I didn't know.

"Maybe," I began, but my voice was too loud and I lowered it. Quiet, like sleep. "Maybe, at the end of the night, he will even give me a . . ."

"Kiss?" Mama finished for me, just as the brushing was done. One hundred slow strokes, no more and no less. My scalp tingled where the bristles had been, almost painful. Mama looked at me in the mirror, unsmiling, tilting her head so that a lock of dark hair fell across her neck like a wound.

"Go to bed now," she said. "Sleep well."

Strange, but when she said these words I was still sitting on the stool, and the next moment I was tucked up in bed. I didn't remember the walk up the stairs or changing into my nightgown, or even laying my head upon the pillow. I had been telling her something while she brushed my hair—but what?

That night I dreamed of berries, crushed underfoot.

IN THE MORNING, a Saturday, I wanted to play outside but Mama said no, she needed help in the shop. I asked if I could go out after and she said all right in a voice like melted ice. Dusting, it was always dusting she wanted me to do, and there was always so much of it. In school, while I sketched a boy

wearing a crown of leaves in the margins of my Lisa Frank note-
book, we learned that dust was just bits of skin that flaked and
fell off and settled on every surface because it had to go *somewhere*. I only wished it could float on the air and stick to the
ceiling instead, and we could all just politely agree to look anywhere but up.

Mama sat in her office with the door open, going over accounts. It seemed like she was always going over accounts, or
else talking on the telephone in a tone too whispery for me to
understand. I grabbed the duster off the hook in the closet and
then I started in the back of the store and worked my way forward. The space was so crowded it was easy to miss things, and
I carried around a small stool to stand on when items were
piled too high. There was little logic in the way the shop was
arranged: tea sets next to crumbling texts next to bookshelves
next to an armoire. A hand-cranked Singer sewing machine, a
chess table, even an ax, slightly rusted around the edges. There
were hats with feathers around the brim and ribbons to tie it
under the chin, and a line of dress forms wearing lacy, yellowed
wedding gowns. I noticed patterns in the dust, thicker in some
spots than in others, the places I had missed the week before.
Sunlight came through the windows, but it was the kind of sun
you only see and don't really feel on your skin, an empty glimmering. I moved through the shadows, shivering.

I saved my favorite room for last. The Glass Room, I called it,
because there was nothing else in it but mirrors and chandeliers. Blackout curtains were closed tightly over the windows so
that the chandeliers could shine. And the many mirrors of all
shapes and sizes reflected the glow, intensifying it: like standing
close to the stars, or inside a kaleidoscope. I used to think it was
a portal to some strange and radiant world.

Lots to dust in the Glass Room—each arm of the chandeliers, plus the frames of every mirror. There was a smell of lav-

ender about the room, dying petals, delicate rot. My arms were aching by the time I was done, and I wished—I *wished!*—that I had a little brother or sister to help me with the cleaning. Or to do *all* the cleaning, since I would be the elder and could boss them around. I would make them do the dusting while I went to play in the woods in secret.

I was not allowed to go into the woods because of the monsters there. I didn't know what a monster was; only that it would speak in a voice like deep water, and when it called to you it was impossible to resist. Always in shadow, one step ahead, so that you were achingly curious to draw closer, to see what couldn't be seen. With its voice of black and blue, the monster would lead you into the dark and into the trees, a long and winding way, far from home and far from the path. And those who wandered never came back.

Fearsome, Mama said, meat of nightmares, ax on bone. But, oh—how I longed to go and see it for myself! To know just what it was that separated a fairy tale from every other kind of story we tell. I begged her to show me but she wouldn't—or couldn't—and sometimes, in my most secret heart, I suspected that this was because she was making it all up. Like how pirates bury their heaps of jewels and coins on a faraway island and then draw dragons on the maps between here and there so that others would be too scared to sail through those waters and steal their hidden treasure.

What was Mama hiding in the woods?

An hour passed, maybe two, before every mirror and chandelier was crystal clean, spilling diamonds of light on the dark wood floor. A treasure room, with my face reflected all around and everywhere. I smiled at myself, a many-headed creature, and gave a little bow. *Ta-da! The End.*

I heard something then. A voice, Mama's, and at first I

thought she was singing to herself . . . but no. There was another voice, one I didn't recognize right away. Soft, but echoing.

"Virginia, I may have a lead."

The shuffle of papers, a chair scraping against the floor. A little cough, a clearing of the throat. Mama took her time to reply, but when she did her voice was steady. "You're sure?"

"Yes. I should know in a week."

"My God," Mama murmured, and I tiptoed out of the Glass Room, edged around an armoire, and crouched behind a bookshelf filled with tomes so old that they didn't even have titles on the spines. In my hands I clutched the duster like a magic wand; my fingertips felt numb. I had thought there was someone in the office with her, but it was just the telephone on speaker.

"My God," Mama said again. "This could all be over in a week?"

I peeked around the bookshelf and saw that she had her hands over her face, bony fingers splayed wide, but then she peeked through her fingers and saw me. She clicked a button to take the phone off speaker and I shrank back behind the bookshelf, feeling like a naughty sneak.

"Thank you, Clarice," she said formally, and the name sent an ache through my heart. She was talking to my grandmother, who I hadn't seen in a while because she was "away." Almost a year, actually. When I asked Mama where she was and when she was coming back, all she said was *hush*.

Already my grandmother's face had started to fade from memory, but I still remembered that she wore dark pink lipstick and that her smiles were like shooting stars: rare and hard to find but dazzling if you were lucky enough to catch one. She was always touching the top of my head, pressing her cold palm to my crown and asking wouldn't I like to cut my hair so short

I would never need to brush it? Easier to take care of it that way, she said, but I didn't want to look like a boy and also what would I do with all my scrunchies if I couldn't wear a ponytail? I told her this and she nodded like she understood. *All right.* But later she'd ask again.

With my head bowed, I slunk back to the Glass Room.

Mama found me there. I pretended to dust a gilt-framed mirror I'd already dusted, acting like I'd been there the whole time and not spying on her phone calls. I prepared to be reprimanded and sent to my room.

"Not finished yet?" she said behind me, and when I turned at the lightness of her tone I saw a laugh in her eyes that didn't quite make it out of her mouth—but still, it was there, shocking me into silence. "Go ahead, Gem. Go outside and play."

I SAT ON the little stool in front of the mirror, but my legs felt wobbly—even while sitting—and I couldn't stay still, knees bouncing and fingers twitching. Mama saw and paused with the bristles of the brush still buried in my hair, my scalp tingling where it touched. I had lost track of the number of strokes.

"Gemma, is something wrong?" said Mama, and I couldn't tell her about this afternoon—it was too frightening to recall!—but I *had* to, didn't I? It made me so itchy to keep secrets.

"Well," I said, trying so hard to hold it in. But it was like trying not to throw up when you had a bellyache. The story came pouring out, burning my throat and my mouth. *"Well."*

Earlier, after I had dusted the Glass Room and Mama let me play, it had started to rain. Just a drizzle, but I didn't like to be wet and I didn't want to go back inside where there was little to do and the air was so stuffy and smelled like all the old objects filling it from floor to ceiling. A curious thing, though: It was raining in the backyard, but it wasn't raining in the woods.

There was sunlight slanting between the branches, and as I crept closer to the trees, I could even feel its warmth. Would it be so terrible, really, to seek shelter under the leaves, just for a moment? *No,* I decided as I inched beneath the nearest tree, careful to keep an eye on the house behind me. *It's only for a moment.*

But I was in the shade, and it was a little cool there. Only a few feet into the woods there was an unfiltered patch of sunlight—close enough to where I stood that I would still be able to see the house, so what was the harm in venturing just a little farther inside? I stepped over a fallen log and went to stand in the sun, the light like a warm hand on my forehead, comforting and bright. The rain continued to fall beyond the edge of the woods, coming down harder now. I backed up a few more steps, just to be entirely clear of it. Then I heard a sound behind me—a sniffling, snuffling sort of crying—and I thought I'd better follow it to make sure whoever was making it was okay. That was permissible, wasn't it? Noble, even? To want to help someone who might be in distress? It was a quest, and quests were always noble. (Someone told me that once, but I couldn't think who.) I left my patch of sunlight, my heart thumping like a rabbit on the run, and walked swiftly toward the sound.

It had not seemed far away from where I had been, but I walked for a very long time, the sniffling growing louder but its source still out of sight. Finally I came to a clearing, where a very thin woman knelt with her head bowed among some of the strangest things I had ever seen growing in a twisted kind of garden. Short plants with leaves that looked very much like skin; a bone-white tree bearing brown fruit that twitched as if from muscle cramps. Mushrooms oozing something sticky and rust-colored from their caps; flowers whose petals opened and closed as if with a breath. When I peered closer, I saw that there was a tiny pair of brown lungs attached to each stem, filling and deflating and filling again. Trying to ignore what looked very much like dirty human fingers protruding from the dirt not three feet away—roots, they were only roots, I told myself— I called to the woman, whose face was obscured by a thick curtain of long white hair glowing almost blue in the light.

"Hello, are you all right?" I had not thought to be afraid, despite the strangeness of the scene, but then my whole body went cold and clammy and I realized that maybe I had made a mistake. I stayed to the side of the clearing, not daring to enter it, and I was glad I didn't when the woman looked up, her hair falling away and over her shoulders. She was beautiful, but in the way a poisonous flower is beautiful, or a brightly colored venomous snake—beauty to tempt and reel you in before it strikes. I had the peculiar sense that she wasn't young even though her skin was smooth and unlined. Her eyes were silvery-blue, her lips red and curved into a smile like a cut.

"Oh, what a pretty little thing you are," she said, her voice as high and clear as a songbird's trill. "How old are you, my sweet?"

"Twelve," I said, mesmerized. I had the uncanny feeling that I was talking to a phantom, something dead that had come back to life. "And a half."

"A wonderful age, your magic just about to bloom." She closed her eyes and sniffed the air. "Yes, yes—I can smell it on you."

"I don't have magic," I said, taking a step away.

"Not yet, but it will come. The Touch is like that; it develops in adolescence." The woman's eyes flashed gold and red before settling back into silvery-blue. "You're a bit skinny for my tastes, but I like the bones best anyway. Ah, how fortunate for you that I already ate."

A whistle came from somewhere beyond the clearing and I jumped. I was already stepping backward, readying to run as far and as fast as I possibly could. The woman stood, unfolding, and she was taller than any woman I had ever seen—a giantess looming over me even though she was still halfway across the wide clearing.

"My handler's coming. Don't tell her you saw me." And with that, she sped off on her very long legs into the shadows of the trees. I wasted no time in leaving that strange place behind, sprinting back the way I'd come, and I did not stop even as the rain hit my face and soaked me to the bone.

Now, in the mirror in my room above the stool, Mama's face had gone pale as I told my tale. She started brushing again, faster, my head pulling back as the bristles caught on the tangles and knots. My brain went cloudy, sort of numb, and in another moment I couldn't remember what story I'd been telling, or if I'd been saying anything at all.

"You are not to go in the woods, Gemma," Mama said, and she sounded very far away even though she was only right behind me. In the mirror, I watched her touch a spot on her chest, pressing a fist to it like it hurt. "How many times must I tell you that?"

"What?" I said, confused, because I had never been to the woods. I had never seen a monster there, though I so desperately wished to meet one. How would I know what makes a hero if I'd never encountered a hero's equal and opposite?

"*Hush*. Go to bed now," Mama said in a much gentler voice. And I was so tired suddenly, so tired I almost didn't make it to bed before I fell asleep. Before that one word echoed across my dreams.

Hush.

2

Virginia

I T WAS THE MOST UNPLEASANT PART OF MY DAY, brushing my daughter's hair. It shined in my hands; it gleamed. Surely, if this were a fairy tale, a rich king would fall in love with such hair and never look her in the eye all her life; all he would see is the dark of it, the fantasy. One hundred perfect strokes, and I could think of nothing but one hundred ways she could lose her heart. And with every stroke my chest burned, the magic extracting a bit of my vitality in exchange for the memories I stole. It was unpleasant, yes, but I had to do it. It was best to forget the woods and everything in it; best to shove the monsters back into the shadows where they belonged. Best that she never think about monsters at all. Some memories were too frightening to keep, and so I unburdened her of them, one brush stroke at a time. One hundred to complete the spell and a fog came over her eyes, creating gaps in her mind that she would fill in time with pleasanter things: open skies and summer nights, future hopes and dreams. No fear, and no nightmares either. The spell wouldn't last forever—like all things, even magic decays—but it was enough for now.

Then I put her to sleep.

These evening hours were mine, the only time that no one expected anything of me. I put the hairbrush away under the glass in the counter at the back of the shop, where everyone could see it but no one could buy it. A private little joke, it was my way of taunting the one I had stolen it from. I weaved between the tight aisles of antiques, some of them scuffed and some pristine: end tables and china cabinets and Tiffany lamps, carved music boxes and Madame Alexander dolls with bright painted cheeks. A jewelry box, a grandfather clock, and everywhere dust and creaking.

Precious, pretty things. All of it useless to me.

I stepped out onto the porch and closed the door behind me with a faint ring of the bell. The air was cool and damp, and when I passed from the wooden stairs to the grass a shiver went through me. The road beyond was silent; it was the one good thing about living at the end of a dead end. The only ones who used this road were the ones that came to my shop. A lonely life, but I preferred it. And I wasn't alone, not really. There was my daughter, and the wind, and the birds.

And the woods.

It was dark as I walked around the side of the house. Cold, pale stars. Fading moon. And all around me trees, quiet and still.

On the east side of the house I stopped and looked up to Gem's bedroom. I made sure that there was no light behind her curtain, that she was asleep and not simply staying up past her bedtime to read. She did that sometimes—flashlight under a blanket, an old copy of *The Perilous Gard,* dog-eared and beloved—and she thought I didn't know. I didn't mind it really, as long as she was not by the window.

But the room was dark and I exhaled, goosebumps rising along my spine. I faced the woods and waited.

There was movement at the edge of the trees, but it was too far away to see clearly. I stood still and didn't take my eyes from the spot.

I was lost in these woods once, years ago. There was this game I used to play with myself after my mother forbade me from entering the woods but before I believed that monsters were real. (Before she *made* me believe.) How far was I willing to go to defy her? How far into the trees and the shadows between? I would step backward into the brush, feeling behind me with my feet and my hands, careful not to stumble on a fallen branch or boulder. Eyes fixed ahead (behind?), locked on the clean light at the edge of the woods from which I had come and to which I would return, always in sight even as I ventured farther.

When I could no longer see the light I would pause a moment, listening to the scurry of small creatures, the whisper of leaves, the reverent song of the birds. I imagined a monster creeping closer behind me, dark eyes glowing hot in its head, knees bent backward, and pale skin draped like curtains over the ribs. The Hunting Beast as I pictured him to be, a creature straight from a nightmare. And when the thrill of it—the terror—became too much, I released my breath and ran fast along the path I had made, bursting back into the bright. I would laugh, high and shaky, triumphant over the "monster" I had thwarted, unable to follow me and capture me there in the daylight.

A game of imagination, it was always the same. Until the time I took one step too many and felt a cold hand wrap around my wrist.

Now, standing beside the white brick Victorian where I had lived all my life, I watched through the dark as a figure stepped from the trees. Too tall to be a man, too thin to be anything else. Gnarled hair, twisted antlers like a deer's, a slow and scraping gait. Precisely the monster I had envisioned, once upon a time, now here in the flesh. Not the Hunting Beast—I'd never actually encountered *him,* only his victims—but a monster all my own. He crossed the distance between us, but before he was even five feet past the trees, I was walking—then running—toward him to meet him halfway. Just like the night before, and the night before that, stopping just short of running into his arms the way I would have done if he had not forbidden it. The last time I'd tried—years ago now—my cheek had been pierced by the thorns that jutted from his shoulders like those on a rosebush, and the skin of my arms had been scraped from moving against the roughness of his own, coarse and furrowed like bark. So we didn't embrace, but still I reached for his hands and he reached back, the heat of him flowing into my palms, close to burning. His long fingers curled gently around mine before squeezing once and letting go and my heart fell. Too brief a touch. It wasn't enough—it would never be enough—and I didn't care if it hurt me. I just wanted to be near him.

As if sensing my longing for more, he took a step back, cloaked all in shadow except for the eyes that glowed, and waited for me to say that I had found the thing that would save him. *A mirror to show one's true reflection.* We had two and a half years left, but the days were slipping away so fast. So little time before he became a monster in full, in his *soul.* So little time until he would hunt me down and eat my heart, whether he wanted to or not.

"Not yet," I whispered, and he bowed his head. I wanted to keep from crying, so I made my voice hard instead. *"Not yet."*

IT WAS THE longest week of my life, the one after the call from Clarice. That infernal woman—maybe she *would* be the one to save me, after all. Isn't that, really, what mothers are for?

By the end of the week I couldn't concentrate on anything,

least of all Gemma, who had been particularly restless of late. She flitted around the shop after school, rearranging the dolls on the shelves or playing chess with an invisible partner. She probably sensed that something was amiss, but I had kept her in the dark all her life and she would just have to stay there a little longer. Her father and I had agreed long ago that she would never know him until the curse was broken.

Soon, I thought. *Please, God, let it be soon.*

"What's that you're singing?"

Early Thursday afternoon Gemma came into my office, where I sat with a sheaf of papers in front of me, though I couldn't remember what they were for. I had been humming a tune without realizing. A sad, soft one that often escaped me when I tried to focus on it too intently. Behind my eyes, I couldn't stop seeing the beast at the edge of the woods. The song was for him. For us.

But I couldn't tell Gemma that, so I didn't tell her anything.

"You're home early." The shop was dim, but when I looked at the clock, it was only a little past noon. My hands shook as I gathered my papers into a pile. "Has something happened?"

Gemma tipped back on her heels and shrugged, her hands clasped behind her back. "Well. No."

I waited.

"Well. Yes." The pink ribbon I'd tied in her hair that morning to match her dress had come undone, the bow unraveled and the knot precariously loose. "I felt like I was going to throw up all morning, so I went to the nurse's office and she sent me home. That's all."

"You're sick?" I reached across the desk and lay my hand against her forehead. The skin was cool and dry. "You don't look sick to me."

"I feel much better now that I'm home. I just needed some

fresh air." As if to demonstrate, she took a deep, noisy breath. "See? No more bellyache."

"Hmm." I propped my chin in my hands as I pretended to consider her predicament. I knew she was lying; I just didn't know why. "What do you think made your belly ache in the first place? Was it something you ate?"

"No." She shook her head so hard the ribbon fell out of her hair and onto the floor. "Not that."

"Did something at school upset you?"

"Nuh-uh. No."

I waited, and after a moment she sighed.

"Really, Mama," she said, her gaze sliding away from mine. "Just a little stomach bug or something."

I looked at her a moment longer, but her attention was already drifting elsewhere. I relented with a nod and she smiled in a way that made my heart tight and cold. Otherworldly, that mouth of hers. I knew where she got it, that shimmer and gleam, and—my God—it wasn't from me.

"The school never called me." I took an idle sip from the mug balanced near the edge of my desk. The coffee had gone cold and I wondered how long it had been sitting there. I didn't remember making it. "Wait—how did you get home?"

Gemma put her elbows on the desk and leaned across toward me. "They did call, but you didn't answer. Carly's mom was finished with lunch duty, so she drove me home."

Had I really been that wrapped up in worries about Clarice's lead that I hadn't heard the phone ring?

"Well, I'm glad Carly's mom was there to help." I realized I was angry, but not at Gemma. At myself. I should have been there for her and I wasn't.

I should have ended this nightmare that my life had become years ago—for both of us—but I hadn't. It just went on and on.

"Why don't you go lie down in your room until I call you for dinner?" I said. It was a dismissal and it sounded like one, but I needed a moment alone.

Still that fey smile of hers; it turned slick and sly. "Can I go outside instead?"

I almost laughed and let her. How bold she was to ask such a thing after the day she'd had. But if I capitulated she would think it was perfectly fine to lie about a bellyache so that she could ditch school and come home. Besides, she was just as likely to wander into the woods as to stay on her swing like she was supposed to. Really, she was only in a little danger in the woods, what with her father watching out for her, but it would make the brushing of her hair in the evening that much more difficult for me if she did. It was not a simple magic, the stealing of memory.

"No," I said, bringing a hand to my chest and tracing the raised, white line that crossed over my heart. Not a wound, or a scar—a *crack*. Bloodless but sore, throbbing in time to my pulse. The magic lived in the hairbrush, but it was I who paid the price. "To your room."

"Can I at least play my Game Boy?"

"No. If you're sick, you need to rest."

She slumped her shoulders as she glided out of the room but didn't argue with me. A moment later I heard her on the stairs, and her bedroom door closing with a soft click. She was a good girl, despite her best efforts to go feral. Sometimes I wondered why I bothered getting in the way of it. Sometimes I wished I'd been as feral as her.

The phone rang then, jarring me. I wanted to pick it up and slam it down again, assuming that it was Gemma's principal following up, but I forced myself to take a breath and answer it. My heart skipped faster at the voice on the other end.

"It will arrive Saturday," Clarice said without even a greeting, her voice clipped and professional. "My contact is quite certain this is the one you seek."

My throat was so dry that I couldn't speak even if I could think of a single rational thing to say. *Saturday*. Only two days away.

"Gigi?" I could almost feel the brush of Clarice's breath on my cheek through the phone line. "Are you still there? Did you hear me?"

She knew I had, but I confirmed it anyway. "Yes," I said, my hand sweating around the plastic curve of the phone. "Yes, and—and thank you."

Crackling silence gathered down the line. She paused, and I thought she might tell me she loved me. I held my breath to hear it, but instead she said to be careful.

It was close enough.

"I am sorry your nightmare has run so long, and I am sorry to have been yet another monster in it."

There was a pause, and then the click that let me know she had hung up. I held the phone to my ear for a few seconds more before I gently placed it back in its cradle. Then I put my head down on the desk and wept.

IT'S AN OLD story, isn't it? A mother tells her daughter not to open the door at the end of a long dark hallway and the daughter does it anyway because she'll never really believe her mother until she experiences the room beyond it for herself. The daughter steals the key and unlocks the door she is not allowed to unlock and whatever she finds behind it marks her in some way, indelibly. One day she'll tell *her* daughter not to look behind the door, but even as the new mother warns her young daughter, she knows there's no place on earth she can hide the key where her daughter can't reach it eventually. A truly curious girl will never cease her pursuit of the unknown, even if it means she must whet her fingernails to bloody points as she claws her way through the wood of the door. And so the cycle continues, because simply telling someone about a monster isn't enough. The same way you can explain that a stove is hot, but you won't really know until you've been burned. And it's terrible, isn't it? We try so hard to save each other when really we're doomed from the start.

On Friday, I needed to get away from the woods. Not far, and not for long, but well out of sight. It was my own curse of sorts that I couldn't sever myself from the woods entirely, and nor could I live inside them fully. Long ago my mother had made a little monster of me—of my heart—when she brought me to the woods to see its wonders, only to decide later, when I was eight years old, that it wasn't worth risking its horrors. I had danced and dined with the queen of the Forest Fey; I had gone to the panpipe concerts of the satyrs in the fairy village square, and played hide-and-seek with a group of fairy children in the woods. And in all that time I hadn't felt anything but safe and full of stars, drunk on magic and stumbling with wonder. So when my mother first forbade me from it, I didn't understand the frightening things she said about monsters. How could I? I had never met one. I didn't *believe* in them.

Oh, Gigi. I'll show you if you don't believe me . . .

I learned that fear is stronger than anything else. Even joy, even love.

In the morning, after Gemma had left for school, I drove into town and bought a latte from the tiny café on the corner across from the only movie theater around for miles. There were a million little towns just like this one all across Michigan, with Kilwins fudge shops and novelty souvenir stores, ice cream parlors with a dozen different flavors, clean family motels with bright beach themes and an outdoor pool with a slide. Slightly grubby but still charming, beset with tourists every summer. Though we were more than an hour away from either of the Great Lakes, it was considerably less expensive to stay here than to book a hotel closer to the coast, and besides, we had our own small lake nearby that was good for camping and fishing (or so I'd been told). I didn't mind the tourism, as it drove business to the shop. But here on the sun-touched streets, crowded even in the earliest days of the offseason, I felt crookedly out of place. Among but not part of, lonely but not alone. Still, being there reminded me that there was more to life than monsters. There was sunshine and warm beverages and the laughter of strangers; errands and tip jars and cars braking too suddenly. *Normality.* If I couldn't be part of it, at least I could observe it. I sat on a bench on the sidewalk beside a single maple tree, feeling steadier in my proximity to root and bark and leaf, and drank my latte slowly, every drop too hot on my tongue.

"Virginia! Hello!"

I startled at my name and didn't recognize the speaker: a woman wearing a dark suit and a large red purse hooked over one shoulder, waving to me as she waited for a car to pass so that she could cross the street. It took me a moment to place her, and by the time she reached my bench and sat down beside me I had only recalled her surname—Clemens—and that her daughter Carly was in Gemma's class. Her husband owned a car dealership, I was almost completely certain.

"Hi," she said, a bit out of breath. She set her purse on her lap and rummaged through it until she found a compact mirror and a tube of Revlon lipstick. "So good to see you. I've been meaning to talk to you for a while now. How are things? Is Gemma all right?"

"Why wouldn't she be?" Between my confusion—why would this woman I barely know want to speak with me?—and a sudden stab of dread—what did Gemma have to do with this?—my voice sounded hard and unfriendly. I watched as the woman reapplied a pale shade of pink to her lips, her eyes laser-focused on her reflection.

"Oh?" She clicked the compact closed, blinking in genuine surprise at my vehemence. "Carly told me that Gemma is being picked on in school. Says she tells these fabulous stories about that little strip of woods out near your house. Says there are fairies or elves or some such thing living in the hollow of every tree. Sounds quite cozy to me! Carly, for one, admires Gemma's wild imagination, but some of the other children . . . well, *don't.*"

Little strip of woods. I almost laughed. But that's the thing about enchanted places: They're never quite what they seem. Perhaps from the outside the woods appeared small—*cozy,* even—but once you were inside, the trees went on and on. Mercilessly.

The rest of her statement sobered me, though, and I tightened my grip around the cup I held in both hands. How many times had I spoken with that clearly incompetent principal about the snide remarks, the little shoves Gemma received in the hallways, the tugs on the end of her braid? And yet, nothing at all had changed.

Buck up, my own mother would have said, giving me a stern nod. Not in expectation that I would fight my own battles, but that I would quietly weather the storm. *Remember what I told you about sticks and stones?*

I wouldn't tell Gemma to simply keep her head down. I would go to the school and speak with the principal in person, demand *discipline.* Perhaps I could not prevent my daughter from being eaten by monsters one day, but there was no way I'd let her be picked apart by creatures without any claws at all.

"I wish I still believed in fairies," Carly's mother said with a sigh, dropping the compact and lipstick back into the bottom of her purse. "To be young again, to believe that there could be something so pure and *good* in the world."

"Fairies aren't good," I said without thinking, and the woman smiled at me sideways, as if we were suddenly in on a joke together.

"Oh, you too? Well, I see now where Gemma gets her stories."

"We choose which stories to tell our daughters," I said, looking down at the cup in my hands, "but not which ones they'll believe."

The stove is hot. The monsters are hungry.

I'll show you if you don't believe me.

"True enough." My unsolicited companion hefted her purse onto her shoulder and stood. "Well, I have to get going. It was nice talking to you, Virginia. Please let me know if there's anything Carly or I can do to help Gemma, or you."

"Thank you," I said, and truly I didn't resent the offer, only that it was warranted. As I threw my empty cup into the trash bin and walked back to my car, I wished—not for the first time—that I could have confided in someone like Carly Clemens's mother, and not because our daughters happened to be in the same class, but because we were actually friends. But it was difficult to grow close to someone who would not understand who you were and where you had been. Maybe she did want to believe in fairies, at least in the abstract, like ghosts, but that didn't mean she would *actually* believe if confronted with evidence of them. *A little strip of woods.* I shook my head, and now, alone, I really did laugh. A laugh that would have become a cry if I let it.

My only solace was this: Once the curse was broken and my monster was human again, I wouldn't need friends. Or lattes, or benches on a busy street to ground me. I would have *family*—Ash and Gemma and me—and we would carve our own path through the woods, find a place where we could be safe. And though there were only rumors of the existence of the *eastern* edge of the woods—the woods being only a bridge to other lands that lay beyond it—I knew that together we could emerge out the other side, into a world that was perhaps kinder, where the monsters were scarce but the magic plentiful. Where there would be other people like me, a sanctuary for those living with one foot in fairyland and the other in reality. Where there would be a school for Gemma that taught math and science, but also how to break a witch's curse. The woods couldn't possibly go on forever. Eventually, out of the dark, there *would* come a light.

THE PACKAGE ARRIVED the next day, just as Clarice had promised. It was smaller than I'd anticipated, and perfectly round. I was careful not to look at its surface as I unpacked it on my bed with the door firmly closed, unwinding layers of tissue paper and bubble wrap, leaving it facedown. I closed the shop and sent Gemma outside so I could be alone.

A mirror to show one's true reflection. I had sought it half my life, contacting museums and antiques dealers and private collectors around the globe, but it was nearly impossible to locate an object of magic in a mostly mundane world. A world where bad dreams ended for good when you opened your eyes, and anything unordinary was whispered through a story. I had come close, but the mirrors I'd procured in the past were never quite right.

I had an entire room in the shop dedicated to my failures, the one Gemma called the Glass Room. The chandeliers were innocent of all of this, but at some point every one of the mirrors had filled me with hope, and every one of them had shattered it.

This time would be different. It *had* to be. All that was left was to wait until dusk.

3

Gemma

SOMETHING WAS WRONG WITH MAMA.

All day she'd been agitated, pacing and sitting and standing, even dusting—*my* job—and finally, after the third time I asked her what was up, her eyes sparked and in a strained voice like she was trying to speak through a spike of pain, she told me to go outside and play. I obeyed and went straight for the swing, the one Mama had strung for me from the thickest branch of the ancient oak that grew apart from the woods, as close to it as I was allowed to go. The ground rushed up and then away again beneath my dangling feet as I pushed myself higher into the air. Hazy afternoon, the sky so low I could breathe the clouds, thin golden light falling on folded leaves. My hands burned against the fraying rope that tied the swing to the tree, but I didn't let go or loosen my hold, didn't let it stop me from closing my eyes and pretending I could fly. Wind in my hair, sky in my throat. But when I opened my eyes I nearly cried to find that I had gone nowhere; I was no closer to anywhere I wanted to be. Gradually the swing came to a halt, and that was when I looked to the woods with longing.

There was a boy at the edge of the woods. I didn't notice him at first because he wore a cloak like a shadow and he stood as still as a tree, watching me. I didn't move or even blink—afraid he'd disappear, only a figment of my imagination. The boy took shape slowly in the darkness: here an eye and there a lock of curling hair; another eye and jaw and chin, shoulders, hands, and knees, until he was all I could see, so distinct and sharp and angular that it seemed silly—impossible really!—that I could ever have mistaken him for anything but a thing of flesh and bone like me. I stared at him, and he at me, and then something wonderful happened: He smiled.

"Gemma!" he called, in a voice that opened like the first bloom of spring, and I started violently. How did he know my name? I held tight to the ropes of the swing and did not let go. The boy spoke again, and this time he sounded almost cross. "Gemma, come here! What are you doing gaping at me like an owl at the sun?"

I shut my mouth at once; I had not known that I was gaping. It was only that he looked so familiar, like a character in a movie or a model from a magazine. He was a stranger, and yet he knew my name, and though I knew I should probably turn right around and dart into the safety of the house, bright curiosity burned like an itch on my heart. Leaving the safety of the swing I took one step toward him and the woods behind him— one step and another step until I was nearly halfway there. It wasn't so far to go, not really, but oh!—I couldn't do it. Mama might kill me or—worse—never let me even slightly near the woods again, not even to the tree with the swing. Duster in hand, I'd be consigned to clean forever, until I was nothing but dust myself. I glanced back to see if she was watching at the window, but the house was dark and shut up tight. Still I went no farther, and the boy crossed the distance to stand right before me.

"Why do you not come?" he demanded, and I merely blinked at him, still mesmerized by the way he had walked, as if he did not touch the ground but merely skimmed it. His cheeks glowed rose and gold, and I began to suspect, in my secret heart, that he was a fairy and a prince. He wore a crown of silken leaves, and held his head so high.

"How do you know my name?" I said, and shivered. My sweater and leggings weren't really warm enough in the chill of the woods' shadow, and I tried very hard not to shiver again before this boy who had come from deep within the darkness to shine his dazzling light on me.

"Silly Gemma Belle," he said, with a laugh like a clear sky. He took my hand without asking, as if he'd done it many times before. His skin was soft and warm, and in an instant I was no longer cold. "Why do you always say that? Come now, I have something to show you."

He tugged me toward the trees, heedless of my whirling heart and the deliberate dragging of my feet.

"I'm not allowed to go into the woods!" I cried, and the boy stopped, but never relinquished my hand. He was several inches taller than me, and his clothes were like those I had seen only in illustrated tales that told of long-ago princesses trapped between walls made of night. Tight pants and a velvet tunic, a cloak that fell to his knees.

"Because of the monsters there," I added quietly, my eyes on the ground. A cluster of dark birds nearby took to the air and plunged into the woods. With his other hand, the boy gently placed his fingers beneath my chin.

"I will protect you from monsters," he said, raising my head to look up at him. His eyes were bright, but not like stars—like something older. Something truer. "Remember? I am the warrior destined to kill the Hunting Beast."

"The Hunting Beast?" I said, but it was only a breath that barely passed my lips. The boy squeezed my hand and pulled me along after him.

Was I frightened? *Yes*. But it was more like the fright that comes before riding a roller coaster—*thrilling,* a safe kind of scare. Beneath the boy's cloak there was a sword at his hip, and on the boy's face a grin on his lips, and if I was going to have nightmares that stripped me bare and ate me alive, at least there was a hero at my side to slay the monsters before they could sink their teeth into me.

Mama, forgive me, I prayed as I followed the boy, hand in hand—easy, so easy—where I was not allowed to go. But also I prayed she would never find out. How could she if she was still in her office going over accounts? Whispering to Clarice on the telephone, wrapping her wrist in the spiraling cord, saying things to her that she would never tell me? She had secrets. Why couldn't I have secrets too?

Soon we crossed the threshold and then we were gone and there was no going back; tree line, skyline, moss, and damp. I had done the thing I could not do and I would be punished for it. Maybe not today or even tomorrow, but eventually. I knew it in my bones, and I didn't care, because the boy who was maybe a fairy and maybe a prince had his hand in mine and I was with him in the woods.

It was so dark I couldn't see; time worked differently between those trees, said the boy, days and nights flowing in their own peculiar rhythm. And for a moment, in the darkness, I felt like I sometimes did in bed when there was no monster but still I was afraid—breathless, flushed, my heart too full to fit inside me, a beat from breaking open. But soon it passed, as it always did—somehow—leaving sweat on my brow and the slightest of tremors hidden in my fingertips. The woods were dark, but it was a darkness I decided I could keep.

"Where are we going?" I said, but the boy didn't answer. Faster now.

How long before I noticed that my feet, like his, barely touched the ground? How long before I knew that I was floating? Weightless, almost, with him ahead and me behind, traversing a path that only became a path as we hurried along. Narrow and curving, the trees parted like shadows that stepped backward and bowed, branches bending to form an archway over our heads. Moths and rabbits and spiders' webs; a smell of old rain and more to come. In the earth beneath us there were broken slabs of colorful stone arranged in a pattern to create a gorgon's head, snakes for hair and a gaping mouth, catching my eye so that I didn't notice when exactly the trees stopped being trees and became carved stone columns instead. When the leaves turned to billowing curtains, and the woods to an ancient city at night, stars like thorns in the palm of an open hand. When we had passed from the world I was familiar with and headfirst into *this*.

A spectacle, to be sure: The colonnaded path opened into a fire-lit piazza, stone buildings rising all around and a gushing fountain at its center, the water glowing pinkish gold as it arced toward the midnight sky and fell with a bell-like splash into the basin below. Market stalls were set up along the cobbled street, selling all manner of cloth and tools and delectable treats: twists of bread and cinnamon, papier-mâché masks encrusted with jewels, daggers and feathered pens and bubbly potions sealed in tiny glass jars. A press of people—shouting voices and shivery laughter, children licking sticky fingers. Girls twirled in delight and boys shoved one another in line, all of them dressed similar to the boy—my boy—in tunics and velvet and cloaks falling to the knees. There was something different about them—different from me, I mean—a sort of shimmer beneath the skin, but I never really got a good look. The boy didn't stop or slow as we approached; with a grin tossed over his shoulder, he adjusted his grip on my hand and pulled me through the crowd. We moved so fast that our surroundings became a dizzying blur.

We didn't hit anyone, or collide with a cart, and quite honestly, I don't know how we managed it. Or how *he* managed it, for clearly it was all his doing, and I was only along for the ride. He let out a whoop of joy as we ducked and dodged, and my heart swooped inside me like a baby bird flying for the first time. We wove through the crowds and through thin alleyways; past canals whose waters were thick like clouds in the moonlight, wooden gondolas rowed languidly with plenty of assistance from the wind. Someone, somewhere, called out a name—*"Silvanus!"*—and the boy turned his head, his crown slipping down over one ear. But he only laughed again and led me around a corner—a dark one.

It was a dead end, I noticed that right away, but the boy didn't seem especially concerned as we sprinted faster than ever before toward the very solid ten-foot stone wall. I didn't even have time to scream before the boy wrapped one arm around my waist—surprisingly secure for one so skinny—and then we were somehow gliding over the wall, the ground falling away beneath our feet. I closed my eyes, certain we were about to splat, but instead of sudden death we landed lightly on the other side, our toes touching the grass as softly as if we were simply stepping out of bed in the morning. The boy's arm disappeared from around me and I sank slowly to my knees, boneless and breathless and half-wild with recklessness.

"Everything is fine, Gemma," the boy announced. "You can open your eyes now."

I opened them tentatively, not sure what I would find. But there he was, filling my whole vision: crouched in front of me with his elbows propped on his knees. His crown was still crooked, but he held his chin high. His smile like cool summertime washed over me.

"What was that?" I said. Suddenly I felt as if I could eat a star and live forever. Or dance and dance and never tire.

"The quickest path," he said, with a little wink. "Come, we're nearly there."

We were in the woods again, but here the birds were silver, stark against the sky, and the wind sounded like a song I'd heard a long time ago and forgotten. The city at our backs, we walked only a little way into the trees before coming to a glade with a perfectly round pool of water at its center, steam curling from its surface and dissipating into the open air.

"What is this place?" I asked, wary and enchanted at once. The pool had no beach or banks, no sand or rocks or slopes to mark where the ground ended and the water began. Like a hole dug into the earth, not a natural lake.

"It is a wishing well." The boy knelt beside the water, and I knelt next to him, the steam brushing my cheeks and clinging to the wisps of hair around my face.

I peered at the steam with skepticism. "It doesn't look like a well to me."

The boy pinched me lightly on the cheek. Easy, as if he'd done it before.

"And what would you know about it? Silly Gemma Belle, who always pretends not to remember me, and who does not even know how to properly jump over a wall. Here, I will show you," he said, then took a deep breath.

When he released it, a gust far greater than should have been created by such a thin body came rushing out of his chest— a mighty breath that blew the steam away, leaving the surface of the water clear and still.

"Now watch," he said. And as I stared at the water, I began to see shapes. Dark shapes, like shadows but more substantial— people dancing, gleeful, weaving in and around, touching hands and spinning feet. Music I couldn't hear but that I could feel, moving through me like a ripple.

"It shows you your greatest wish," the boy said beside me,

hushed and reverent. The trees swayed around us, and a bird called hoarsely from far away. "This is mine, you see. Triumphant revelry."

"It's lovely." But when I reached to touch the water and the shapes still spiraling there, the boy quickly grabbed my hand and pulled it back.

"Don't disturb it," he said, "or it won't come true."

"Oh! I'm sorry." I tucked my hands beneath my knees.

"Would you like to see yours?"

I looked at him. "My wish?"

He nodded.

"Yes, please," I whispered.

He shifted closer to me. "What you have to do is—"

But I never found out.

The boy stiffened suddenly, rising a little onto his knees. "Your mother is looking for you." He stood, and the shapes on the water dissolved into nothingness. Slowly, steam began again to rise from its surface. "We'd best head back."

"How do you know?" I leapt to my feet so fast my head felt light and heavy at the same time. "How do you know Mama is looking for me?"

"I hear her calling you." He tugged on his earlobe, righted his crown. "I've been listening."

I began to walk back the way we'd come when I realized I didn't know which way that was anymore. The wind was cold and I shivered; once I started I couldn't stop.

The boy stepped behind me. I tried to face him but he stopped me. And when I asked why, he said to stay still, please.

"I'm not supposed to do this," he said and put his hands over my eyes. My lashes just brushed his palms. "But for you, I will risk breaking a rule or two."

A sensation of spinning, even though I didn't move. For one second, two, three, and then the boy pulled his hands from my eyes and the spinning-not-spinning ceased. The trees around us were duller than they had been—a missing shine I only noticed when it was gone—and thickening clouds cluttered the sky. Through the branches I saw my house, curtains like eyelids shut against the coming evening. The boy was still behind me, very close.

"Are you a fairy prince?" I whispered, and his reply came at my ear.

"Always you ask me this." His laughter floated away on the wind. "My Gemma Belle, so forgetful. Perhaps this will help you remember."

Before I could really comprehend what was about to happen, the fairy prince spun me around by the shoulders. He put both his hands on my cheeks and kissed me—quick—right on the mouth.

And then I was alone. Alone in the crust of the woods, with my head drifting away on a dream.

AT LEAST FIVE old clocks in the antiques shop chimed the hour downstairs, echoing through the halls. It was late, but not late enough for sleeping, only for brushing. I sat on the stool in front of the mirror while Mama dragged the bristles through my hair.

I hadn't intended to tell her anything about earlier; but it was like breath, I couldn't hold it in. And so I told her that I saw a boy at the edge of the woods. Not that I went into the woods—that would be dire to tell!—but only that I saw him. Just your imagination, she replied lightly, and I said no, it wasn't my imagination; he was real. He held my hand and was real.

Mama paused for a moment and my scalp tingled. "Often phantoms feel real when we think about them too much."

Was a phantom the same as a ghost? I wondered, as I sat very straight and still. What about a spirit? A specter? Why did we have so many words for things that weren't there but still scared us anyway? The boy wasn't any of those, but I didn't protest. I didn't say anything, because sometimes talking to Mama was like chewing ice between my back teeth. Pointless, and it hurt. (*Tell me about the monsters.* If I do, you'll be afraid. *But I can handle it!* No. *Please?* No. *I'll die from not knowing!* No, you won't. *Yes, I will. I'll die and you'll be sorry.* I won't let you be afraid, Gemma. Not like I was. Not like I *am*.) Whatever Clarice had told her this morning had lifted her mood—she swayed her hips while she walked and hummed to herself, and fresh flowers had appeared on the windowsill—but suddenly I wanted to destroy it.

"Well, I went to the woods and guess what? I didn't see any monsters there. Only a fairy prince who held my hand and an old city at night and a pool of still water that he said was a wishing well—"

"*One hundred,*" Mama gasped with a huge, shaky sigh of relief, and suddenly I couldn't remember what I was saying anymore, could only sink into the feeling of her soft skin as she pressed her cheek to mine. After a minute she said to go to bed. I did and it was soft there too.

Hush.

4

Virginia

WHEN I THINK OF MY CHILDHOOD, I PICTURE A bright golden light under a door I cannot now open. There were shadows, of course: my mother's general unhappiness that seemed only to fall away in the woods, or the friends I failed to make at school because I was quiet and shy and my head was too full of fairy tales, my belief that they were *real*. But what were a few shadows compared to long afternoons playing in a fairy garden, chasing rabbits until they burst into a thousand flakes of glitter and flittered out of reach of our grasping hands? Or to the shape-shifter that would babysit me while my mother ran errands (or visited a certain witch, as I would learn only later), transforming into a cat or a weasel or a wolf pup and hiding behind the antiques while I called out ready or not? It was a childhood of wonder, constantly discovering new things. It was a childhood of believing in magic but not in monsters, before I learned the devastating truth that there cannot be one without the other. It was a childhood before I worried, and gnawed myself to bits.

Was I romanticizing it? Probably. Especially because there were always horrors lurking around the edges. I just didn't know it yet.

Earlier, while Gemma was playing outside, I dug out the phone book and flipped through the thin pages to the listings under *C*. With a sweat-slick hand I picked up the phone and dialed slowly, punching each number with more force than was necessary. I chewed my cheek while the phone rang and rang, my heart lurching as the call went to voicemail. Did I want to leave a message? No time to decide. Carly Clemens's achingly cute, high-pitched greeting told me to start recording after the beep, and then the beep came and there was only the sound of my breathing.

"Hi. Jenny? It's me, Virginia Cassata. Gemma's mom," I said, proud of myself for finally remembering the woman's name. "I just wanted to . . . to thank you. For the other day. For driving Gemma home from school, and for making sure she was okay. I really do appreciate it." I paused, feeling awkward and unsure. "Also it was good to see you the other day. I get so wrapped up in my work sometimes that . . . Well, it was nice talking to you. Maybe we could grab a coffee sometime?" The words were stiff and stilted; I hadn't meant to say them. Why would I need to grab a coffee with her after tonight? Everything was going to be different. Better. *Magical*. "Anyway, thanks again. Bye."

After I hung up, I sat in the silence, torn about the call. Before I'd done it I'd thought of it as a last goodbye, a final expression of gratitude before Ash was returned to my side and together with Gemma we set out to make a new life. But now I wondered if I'd meant the call not as an ending but a beginning. Just . . . in case. In case everything went wrong and we were still stuck here, Gemma and I, fighting to find our place in a mundane world with the echo of magic in our veins. It would be nice to have a friend, wouldn't it? It would be nice not to be so alone.

It felt like a betrayal to think like that, and I suddenly felt guilty for it. I had to have faith that the mirror would work, that the curse would end, that the life that was stolen from us would be ours again. If I didn't have faith, what did I have left?

It was time to summon Gemma inside for dinner. I could barely think of eating, but I still had to feed my daughter. I still had to be a mother. I still had to go through the motions, even if I was dying inside. I opened the back door of the house but I didn't see her in the yard, and my heart skipped a beat.

"Gemma! Gemma, it's time to come in!"

Nothing. My stomach flipped; I didn't need this today, of all days. It was wriggling under my skin, the impatience, the longing for night and for Ash and the moment we'd discover if I'd succeeded or if this was only another failure.

"Gemma? Gemma, come on! This isn't funny!"

Another moment passed, and then suddenly she burst from behind the old oak tree, her eyes bright, her hair and clothes disheveled. I knew at once that she had gone into the woods where she was not allowed to go. But I couldn't feel angry with her, only with myself. All of this, *everything,* was my fault.

"Oh, Gem," I said, opening my arms. She skittered into my embrace, her skin overly warm. "Oh, Gem, what have you done? Your hair is such a mess. Here, let me brush it for you. Come on."

WHEN THE SUN was gone and the sky had dimmed, I crept down the stairs and out the back door so that Gemma wouldn't hear me; she was already asleep in her bed. Too early, but I could wait no longer. I shut the door behind me and made my way to the woods.

He was already there waiting for me, as if he knew that I did not come empty-handed this time. The grass was high and the woods were dark and I forced myself to walk evenly over the uneven ground, not falling in a rush to get to him. *Please let this be it,* I prayed as I came to stand in front of him. *Please let it end.*

"Oh, Ash," I said. "I think this might be it."

Then I took the mirror cradled to my chest and raised it high over my head.

5

Gemma

I WOKE WITH A START. I'D BEEN FALLING. FALLING DOWN a hole or a tunnel or—or a wishing well. I remembered the splash, the wet, the feeling of the water closing over my head. I touched my hair, but it was dry. Just a dream. But even a full minute after I woke, I still felt strange, like I might be about to drown. I climbed out of bed, shivering, and went to find Mama. I didn't want to be alone.

I tiptoed through the whole house, but I couldn't find her anywhere. Not in her room or the bathroom or the office or the Glass Room. Not in the kitchen, or even out on the porch. I went back to the kitchen and sat at the table and stared at the door to the basement. She must have been down there; it was the only place I hadn't checked. The only place I *wouldn't* check, because I didn't like it, spiders in every corner and enough dust to keep you up coughing for several nights in a row. That was where we kept the oddities, the things most people did not like to buy: paste jewelry and bell jars and love letters tied in a bundle; skeleton keys without a lock to open. Sometimes people left things on our doorstep unsolicited—those objects they could not bear to throw away and yet could not stand to keep. We stored them in our basement—relics that meant nothing to anyone anymore. Someday, maybe, we'd throw them away, but someday had a habit of never quite arriving.

A minute passed, and then several minutes, and I was cold. I stared at the door but she wasn't coming and wasn't coming and the silence stretched like a wicked grin. All week I had tried to be good and quiet because I'd heard Mama crying behind a door in the middle of the day, but somehow I ended up always "under her feet": in the kitchen filling a glass of water when she was waiting to strain a pot of noodles in the sink, or setting off a music box when I lifted the lid to dust it while Mama spoke nearby with a client. To atone, I'd kept to my room for most of the week; and today, as I often did on the weekend, I cleaned the shop with my head down and my heart down too. Until she'd sent me outside to play—and I must have been very distracted, because the afternoon had become a blur. I remembered sitting on my swing by the edge of the woods, and then somehow it was bedtime and Mama was brushing my hair. Worry so big it swallowed everything, even several hours of the day. I hadn't heard her crying again, but that didn't mean she was done, only that I hadn't heard it. And I was only half-certain that I was not the cause or the reason.

Now, the shadows stretched, and my worry with them. I went to the window, and the moon was a silver stone high above the woods. By its light I could see my oak tree with the swing swaying in the wind, and the overgrown grass rippling as if someone walked there but no one did. Suddenly, a door downstairs banged shut with a thud that shook my teeth down to the nerve. Mama? It must be. I crept out of the room and lingered at the top of the narrow stairs that led to the back of the shop.

I couldn't see much of anything. Slowly, like melting, I crouched, balanced with a hand on the floor, and peered into the shop. I listened, waited for footsteps, but none came. Only silence: around me, inside me, under my skin. Had Mama come in or gone out?

Down the stairs and through the shop, the beating of my heart like a magic spell in my ears. I wound through the antiques on fast feet, nearly knocking over a chair with my hip and a vase on a high shelf with my shoulder. I kept as quiet as I could, but my breath was a messy thing in my mouth and my footsteps stole the silence out from under me, and anyway, I was right; no one was here. It was dark, and when I reached the front door I thought it looked like the lid to a coffin, all sealed up and secret. But it was unlocked and opened easily. I stepped through and into the wind.

At first I noticed nothing, no one, and dark clouds gathered around my heart. Where was she? Was I alone? What should I do now? I was about to call out for her but stopped, my voice curling tight in my throat the second before I saw her. *Hush.* There, by the woods, a shadowed figure. Waiting, I thought, but not for me. I tiptoed off the porch and into the long grass—closer, but not too close. Above me, it was like the whole sky held its breath.

A monster stepped from between the trees. At least, I thought it was a monster; I had never seen one before. It was so tall and spindly, almost like a tree itself, though it moved gracefully despite the deep bend of its knees. Twisted antlers protruded from the head, and I was certain that if it opened its slanted mouth it would reveal sharp white teeth and saliva would drip from its bruised red lips, a venom full of forgetting. I wanted to yell at Mama—*Watch out, turn around!*—but she surprised me by taking a step toward the creature, not back. I did not even think to be afraid. I crouched in the grass as I had on the stairs, listening.

"Oh, Ash," said the shadow that was Mama, and in her arms she held something that I had not noticed before. Fairly flat, it was pressed to her chest, but as she turned it around the moonlight reflected off its silver surface and I saw that it was a mirror. "I think this might be it."

She raised the mirror over her head so that it was at a height with the monster's terrible face. The monster—Ash?—stayed perfectly still except for the curling of its clawed fingers, its eyes on its eyes in the mirror. I waited, wondering if it might turn to stone, or into a prince, or something equally magical, but nothing of the sort happened. Nothing happened at all. Eventually Mama lowered the mirror and released a tangled cry.

I jumped to my feet to run to her, but of course the monster was already there. Instead of clamping its jaws over her face so that she would not make such a dark sound it put its eerily long, thin arms around her. An awkward embrace, as it tried to avoid impaling her with its thorns, but an embrace nonetheless. Stunned, I sank back into the grass, a few lunges nearer than I'd been before. Their embrace was only broken when a high trill came from the woods, like a bird imitating a human laugh. The sound scraped over my bones.

The monster let go of Mama, but Mama did not let go of the monster. It spoke, and its voice surprised me: light, like rain, or the rustle of pages in a yellowed book.

"The Slit Witch is coming," it said. "Go now."

Mama clung to the monster.

"I can't do this anymore," she said. "Let me face her now and be done with it."

"There is Gemma to think about."

A chill bit into my heart: *The monster knows my name*.

"Gemma, Gemma—I think of nothing *but* Gemma! And you, always you."

She said my name as if it were glass and she was trying very hard not to shatter it. I stiffened like a cat in cold water.

"Two and a half more years and she'll be fifteen," she said, and I wondered why that should matter. "Only *two and a half*."

That horrible grating call came from the woods again, much closer now than it had been. Something was coming, and it was coming for Mama and maybe for me; I knew it like I knew I would die one day, with an awful certainty. The monster knew it too. It pushed Mama with enough force to make her stumble away from the trees.

"Go now," it growled—a proper monstrous growl, so sharp it could sever a shadow from the body that had cast it. *"Now,"* it said again, just as something else stepped from the trees, and when I saw it I thought that maybe I did not know what a monster was, after all.

A woman, tall and thin, with long gray hair that looked and moved like smoke. Her eyes were dark but not in the way mine were dark. Almost, they looked like rolls of wax: shiny and without pupils or irises. And except for her hair curling over her shoulders, the woman was entirely naked. It was not just that she did not wear any clothes—she also did not wear much skin.

It was as if she were rotting, her skeleton glowing through large gaps in her flesh, sinew hanging like scraps of cloth from her bright white bones. Her right hip, both of her knees and each of her shins, her chest and half her face—skinless, blood-less, a dead thing that refused to believe it was dead. Her voice when she spoke was like a knife cutting across a throat and I understood at once why she was called the Slit Witch.

"Ah, Virginia, it has been too long. Twelve years and then some, I should think." She smiled, or tried to smile; her mouth was merely a cut on her face. "You see? I have been counting every one."

The monster—the one named Ash—stepped in front of

Mama, a shield between her and the witch. I was glad Mama had someone to protect her, though I wished that person was me. I only cowered in the grass, making myself small.

"Two and a half more years," said the Slit Witch in her strange sliding voice, her heart like a bloody fruit hanging from the branches of her ribs. "Why extend your torment? Perhaps now is the time to give up. To rest."

Ash fell into a crouch—I don't know how he did it with all those strange bends in his limbs—and snarled. The force of it shook the ground.

But the Slit Witch only laughed. "And what will you do about it, beastie? Tear off my skin? I'm afraid there isn't much left."

The Slit Witch bent down and peeled a strip of gray skin from her kneecap, dangling it in the air like a delectable treat. But when he didn't reach for the bait, she shrugged and let it fall to the ground.

"I will never give up," Mama said, and—as if to emphasize her point—the monster Ash growled again. "Not on Ash, and not on myself."

The Slit Witch laid a hand over her heart. She actually touched it, that slick, beating thing.

"Oh, I love a good tragedy. What do they call it in stories? Star-crossed? Hmm, more like legs uncrossed. You and your desires; it's all you humans ever think about." The witch's smile fell from her lips and she spoke through teeth that grated like stones. "You stole from me, girl, and so you will pay."

Mama stepped around the monster. He never took his eyes away from the witch but tensed when he felt Mama beside him.

"Like you said, I have two years yet to break the curse," she said.

The Slit Witch inclined her head. If there is such a thing as a wicked gleam, she possessed it at that moment. "You won't break it."

Even in the dark, I could see Mama's face going pale. When she spoke, it was a whisper, barely there. "Did you make the deal in bad faith? Does the mirror even exist?"

"Oh, it exists." The Slit Witch slid closer to Mama, out of the shadows so that the moonlight refracted against the bones of her cheek. The hole for the nose, the extra-long teeth. "And that, in fact, is why I am here. I'm afraid you're getting a little too . . . close."

Mama inhaled, her eyes going wide in shock. The witch reached out as if to touch Mama's face, but Mama leaned back and away. At her side, Ash rose to his full height. A figure looming like the trees—rootless, though, and deadly. The grasses curled around me in the wind, and the dark sky above looked farther away than it had ever been. Like a dream I'd had once, and might never have again. Did I still have a heart? Yes, but I barely recognized it. It didn't beat so much as tear through me—my chest, my wrists, my throat.

"You should have listened more closely to your daughter's stories, Virginia, before you made them disappear."

The Slit Witch shook her head slowly, and I sucked in my breath so fast I almost choked. *The Slit Witch knows about me! And what does she mean that Mama should have listened to my stories? What stories?*

"Oh, but you have a witch's heart. You steal, and you conceal, dressing the truth in pretty dresses to hide the rotted skeleton beneath." The Slit Witch smiled again, and I really wished she wouldn't. Her gums had receded so high that her teeth looked even longer and pointier than they should. "I suppose I can wait two and a half more years. Perhaps dear Gemma will succeed where you could not. If she finds the mirror by her fifteenth birthday, the spell will be broken as promised. You see? I can be reasonable. I can be fair."

Now it was Mama's turn to snarl, but it was like a ribbon

half-frayed; it couldn't hold anything together. Too soft, and too human. "You leave Gemma out of this."

"Ash," said the Slit Witch, and the monster curled his claws. A red light shined behind his eyes that was not there before. "Seize her and go. We are finished here."

Ash struggled against the command, his whole body trembling, but in the end the witch's spell was too strong. He scooped Mama up and held her tight to his chest. She flailed, lashing out, but the monster was immovable.

"Gemma is only twelve years old," Mama cried as the monster carried her toward the trees. "I can't leave her. I won't!"

"You will," said the witch. "And she won't be alone. I shall see to it personally."

Locked in the monster's arms, her head thrown back in a howl that should have split the stars, that should have torn the world in two—but didn't—was the last glimpse I had of Mama before she was carried away. Of course I had always known that she was a thing made of flesh and bone like me, but I don't think I believed it until that moment. Flesh could rip and bone could break and there was nothing I could do against a monster and a witch and the woods where I was not allowed to go. (Because of the monsters; *these* monsters here.) Did I dare to follow, to attempt a dangerous rescue? I thought maybe I could best the creature—were my teeth not at least a little sharp too?—but I could not outwit the witch. So I stayed out of sight and waited for her to be gone.

But the witch didn't leave, and through the darkness I saw that her lips moved very fast. It was a spell she was casting, too quietly for me to hear. Soon there was a prickling all around me, on my skin and in the air. I waited for something to happen, and when it did, it was more terrible than I could imagine.

The smoke of her hair slid off her scalp, leaving behind only a wisp around her head. But it didn't dissipate, as normal smoke should. It billowed and became darker, more solid, stretching and re-forming into an eerily human shape.

And then . . . the smoke became skin, pale in the light of the moon, and soon it was Mama standing before the witch, or a near-perfect approximation: dark eyes and dark hair and the upward curve of her lips. She wore the same red dress Mama had been wearing, the same gold bracelet glinting at her wrist. And when she spoke, it was with Mama's voice too.

"Good evening, my lady," said Not-Mama, and curtsied to the witch. "What can I do for you?"

"Keep an eye on our precious little gemstone," the Slit Witch said, and a shiver like all of winter went through me. I didn't wait to hear more but turned back toward the house and ran.

IT WASN'T SO very far, but until I crossed the threshold I didn't think I would make it, like a terrible dream where the end of the hallway stretches into infinity. I shut the door as quietly as I could with my hands trembling and then I locked it. Maybe it wouldn't stop her, but it would slow her down. The shop was a dark labyrinth as I sprinted through it, dodging around the antiques, and somehow made it to Mama's office without disturbing anything. That door I locked too. I snatched the telephone receiver from its cradle and held it to my ear, pressing the button for speed dial number one. It was my best guess, but as the phone rang and rang, I began to lose hope. I heard a clatter at the front of the shop, the fierce rattling of a doorknob.

"Please, please, please," I whispered, wrapping the cord around my wrist. "Please—"

"Yes?"

Not even a hello, but it was a woman's voice, deep and assured, and I held more tightly to the phone as my palms began to sweat.

"Grandmother? Clarice? This is Gemma calling. I—"

"Gemma? My God." Her voice cut across my stammering, but I wasn't finished, I couldn't let her interrupt. "What is it? What's wrong?"

"Please, I need to tell you—Mama is gone! I know it sounds mad, but a witch came and took her into the woods and now there's a lady of smoke that looks like Mama and talks like Mama and she's trying to get to me—"

"Slow down. Start from—"

"I can't!" I cried and felt the house shudder around me as the front door swung open wide, so fast and hard it hit the wall behind. "She's coming right now, this thing that's not my mama—"

"All right, listen. Listen to me." My heartbeat and my messy breath blurred in my ears, so loud it was a wonder I could hear her or myself. "Gemma, the creature you speak of, I think it's some kind of mimic. Dark, dark magic, and very old. It won't hurt you as long as you act like nothing is amiss. You must call it by your mother's name, and don't pull away when it tries to kiss you—okay? Wait right there, and do not let it know that *you* know it is not your real mother. Do you understand? I'll come as soon as I can."

I nodded and realized too late that she couldn't see me. "I understand."

Footsteps through the shop, so soft I almost missed them. My grandmother bid me again to wait for her and was about to hang up when I remembered something.

"Wait! The witch said that there's a curse, and that I have to break it. Mama was looking for something and now I have to look for it too. Do you know what it is?"

"A mirror." The footsteps stopped on the other side of the office door. "A mirror to show one's true reflection. But, Gem—"

I slammed the phone receiver back in its cradle just as the door before me opened. The thing that was not Mama stood on the other side, and in her hand she held a long silver key I'd never seen before. I thought, perhaps, it was a key that could open any door.

"Gemma," she said with a note of annoyed surprise, "what are you still doing up? Can't sleep? Would you like me to brush your hair?"

"Just a bad dream." I'd never been very good at lying, but there was truth to this and that made it easier. I came around the desk and edged past the creature in the doorway with my eyes downcast, as if I were afraid of being reprimanded and not afraid of the creature itself. She even smelled like Mama—apple blossoms and cinnamon, black coffee and the woods after a heavy rain—an illusion so thorough I could almost forget that it was one. "I'll go back to bed now. Good night."

Just as I was about to dart out of arm's reach, the mimic placed a hand on my shoulder. I bit my lip and tried not to cry.

"You are such a good girl, Gemma," she said, and her breath brushed my hair. Sickly sweet. "I love you."

I closed my eyes and made a wish. But when I opened them, everything was just the same. The darkness and the shop and the hand pressing down, down, down on my shoulder. How could a hand be so heavy?

"I love you too," I said. Then, "Mother."

It was the deepest of betrayals, and I felt it like a blade cutting into my own throat, blood in my mouth I could not spit out. I ran up the stairs and locked myself quietly into my room. I could pretend, sure. But I would *never* forget.

6

Virginia

ASH HELD ME AS GENTLY AS HE WAS ABLE AS HE RAN
with me through the woods, and it was that more than
anything that made me weep. I could not even think of Gemma
and of how frantic she would be to find me gone. Hopefully she
would call my mother, and they would take care of each other.
But Gemma was a clever one, and though I could not believe she
would ever find the mirror—it was a near impossible task, the
witch's vilest trick—I did believe that she would persevere. Often,
I thought of Gemma as the sea (and myself as the moon, dictat-
ing the tides): terrifying sometimes, but beautiful always and
deeper than imagining, possessed of an open embrace and a will
of her own. My girl would be all right; the sea bows to no one.
Magic can be cruel, but even the sharpest knife cannot cut water.

I hadn't entered the woods since a boy who was almost a
man had taken my hand in the darkness and pulled me in so
deep it took a misguided quest to help me find my way out
again. But here it was, unchanged: black trees, spiderwebs long
and thick enough to ensnare a deer. Nightshade, thistledown,
roots protruding from the ground. Shadows that did not move
like shadows.

I felt as though I were nineteen again, home from college for
the summer and trying to figure out how to tell my mother that

I didn't want to return to school in the fall. I had only wanted to disappear for a little while. Amazing how only twenty little steps backward into the woods had changed my life so completely.

Though I was not the one running now, I could not catch my breath. Ash weaved between the trees and the bracken with something close to abandon, tearing through bushes so tight and barbed with thorns that I was sure we were not going to make it . . . until we did. Ash shielded me with his body, but he could not shield me *from* his body, and deep scratches opened on my arms where he touched me, his skin so coarse and grating. When I peeked up at him, his mouth was twisted, but not in pain, more like determination; his eyes wide and focused straight ahead.

"Where are we going?" I cried, trying without success to twist out of his arms. "Ash, where are we going?"

"I will hide you," he said, and slowed. In the absence of his heavy footfalls, I heard a rush of water. "I will hide you where she cannot get to you, down in the Woods Below."

"The Woods Below?" The thought of another woods below this one was terrifying enough, but I was more afraid for *him*, of what the witch would do in frustration when she found she couldn't reach me. "No, Ash. *No*. She'll punish you!"

"Look at me." He stopped suddenly and set me on my feet. We stood on a mossy, sloping bank, my back to a curving river. He kept his hands on my waist, for which I was grateful. Dizzied, I would have fallen without him. "I have been punished before. I will endure."

I looked at him, and I could not think how we could go on living like this. I opened my mouth to tell him to take me back, but he took my face in his hands and kissed me.

Ash kissed me for the first time in thirteen years, and not gently at all, his mouth as rough as bark. It was only a moment, both too long and not long enough, but his lips came away bloody and he licked them, eyes closing, unable to help himself. I didn't feel it right away, how much the kiss had hurt. I raised a hand to my lips, and my fingertips knew it first: I had been torn open.

A high, crow-like call splintered the silence, and I knew the Slit Witch was near. I wanted to cling to Ash and never let go— not this time, not again—and when he reached out his arms I stepped into him with a sigh. But he did not move to embrace me, only to place his hands on my shoulders, his claws curling into my skin.

"Be safe," he said, as if I had any choice in the matter, and then he pushed me—a hard shove to throw me off balance— and before I could even cry out I plunged over the bank and into the water waiting below.

The cold of the river seized me so quickly that I barely had time to feel it before my entire body went numb. I waited for death, but death didn't come. The blood from my lips swirled in the water around me—much more blood than I had thought there was. Little lights glittered on the black surface above, growing smaller as I fell deeper, until I could see or feel nothing at all.

Until something warm and slimy like seaweed wrapped around my ankle and pulled me forcefully into the dark.

PART TWO

7

Gemma

THE WEEK BEFORE MY FIFTEENTH BIRTHDAY, MOTHER made me a cake. A delicious gooey one, chocolate with chocolate buttercream frosting and a strawberry on top, the whole thing only as wide as my hand was long. It was a practice cake in preparation for my party next week, the one to which she had invited Carly Clemens and a bunch of other kids from school at the urging of Mrs. Clemens, who Mother now met for coffee every week. I had told Mother again and again that though I liked Carly well enough, she and the others weren't really my friends. *You need to make more of an effort, Gemma,* Mother had said. *You need to get your head out of the clouds and your feet on the ground and join us here in the real world.* She wouldn't listen when I said that I didn't want a big celebration. That, in fact, I wanted no celebration at all.

Mother sat across the table and watched me eat with a serene smile, the last of the sunset light bleeding crimson around the edges of the curtains drawn over the windows behind her. She didn't ask for a single bite, not even a taste, but I wouldn't share it with her anyway. Mother didn't eat much. Only rats from the basement, and she usually waited to eat until after she thought I was asleep and couldn't hear the snap-*crunch!* of little bones between her teeth.

"Good?" she asked when I set my fork down onto the plate with a clatter.

I smiled with sticky lips. "Very."

She took my fork and empty plate, sliding it across the table between us. "Don't worry about your chores tonight, Gemma dear. It's nearly your special day."

"Thank you, Mother." I stood and walked around the table to kiss her cheek. It was soft and warm and real—too real. I touched her dark hair, so like my own. "I'm going to sit outside for a bit. Just until it gets dark."

She grabbed my wrist, a tender touch, and squeezed. "Whatever you want."

The shop was quiet, closed for the evening, and I wondered if, after this day, it would ever open again. All those antiques rotting away like flesh in a grave, a history that no one wanted or cared for anymore. The Glass Room was closed and locked, and I shuddered to think of the piles of dust gathering behind those doors, clouding up the crystal. But there was nothing much I could do about it. I was no longer allowed to go into the Glass Room (Mother's rule), just as I was not allowed to go into the woods. Good girls do not break the rules, and I was a good girl.

The very best.

I left through the front door, and on the porch I stood a moment, listening. The windows on the second floor were pushed wide open and I could hear Mother above me, humming in the kitchen as she washed the dishes, as she tidied the already tidy room and took her place again at the table with her hands neatly folded and her back very straight. Waiting for me to return so she could tuck me in for the night. But it wasn't time for bed yet. There was still gold in the sky, white clouds flushed dark pink at the edges, and the air was still warmed by the ever-falling sun. The wind seemed almost to whisper my name, and when it tugged at my clothes and my hair, I let it lead me across the winter-brown lawn, all the way to my old oak tree.

I sat on my swing facing the woods, and let my head fall against the rope as I breathed in the chilly air and felt the soil soft beneath my shoes. The winter had been long and snowy, and though we were well into April now, the crust of it lingered still; the first spring blooms had only just begun to poke through the mud. I swayed there, licking the sugar off my lips, until it grew dark and darker still.

It was a night with no moon. In the last few weeks I had watched it fade to a sliver and my heart had faded with it, so that there was no beat inside of me—only silence in which to do what must be done. Shielded by the shadows, I crouched by the base of the oak tree, feeling with steady hands for my hiding place, a hollow under a root as large around as my thigh. When my fingers wrapped about the handle of the small ax Mother used to chop the rats in the basement—the one that used to be in the shop—I pulled it out slowly so as not to cut myself on the blade and stuck it under my sweater along my spine, secured in place by the tight waistband of my leggings.

Tonight was my very last night of pretending.

With the sun gone it was too cold to linger and, of course, too dark. There were monsters in the woods, and the monsters were hungry, and the most delicious meals for hungry monsters were good girls like me. Fleshy soft and sweet, stuffed to the brim with cake.

Humming Mother's same tune, I went inside to brush my hair and ready myself for the night ahead.

"GEMMA, DEAR, WOULD you like some help?" Mother stood in my bedroom doorway, wringing her bony hands. I don't

think she even realized she was doing it, twisting her nerves
into knots. I watched her in the mirror, like Perseus tracking
Medusa. Except I did not have a sword or a shield and I was not
a hero—not yet. To be a hero, one must first complete a quest.

(Someone told me that, the thing about quests, and I think
it must have been Mama, because—who else? It was like a gap
in my brain when I tried to remember, like trying to hum a
song I'd heard once on the radio ten years ago. But no matter—
I felt the truth of it in my soul.)

"No, thank you," I said, even as the bristles of the brush
snagged a tangle on the back of my head. The handle was icy
cold, but I clenched my jaw and kept ahold of it. "I'm almost
done."

"Oh, you're hurting yourself." She hurried forward to pry the
brush from my hands. Her touch was gentle but firm, and I
relinquished it only half unwillingly. She gathered my hair like
a bouquet in one hand and then spread it over my shoulders,
admiring. "Remember how I used to do this when you were
little? How I used to brush your hair every night?"

I smiled at her in the mirror, and Mother smiled too. "I do."

"And now look at you. Fifteen years old."

"Not yet," I said, and she brought the brush to the crown of
my head. "Not until the twenty-second."

"Only days yet."

I sat with my hands pressed between my thighs and waited
for her to be done. I counted one hundred strokes, my scalp
tingling as I anticipated the strange but familiar dreaminess that
accompanied the brushing, making me feel hazy and faraway,
but it never came. When Mama did it, the ritual was like a lullaby, putting me right to sleep. But with Mother brushing my
hair, not Mama, I felt clear and wide awake. Mother ran her
hand idly over the yellowed bristles, petting it like an animal.

"Mother," I said, turning to face her, and she jumped as if

she'd forgotten I was there. "Do you think there are fairies in the woods?"

She set the brush down on my dresser and looked toward the open window, the glass fogged as if with a breath. "Oh, I don't know. I suppose anything is possible. Why do you ask?"

I stood and crossed to the window, closing it. Mother pressed her lips together but did not protest. "I just think that if there are monsters in the woods, then there ought to be something good too. Something made of light to bring balance to the darkness."

There was silence for a long moment. And then Mother laughed, somewhere between mirth and admonishment.

"Oh, Gemma. Fairies aren't *good*."

My heart knocked around inside of me. "How would you know?"

"From stories, of course."

That silence again. It would choke me if I let it. Instead I gave my best snarl and held my hands up like claws, hissing like a deranged thing, and spoke in a deep Dracula voice. "Do they eat little girls like a wolf in three bites?"

Mother laughed again, and this time there was no restraint in it.

"No," she said. "Much, much worse. They'll kiss you until you forget your own name."

I stood from my chair and rolled backward onto my bed to stare up at the ceiling. Mother hovered near the doorway, wringing her hands again. Her smile had begun to slip.

"I know my name," I said quietly. "*Gemma Ashley Cassata*. I don't think it's something I could ever forget."

With the gliding walk of a ghost, Mother went to the lamp and switched it off. Instantly I felt more like myself in the dark. Sharper. No pretending.

"Well, dear," she said, "I'll make sure of that."

* * *

MOTHER FELL ASLEEP at midnight, when all the clocks downstairs struck twelve at once. It always woke me up, that noise like a round of haunted church bells—but not tonight. Tonight I was already awake. I was ready to go into the woods where I was not allowed to go, and bring Mama back.

In my room I picked out the clothes I would have worn for my birthday party. First, a magenta sweater Mama bought for me before she disappeared. It was long and roomy when it was new, frequently slipping over one shoulder, though now that I had grown it was tighter and shorter, only just reaching my hip bones. Then I pulled on a thick pair of leggings, black with little pink polka dots, and a sturdy pair of gym shoes in case I needed to run fast—the only part of the outfit I wouldn't have actually worn for the party. It felt gravely important that I look nice when Mama and I were reunited at last. It was important that I look like someone she would recognize.

When I was done getting dressed, I walked down the up-stairs hallway with Mother's little ax clutched in both my hands, holding the blade sideways to my heart. The metal felt like ice against my skin, almost as if it might melt. All was quiet in the house except for my breath, a warm blur between my lips, and the creak of the floor beneath my gym shoes. I was sticky-hot inside my sweater, and I wondered if I had made a mistake in choosing my favorite. If there was blood, it might leave a stain. If there was lots of blood it might never come clean.

The door to Mother's room was open and I let myself right in. How trusting she was! But, why not? Hadn't I told her every day for the last two and a half years that I loved her? I could still taste the cake she'd made me in the back of my throat. I crept to the bed where she lay on her back with her hands folded over her belly, her long thin fingers interlaced. I thought

maybe I should say a few words as I raised the ax high—
a prayer or something of the like—but all that came to mind
was one word.

Hush.

When I chopped off Mother's head, she left a horrid brown
stain on the sheets of the bed—not blood and torn sinew, but
smoke and dirt, flesh crumbling instantly to ash. She did not
even open her eyes one last time.

I had thought—*before*—that I might scream when the deed
was done, but then—*after*—I did not feel like screaming at all.
There was no blood on my favorite sweater, no flying chunks of
flesh in my hair. I tucked the ax into the bag I had packed so
that the blade stuck out the top and then I hefted it onto my
shoulder, so much heavier than it had felt this morning. I had
forgotten to kiss Mother's cheek one last time before I brought
the ax down on her throat, an apology in case she would feel
any pain, but now there was no cheek left to kiss and I didn't
really know what to do. I hadn't wanted to cause her pain, only
to cause her to be gone. *Murder* was not a word I liked, but it
was the word that was true. *Glorious* was a word I did like, but
I did not do this for glory; I did it to be free.

It had not been an easy decision, but don't heroes have
swords for a reason? There was no other purpose for a weapon
but killing.

I did not know what was going to happen now. I knew only
that I had failed to break a curse I knew very little about, and
that my mama—the real one—had not come back. For a while
I had kept my hope burning for my grandmother, Clarice, but
she had never appeared; I called her dozens of times, left countless messages on her answering machine, but I never reached
her and she never reached me. I asked Mother about her, just
the same as I would have asked Mama—*Why hasn't Grandma*

visited in so long?—but Mother only stroked my hair and said, "She'll be back. Once she's paid her debts."

Debts? But Mother would explain no further—always, I was kept in the dark!—and so I'd been forced to conclude that she had been taken just like Mama, captured by the Slit Witch or some other fearsome entity. It was part of my quest now to rescue her too.

But I hadn't forgotten what Clarice had told me the night I'd called her frantically, and it gave me something to focus on. A mirror, she'd said, a mirror that showed one's true self. Sneaking around Mother had been difficult. Over the years she had signed me up for a myriad of activities—ballet and piano lessons, soccer and martial arts—that sucked up all my free hours. Some of it I liked—karate especially, as it gave me confidence that I could fight a monster; and dance too, because it made me strong—but most of it was tedious and felt like a waste of time. Which, of course, it was. Nothing that I did in the world outside of the woods held any consequence for me. It didn't even feel real, only pretend. A performance—one I steadily grew tired of as I stealthily searched for the mirror, skipping out on play practice to take the bus to nearby towns, avoiding the side-eye of the drivers as they wondered why a young teen was traveling alone. I went where I could, never more than an hour or two from home, visiting antiques shops and museums, historical societies, and even some private collections. I couldn't afford to buy any of it unless I was certain, and I wasn't so I didn't, always returning home empty-handed. I had this conviction that I would *know* when I saw it, as if the mirror would speak to me as clearly as saying my name. When visiting other shops turned up nothing, I stole Mama's phone book from her office and got in touch with her old contacts. Some of them bargained with me in exchange for pieces we had in the shop, sending me mirrors from around the world that were rumored to contain dark magic: pieces no one wanted to buy for fear of an ancient curse. But when they arrived, they felt absolutely ordinary, every single time.

But even if I had located the mirror in question—and I did not believe I had, for none of the mirrors I acquired ever showed me anything but my own face, unaltered—I wouldn't have known what to do with it. No matter where she was or what she was doing, whenever I had taken even half a step into the woods, Mother would materialize behind me as if she had been there all along. She would take my hand firmly with a smile and lead me back into the house, chattering as if nothing were the matter. There had been no way to foil her in this. It was like she'd had a secret alarm that let her know every time I strayed too close to the trees and the darkness beyond. The woods were barred to me as long as she was living.

But now, at last, she was gone, and I had not wanted to do it—I had put it off for as long as I could!—but it had to be done. I was free to rescue Mama and bring her back shortly before the curse took effect. Neither of us had succeeded in finding the mirror on our own, but maybe if we had worked *together* . . . Well, we would be together soon. And once we were reunited, we'd figure out what to do.

I still didn't know exactly what the curse *was*, or what would happen on my birthday without the mirror to break it, but I suspected it had something to do with Mama and the monster named Ash. And that if the Slit Witch was involved, then it could only be very, very bad.

Would Mama turn into a monster too?

It was harder than I'd thought it would be to leave the house and lock up the shop, to drop Mother's skeleton key in my bag, letting it sink down to the bottom. And that was saying a lot, because I'd known it would be hard; I just didn't know it would be like removing a vital bone. And not that the house was the bone—*I* was the bone, and I feared that when I stepped off the porch and into the crisp, crinkling grass, the whole structure would collapse without me. Somehow it didn't, though, and that was the most devastating thing of all. The house didn't need me as much as I'd needed it—something I'd suspected and now was confirmed. The antiques had been in existence long before I ever was, and barring a violent fire or some other disaster, they would be here long after.

I stood a moment on the lawn and looked up at the sky before I remembered that it was a no-moon night. There weren't even many stars, just a sprinkling here and there, like someone had swept them all aside with the back of their hand. The wind curled into my neck like a nuzzling cat and I shivered, but not with fear—anticipation, and even some perverse sense of excitement. Hadn't I been practicing my wolf-smile in the mirror? The one that showed all my pointiest teeth? I had Mother's ax and my hairbrush in my bag—just in case Mama didn't recognize me, I would show her the brush and she'd know me at once—a few apples and granola bars, a bottle of icy cold water. I would miss school, but getting Mama back was all that mattered right now, and no amount of converting radians to degrees would help me in my task. If the school called or came to check on me, all they would find was an empty house and lonely antiques. After two long years, I was ready for the woods. I knew what a monster was now, knew what it was made of. Flesh like mine, and blood like mine too. Which meant a monster was something that could be killed. A monster was something that I could make *gone*.

I took a deep breath, and another. With my ax and my wolf-smile, I started toward the trees.

8

Virginia

SIXTEEN YEARS AGO NOW, I HAD EXPECTED MY FIRST year of college to be freeing. It was my first time away from the woods and the threat of its monsters. Of course, that also meant I would be far from the fairies and the wonder, and I was not prepared for the intense loneliness that throbbed in my heart, as if the devil had gotten his teeth into it. It was inescapable—a terrible pressure in my throat. I went from class to class and did not make eye contact with anyone; occasionally I would return the smile of the librarian when I checked out the same volume of Keats for the third time in a row that was not for any assignment. But even this I could manage only after dark when the lights hovering close above the shelves glowed unnaturally through the high glass windows and spilled onto the quiet campus sidewalks strewn with leaves. I felt like a ghost. Like I simply did not exist without the woods nearby.

Hope College was only three hours from home, but somehow it felt much farther. I had never been one to make friends easily—I was naturally shy, and I quickly realized that not everyone lived beside an enchanted forest, and if you talked about it excessively, the other kids were not very kind—but in that place where the sun seemed to set so early and yet the days stretched so long, I found I could not make friends at all. I couldn't make sense of the wider world.

My roommate was a girl from Ann Arbor with hair so blond it was almost white, and who wore thick sweaters even when the weather was warm. She kept odd hours and behaved in ways that were incomprehensible to me, staying up all night and sleeping in snatches between classes. She never ate breakfast and always went to bed with her hair still wet from the shower. She clipped her toenails over the sink in our room, and cleared her throat every time she turned a page of her textbook while studying. She smoked cigarettes while she watched reruns of *Bewitched* on the grainy TV she'd brought with her, and left countless voicemail messages for someone named Timothy who only called back when he knew she would be away. I dutifully wrote down the time and date of his calls on a notepad for her, and I always found my notes crumpled up in the trash the next day.

There were clubs and meetings and auditions all over campus, sororities I could seek to join, volunteer organizations recruiting new members. Musical theater and book club and cooking contests and stargazing and concerts and soup kitchens, and even whispers of a secret society. Endless opportunities, and yet I couldn't bring myself to explore a single one. All of them would be filled with more strangers doing strange things and I could not be one of them because I was just a girl from nowhere who'd grown up with her mother over an antiques shop next to the woods where she was not allowed to go because of the monsters there. A girl who knew what a monster was; knew all the ways it could hurt you. Not to kill you, but to *keep* you.

Ink on my hands, bedsheets tangled around my ankles, sweat and dreams of growing things: vines choking my throat, weeds sprouting beneath my tongue. I would walk from one end of campus to the other and not remember how I had gotten there; I would fall asleep while studying at a desk in the far corner of the library. I turned in all of my schoolwork on time, but still my grades slipped lower than they had ever been and I couldn't bring myself to feel ashamed. Some days I ate nothing but bread and butter, drank nothing but coffee without any cream or sugar. I cried when my roommate was away and I was alone. Blissfully, terrifyingly alone.

I called my mother every night at nine.

"I want to come home," I said, curled on my side with my old stuffed rabbit tucked between my knees and my chest. It was dark, and I couldn't tell if my roommate was out or if she was sprawled beneath the puffy comforter on her bed.

"Just give it a little more time."

Always she said this: *a little more time*. First that meant a week, and then another week. Then a month, then three months, and soon it was winter break and spring break, and each time I came home and had to leave again it got harder. Why did I have to leave at all?

My mother hadn't gone to college. She was the youngest of four children to a widowed mother, and there'd been no money for it. She'd married young, and moved with my father from Chicago to the antiques shop in Michigan that his retired parents had owned and that for all my life I would call home. I was born a few years after, but when I was still too young to remember, my father filed for a divorce. *We didn't understand each other,* she said when I asked her why. *He wanted things that I didn't.* In the settlement she was granted ownership of the shop; my father didn't want it, or us. So for most of my life it was just my mother and me—and my mother's dreams of me earning a college degree.

And getting away from the woods.

Summer on campus set in, and I reveled in the warmth of the sun on the back of my neck as I studied outside on a bench among the flowers. I made it through finals and then I was free—for three whole months, at least. When at last I came home, I knew I wasn't going back.

How to tell my mother, though?

I fell into my old routine as simply as slipping on a pair of well-worn shoes: sleeping late in the mornings while my mother spoke with clients downstairs in that low, professional tone of voice she could never quite cast off, even when we were alone; pulling on a cotton sundress and wandering barefoot into her office with an apple to balance her accounts all through the afternoon; minding the shop into the early evening while she cooked dinner upstairs, the scent of simmering garlic seeping through the floorboards and making my stomach clench with hunger. Sitting in the window seat in what would eventually become the Glass Room, and watching the sun set over the trees.

One week passed in this manner, and then two. All year I had ached for home—the shop, my bed, and my room—but what I had really ached for was the woods. Or rather, for my *memory* of the woods. For the magic without the monsters, and for my childhood. For the time before I was severed from them, before it was a place to be feared. More and more I wandered to the window throughout the day, just to look. To lose myself. To watch the shadow of the woods stretch toward the house.

I was so young—barely able to walk on my own—when my mother first took me with her into the woods that my memories of that time tend to blur together. But there is one memory from shortly after I turned eight years old that shines brighter than the rest. Wearing a new floral dress with a wide skirt and a giant white bow in my hair, I walked with my hands clasped behind my back at my mother's side, my footsteps so quiet she kept glancing down to make sure I was still there. It wasn't far, a half hour's walk, but though my feet began to cramp I didn't dare to complain. My mother said complaining was useless because it only made you feel more sunken in your misery. So I swallowed it down and let my mother lead us through the woods, each tree as distinct to me as a human face. The sky was a bruise and the sun had only just begun to set, shadows pale in the twisted blue twilight. A bird rushed overhead, rustling the leaves on the nearest tree, and when I looked up, I tripped. Little more than a stumble, but my mother's glare pierced me like a needle.

Silence, Virginia. Or the monsters will find us.

I knew what a monster was—she'd told me all about their snapping tails and rotting breath—but I couldn't quite bring myself to believe her. Not that I thought she was lying—it's like how some people believe in God, and some do not. For me it just didn't make sense. There was no *reason* for monsters to exist—not outside of the stories they were in.

I didn't really think there were monsters about to abduct us, but I stayed quiet anyway because I was good at it, generally. The world was too noisy in my opinion—cars and lawn mowers and electric lines buzzing—and that was why I preferred the serenity of the woods. A wolf, for all its fierce howls, would never be as loud or grating as road workers breaking up concrete to lay a new road over the old. There were no roads at all in the woods, no paths. You either got where you were going, or you didn't. But my mother knew the route to the fairy village by heart, or maybe by muscle memory; either way, we arrived minutes before the ceremony began.

Even after so many years away from the fairy village, how could I ever forget the river? A floating glass floor was set up over the water, held aloft by fairy magic, and there were plump, tasseled cushions laid out for the guests to sit on facing a dais crowned by a triumphant arch of golden flowers. The air smelled sweet, as if dusted with sugar, and I could see the glitter of magic on the wind. The sky above was clear, speckled with stars as day gave way to night. There were fairies all around us, and they could have passed for human but for the deep shine to their skin, the magic just below the surface. And though I had no magic of my own, I felt their magic surrounding me, warm and clear and tingling. It made me feel as if I could do anything. Even fly, if I tried to. My mother found two vacant cushions for us near the front, and we settled in as the music began.

It was a wedding. And not only a wedding, but a royal one. The fairy queen was marrying her longtime love, a fairy woman with high cheekbones and a long silvery braid draped over one shoulder. I had never known two women to marry before—not in our world—but things were different in the woods. As they pledged their hearts to each other, I glanced over at my mother and saw silent tears streaming down her cheeks. I had never seen my mother cry, and I never would again. But that day she was crying and *smiling*, a joy so radiant that I could feel the heat of it.

There was feasting afterward, and dancing too, and my mother held my hands and twirled me around the floor, laughing so freely it was like she was an altogether different person. I wished this version of my mother would be with me always, and not the severe one who whispered of monsters and hardly ever smiled back home at the shop. Who was always so hard at work and had no time for play. We spun around and around until a dark figure bumped into her shoulder, a woman—not a fairy, I could tell right away from the dullness of her pale skin—and my mother dropped my hands abruptly.

"Nicasia," said my mother, bringing a hand to her heart as if startled. The woman was dressed all in black—a tightly laced corset and long pants—as if she were an attendant at a funeral and not a wedding at all. She smelled smoky, like a wildfire, and at first I thought she had a long scar that ran from her chest up her neck to her jaw. But when I looked again, I saw that it was not a scar but a *crack*, as if she were made of glass. The same kind of crack that would open across my own chest with each stroke of the enchanted brush through Gemma's hair. "I didn't know you would be here."

"No, but I knew that *you* would be." There was nothing scary or strange about her voice, but I shivered all the same. "Clarice, I know you despise me now that you've discovered my secret, but I really must talk to you."

"I don't *despise* you," said my mother quietly, almost tenderly, brushing a stray hair from her face with a shaking hand. I had never seen her like this. So emotional. So open. "You're just . . . not who I thought you were."

The woman shrugged, and a small smile curved her lips. It was not a kind smile. "Love is blinding, or so they say."

"It wasn't love." My mother's voice was barely a whisper. "It felt like it, but it wasn't. Our story was false from the start."

The woman was silent for a long moment. I couldn't read her expression; she gave nothing away. "If you say so."

It was then that the woman's gaze slid down to me, and I froze. The woman tilted her head, her brows drawing together as she slowly lowered into a crouch and only stopped when we were eye to eye.

"I didn't know you had a daughter, Clary." Though the woman's tone was light, it sounded like an accusation. The woman reached out and pressed her thumb to the center of my forehead.

I gasped. Her skin was cold, but it was more than that; I felt somehow as if she were touching my very soul, as if she were reaching inside me and grasping for something I did not want to give. Distantly I was aware of my mother's hands on my shoulders, and then I was jerked away, the connection severed. My mother pushed me behind her and lifted her chin.

"I told you I would no longer—no longer do business with you." My mother's voice skipped in the middle and I wondered at that. Was she afraid? Was I? I felt numb where the woman had touched me; I couldn't feel my heart beating.

The woman straightened to her full height. The party was still going on around us, no one taking notice of the confrontation in their midst.

"One more favor, and then I shall leave you alone forever," the woman said, waving a hand in the air, as if she didn't believe that my mother would really want to be left alone forever. "There's a spell I'm trying to cast that's giving me a world of trouble." She ran a fingertip over the crack in her chest and I recoiled, as if I had touched it myself. "I require an object to channel the enchantment through, something from your shop. Fetch it for me, and our *business* shall be at an end."

My mother leaned down and brought her lips very close to my ear. "Wait for me by the dais, Gigi. I'll be there in a moment."

I needed no further prodding than that. I ran, shoving through the crowds of drunken fairies, straight for the dais and the golden arch. The fairy queen came and patted my head, told me how pretty I looked. I had always liked her, and she seemed to hold my mother in high esteem, delighting in the antiques my mother brought to sell to her. I stammered a thank-you and stayed right where I was until my mother came and whisked me out of the woods, far from the fairies, to our house above the shop where she said we'd be safe. I watched from my bedroom window as she sprinkled a circle of salt around the entire house, and scrambled back to bed when at last I heard her footsteps on the stairs.

"Was that woman a monster?" I blurted as she came into my

room, the covers pulled up to my chin. I still didn't believe monsters were real, but that woman was as close as I had ever come to one and I was shaken. My forehead was still numb, as if she were touching me even then.

"I . . . I don't know," my mother said, kneeling by the edge of the bed.

"I saw the crack on her chest." I shuddered, despite my many blankets. "Like she was breaking apart."

"Yes, that's because of her magic. It unravels her a little bit more each time she uses it. Some magic, like some people when they fulfill a favor for you, ask for nothing in return. But there are other kinds of magic that ask for everything, and more besides. But listen to me, Gigi. You are not to go into the woods anymore. It isn't safe."

At that I sat bolt upright. "What? But—but—you can't visit the fairies without me! They're fairies, they're not—they're *good.*"

"Fairies aren't good," my mother replied sharply, but softened at my incredulous expression. "Like you and me—we aren't *all* good or *all* bad. I know that being near fairy magic *feels* soft and good, but magic isn't . . . It's complicated. It can be used for good or ill. And there are many more people with ill intent in the woods than good, which is why you must stay away."

It felt as if my heart were collapsing in on itself. "But—"

"No, Virginia. I see now that it was a mistake to take you to the fairy village to play. The fairies aren't good, necessarily, but they are the least dangerous of all the woods' creatures, and that's *only* because I'm on good terms with them. They can, and *have,* ensorcelled other humans, taken them away from the world and scrambled their brains with magic, or traded years of a hapless human's life for wares in the fairy market. We were protected there. But even the fairies cannot protect us from—

from the woman you saw today. I'm taking one more trip inside, and then I promise I will stay away too. No more woods for us, Gigi. We don't belong there. I wish we did, but we don't." My mother sighed, her breath hot against my cheek. "Do you understand?"

I nodded, because I knew she expected me to. But I didn't understand, not really, and after she had left I buried my face in the pillow and cried. Or tried to cry; the tears were few, frozen behind my eyes. I felt numb and empty, and knew with a wordless conviction that I would stay that way for the rest of my life without the woods to warm me.

But even all these years on—and though my mother had made certain, in the time between, that I was thoroughly afraid of monsters—I still could not forget the feel of magic, the warmth and sparkle suffusing the air, the quiet and peace of those walks to the fairy village, how everyone and everything seemed *brighter* there than it did here. I knew I couldn't leave again, even if school was only three hours away. I belonged here, no matter what my mother said. Even if I was consigned forever to the edge, I couldn't pretend that magic—and monsters— didn't exist. If they didn't, then I didn't either.

SOON IT WAS mid-June, a few days before the summer solstice. I waited until after the final sale of a genuine Queen Anne Chippendale corner chair that my mother had been stressing over for a month to tell her that I had no plans to return to school in the fall. I knew it was sneaky of me, but she was in such a state of elation the evening of the sale that I thought nothing could possibly deflate her, and that, drunk on the high of her victory, she would be more willing to understand why I wanted nothing more than to stay with her and help run things here.

Like an apprenticeship, I thought as I practiced my speech in the mirror, raking my hair up and pinning it high on my head the way my mother liked it best. So much more practical and economic than a degree that wouldn't serve me in this field. Why should I spend four years learning how to do this job at a distance when it made much more sense to gain practical experience? I was good with numbers and knew already how to manage her finances. What I needed now was social knowledge. Namely how to buy from and sell to clients. Customer service, that sort of thing. After spending the first eight years of my life with fairies as my best friends, even if I didn't see them as often as the kids at school—kids who did not believe me when I said fairies were real—I'd never been particularly adept at *human* interaction. But it was a skill like anything else, and I just needed to convince my mother to teach me.

That evening she cooked up a feast to celebrate the sale: wood-fired ricotta drizzled with lemon, and bruschetta baked with rosemary and olive oil to scoop it with; balsamic vinaigrette salad with crunchy homemade croutons dusted with Parmesan; hand-rolled gnocchi with marinara made from scratch. Coffee and chocolate chip cheesecake for dessert with a tiny scoop of vanilla gelato. One shot of after-dinner grappa that nearly corroded my esophagus to nothing, clinking our glasses with a joyous *"Salute!"* Through the kitchen windows, the last of the daylight lingered on the horizon like a bloodstain.

We pushed our dirty dishes to the side, not quite ready to leave the table, not with the grappa still warming our full bellies and the hard gold sunlight still slanting over our shoulders. The windows were open and the classical station on the radio was playing a bunch of commercials; it seemed like it had been playing commercials since we'd turned it on. I felt vaguely queasy, like I'd just spun in circles while holding my breath, and I wished a song would come on, something soft and dreamy. One of Chopin's nocturnes maybe. My mother wore a faraway smile as she sat with her chin propped in her hands, and it almost looked like she was about to fall asleep right there with her eyes half open.

"Ma," I said, and her only response was a murmured *hmm-mmm?* Her toes were tapping underneath the table to the tinny jingle on the radio.

"Ma," I repeated, and her eyes swiveled to me. I'd never seen her like this, so unguarded, so . . . content. Another moment like this wouldn't come again. "This past year has been really hard for me—"

"I know, Gigi." She straightened in her seat, adjusting the lapels of her suit dress, which she had been wearing since before dawn that day. Despite her best efforts with the curling iron, her dark hair had begun to frizz wildly in the humidity. "But you made it through and I'm so proud."

This pronouncement stopped me cold. When had my mother ever said she was proud of me? Tears gathered behind my eyes, but not because I was touched or moved or *happy*. My God, how frustrating that she should say such a thing *now,* the very moment I was about to disappoint her terribly? And then she did the most vexing thing of all: *She kept going.*

"Have you given any more thought to your major yet? You're so good with numbers that accounting seems like the obvious choice. But I was just reading an article in the paper about computer coding and I really think—"

"I don't want to do computer coding," I said. My carefully crafted speech was stuck like a piece of half-chewed food in my throat. I was either going to have to swallow it or heave it back up.

"Oh, but computers are the wave of the future, dear. You can make good money if you—"

"I don't want to study computer coding or anything else." A song finally came on the radio, Stravinsky's something or other from *The Rite of Spring,* and it was horribly, cataclysmically, absurdly *wrong.* I wanted the advertisements back, the earworms and the barely intelligible terms and conditions—normality, nothingness. "I'm not going back to school in the fall."

My mother took a slow deep breath, pressed her shoulders down, and sat back. So smooth and sudden was the transformation from relaxed mother having a celebratory dinner with her beloved daughter to assessing, sharp-eyed professional that I wondered if the laughter and the lightness of a moment before had all been an act. Who was this woman, really?

"What will you do instead?" She didn't sound angry, just coolly neutral, as if she had no stake in the situation. Or as if she wanted me to *believe* she had no stake in the situation.

"Well." I folded my hands on the table, matching her businesslike demeanor. "I know so much about the finances of the shop already, but I really want to learn about the mechanics of it. How to buy, how to sell, how to—"

"No." Detached, cool, she cut me to the bone. "You're not staying here."

"What?" I had expected disappointment, rage, even sadness, but not this quiet, firm refusal, this quick and gutting dismissal. I thought my confession would finally be the thing to break her open. "But I—"

"You don't want to go back to school. Fine." The last of the light leaked from the sky and we were left in darkness. "But you can't stay here."

I curled my hands under the table; I clenched my fists as if there were something there to hold on to. "Where am I supposed to go then?"

"That's for you to decide." She stood with her palms pressed flat to the table and looked down at me. "I will not let you waste away here among a bunch of old junk that is centuries older than you. You're too smart for that. You're so much . . . *more*."

My mother left the room. She left me at the table with the dirty dishes piled high, and she did not return. I waited until the sky went to black and the music faded out on the radio, replaced by more commercials. I waited until my breathing slowed and my heart quieted. I sat there until I felt completely see-through, and then I left too.

Down the stairs, through the shop, out the door. I walked across the lawn in the dim, all the way to the old oak tree at the back of the yard, set apart from the surrounding woods as if it had been banished long ago. My bare feet were cold in the dry grass and I shivered without a jacket. But I was not going back. I edged around the oak tree and pressed my spine to its bark, facing the woods. All was dark and still; even the wind didn't dare to howl here. *Silence, or the monsters will hear you.*

I had listened to my mother after she forbade me from entering the woods—but only for a little while. Weeks, months, a year had passed, and though I never forgot the strange woman with the crack across her chest and her numbing touch, the memory had softened around the edges until I couldn't quite recall the terror that had accompanied it. *There's no such thing as monsters*, I said to myself, and while my mother was busy with work, I played a game I'd only just made up, creeping backward into the woods as far as I could go and still see out beyond the trees to the backyard. With my heart about to burst, I took one step after another, until the thought of a monster hovering right behind me sent me tearing back the way I had come. Yet I saw this as further proof that there were no monsters, because none ever came to snatch me. How clever I had thought myself then. How brave.

My mother caught me when I was twelve. Four full years had passed since I'd last visited the fairy village, since its magic had embraced me like the sun on a warm summer day. So much of what I had seen of magic had already faded from memory, but the *feel* of it hadn't. My mother was shaking so hard with fury that I felt the tremor up my arm as she grabbed my wrist, guiding me back toward the trees.

Oh, Gigi. I'll show you if you don't believe me. Then you'll be afraid! Then you will obey me!

I hadn't played the game since that day. But now, after our fight, I was tired of being afraid and subjected to her control. Shaking with fury of my own, I walked to the edge of the woods and turned my back to the trees. I looked once at the dark sky, and then I stepped over the threshold, backward into the brush where it was cold and quiet. My heart leapt into my throat, each careful step bringing me farther from the open space that meant safety on the other side of the trees. I imagined monsters keeping pace with me, slavering to touch my cheek, and when I couldn't stand it any longer I stopped. A pause to revel in the thrill of it, the tautness of my nerves like a string about to snap. The shadows crowded close. I licked my lips and bent my knees, readying to run.

One. Two. Th—

A hand reached from below. It grabbed my wrist, strong and cold, and pulled me to my knees.

9

Gemma

I WISH I COULD SAY THAT I WENT INTO THE WOODS where I was not allowed to go and the darkness there was like a familiar hand slipping into my own. I wish I could say that my eyes adjusted easily to the dim, enough to make out the path twisting like a dribble of dried blood before me, leading me far away from the only life I had ever known. I wish I could say that I was afraid, but that my fear was like a locket hanging heavily around my neck: close to my heart, but not quite touching it.

I suppose I could say all that, but it would be a lie. And good girls don't lie.

So I will tell a different story instead.

Once upon a time a girl went into the woods with the pulse in her neck fluttering like a little bird's wing, and her unquiet breath was a song that only she could sing, and when she looked at the sky the branches above were like the bars of a keyless cage. But somehow she had never felt so free, and the freedom was as crushing as it was thrilling: which way, and where to go, and what to do if she began to hear footsteps behind her—footsteps that were not subtle at all, footsteps that matched hers beat for beat?

And if she turned around—what would she see?

Nothing much, not at first. Shadows upon shadows, undulating like the layers of a lake. The snapping of twigs, the crunching of leaves, the kicking of rocks that *clunk-roll-thunk* in the dirt. And a voice like cold water that seemed to drip from nowhere and everywhere at once.

"*Murderess,*" it hissed. Everything in the girl went rigid, but somehow she suspended her terror long enough to bend her arm up over her head and grab the ax from her pack. Once it was in her hands, she spun this way and that, searching for someone—a monster, maybe, or a demon—but she couldn't see anything. Only darkness. And then it came again, like an icy trickle down the back of her neck: "*Murderess.*"

"I'm not!" the girl cried, holding the ax to her chest, the blade cold and reassuring against the burning in her heart. "I'm a good girl, and I'm going to get my mama back."

"*You killed your mother. You made her dead.*"

"No!" She shook her head so hard she saw stars. "She wasn't my mother and she wasn't *real*. She was—"

"*Magic?*" A pause, and the only sound was her heavy breath. "*So magic isn't real?*"

The girl bowed her head. It was dark and cold, and she couldn't see more than a few feet ahead. Who was it that tormented her so? Dizzy and disoriented, she stumbled backward until her spine pressed against a tree. She had not thought her journey would go like this. She expected monsters, yes—but none that chose to remain in shadow. How could she fight something she couldn't see?

"No, it's real," she said, and felt stupid—and cowardly—for the way her voice trembled. "Magic is real. It's just—"

"*Inconsequential?*"

She wanted to clap her hands over her ears, but that would

mean letting go of her ax and that she would not—could not—do. "Mother was made of smoke and witchery!" she shouted into the shadows. "Not flesh and blood like me."

The voice was close. It was in the tree above her; it was on the ground at her feet. It was right behind her, at her cheek. *"Are you so sure of that?"*

"Yes. I was there. I saw how the Slit Witch made Mother from her hair. I heard her say the spell, I—"

The voice laughed. Slowly, like thunder. *"I mean you, Gemma. What are you really made of?"*

A girl went into the woods and found no monster there but a mirror. She didn't recognize herself. There, in the dark, she was as long as the longest shadow, as tall as the tallest tree. As proud as the proudest predator, as terrified as the hunted prey. As small as the smallest stone, and as lost as she'd ever be.

She understood too late that the voice was her own, that it came from within. She ran from it, or tried to—through the trees, over dips and fallen branches, faster than she ever thought she could go.

Eventually, she stumbled. It was bound to happen—roots and branches everywhere. She skinned her knee, a rip through her favorite leggings. She felt the blood but couldn't see it. The darkest dark—in her ear it called her names. Names like *silly girl* and *scaredy-cat,* like *lonely girl* and *murderess.* Her chest went hollow and it was coming, it was coming, the terror inside her, worse than any monster, feeding from the inside, starting with her heart. *You will have nightmares, ax on bone.* And she knew now that Mama was right and she was wrong. Mama hadn't been hiding anything in the woods from her. Mama had been hiding *her* from the woods.

The girl couldn't breathe; she was dying. This was it, this was the end, and all she could do was lie on her side with one cheek to the dirt and the other to the sky and close her eyes and let it come. Her ax was useless, lying on the ground beside her. This was not a monster that could be killed.

But.

It was a monster that could be lived with.

One breath came after another. Finally, the girl rolled onto her back and focused on the pull and push of air, the rise and fall of her ribs. She focused until her mind went gray, floating in a calm sea. And soon her heart rate slowed, and her hands stopped shaking, and she began to feel like herself again, not like a girl in a scary story.

The girl, of course, was me.

At last I sighed and sat up, my knee still raw and stinging. I looked to the trees and saw a pair of golden eyes watching me. They glowed like little moons.

A creature stepped slowly from the shadows, one giant paw and then the other. My throat went dry, and though I wanted to scream, I held my breath instead. I actually had time to think, to say to myself, *Gem, please, it is best not to scream,* and time enough to agree, very sensibly: *Yes, Gem, you're absolutely right, you are full of the most wonderful thoughts and ideas.* Time seemed to have slipped sideways and meant very little to me now. It could even have been going backward and I would not have noticed. *Don't scream, don't scream, don't scream, don't—!* Who knew what *else* the echo of a lost girl's distress might attract in the woods? Though surely nothing quite like this.

It was a wolf.

A wolf with black fur.

A wolf with black fur and a long snout and those glimmery golden eyes.

A wolf with black fur and a long snout and those glimmery golden eyes *fixed on me.*

He was enormous, larger than I had imagined any wolf to be.

"Good evening," said the wolf, in a voice that scraped very

close to the bone. I stared, and reached for the ax without turning my head. "Is that blood I smell?"

I PREPARED TO be eaten. I hoped it would be painless, and I hoped it would be quick. The great face loomed over me and I closed my eyes so I wouldn't see it, the dark fur and the long wet snout. I waited for lips, for teeth, for foul breath. For the bone-crunch and the throat-snap. I waited for endless night.

It didn't come.

I opened my eyes as a warm exhale rolled over my face. The wolf crouched and blinked his large, luminous eyes at me, squinting carefully at my grazed knee. "You will want to wash and bandage that. Otherwise it will fester, and the stink of it might attract a predator. Though you don't look like much of a meal—skin and bones and not much else."

It took me a long moment to find my voice, and even then it was thin and small. I looked down at my torn knee, but I couldn't feel the sting anymore, as if it no longer belonged to me.

"But it's . . . not very deep," I said. "The wound, I mean."

"You cut yourself on a stick." The wolf's voice was scratchy but somewhat kind—as kind as it could be with all those teeth. "The forest is in you now, in your flesh. Be sure it doesn't spread."

I kept a wary eye on the wolf as I reached into my pack for an antibacterial hand wipe and used it to clean my knee, careful not to rip my leggings even more than they were already. It did the best job a half-dried-up antibacterial hand wipe could do, and when it was thoroughly crusted with blood I crumpled it up and stuffed it back in my pack. The wolf watched me all the while—not hungrily, but with intent curiosity. When my knee was clean, the wolf straightened to his full height and said, "Try not to take any more tumbles in the dark. Keep your blood in your veins, where it belongs."

"I'll try." And then, because I had the sense he was about to leave me there, alone and more lost than I had ever been, I said, "Excuse me, but—what is your name?"

The wolf rose to all fours and began to pace. He was still taller than me, even hunched and with his head bowed.

"No name your human mouth could pronounce." And he snarled what I assumed was his name—a deep growl that shook the nearest trees. It shook my heart too, every string.

"Oh, it's lovely," I said, and stood quickly. I felt like I should curtsy, so I did, bending with a dip of my chin. "It's very nice to meet you."

The wolf huffed. I chose to believe it was a huff of approval.

"I am the guardian of the forest's edge. I make certain that those from beyond stay out—and those from inside stay in." The wolf paused in his pacing and eyed me again. "You do not smell of the forest, child. Who are you, and why have you come here?"

I swallowed, feeling very small. "My name is Gemma Belle. I'm the guardian of, um—antiques."

Only once the words were out of my mouth did I realize I'd introduced myself as Gemma Belle. Belle was not my last name (Cassata), nor my middle (Ashley). But Belle—*Gemma Belle*—sounded so natural rolling off my tongue that I stood for a moment bewildered, wondering where it had come from.

I shook my head to clear it and hurried on.

"I'm looking for my mother. She was stolen by the Slit Witch, and a monster that looked like a tree but was not. With antlers and claws and great sharp teeth." I paused to catch my breath. "Please, Sir Guardian, do you know where I might find her? The Slit Witch, I mean. I'm determined to reach my mother, even if it means I must fight to win her back."

The light behind the wolf's eyes flickered like a firefly's.

"I know of no such creature by that name. Does she have another?"

"If she does," I said, "I don't know it."

It was a long moment before the wolf spoke again. "There was an incident near this edge of the forest several years ago, which is why I now must guard it. If the one you seek was part of it, I suggest you leave the forest and return home."

"Thank you, Sir Guardian," I said, and once again shouldered my pack. "But home is empty for me now. I can only go forward, not back."

"I am sorry to hear that." The wolf walked some distance away, and I thought that this meant our interaction was over. But in a moment he returned, a familiar object clenched between his teeth. He set it carefully into my waiting hands, and I curled my fists around it—the handle of my ax.

"Be careful of the blood you shed," he said. "Most especially your own."

I almost wished he could come with me, wished that he could stand so tall and terrible at my side and protect me from my enemies. But I knew that he could not. He was the loyal guardian of the forest's edge, and I was on a quest. I left him behind with a little wave over my shoulder, the lights in his eyes as bright as they ever were. My knee still hurt, but less like a scrape and more like the memory of one. With my eyes wide open, I ventured on into the dark.

10

Virginia

IT WAS A BOY THAT GRASPED MY WRIST THAT DAY. A boy that was nearly a man. In the dark I couldn't see much of him, but that didn't stop me from staring. His hair was longish and windswept, and he had a scar along the curve of his jaw, a slash that was paler than the skin around it. His eyes were focused not on me but straight ahead, and I wondered how I could fix that. With a finger to his lips, he pulled me down beside him, behind a hollow log.

"*Shh*," he whispered. Our faces were so close I could feel the warmth of his breath. "They'll hear you."

I looked to where he nodded and saw nothing. Only trees. It was better to look at him, so I did. He had gone as still as a stone at the center of a rushing stream: shoulders taut, gaze alert, and though his breath came hard and fast, there was more of fascination in his posture than fear. Beside him, I barely breathed at all.

"Who will hear me?" I asked, so dazed that I forgot to lower my voice.

"*Shh*." He crouched even lower, and I crouched too, drawing toward him without realizing until our shoulders touched.

"*Who* will hear me?" I said again, but just at that moment, I saw them: tall, thin creatures walking close together, moving in a pack. Slowly but stiffly, as if they hadn't exercised in quite some time and now their limbs kept locking up. They were shaped like trees, like the shadows of trees, dark but translucent if you stared hard enough, which I did, both fascinated and repulsed. Their joints cracked like the snap of branches in a storm, and a heavy, wet smell rolled through the air around them. I held my breath until they passed. I held it for as long as I could.

"What were they?" I whispered when the creatures had gone. The boy rose to his knees behind the log to make sure the coast was clear. I thought at first that he hadn't heard me, and was about to inquire again when he crouched back beside me.

"Dryads. Tree spirits. Their nails are as sharp as knives." His eyes were bright as he leaned closer to me and dragged a fingertip across his neck. He still wasn't quite looking at me, keeping a vigilant eye on the vicinity. "They'll slit your throat and drink your blood while you're still alive."

My heart thumped. *"Really?"*

"Absolutely." For the first time he turned his attention on me fully, and he must have seen the alarm written plain on my face. He grinned, reassuring, and my wild heart sprang into my throat. "But don't worry. You're perfectly safe with me."

I wanted to believe him. He'd saved me, hadn't he? Pulled me into the shadows, hidden me from monsters. With my shoulder against his, I'd felt his heat and solidity. For one mad second I imagined wrapping my arms around him, burying my face in his shoulder and letting him hide me from the woods, from the world.

From my mother, and from myself.

"I'm not sure I'll ever feel safe again," I said, shaking the thought away. The boy stood and held out his elbow for me to hold as I unfolded my legs, my knees numb from crouching for too long. I wrapped my arms around my middle, shivering in my thin, inadequate dress. "This forest is haunted."

He shrugged. "No more haunted than anywhere else. It's just that here the phantoms aren't shy about showing themselves."

A moment of quiet as we regarded each other, two strangers whose paths should never have crossed. Though I had questions—*Who are you? Why are you in the woods? Do you* live *in the woods?*—I didn't really know what to say or do, and was about to wave an awkward farewell and leave the whole incident behind when the boy stuck out his hand.

"Hello, and nice to meet you," he said, a grin splitting his face again. "My name is Ash."

"I'm Virginia," I said, and clasped his hand for an all-too-brief moment before dropping it. His palm was warm, and mine fit into it like a head on a pillow. Comfortable. "It's nice to meet you too, but I'm afraid I have to go."

"So soon?"

I looked in the direction the dryads had gone. Thankfully it was in the opposite way of home.

"Not soon enough," I said. "I have to get home. My mother will be worried."

I wasn't sure this was strictly true. If I stayed out all night, then yes, she'd worry; but for an hour or two? I was a grown woman in her eyes; I could do as I pleased.

Anything except drop out of college, that is.

Or venture into the woods.

"Well," I said to Ash, hunching my shoulders a little as I turned away. "Goodbye."

I began to walk toward home. Or where I thought home might be. In the dark, every tree looked the same. I only made it a few feet before Ash called out to me.

"Will you come here again?"

"After that?" I stopped, and waved a hand vaguely toward the path the dryads had taken. "No," I said, "never." And I meant it. I meant it with everything in me. *Never, never, never. My mother was right.*

My mother was right about the woods and I still resented her for it.

"It's true that here there be monsters," Ash said with a measure of grandiosity. "But *I'm* here too."

"Perhaps you shouldn't be." What did his face look like in the sun? A coil of regret sprang loose in my chest to think that I would never know. You *could come to* me, I thought. *We could meet outside of these woods, where the light shines bright and warm.* I didn't dare to say it, though.

I left him behind, or tried to; I admit that I looked back once, just a tiny peek over my shoulder. And that was what doomed me, I think. The forest felt my longing and curiosity and seized on it, tightening like fingers entwined in a long chunk of hair. I walked for five minutes, and still there were only trees around me and no sign at all of home.

I was going the wrong way. There was no explanation but this. Before I could make the conscious decision to stop and turn around, a figure jumped out at me from behind a fallen log. I started to scream until I realized who it was, and the sound that came out was a hiss of hot breath.

Ash.

"What are you doing?" It was something of a whisper-shout. I should have been home by now. I should have been safe. "Were you following me?"

"How could I be following you? I haven't moved from this spot." There was something in his hands that glinted silver as he tucked it back into the leather sheath at his hip. *A knife.* "You really ought to be quieter, though. You were so noisy approaching I thought you might be a weeping wili. They're undead shades that—"

"Oh God, don't even tell me." I wrung my hands, my heart fluttering. "Can you point me in the direction of the woods' edge, please? I must have gone in a circle."

"The woods' edge?" he said, as if he'd never heard of such a thing.

I took a deep breath. Suddenly it was hard to get enough air. "It's all right. I'll find it. Goodbye, Ash."

And I left him there for a second time, determined that it should be the last.

It was not.

"You're doing this!" I cried as I came upon Ash again, and in less time than before. My voice was too loud, but I couldn't hold it in. The dark of the forest held me as if in a fist.

"I'm not," he said. "I swear I'm not."

I was breathing so hard that it was almost painful to speak. My throat burned. "Then why do I keep coming back to you?"

There was silence as we looked at each other, and for a moment I was glad that I wasn't alone. But then I remembered that I couldn't trust him; he was a boy with a knife in the woods, and although he looked human he might be something more—or less—than that. How else to survive being surrounded by monsters than to become a monster yourself?

"If you can't find the way out," Ash said, his voice going so low that I shivered, "then the way out doesn't want to be found."

"What do you mean?"

Ash took a step closer to me and I let him. I let him take one step closer than he was before. But no more.

"You must complete a quest." He was tall, nearly a head taller than me; I felt that if he wrapped his arms around me, I would disappear entirely. And, oh, how I longed to disappear. "Fight your way out of the forest."

None of this felt real. His words, or my answer. "What kind of a quest?"

His smile now was grim. Grim but determined. "To best the Hunting Beast, of course."

MY HEART WENT still. *The Hunting Beast.* No. No, no, *no.*

Oh, Gigi. I'll show you if you don't believe me. Then you'll be afraid! Then you will obey me!

My mother took my wrist and pulled me into the woods, her steps steady but wooden. Down a path we had never taken, over a stream and past trees stripped of their bark, deep gouges secreting sap like sticky, dark tears. I wondered how she knew the way, but didn't dare to ask. No birds called here, and the leaves did not even rustle in the wind. The world was holding its breath. *Hush.* It was so dim I could barely see my mother beside me, but gradually the sky above us lightened. The trees thinned as we went up a hill—I had not known that the woods were anything other than completely flat—and as we crested the rise, I had my first glimpse of it: a burial ground, the place of the Hunted.

"Victims of the Hunting Beast," said my mother, still holding my wrist with her cold fingertips. "The most fearsome of the woodland monsters, and the most cruel."

It was a valley of death before me. A valley of death and the life that grows from the rot, only it was all *wrong.* The bodies in the valley, they each had their plot—shallow graves, half-submerged. Hands and knees pushing up through the dirt, faces and rib cages, bloodied throats and organs scattered carelessly: here a liver, there a heart. The hearts, covered in grime, still beat, and the eyes in the faces still blinked, and the fingers of the hands flexed as if reaching for another hand to hold, and the people were dead—weren't they? Oh God, *weren't* they?—but the pieces of them were still—they were still—

"It's the venom," my mother said, as if she could read my mind. "The Beast's venom keeps them alive."

More like a-*writhe*. A tapestry of agony, broken limbs and torn-open skin. The bites they'd incurred from the monster's mouth were still bleeding, and from the wounds on chests and cheeks and throats grew strange, prickly things. I hesitate to call them plants, though some of them had flowers and even fruits. From one woman's open belly sprang a fountain of leaves made of flesh, blue-black veins pulsing beneath, and from one man's empty eye socket bulged a round bubble like a spider's egg sac, with something twitching inside it. A rabbit with jewel green eyes calmly chewed the thistles jutting from a spilled pile of viscera. There were strange marks in the dirt around it, as of claws and knees, signs of someone crawling desperately away; the person the viscera belonged to was nowhere in sight.

The smell rolled over me as I took it all in, metallic and burning, like fire and blood. The sound of it too, a chorus of low groans and spittle-filled moans. I felt a scream in my throat, but my mother's grip tightened and I pushed it back down. I turned away and heaved, bile and chunks deposited at my feet, and when I was done my mother hurried me back the way we'd come. I didn't remember the journey. The next thing I knew, I was tucked in bed with a terrible taste on my tongue.

My mother knelt beside me. I couldn't look at her as she handed me a glass of water. I took it but didn't drink.

"Do you believe me now?" she said without any inflection at all. "Will you promise to keep away from the woods?"

I nodded; it was all I could manage. I felt the water glass slipping from my grip, so I set it on the nightstand. The room was full of shadows as she told me the story of the Hunting Beast.

Long ago when the world was new and the woods were young, the most powerful one among the clan of the earliest nightshades—creatures born of the first man to enter that place of wild branches and brambles, and the living shadow cast by the very first tree that grew there—was named prince and steward of the woods' sacred magic by the trees and rivers and stones.

Handsome and strong, he could win any fight; intelligent and keen, he could win any argument. He was not brave because he had no fear; he was not wise because he never failed. But he was charming and nothing stood in his way. He guarded the magic from outsiders who might wish to twist it for their own purposes, to smuggle it beyond the borders of the woods where it would warp and rust like iron in the rain. His might was prized above all else, and that was the woods' first mistake.

The woods thrived for a time. The trees grew thick and tall, the rivers flowed lush and quick, the stones tumbled and gathered strength. Firebirds began to nest, sprites bathed in the clear waters, and fairies built cities that would stand solid for centuries. Human in visage, but pure magic in their hearts, the nightshades protected the woods and everyone in it. The prince was revered among them, beloved by all.

But there was one who loved him above all else. She was a fairy, beautiful and kind, and the nightshade prince could not help but to fall in love with her too. They were married and soon expecting a child: a half-nightshade, half-fairy who, the oracle of the nightshades declared, would be the most powerful being the woods had ever seen. This angered the prince, and worried him, and after the child was born he snuck into the nursery and devoured the child in one gulp.

Well, it's a perverse and wretched thing to consume the flesh of your kind, and doubly so for one's own child. From the very first bite, the prince was cursed. His wife grew afraid of him, hated him, and soon he ate her too, beginning with her heart. Wasn't it his, by rights? Then he ate the other nightshades, so that none of them might lay with the fairies and produce children more mighty than he. He grew more monstrous with every twisted meal, until soon he was unrecognizable—as well as indestructible. For a dozen centuries, brave knights tried to best him, but the scales on his back and his belly were impenetrable, and the horns on his head were a foot and a half long. His teeth were as sharp as any sword, and his claws could rip through stone. He had no soul, and if he had a heart, it was a heavily armored one. Nothing could pierce it. It was foolish even to try.

For centuries he went on this way, eating anyone who crossed his path, but eventually his hunger turned against him. The taste of flesh began to sicken him, even as he craved it. Disgusted but starving, he ate merely one or two bites—just enough for him to survive—before he discarded his prey, leaving them pumped full of his venom, neither to live nor to die. And that was the graveyard that I had seen, the enduring agony of the Hunting Beast's feasts.

"Why did you bring me there?" I whispered when the story was done. "What if the Beast had gotten us?"

"You needed to see. You needed to *know*." My mother's gaze was steady and severe. "Now promise me, Gigi. Promise you won't ever go in the woods again."

There were tears in my eyes. I couldn't help it. "Why don't we just move away? Far away, where the monsters can't get us?"

Even as I asked it, though, I knew it was no good. This was our *home*. The house, the shop, and, yes, the woods too. I knew it in my bones. Once you had visited fairyland, there was no way to pretend that magic did not exist. That monsters didn't either. It would be like denying myself breath, or like living without dreams, cold and empty. Why must the terrible and the terrific be one and the same?

"Promise, Gigi. Say it."

Finally, I looked at my mother. Her dark eyes, her round face, the lines around her mouth that revealed her age. And in that moment I hated her, truly and completely: for scaring me, for showing me monsters, for the fact that monsters were real at all.

"I promise," I said, and rolled to my side away from her. I hated her as she sighed, and as her footsteps retreated, and as the door closed—the last time she'd really come fully into my room, deciding it was time to give me privacy, like I'd grown up that night. I hated her as I fell asleep, and as I dreamed, and when I woke in the morning to soft sunlight. Monsters were real.

They are real.

And wasn't it, a little bit, her fault?

"Not the Hunting Beast," I said now to Ash, in the woods, after I had defied my mother and plunged so deeply into the shadows that I could not get out. "I'll face anything but that."

"You know of him?" Ash sounded surprised, and almost . . . Was he upset? As if he had hoped to shield me from how terrifying this task would be?

I could only nod, seeing again the broken necks, the growing things; the blood in the dirt, the flickering eyes, abandoned bodies at once dead and alive. Though the nightmares of that place I'd had in the weeks, months, *years*, to follow had faded in time, the memory of that day stayed with me always. A memory my mother gave me.

"Oh, God," I said, covering my face with my hands. Would I really have to face the monster that had caused all that carnage? Was this truly the only way out? "What have I done? My mother warned me about the Hunting Beast and his victims, his graveyard, and now I'm about to become one of them!"

"Oh, is that what you're worried about?" Ash stepped toward me and lifted his arm as if he were about to put it around me, but dropped it back to his side at the last second. "Virginia, that place is nothing but a myth. I've lived here my whole life and never could find it."

"No, it isn't." I was shaking now; I couldn't stop. "I've been there. I've seen it."

The muscles of Ash's throat rippled as he swallowed hard. "Well, the Beast is old now. Retired, really. It's still a risk, but not so dire as you believe. Trust me." He smiled, and for a split second—the blink of an eye—I had this feeling like I didn't need to go home, because I already *was*. But the moment passed, leaving only dread. "I promise you'll be all right."

I lowered my hands from my face and looked up at him. *Don't cry, don't cry, don't cry.* "Is there truly no other way?"

"If there's another, I don't know it." Ash turned to me and took my hands. I was so startled that I didn't pull away. I didn't want to. "Virginia, I know we just met, but I won't let anything happen to you. Not until I've gotten to know you better, at least."

He squeezed my hands and dropped them. I managed only a feeble laugh.

"Anyway, I'll be right beside you," he said, and I inhaled sharply. It had not occurred to me that he would help me. That I would not have to face the monster alone. "But since this is your quest, you'll have to do the trickiest part. Okay?"

At this my stomach tightened. I just wanted to go home. But here I was, deeper in the forest than I ever thought I would go, with a strange boy telling me that the only way to escape was to trick the most cunning, most ravenous monster ever known.

"Okay." I nodded, determination shoving aside the dread. *Don't think about the bodies; don't think about the bites and the blood and the macabre growing things.* "What do I have to do?"

11

Gemma

I WAS LOST AND I WAS HUNGRY AND I WAS COLD. THAT was the state of things. The woods went on and on, and it occurred to me that I might be walking in circles but there was no way to tell. It all looked the same—the black trees and the gray sky and the shivering leaves. A smell of damp earth, of wet leafy greens—a heavy scent, but so monotonous that eventually I ceased to smell it. After a few hours I had gulped all the water in my water bottle; a few more and I had devoured every granola bar I'd put in my pack. My throat was dry and my belly rumbled, a slick feeling of nausea rising in my chest. I needed to drink something, to eat something—and soon!—or I would pass out. Maybe die.

Why had I thought this would be simple or quick? Find the witch and free Mama—that was all I had to do. In the stories I read, the heroes only had to be good and brave and all their wishes came true. Was I not good? Was I not brave? Why, then, was I still wandering the woods alone?

With a blister on my heel and a dizzy lightness in my head, I walked on. Soon it was night again, the sky dark violet. Occasionally a rabbit hopped across my path, or a squirrel. Sometimes a bird watched me from a branch. But other than that I was alone, or appeared to be alone, and I think that was the worst part—the loneliness. At some point I started to hum to myself without realizing I was doing it. When I did finally notice, I thought it would probably be best to stop—that the sound of a girl singing might be worse than a girl screaming, because a predator might hear it and think: *Why is she not afraid?* I couldn't give it up, though; I couldn't force my throat to close. It was a quiet kind of comfort, like a cat purring to heal herself. So I kept on with my humming, but softer.

After a while I heard running water. A stream maybe, or a brook. (*Are those the same? What about a creek?*) I stopped dead, listening. Whatever it was, it was close.

The energy that came over me then! You might have thought I'd just sprung up from bed. I *galloped,* I *flew;* I held a sudden, irreversible conviction that the creek-stream-brook was right around the corner, just up ahead, beyond the next old oak. The rush of water grew louder, until I couldn't understand why I wasn't standing in the middle of it, already wet from head to foot. Cool, clear water, so refreshing it bordered on divine.

Eventually the trees thinned out into a clearing, but no water was there either. I stopped, my palms sweating around the handle of my ax. There was a little light to see by from the glow of the sky, but it only made the trees a darker silhouette around me, more sinister and knotted than ever. I turned in a slow circle, quickly losing hope. But just when I was about to give up on ever finding the water I saw something—a gap in the underbrush, a tangled arch of sticks and leaves. I approached the tunnel cautiously, in case it was really a cave or the nest of some formidable creature, a mother protecting her babies. Slipping my ax into my pack, I lowered myself to my knees and peered inside. I don't know what I had expected to see, though; it was only darkness all the way through.

I decided what to do in an instant, because it was not really a decision at all. I took a deep breath and crawled into the tunnel.

It didn't take long before I was completely coated in mud up to my elbows and caking the ends of my hair. The hem of my sweater was soggy with it, my shoes clogged with it, and even though I never opened my mouth I could taste it, wet and heavy and bitter as coffee. I felt something squishy and squirmy under my hands, but I tried not to think too hard about it. The underbrush snagged at my hair, and several times I paused to untangle it. I'm sure I left more than a few dark clumps behind.

At last I reached the end and emerged into a clearing glittering with sunlight behind a fluffy white cloud. Daytime had arrived, suddenly and without warning. I blinked and raised an arm to shield my eyes. So jarring was the brightness that I thought maybe I had fallen asleep somewhere along the way and this was just a dream. But as I stood and wiped my hands on the front of my ruined sweater, the sun on my skin burned hot and pleasant, and the wind was warm and tickled my cheeks. Bits of cottony fuzz floated on the air and I smiled. If this was a dream, then so be it; I didn't want to leave. Especially because before me was the thickest tree I'd ever seen, its bark so white it was almost pink, and every branch was bowed with dozens of apples gleaming golden in the light.

I nearly wept to look at them, those plump shiny apples hanging just above my head. They were almost *too* pretty, too perfect to be real, and it occurred to me that this food might be fairy-made, meant to ensnare the trespasser for some nefarious purpose. A trick, a trap, a ruse, that might even spell a fate worse than death. But I was hungry, so I reached up and plucked an apple from the tree, sinking my teeth into it before I could panic or change my mind.

But instead of a juicy golden apple, I bit—*hard*—into my own hand.

In an instant the sunlight was gone, the clouds and the apples and the fluff dancing in the air—all gone. The tree was still there, but it was sickly now, its bark peeling in places to reveal deep gouges like scars. My hand was empty; hot blood glazed my lips. I stared at the puncture wounds between my thumb and forefinger where my teeth had cut deep. I knew it should hurt but it didn't yet, as if the pain had gotten lost in translation somewhere between my hand and my head, a signal blinkering out somewhere around my heart.

The wind picked up, and with it an ominous rattling. It took me a moment to realize the sound was that of the branches above me, thin shoots of wood clicking together like fingers. The tree bent toward me then, the branches sweeping like a dozen arms around me; they pushed at my back and sent me stumbling forward, into the trunk. I braced my hands against it to keep from falling, leaving a smear of blood on the bark. A sound like a sigh—a deep and relieved one—and I watched as my blood soaked into the tree, absorbed far too quickly. I lashed out with my ax, but when the blade met the bark it didn't chop like wood—it split like *skin,* dark sap oozing from the shallow cracks. The clicking began again, and terror swept through me. There was a word on the wind and that word was *more.*

The tree meant to eat me, to drink all my blood. Roots burst from the ground and twined around my ankles, so tightly they cut through my skin. The branches chafed and trembled around me, and I kept hitting the trunk with my ax, but despite the many gashes I inflicted, the tree seemed to barely notice. If the tree had a heart, my little ax wasn't long enough or sharp enough to pierce it.

I wish I had a sword that could slice through the tree and set me free.

It came from my heart and not from my head, that little voice making a wish in my last moments. It was quiet compared to the screaming and the terror, but it was clear and concise and true. The ax in my hand grew heavier, the blade thinning and lengthening, until I was no longer holding an ax at all but the hilt of a sword.

Was it real, or only my imagination? I supposed it didn't matter. The tree had created an illusion to lure me close, so why couldn't I conjure one too? The roots twisted around my waist, holding me there almost tenderly. The blade of my ax-turned-sword flashed silver in the low, gray light, and for a moment the tree's grip on me slackened, trickles of blood running bright down my ankles. With two hands, I raised the sword high over my head and brought it down on the roots nearest my feet. I used all of my strength and every last bit of energy I possessed.

The tree released a terrible screech—pain and sorrow and fury. I hadn't known a tree could make such a sound. I hacked through the roots, even as more of them sprang from the ground like the severed heads of a monster, regenerating and multiplying every time they were sliced. The branches above dove down and scratched me in retaliation. I swung my sword at them, but they just kept coming, kept swiping at me, and in a last act of wild desperation, I plunged the sword at the trunk of the tree—where I imagined a heart might be, if it had one. The blade sank into it as if it were flesh, and I pushed all the way down to the hilt.

The entire tree shuddered; the roots recoiled and the branches retreated. I pulled the sword from the trunk and a dark, sticky substance leaked from the wound, thick and shiny, like blood and sap mixed together. The tree slumped and went still, and I fell to my knees, my legs completely numb. The sword transformed back into an ax, and I cried when it crumbled to dust in my hands. Exhausted and stunned, I watched as a hand reached from the hole I had made in the trunk with my sword. Another hand joined it and began to peel the bark apart like ripping a piece of fabric in half. A woman stepped from the tree—a very tall, very thin woman, her hair long and white with a bluish tint, and wearing an odd dress of leaves. Her limbs were as spindly as branches; her feet were entirely bare. She raised a hand, pointing at me with a long, skinny finger, and I eyed her nails warily. They looked exceedingly sharp, curved at the tips.

"You have the Touch," she said in a voice like boiling water. It bubbled, spit, and scalded. "A Touch of Magic, my sweet."

12

Virginia

"THE FEARSOME HUNTING BEAST LIVES IN A STORY-book cottage? With a little smoking chimney? And a beautiful garden? Have I got that right?"

Beside me, Ash snorted. Together we peered around a thick tree at the edge of a clearing strung with strands of tiny fairy lights, a cozy-looking stone cottage at its center.

"It's like I told you," he said. We were so close that the heat of his body warmed mine, but still I shivered and felt frozen. "The Hunting Beast is enjoying his retirement."

None of this seemed right, but the fear was overwhelming and it was hard to focus on anything else.

And why, I couldn't help but think, an old familiar rage boiling up inside me, because it was easier to be angry than afraid, *am I even trying so hard to get back to my mother? Isn't all of this her fault?* She never let me make my own choices. Not about the woods, or school, or my life. Sometimes it was like I was little more than a doll in her shop, rosy cheeks and painted smile, positioning me in any way she pleased without ever asking what I wanted, how *I* felt about it.

If I was eaten by a monster now, would she even care?

I took a deep breath and shook away the thought. I knew I was being unfair.

"And all I have to do is get the hairbrush and get out?" I asked Ash, for what must have been the tenth time. I was stalling, and I was pretty sure he knew it.

"Just like we talked about." His jaw was set with determination, but his eyes were soft. "Trust me, Virginia. I'm right here with you."

I looked at the sky, tipping my head back with a groan. Trust him, he said, as if I had known him for years and hadn't just met him an hour before. Trust him, he said, as if it were as easy as breathing, as simple as giving him my hand to hold.

Trust him, he said, and I did, because what other choice did I have? I wanted to go home.

I took a deep breath and started toward the cottage, with Ash close behind me. The whole scene appeared so harmless, the front lawn wild with roses. It smelled like springtime and the Baby Magic lotion that came in a pink plastic bottle—the kind my mother slathered all over herself when she came out of the shower. The fairy lights in the branches swayed with the wind. I held my breath as I walked up the dirt path to the front door, careful to avoid making any noise by stepping on a twig or kicking a stone. Every window in the pretty little house was dark. My mother had told me the story of the Hunting Beast, of course, but I couldn't recall any sort of hairbrush being involved. Before agreeing to do this, I'd asked Ash to explain it.

"After he had eaten everyone he knew," he'd said, "the Hunting Beast sold his soul—what was left of it anyway—to a witch in exchange for a hairbrush enchanted to steal memories with every stroke, so that he would not have to live with the misery of what he had done. And I'm happy to say that it worked! He forgot he was ever a prince, ever a monster, or that he ever devoured hundreds of people, including his own flesh and blood."

This addendum to the tale hadn't made sense to me then, and it didn't make sense to me now. But Ash had already started

going on about how the brush was an Object of Great Signifi-
cance and that surely retrieving it would fulfill the terms of the
quest. The door to the cottage was unlocked, as Ash had
guessed it would be. Why lock the door when you are a beast
that cannot be beaten? The interior was dim and smelled bit-
terly sweet, like chocolate and cinnamon laced with the smoke
from a fire burning in a room off to the right. As we passed by,
I saw that something was roasting, though it didn't look like a
person, thank God. More like a chicken. The hallway leading
deeper into the house was narrow, piled with books and boxes
and other paraphernalia, jars and notebooks and candles half-
melted, drips of white wax. It did not look like the home of a
beast, but more like the home of a witch. I stepped carefully,
quietly, holding my breath. Though Ash's presence beside me
was solid and comforting, my heart was not okay with this. It
pounded like an alarm inside my head as everything in me
screamed to turn back.

But I kept going. I found the stairs at the back of the house,
and at the bottom Ash nodded at me. *This is as far as I go; the
rest you must do alone.* I climbed the stairs slowly, testing each
step before I put my weight on it. At the top I paused and took
a moment to exhale, looking back to Ash for reassurance. Another nod, a little half-smile; my heart tripled its speed.

Ash said the hairbrush would be on the second floor, in the
room where the Hunting Beast was asleep. When I asked him
how he knew this, he said only, "Legend." And I supposed it
made sense that the Beast would want to keep a precious object
so close. I crept to the door at the end of the hallway; it was
open only a crack. I pressed my hand against the wood, pushing it open a few more inches, until there was just enough space
for me to slip inside.

The faint lights from outside cast the room in a gray pallor
through the single window. Scratched floorboards, heaps of

dark clothing, a round mirror hanging on the wall. The snoring lump in the corner on the bed was not as big as I had imagined the Hunting Beast to be. In fact, it seemed no larger than me when I was curled up under the blankets, my knees tucked into my chest. This brought me little comfort, though. What did the beast's size matter when its claws were sharp enough to cleave me in half with one swipe? The hairbrush glinted silver on the nightstand, very near the Beast's covered head. I pressed my hands to my cheeks, the coolness of my palms steadying me. Then I took one step forward. And another.

I barely remember crossing that room; I think I almost blacked out. All that mattered was the hairbrush, the stupid hairbrush that somehow spelled my freedom. When I was still a foot away I reached for it, leaning forward at the waist. I closed my fist around the handle and gasped.

The metal was cold. Unnaturally icy cold, as if it had been chilling in a freezer for hours. I hadn't expected that, and it slid right out of my hands.

I had never heard such a sound. The clatter of it hitting the floor was shattering. I went absolutely still, grounded to the spot. The Hunting Beast sat up in bed, the blankets falling away to reveal that it was not a beast at all.

It was a woman.

"Ash?" she said, rubbing her eyes. Her voice was choked with sleep. "What are you doing?"

I didn't stick around long enough to get a good look at her. No thoughts in my head, I snatched the hairbrush and I ran.

"*Wait—*" said the woman, fully awake now; her voice was high and harsh. I held the hairbrush against my chest with my forearms crossed in an X, the handle still too cold to touch as I sprinted out of the room and down the stairs to where Ash was waiting, springing into a run when I reached him at last. I heard her coming after me, horrible thudding footsteps that sounded much meaner and heavier than one small woman could make. In the hallway I bumped into a stack of books and sent it toppling; I tripped over a basket filled with yarn. Ash grabbed my elbow to steady me, and together we flew out the front door. At the tree line he stopped, though I couldn't think why; when I tried to continue on he placed a gentle hand on my shoulder. His eyes were wide.

"You did it," he breathed, staring at the brush that I still hugged against my chest. "I can't believe—"

"*Ash.*" The woman stood in the doorway. Her hair was long and silvery and fell over her shoulder; her skin was so pale it was nearly translucent. And in her chest was a long crack, as if she were made of glass.

I know this woman, I thought, now frozen to the spot, seeing a phantom version of the fairies that had danced all around us at the fairy queens' wedding, feeling the cold that had pierced me at her touch. The crack in her skin was wider than it once had been, with smaller, spidery fissures spreading out toward her shoulders, and through it all I could see her heart. Mesmerizing red, a bloody gem. I stared until Ash spun me around by the shoulders, his breath in my ear.

"Run," he said, and I needed no more encouragement than that. Into the woods and away, sprinting as the woman behind us shouted something, a word in a language I didn't recognize. A second later the ground rippled beneath us like an ocean wave and knocked us off our feet. Somehow I managed to keep hold of the hairbrush as I landed hard on my knees. Before I could even really register the pain, Ash had grabbed my arm and yanked me to my feet.

"Sorry, I'm sorry," he said as I yelped, and then we were off again. There were footsteps behind us—too close—and Ash glanced over his shoulder. Without stopping, he shouted something in the same language the woman had used. The air crackled and a gust of wind more powerful than any storm could produce blew past us and bent the branches of the trees. The hairbrush tumbled out of my arms, and I scooped it up in one hand without stopping. After a few minutes I could no longer tell if the brush was warming to a natural temperature or if my palm had simply gone numb. Eventually the woman's footsteps fell away, and we were alone.

"Ash, who was that?" We were running hand in hand. I didn't know if he had taken mine or if I had taken his. Perhaps we'd reached for each other at the same time. "Ash, that wasn't a beast."

We kept running. Wet leaves beneath my feet, branches scratching my cheeks.

He didn't answer me.

"Ash," I said again, and pulled my hand from his. "You *lied*. *Who was that?*"

Breathing hard, he swung around and stopped in front of me. "You're right, you're right. I'm sorry."

Ash bent forward, his hands on his knees. He wouldn't look at me.

"Virginia," he said, and I stiffened, waiting. "That was not the Hunting Beast. That was a witch."

My heart dropped to my toes. This was bad. But then it got worse.

"The witch is also my mother."

THE RELIEF I felt at the sight of the woods' edge and my house beyond was unparalleled—truly, like waking from a nightmare. Like opening your eyes and finding that it wasn't real, that you'd never have to think about it again. When I was close, I was about to make a break for it, but a soft voice behind me said simply, "Virginia."

Ash.

It wasn't that I had forgotten him, exactly; I was simply pretending that he wasn't there. After he'd admitted that the woman in the cottage—*the witch*—was his mother, I had stared at him for a full thirty seconds and then turned abruptly and walked away. Not quickly—I was tired—but I was going home. And no boy or beast or witch was going to stop me now.

"Virginia," he said again, and though I paused I didn't turn around. Truthfully, I hadn't known for sure if he was behind me. He hadn't called out or tried to explain. Only the occasional crack of a branch several feet in the distance had alerted me to the possibility of his presence at all. Now, though, he said my name for a third time, like casting a spell. "Virginia, please. Can we talk about this?"

I could have kept walking.

Instead, I turned around slowly.

"Everything you told me was nonsense." I tried not to sound too angry. But then I wondered why I felt the need to restrain myself. After all, I *was* angry. I was still holding the hairbrush—the stupid hairbrush!—and I very nearly threw it at his head. "The Hunting Beast's hairbrush and the *quest.* Well, I mean, I must have completed it because—look! There's my house. So I'm not really sure what's left to talk about." I laughed, but not because I found anything particularly funny. In fact, it was all so absurd and traumatizing that if I didn't let out *something*—a laugh, a cry, a scream—I might have imploded. "Ash, you made me think there was a monster in that house that might *eat* me."

"I know, and I'm sorry. Really, I am, with all my heart I . . . hadn't expected you to know about the Hunting Beast, and I was afraid that if I told you the truth, you wouldn't have done it."

I laughed again. "Yeah, no shit."

Ash ran a hand through his hair so that it stuck up in several directions. "I needed that hairbrush, Virginia. The witch put a spell on it so that I couldn't touch it. Trust me—I've tried. I've been trying to get at it since I was small. She's been using it to steal my memories."

"*Steal* your memories?" My mother was controlling too, but even she wouldn't do that.

At least, I was pretty sure.

Somewhat sure.

Well . . . I was *completely* sure she would never use magic.

"The witch is my mother, but not through blood," he said. "My birth mother gave me up to the witch as part of a bargain: her firstborn child for a chance at true love."

I looked again to my house through the trees, reassuring myself that it was still there. Then I sighed and sat on the ground, too tired to stay standing to listen to his story. After a second's hesitation, Ash sat too, facing me. Our knees nearly touched, and I could feel the heat from his skin.

"This sounds like a fairy tale," I said, with more bitterness than I'd meant to inject. I finally let go of the hairbrush, tossing it in the dirt nearby. My hand was cramped from the cold of it. "I'm too old for fairy tales."

Ash looked up. "Are you sure about that?"

I was quiet. Suddenly, I was not so sure at all.

Ash bowed his head. "I don't know much about my birth mother, which is all part of the problem, as you'll see. This is the story the witch told me when I asked about her, so take it with a grain of salt, okay? She only told it to me so that I would stop asking questions."

He rubbed his hands on his knees, taking a breath.

"My mother was a water sprite, so she could only leave the river where she lived for a few hours at a time. One day a man wandered into the woods searching for his dog that had escaped the leash. He paused to drink by the stream and another sprite pulled him under the surface, meaning to drown him for stealing a precious handful of clear water. My mother saw and saved him. They, uh, spent some time together after she rescued him, but then it was time for her to return to the river, and for him to head back home.

"Lovesick and heartbroken, my mother went to the one they called the Slit Witch to ask that she be transformed into a human, like him. Or at least, human enough that she could stay out of the water as long as she liked without drowning in the open air. The witch agreed to cast a spell, but only in exchange for her child. I don't know why the witch wanted me, then or now. Often she doesn't seem to like me very much.

"Anyway, that was how the sprite found out she was pregnant with me. When I was born, she dutifully delivered me to the witch. She drank a potion to turn human and went to find my father. She left, just like that—and she never looked back."

I wrung my hands in my lap. It was a sad story, and I wasn't in the mood for sadness. I still wanted to be angry. It was easier. And so I didn't look at him as I asked, "But did the man ever find his dog?"

Something unexpected: Ash laughed. "Yes, I'm certain he did. Let's not make this *fairy tale* more depressing than it needs to be."

I smiled a little, but it was more of an automatic response to his laughter rather than an honest gesture, and I quickly dropped it, forcing my face blank. "Why do they call her the Slit Witch?"

"They call her the Slit Witch because her magic is older than the woods itself, and stranger and more volatile than most other common forms of magic. If you are careless of keeping the balance, of taking without offering anything in exchange, then the magic will strip you to pieces. Her kind of magic is called the

Touch, and the molting doesn't happen right away. It begins very slowly at first, but much faster and sharper as time goes on. She's missing much of the skin on the back of her scalp, though she hides it well."

Oh God, why did I keep asking questions? I should have surmised by then that asking would only lead to learning things I didn't *really* care to know, or even to think about ever again. But I was curious—how could I not be?—and so I left that line of inquiry behind.

"All right," I said, combing through all he had told me. "But what does the hairbrush have to do with the Slit Witch and your real mother the water sprite? And with you?"

"Oh. Well, the thing is, I *remember* the water sprite. Her laugh, her smile, the sound of her singing me to sleep. Little flashes, here and there, but I knew enough that when I asked the witch about her, she became angry—angrier than I had ever seen her. She sat me down and told me the story of how I had been bargained away, abandoned, left in the witch's care without a thought. But the story didn't make sense, because how could I remember her if I was only a baby? So I pressed harder, asked more questions. 'Remember her no more,' the witch said. 'She is not worth the time it takes.' But I couldn't let it go. I needed to *know*."

He stopped and sighed so hard he shuddered. I sensed that this would be the hardest part. The part that mattered most.

"One evening, after I'd asked again after my mother, she sat me down and produced a sterling silver hairbrush I'd never seen before. I was only nine years old at the time. She ignored my questions and began to brush my hair, and soon I didn't remember what I was asking anymore. I felt strange. Outside of myself. Then she sent me to bed.

"I didn't realize at the time what she had done. I didn't ask about my birth mother for a long time. In fact, I'd forgotten her.

It wasn't until a few years ago that a memory resurfaced, even blurrier than they had been when I was still a child. Remembering again was like—like looking into a mirror, seeing a person behind you, or a whole scene playing out, but when you turn around, there's nothing there. It was a smell that triggered it, that time. Just the right mix of lemon and damp earth, of wood smoke and salt. It hit me so hard that a woman's face jumped into my mind—because the smell reminded me of her, of her hair tickling my face. When I asked the witch about it, she brushed my hair again. The next time I remembered her it was a sound—the precise pitch of an owl's hoot over the western wind. It conjured up a lullaby, the shape of her lips.

"I've lost count of how many times the witch has stolen my memories, but the last time, only a few months ago, I finally realized what she's been doing to me. I believe the hairbrush is enchanted not only to steal memories, but to hold them as well. And if I can just figure out how to crack it, perhaps I can recover the lost memories I had of my mother. I can figure out why the witch has been lying to me."

My hands were trembling. My breath was too. I tried to wrap my head around all of this, and found that I couldn't. Not quite.

"The witch seems very powerful," I said. "How do your memories keep breaking through the hairbrush's spell?"

"A fair question," Ash said, leaning forward over his knees. Almost as if he . . . longed to touch me? Or was that only my imagining? His fingers found a small rock in the dirt, turning it over and over. "Time is one factor. No spell lasts forever, just as nothing in the natural world does. Not us, not the birds, not even the trees. But also, I think it comes down to the *nature* of memory. I used the wrong word, before, when I said she *stole* them from me. How can a memory be stolen, really? Surely you'd have to cut out a part of the brain to do that. People forget things all the time, but it's all still *there* inside, isn't it? Somewhere? It's more like she concealed them. Cast her shadow over them."

"I . . . see," I said—though did I really? It frustrated me that I was only part of this world of the woods by half. Enough to know that magic existed, but not enough to grasp the mechanics of it. I knew so little, and yet what I *did* know tugged ceaselessly on my heart. Isn't that why I played my game today, crept backward into the place where I was not allowed to go? I was a creature banished to the shadows, not unlike Ash's memories.

Ash wound back his arm and tossed the little rock in his fist far into the trees, watching it sail until it disappeared into the dark. "The witch likes to think she's infallible, but no magic is. I even found a way around the enchantment that I couldn't touch it. The hairbrush, that is."

He gave me a grateful smile, but I couldn't return it. I glanced toward my house and felt instant relief to see that it was still there and waiting for me.

"Well, I'm glad you got your memory-stealing hairbrush back." I plucked the accursed brush off the ground and stood, wiping off the leaves clinging to my clothes. I held it out to him, but he didn't take it. Could he still not touch it? How was he going to get it home?

"Virginia." Ash stood too. "I have one more favor to ask."

I tensed.

"Can I keep the hairbrush with you? Just until I find a better place to hide it?"

His face was so hopeful, earnest and open.

"I don't want any more trouble with the witch," I said. It wasn't a *no* and it wasn't a *yes*.

"She won't find you," he said quickly. "I promise, a thousand times. She doesn't like to leave the sanctuary of the woods. I'm not sure how she does it, exactly, but she draws her strength from the trees."

I swallowed, thinking of the words he had shouted at the witch that had caused the wind to blow like it was the end of the world. "You're a witch too?"

"Not a witch," he said, and his hands twitched, again like he wanted to touch me but didn't dare to. He curled them into fists. "The son of a water sprite."

My heart pounded faster and louder than it had at any point that day. "Okay," I said, and then again, "Okay."

He kissed me then—quick, on the cheek. Almost reflexively I brought my hand to the spot he had touched, my face flushing. "Thank you, Virginia. *Thank you.* Keep it close, and I'll come back for it as soon as I can."

I looked back only once as I made my way out of the woods, at the edge of the trees where the dark met the light, and he was still there, his smile gone, watching me. When our eyes met he nodded, and I took a deep breath. Then I stepped fully into the fading sun and the safety of my backyard. The woods and the witch and the boy with a quest—at once, it felt like a dream.

My mother wasn't waiting for me. She was already in her room and reading in bed as she did every evening, a slit of light leaking beneath her closed door. For a moment I wished I *had* been eaten by a monster, just to make her feel bad. To make her feel *something*. I laid the hairbrush on my nightstand and crawled into bed as well, too tired to do anything else. I felt more alone than I had when I was away at school, and for a moment I wondered if I should take it all back, if continuing my studies was actually the right path.

It's true that here there be monsters. But I'm here too.

No. I knew I could not wrench myself away even if I'd wanted to. But I didn't want to now, and that made it all the worse.

13

Gemma

EVERYTHING AND NOTHING HURT, AS IF I COULD sense my pain but not fully feel it. Cuts and bruises all over, a scrape on the knee, a twinge in the wrist. I thought I was dying or coming very close, or maybe I just needed to sleep. Except I was still lying beside the evil tree that had tried to gut me and the woman with the white hair stood near, gazing at me like a foreign fruit that had rolled into her orchard. As if she might eat me, but wasn't sure if I was poison. She had said something about a Touch of Magic, and I really wanted to know more about that. But it hurt to *think*, let alone to speak.

"Little girl, do you hear me?" The woman lowered to her knees at my side, her eyes a startling silvery-blue. I lay on my back, the sky as gray as smoke. "You have freed me from the wicked tree, and though I am rather wicked myself, I will heal you now in return for the great service you have done me. The debt will be paid, and we will be bound together no more."

I hadn't realized we were bound in the first place. I didn't like the idea of that. But before I could protest or ask any questions, something began to happen: The clouds turned pink, then red, then deepened to black, and a smooth, cool rain began to fall—thick droplets the color of old dried blood. It blistered on my skin and I stiffened, muscles locking as I cried out in an intense discomfort that quickly approached agony. *How is this helping?* But soon the ache washed over and out of me, like a wave of the sea retreating, and my whole body began tingling. I sat up, rolling my wrists and ankles to coax the feeling back into my hands and feet. Blood rushed through me, and I felt whole and new. Clean.

"How did you do that?" I wasn't tired anymore, or even hungry. "Are you a witch?"

The woman snorted. "I am a *warning,* and don't you forget it. I am almost as old as the woods itself, and far more cunning."

She said this last with a derisive look over her shoulder at the tree behind her, dark brown blood dribbling from the giant gap she'd stepped through.

"Okay." I kept flexing and straightening my fingers, in awe of myself. What a rush, to jump from nearly dead to electrically alive! "It's only that I'm looking for a witch, and I thought—"

"My advice? Don't."

This snapped me back into focus. "Don't think? Or don't look for the witch?"

"Both." The woman stood, and I did too, a feeling like an itch in my brain coming over me as I watched her unfold on her very long legs, her towering shadow falling coolly over my skin. It reminded me of something; *she* reminded me of something, and I shook my head, trying to think. But whatever it was, it remained just out of reach. "Witches are troublesome, meddlesome things. It was a witch that shut me all up in this tree. Now be gone with you! I'm hungry."

How rude, I thought, but then, if I had been trapped inside a tree for however many years, I would probably be rude and grumpy too.

"Wait," I said, dusting the dirt off my clothes. "Can you just—"

"No."

"But you said something about—"

"Go! Now! Before I change my mind and eat you!"

I probably should have been afraid, but I was only annoyed. I planted my feet firmly into the ground and lifted my chin—my best imitation of bravery.

"Listen," I said, "I need your help. You said you are almost as old as the woods itself. You must know its paths and passages by heart."

"Have you not been paying attention, girl? I've been stuck in that tree for the last who-knows-how-many years. I'm tired, and I'm hungry, and at this point I wouldn't know sky from dirt."

"Please." I came very close to stamping my foot in frustration, but managed somehow to refrain. Rude people did not take kindly to those who were rude in return, even though it was very tempting to strike them with their own blade. I took a deep breath and began again. "You must know a spell that could help guide me in the right direction."

"Hmm." The woman looked me up and down. Then, "It will cost you."

I swallowed, my throat dry. I only had about fifteen dollars to my name. "How much?"

"Not money, you fool. Let's see . . ." She paced over the split tree's roots, her pale hands clasped behind her back. "What'll it be, what'll it be? A price to pay, a gift to give. Hmm . . . *yes.* Your rib."

My heart thumped once, hard. "My—?"

"Rib, yes. Bottom rib, the left."

I hadn't realized how fond I was of all my ribs—and the bottom left, particularly—until faced quite suddenly with the prospect of no longer possessing it.

"Isn't there anything else—?"

"No."

"Will it hurt?"

The woman grinned. It was a sticky thing, like sap. And me a fly, buzzing willingly into her trap. "No more than a nightmare from which you will soon wake."

I was quiet for a moment, but really, my mind was made up. Before I could panic or talk myself out of it, I looked at the woman and nodded. Her grin—so wide before—somehow widened. She put me in mind of a skeleton.

"Very good," she said, and closed her eyes. "Information for you, and a little snack for me. We have a bargain then."

She didn't utter a single word, only raised her arms and held out her hands, palms splayed to the sky. I waited for the anguish of having a bone ripped from my body, but it never came, not the way I imagined it. Instead, my vision went black, and I felt a not unpleasant prickling all throughout my middle, almost as if it were raining inside me. But then, suddenly, the rain became a crackling storm—lightning strikes of pain, here and there and everywhere, my heartbeat rushing in my ears like the wind.

But like a sudden storm it was quickly spent; it was over in moments. My vision cleared, and all was as it was before except that my lower left side felt slightly numb.

"All right," said the woman when it was done. "Ask what you will of me."

It was smaller than I thought it would be. A skinny white bone with a slight curve clutched in the woman's hands, the end of it a dull point. It made me dizzy to look at, so I focused on the woman's face instead.

"I'm looking for the witch," I said, and swayed on my feet. I had this terrible suspicion that my body no longer belonged to me fully; that any part could be cut out and hauled away at any time, easily. I felt the first flush of panic creep up my cheeks.

"Which witch?" the woman demanded. "You can't turn right around here without smacking into a witch's saggy chin."

I shook my head, took a deep breath. *Steady, steady.* "The Slit Witch," I said.

The woman's face fell into a severe frown, and her eyes widened and looked at me almost—tenderly? Slowly, as if it pained her, she reached out her arms and proffered the rib. Shyly, I took it.

"Go home, little girl." Her voice, once burning, was cool now. "You will not find the Slit Witch if she does not want you to. And anyone who is actively looking for her is someone she does not want to see. Our bargain is broken. I cannot help you."

I glanced down at the rib, so light in my hands. *Mine, it is mine.* I would never let it go again.

"Can't you put it back?" I asked, but when I raised my gaze the woman was gone, as if she had vanished into the very air. I was alone, with a rib on the wrong side of my skin, and I was still lost, no closer to reaching my goal.

A cool breeze blew that felt like spiders crawling over my skin, and I needed no further prompting to vacate that haunted clearing. I slid my rib carefully into my pack and then I left the glade, walking briskly at first, until a howling wind rushed at my back and sent me running wildly between the trees with no hope of knowing where I was going, aiming only for the destination of *away,* far away. My heartbeat knocked about in my head, and my breath came in short, aching gasps. Finally, when I could run no more, I sat down heavily on a fallen log, and folded forward until my chest was pressed to my thighs.

I wish I had a map, I thought, trying to tap into the same source that had transformed my ax into a mighty sword. *A map that would lead me straight to the Slit Witch.*

Nothing happened. Not a spark or a surge, nor a tingle or a

prickle—or whatever magic was supposed to feel like when it rose up inside you. I tried again, thinking the words more slowly and clearly this time, but again nothing. I wished one more time—in stories magical things often happened in threes—but there was only silence and stillness in me.

So much for the Touch.

After a long moment I lifted my head and came face-to-face with my own shadow.

I didn't scream—but I did whimper. I covered my mouth with my hands. Would the strangeness of the forest ever stop sneaking up on me?

I lowered my hands slowly. "Hello," I said—a whisper really—and my shadow took a step closer. I couldn't be sure she was mine—none of her features were defined—but as I beheld her, a solid dark form standing tall, it felt strangely like looking in a mirror. When I stood and tilted my head, she tilted hers too, and when she spoke, it was with my voice, though I didn't recognize it at first.

"You are lost," she said, and it wasn't a question. "I will show you the way."

She turned without a backward glance to see if I would follow. But she didn't need to; of course I was right behind her, pushing branches and bushes out of my way to keep pace. She was the first person who had offered to help, and if I couldn't trust my own shadow, then who *could* I trust?

She began to walk faster, and soon my breath was coming in hard little puffs, while my calves ached in a way that reminded me of meat spoiling. Then we were running, and I lost sight of her between the trees, one shadow amongst many shadows, like trying to follow one drop of water down a stream.

"Wait!" I cried. "I can't go that fast! Please, slow d—"

An enormous wall of white stone appeared, so suddenly that I did not stop in time. Turning a little, I ran right into it, shoulder first, and my whole world went fuzzy around the edges. I fell back in the dirt, landing hard on my tailbone, looking wildly around for my shadow, now nowhere to be found.

I lay back in a soft pile of leaves, clutching my shoulder with one hand as if that would help. I didn't think anything was broken or dislocated, but likely I would have a nasty bruise in the morning—that is, if I made it to morning. I stared up at the wall, which seemed to stretch infinitely from side to side, and wondered what, exactly, I was meant to do now.

14

Virginia

AFTER OUR DISASTER OF AN EVENING, MY MOTHER and I didn't speak for three days. Not during meals or when working in the shop, nor while we ran errands, or before bed, or when we woke up. Silence met silence and refused even to shake hands, stubborn to the last. And as the silence grew, the more unbreakable it became.

It might have bothered me more if I wasn't so distracted with walking past various windows of the house to glance at the woods for an Ash-shaped shadow or consumed by worry about the hairbrush tucked into the top drawer of my dresser. I'd buried it beneath my *unmentionables,* as my mother would call them. (Surely, I reasoned, it is a hideous violation to root around in someone else's bras and underwear, one that would make even an evil witch hesitate.) Only at night with the curtains pulled tight did I dare to take it from its hiding place.

What would happen if I brushed my hair with it? Would I forget the fight I had with my mother, forget that I did not want to go back to school in the fall? Would I forget all the nights I had cried myself to sleep in my narrow dorm room bed, the helpless, clawing realization that I was a thing separate from the rest of the world, that no one on earth would ever feel what I felt in just the same way? Would I forget that no one could know how magic had touched me, changed me, spoiled me, so that I couldn't stop hungering for it even as my mother preferred to pretend that we had made a quick getaway, a clean break? Would I forget my longing for the woods of my childhood, for my life before I knew what a monster was?

Perhaps it would be easier to forget. Certainly, it would hurt less.

But then, what would take the place of those memories? My heart would not simply be emptied. There would be an ache that I couldn't explain; I would always be reaching for something I couldn't recall. Like Ash, struggling to remember his mother, his life before the bargain and the witch. Forgetting was not without pain.

I put the hairbrush away.

On the fourth day my mother cut through the silence, surprising both of us.

"Well? Have you decided then?"

I had been standing alone at the window in what would become Gemma's Glass Room, watching the shadow of the woods crawl toward the house. *Ash, where are you? Will I ever see you again?* I jumped a little as she said my name once and then again. When I turned to the doorway she was only a silhouette.

"Decided what?" I said, though of course I knew. My voice was rough with disuse. I had spoken to no one but myself for three days.

"If you will return to school at summer's end. You have only two and a half months left."

Only two and a half months? The thought of it stopped my breath.

"I don't know," I said, because I couldn't tell her what she wanted to hear, and I couldn't tell her the truth.

She sighed and looked so tired that suddenly I wanted to cry.

"It is a privilege, you know. To learn."

"I *know*." I swallowed, took a deep breath. I was so angry with her—for not understanding me, for not even trying to—and the anger burned. But it only burned me, not her, and so I let it go. For now. "Can we just . . . not talk about it? Until September first, at least?"

Her reply was quicker and easier than I thought it would be. "Yes," she said, and then again, "*yes*. It was beginning to get far too quiet around here. I could hear myself think."

I laughed, and the laughter helped me to push the last of my anger down where I couldn't see it. My mother rarely made jokes, but when she did I treasured them. It was a much-needed moment of levity, and maybe if we had been different people—a mother who knew how to express herself, a daughter who had not defied her—she might have crossed the room and wrapped me in a hug. She was always holding herself away from the world—apart—and in that moment it occurred to me that maybe she wasn't deliberately trying to keep me at a distance; she was trying not to get hurt. It was an ingrained response, a form of self-protection from monsters great and small—the ones that lived in the woods and the ones that lived in her head that I still knew little of. So, no, she made no move for a hug, but she smiled at me and I smiled back, and it was almost the same as an embrace.

Almost.

"Do you want to help me with dinner?" she said. "I could use an extra set of hands."

And though I was reluctant to look away from the forest for even a moment, I nodded and followed her upstairs to the kitchen, where the light was bright and the stove was hot and the radio was just loud enough to cover the sound of our breathing while we worked side by side in companionable quiet. Where things were normal for a little while, and I could pretend that my longing wasn't eating me alive.

* * *

THERE WAS A thunderstorm the following evening. The rain fell so hard and fast beyond the window that I could only see the forest during each blink of lightning, the tops of the trees gilded and stark before going dark once more. It was weather that no one should be caught in, not even the foxes and the birds. So imagine my surprise, as I closed up the shop for the night, when I heard a series of taps upon the door, so soft they shouldn't have been heard. But I was listening, alert for anything out of the ordinary, and I heard it even in the roar of the storm. Or maybe I didn't hear the knocks so much as I *felt* them, like a fingertip tapping my shoulder. Whatever it was, a sound or a sense, I rushed to the door and threw it open just as a jagged knife-edge of lightning split the sky.

I knew it would be Ash, and yet, when I saw him I could hardly move or speak; I could only stare. I had imagined him arriving on my front porch so many times over the last few days that to actually see him there, hunched under the hood of a dark cloak, was jarring.

"Virginia," he said, with a shiver in his voice. His hair was stuck to his face and dripping into his eyes. "Will you let me in?"

I was under some kind of spell; I must have been. It was the only explanation for what I did next. Despite the rain and the lightning, I stepped over the threshold, took his face between my hands, and kissed him.

I hadn't realized until then how afraid I had been that I would never see him again. That the Slit Witch had gotten him, and that she would come for me next.

It wasn't a very deep kiss—a desperate press of lips—nor did it last very long. He barely had time to react or kiss me back before I pulled away, dropping my hands quickly and stepping backward into the shelter of the shop. But it was our first kiss and I will always remember it, the way my mouth came away wet, the little drops of water that had gathered on my eyelashes. And his face, half-smile, half-concern, rendered quite speechless as I grabbed his arm and pulled him inside.

The storm was much quieter with the door closed, almost eerily so. I was shaking, but from adrenaline or from something else, I don't know. A puddle formed quickly at our feet, rain spilling from Ash's cloak as he shoved back the hood and looked at me.

"I'm sorry it's taken me so long to return," he said, pushing damp hair out of his eyes. He grinned, and my heart began beating like a trapped bird's wings. "Clearly, you missed me."

"Not as much as you think," I said, but I didn't mean it and we both knew it. His grin only widened.

"*Gigi?*"

My mother. She called down from upstairs, much too near for my liking. But even if she came into the shop, she wouldn't be able to see us with all the antiques in the way. There was no clear view from the steps to the doorway. "Is someone there with you? I thought you were closing for the night."

I looked at Ash and laid a finger over my lips to keep quiet. He nodded, and I crept through the shop on my own, calling back to my mother as I went.

"No, Ma! I thought I heard someone at the door, but it was only the storm."

At that moment, the power went out. Most of the lights in the shop were off already, but what little illumination there had been was suddenly gone. I froze and blinked furiously in the dark.

"Shit. *Shit.*" There was a thump as my mother dropped something, followed by a scraping sound, and more swearing. She rarely swore, and unease began to brew in my belly. "Gigi, do you need a flashlight?"

"I'm fine!" I called, even though a flashlight would have been nice. But I absolutely did not want her coming down to deliver it. "I could navigate this place with my eyes closed."

This was true. Or probably true. At any rate, she didn't question it.

"Fine," my mother said on a sigh. "Just make sure the front door is locked and come up. I'm going to light some candles, get ready for bed. Let me know if you need anything."

Several tense minutes passed. I waited until I heard her footsteps retreat, and the groan of the pipes as she turned on the faucet in the bathtub.

"Gigi, huh? I like it."

Ash's voice, right at my ear. I spun around, clamping my jaw shut on a shout of surprise, and there he was, standing right behind me.

I recovered myself and lifted my chin, as if he hadn't frightened me nearly to death.

"My mother is the only one allowed to call me that," I said, and he laughed under his breath. "Now come on. I'm going to smuggle you up to my room."

It wasn't so difficult as I'd anticipated. There was no light but the lightning staggering at intervals across the sky, and the door to the bathroom was shut tight with my mother behind it, performing her extensive nightly toilette. She was humming to herself, something sad; she probably didn't even realize she was doing it. That helped, as did the thunder that rattled the windows in their panes to smother the sounds of our footsteps. But still I held my breath the whole time and did not let it out again until I had closed the door to my bedroom and locked it with the quietest of clicks.

And though part of me was grateful that it had been so easy to smuggle a strange boy into my room without her noticing, another part resented it. My mother was obsessed with privacy, but only when it suited her. When it came to the woods or to school—the two areas in which I most wished she would leave me to my own devices—she had very strict and specific thoughts about how I should conduct myself. But here, now, alone in the dark during a thunderstorm, she could barely be bothered to see how I fared. It was like she always did the opposite of what a mother should do.

At least she had left a bunch of candles and a matchbox on the floor just inside my bedroom door. I quickly scooped them up and placed them on the windowsill, lighting each one with a single match. They threw thin, undulating shadows on the walls, dreamy and strange, flitting like creatures that can only be seen out of the corner of your eye. When I turned around, I found Ash examining the books on my shelf, thoughtfully reading each spine. It made me wonder if there were books circulating in the forest that were written by witches and water sprites and fairies, or if all the books he had ever read were ones like my own, having nothing to do with the forest, and so nothing really to do with his own life. There was so much I didn't know about him.

There was so much I did not understand.

"If my mother finds you here . . ." I said, shivering both from the cold of the rain still on my skin as much as from the unreality of finding this boy from the woods where I was not allowed to go now in my bedroom. Which was, after all, not a very large room; I could reach him in three long strides if I chose. "Well, I'm not sure what she would do."

"Then we won't let her find me," he said, as if it were the simplest thing in the world. He turned his attention from the books to me. "I can't stay long anyway."

"Oh." Without meeting his eye, I crossed the room to my nightstand and carefully opened the top drawer. I removed the hairbrush from its hiding place and held it out to him. "I suppose this is what you've come for."

A great surge of wind pushed against the walls and the windows, and the house groaned with resistance.

"Actually," Ash said, as the candlelight danced across the hollowed bones of his face, "I was hoping you would hold on to it a little while longer. I haven't figured out how to unlock its secrets just yet."

"Of course." I all too eagerly put it back in the drawer. With the hairbrush still in my possession, he would have a reason to visit me again. "Ash, these last few days . . . Where have you been?"

"Hiding from the witch." Ash went to the bed but waited for me to nod my permission before he sat on the edge. "She's sent her . . . *helper* after me. A smoke-demon. Not so easy to evade."

"A *demon*?" There were demons in the woods too? How had I not known?

Ash gave a solemn nod. "I wanted to come sooner, but I was afraid of leading the demon right to your door. A storm like this is what I've been waiting for—it provides cover, confuses their magic. Smoke and water don't exactly mix."

I hugged myself around the waist. "So you'll only come here when it rains?"

"Yes," he said. "To keep you safe."

I nodded, absorbing this, but I wasn't thinking of myself and my safety. After a long moment I went to the bed and sat next to him. Our shoulders were just touching.

"I'm more worried about you." I looked down at his hands curled in his lap. "Where will you go? What will you do?"

"I've been searching for someone—an enchantress who might know how to break the spell on my captive memories. She's an expert in magical objects. The fairies call her the Great Ensorceller of the Hidden Moon, or something ridiculous like that. I met her once long ago, when I was a child. She moves around a lot, but I've uncovered a promising lead on where I might find her."

Despite eight years spent among the fairies, I had never heard of this Ensorceller of the Hidden Moon, expert in magical objects. Suddenly I had several pressing questions, none of which I was actually brave enough to ask. Namely, had she and Ash been children at the same time, or was she older, around my mother's age? Or perhaps she was ancient but ageless, with her magic to suspend her in time. What was an enchantress, really, and how powerful was her magic? Did she use it for good or for wickedness? And if it were wickedness, what kind exactly? General, regular evil, or something more specific, like seduction?

"An enchantress?" I said with my gaze still trained on his hands. "She sounds very . . . beautiful."

Ash's eyes slid sideways to me. A sly, fox-like glance. He turned toward me so that our knees were angled together and he could look at my rapidly flushing face. He took my hands in his and held them tight.

"Virginia, I know we've only spent one afternoon together, and that we hardly know each other yet, but may I tell you something?"

I nodded, and he leaned close, his mouth only an inch from mine.

"I really missed you too," he said, and then he kissed me, and it was a much better kiss than before. Not so desperate and flailing, but slow and deep and true. I had never enjoyed kissing until I kissed Ash. I had tried a few times, with a few people, but always found it sloppy and pointless and disappointing. But this was different.

I didn't know what *made* it different, not yet, but still I let myself sink into the rhythm of it, the closeness. The feel of his hands cupping my face, my fingers twining gently in his hair. For the first time in a very long time, I didn't feel so alone.

In fact, I did not feel alone at all. Here, with him, I was not the only one with fairyland in my veins.

It had to end, as all things do, and all the more sorrowful for the sweetness of such a moment. The storm had quieted to a hush, and the rain had slowed to a drizzle. If there was a smoke-demon waiting in the woods for its cue to emerge, it would surely arrive soon; the clouds that were left drifted away on a warm sigh of wind. My mother had long since gone to bed. The power was still out.

I led Ash back through the house and left him at the porch after assurances that he would be careful, and that he would return to me as soon as he could. Our lips met one last time— I did not want to let him go, but I had to—and then he pulled up his hood and disappeared like a shadow among shadows into the dark.

15

Gemma

MOTHER, WHOM I HAD KILLED WITH AN AX, TOLD me a story once about a girl at the beginning of the world who was given a box by the gods and told never to open it. But *of course* she opened it; the gods had known all along that she would, because there is nothing more human than curiosity. They watched from the shadows as the girl pried the lid off the box, breaking the metal clasps that held it shut, and they laughed as all these terrible things came pouring out: grief and sorrow, fear and rage, worry and spite and jealousy. And at the very bottom of the box, trembling and small, was hope. The girl picked it up and it was hot like fire, but it didn't burn her; it was bright like the sun, but it didn't blind her. The girl held it close to her chest, and that's where it stayed, inside the human heart.

But hope was terrible too, Mother said, because it made you believe that you could have things you could never have, or be someone you could never be, and when a hope failed to come true, it was worse than if you'd never had hope at all.

Your grandmother told me that, she added; and it was one of those times when I was almost tricked into believing that all of this was real—that Mother was Mama, and not a smoke-demon doing an imitation. From what I remembered of Clarice, this was exactly something she would say—or what Mama would have told me that Clarice had said. It was eerie how Mother seemed to have access to Mama's secret memories, to speak with her voice.

Your grandmother knew that hope was a trap.

But I still had hope. Even though I missed my bed and my blankets and being soft and being safe. Even as I faced a wall between me and where I wanted to be—a wall with no obvious way around it or through it. I had tried to magic myself a door, but the stones refused to be anything but stones. Yet I still had hope even as I slumped to the ground and pressed my cheek to the wall, the stones so cold that I shivered. Even if it was a monstrous hope, eating me from the inside out, it was still mine and still precious to me.

Having hope didn't stop me from crying, though.

My sobs were so heavy that they hollowed out my chest. My heart thumped and scraped as my ribs heaved, as they hurt in the spot where one of them was missing. I felt like I was being torn open, but just when I thought my tears would last forever, they ceased.

As I wiped my eyes, a cool calm descended over me, and in my lap I found a curious thing: a handful of diamonds, glittering. I picked one up, pinching it between my fingertips. It was solid; I'd half expected it to melt like ice. I brought it to my lips and licked it, and was unsurprised that it tasted of salt. These were my tears, hardened into jewels. I slipped them into my pack and sighed. When I was finally ready, I pushed to my feet and faced the wall again, looking at it now not as an enemy, but as a potential friend.

Hello, I thought, pressing my hand flat against the stones. *My name is Gemma Belle—Gemma Ashley—Cassata. It's very nice to meet you.*

I tried to relax, as much as a girl alone in the wilderness could, and focused on my every breath. I let my mind go blank but not empty. And after a very long while of quiet and still-ness, I heard a voice whisper in the back of my mind—a voice like wind over water.

No way around or through. Only over.

I kept my hand on the wall and concentrated very hard. *Do you mean . . . I should climb?*

Too slippery, too steep. Better to jump.

Jump? But . . .

The higher the jump, the longer the fall. Ask the wind to help you. Should have no trouble at all.

A memory came to me, blurry but full of feeling: my stom-ach swooping as my feet left the ground, a warm hand in mine guiding me over a wall like the one before me to a wooded area beyond. Landing as lightly as a ballerina, a high laugh of relief; a misty pool, perfectly round, steam curling from its surface in luxurious tendrils.

And someone beside me—someone who was familiar in the memory but unfamiliar to me now. A boy as thin as a leaf, with a smile as sweet as spring rain. Who was he, and why did my heart stumble at the thought of him? How could he cause a blush to spread so quickly across my cheeks when the memory I had of him was fractured and incomplete?

Jump, Gemma Belle!

This time it was not the wall that was speaking to me, but an echo from the memory. His voice wrapped around me and *pulled,* and I knew in that moment that I could do it, that I could jump over the wall. And then an idea occurred to me—one that sent a thrill of giddiness and relief down my spine: Was it possible that the boy was waiting on the other side of this wall even now?

I thanked the wall for its help and then I ran away from it—fifty feet, one hundred. I went as far as I could go while keeping the wall in sight, and then I stopped and turned on the spot.

My heart pumped fast but more from the exercise and less from fear—or so I told myself. Anyway, I ignored it. I ignored my heart, and I dug my heels into the dirt. *The boy, the boy is waiting for me.* I knew it like I knew the sound of my own name, and I knew too that he was what my shadow had wanted me to see. When I saw his face in the flesh again, all would become clear; I would know why he called me Gemma Belle, and why I had forgotten him in the first place. And if I found him, perhaps he would help me. He would take me straight to the Slit Witch, and I would rescue Mama at last.

I sprinted headlong toward the wall, as hard and as fast as I could. I summoned the Touch from somewhere deep inside myself and pushed off from the ground, keeping my eyes on the sky as I imagined the path I intended to take through the air—*Help me, air!*—up and over the stones blocking my way. I rose about five feet before I fell, still on the same side of the wall, but the landing was soft and I knew I could make it. Eventually.

Again and again I ran and I rose and I fell, and on the seventh try I cleared the top of it, the heels of my shoes just brushing the stones as I sailed—*soared*—over the wall like a bird, or the ghost of a bird, the wind seeming to rush right through me, cold on my bones. Leaves from the trees brushed the crown of my head, and then I was arcing down toward the ground and the dirt and the worms. The whole time, I held my breath.

The landing on the other side was not as graceful as the one I recalled from so long ago when the boy had assisted me. I stumbled, though somehow managed to stay on my feet. But then it hit me how *tired* I was, and how much the jump had drained me, and I collapsed in a heap anyway. I wanted to lie down and sleep for a hundred years or more, but this was no place to rest.

I was no longer in the woods.

I was in a town.

Well, a town or a city; I wasn't quite sure what to call it. (*A village? What's the difference?*) Certainly it was unlike any place I had ever been, although I had not been to very many places before. I stood at the end of a long cobblestone street lined on both sides by tall stone houses pressed shoulder to shoulder, balconies overflowing with bright flowers and succulents that glowed in the dark. The stars glittered secretly and a full moon hung like a lantern on a hook in a wide-open sky. Arched pathways led to alleys that twisted out of sight, and arrangements of wooden carts were set up along both sides of the street to sell the merchants' wares. Though all the carts were currently closed, a smell of cinnamon and roasted meat, of jasmine tea and fresh fruit, lingered on the wind, making my stomach turn over with longing.

But even setting aside these splendors great and small, there was something in the air—a shimmer, like the crackle before a storm—that I had never seen or felt before, and it took me several moments of contemplation before I realized what it was.

Magic.

A magical village in the middle of the woods! Under different circumstances I would have been thrilled by such a discovery, but as it was, the street was empty and there was no boy waiting for me. In fact, the village was absolutely silent—and not the silence of people in their houses, asleep. It was the silence of absence, of total abandonment.

There was nobody here but me.

I took a step, and another, and my footfalls echoed like the softest, saddest song. If I screamed, would *anyone* come running? On the other side of the wall, letting loose a scream would have been unthinkable. Now, the urge was so strong that I pressed the back of my hand to my mouth just to quiet myself. I was alone in a way that made me afraid, as alone as if the world had ended while I was in the woods and now I was the last person on earth. My shadow had led me here, and I'd thought I could trust her, but who really knew where a shadow's loyalties lay? A shadow was not quite darkness and not quite light—an in-between thing that was always behind or just out of sight. Was this a trick or some kind of trap? I was too drained to leap back over the wall, so I decided to take my chances and go in the only direction there was left to go: *forward*.

I walked down the street, moving straight ahead, too nervous to diverge from the path, and soon came to a piazza with a marble fountain at its center. The bubbling water glowed pink in the moonlight, and though I was thirsty and the water looked clean despite its odd color, I suspected that it might be enchanted in some way and deemed it safer not to partake—especially given my experience with the apple. There was a sculpture of a woman in a long robe rising from the middle of the fountain with her hands pressed together in front of her chest, and I had the distinct impression that the statue was alive in some way—a spirit imprisoned in the stone. Her head was slightly bowed but her eyes were up, and they blazed as if there were a fire behind them. I felt her gaze on the back of my neck as I left the piazza and made my way down another dim street. That street too was empty, as was the next and the next. Soon I realized that this wasn't *just* a village. It was a labyrinth.

And I was lost.

HOW SICK I was of being lost! So sick I thought it would kill me. An infection like any other, and the cure utterly beyond me. In a fit I flung my rib to the dirt; I kicked a small rock with my toe and sent it rolling end over end. I tossed my pack beside my rib, and I threw back my head, and I *screamed*.

I might as well have walked myself into a monster's mouth—straight past its teeth and right down its throat. The scream echoed as if I had rung a thousand tiny bells all at once. Anyone—or any*thing*—in the vicinity would be able to find me now, and quickly. I was too tired to run—or too tired *of* running—and so there was nothing left to do but stand there with my scream in my ears and in the air until the echoes eventually quieted and stopped altogether. Then it was just me and my heartbeat, and if I was to be eaten soon, at least I felt better.

A minute passed, and two minutes, and ten. No monsters came running; no birds had even startled at the sound. I really was the only one around—and there was freedom in that. Terror too, but I shoved it down deep. Locked it in a box like the one the gods had given the long-ago girl, and vowed not to open it ever again. I looked down at my hands—I don't really know why—and they were trembling like the plucked strings of a violin. I didn't feel the vibrations, but I certainly saw them, and I stared in fixed fascination, watching as the veins in my palms and my wrists and my arms slowly turned from violet to blue to a dark, lush green.

The forest is in you now, in your flesh. Be sure it doesn't spread.

I laughed. Like the scream, it was the only other thing left in me. I thought the veins might return to their normal color after a moment, but they didn't, and I suspected they never would. There was terror in that—in becoming something new—but there was freedom in it too.

From this point on, I will be whatever I want to be, I thought with resolution. That was a word I liked—*resolute*. It spoke of someone with something to fight for, someone who was brave even if it was only pretend. Pretend-brave was still brave as long as you did the thing you were trying to be brave enough to do. Besides, maybe I wasn't becoming the forest. Maybe the forest was becoming *me*.

With a sense of calm I'd never felt before—and was a little bit afraid I'd never feel again—I picked up my pack and my rib. I retrieved the rock I had kicked and put it back where it had been (approximately). And that simple act of putting the rock back was like releasing something that had gotten stuck. The very moment the rock touched the cobblestones, I heard it: *music*.

A bright tarantella. As if pulled by a string that could not be cut, I followed the sound through the village. Gradually the lanes widened, and the houses grew farther apart. The cobblestones gave way to briars and sticks and dirt, and I entered a wooded area much like the one on the other side of the wall. Only here the tree trunks were thicker, spaced farther apart, and they grew tiny blue flowers shaped like bells that chimed faintly in the wind. A smell of ripe fruit and berries, of growing things—of life at its most alive. The ground sloped steadily upward and I became winded as I climbed, but the music grew louder and I knew I was close. I walked on, and was listening so intently to the song that I nearly walked right off a cliff.

I stopped just in time, my toes touching the edge. Breathless, I scrambled back and wrapped my arms around the nearest tree while I steadied myself. I had been in mortal peril plenty of times throughout this journey, but being eaten by a wolf or a witch suddenly seemed like nothing compared to a sharp fall from a cliff. I waited until my breathing returned to normal—or almost normal—then I dropped to my knees and crawled forward, coming as close to the precipice as I dared. The music was so loud it was as if there were an orchestra playing right beside me, and my heart danced circles in my chest as I craned my neck to peer over the ledge.

Below was a steep ravine, with tangles of shrubs and vines growing all up and down its sides, fireflies like little stars flitting through the night. And people, so many people—hundreds!—

gathered at the bottom of the gorge on top of a thick glass floor suspended over a river. It was a dance floor, with couples spinning in the center of it, dressed formally in flowing gowns and tailored suits, feathers and jewels and dripping gold bangles. I watched, mesmerized, as the song ended and the dancers curtsied to one another, low and languid. I thought the dancing would start up again, but instead a flock of waiters in identical sparkling robes slipped through the crowd, passing out flutes of pink champagne. The revelers raised their drinks as one and shouted in unison, "To the prince, slayer of the Hunting Beast!" and then they tipped back their heads and downed the glowing liquid in one gulp. A raucous cheer arose, so intense that I clapped my hands over my ears to muffle the noise. Whoops and hollers, rolls of laughter and claps on the back; cries of "Silvanus, Silvanus, Silvanus!" as another waiter emerged. And this time, catching sight of what he bore on his tray, I almost threw up, though there was very little food in me.

A *head*. A severed head on a *plate*. The head of a beast with curving horns and eyes that were open and shining as green as emeralds. The mouth was long and turned down, the lips drooping to reveal a jaw crammed overfull of teeth. I stared at it, horrified but unable to look away, bile creeping up my throat. Especially because it looked a lot like . . .

Like the monster named Ash.

Maybe I was mistaken, though. I'd only seen him once, two and a half years ago, and it had been dark and it had been a very stressful night. I couldn't believe that Ash was the Hunting Beast—not with the way he and Mama had embraced. Hugging did not seem like something the Hunting Beast would do. Mama trusted him, so I did too.

But even as the sight of the head disgusted and confused me, there was something else at work, as if an arrow had pierced me through the heart and now I was bleeding—bleeding memories.

"Are you a fairy prince?"

Like an echo of an echo, I heard my own voice from long ago inside my head, breathless and full of awe. And in answer there was laughter, and another voice, very close to my ear.

"Always you ask me this! My Gemma Belle, so forgetful. Perhaps this will help you remember."

And then . . . and then . . .

A kiss.

"The prince," I breathed, still holding my rib in one hand. I had almost forgotten it; the feel of it had become so familiar in my grip. "Silvanus! He always said that he would slay the Hunting Beast."

Below me, at the celebration in the ravine, another song began. It was the same one that had led me here, only slower and in a minor key. A waltz with a melancholic pulse, it sounded like star-crossed love, like beautiful doom. I didn't really like it, but then, what did that matter? I had to get down there—I had to find him!—but how? As soon as I thought this, a glass staircase appeared, unspooling like a ribbon down the side of the ravine. I tested it with a toe before setting my whole weight on it, and it felt as solid as if it were made of stone. I hurried down the steps as the couples reassembled and started to dance, and in moments I was among them, conspicuous in my dirty clothing but far too distracted to care. He *had* to be here somewhere.

Silvanus, the fairy prince.

Silvanus, my friend and very first kiss.

I wove through the crowd, scanning each face for his familiar one. More than two years had passed since I'd seen him last, but I knew I would know him as soon as I saw him. I tried to ask some of the friendlier-looking fairies where I might find him, but all of them ignored me; curiously, not a single head turned in my direction, not even when I stepped on the train of a lady's long silky skirt, or when I bumped into someone wearing a dragon mask with actual curls of smoke puffing from the nostrils. There were so many sounds—crickets and footsteps and murmurs and music—and so many smells—lemon and jasmine and mint and wood smoke—and it all crashed over me in endless waves, a sea of magic and deep enchantment.

It was dizzying, and I began to feel as though there wasn't enough air to breathe, or enough space for my heart to beat. I pushed my way through the dancers to the edge of the floor and pressed my back to the ravine wall. I skirted slowly to the side, trying to find a path or a way out of the melee, and came eventually upon a dais raised high above the party, with a curving set of stairs leading up to it. I took the steps two at a time, thinking that it would be easier to search for Silvanus from a higher vantage anyway. At the top I stopped so abruptly I nearly fell forward onto my hands and knees. The dais boasted two thrones—and upon them, the queens.

If I were to close my eyes and picture the high queen of the fairies, the one sitting before me was exactly what I'd see: pointed chin and long black hair threaded with jewels, and wearing a medieval style gown of dark red velvet. But it was more than just her looks that gave her an indisputably regal air. It was the way she held herself, tall and proud and sparkling. Like ice, I thought, like ice in the sun that knows it will not melt, because it is as cold inside of her as it is around her. Like it is her will and her right to defy the light that shines upon her. She thrust her chin high and reached across the dais toward the other throne set very close beside her own. The queen's wife— who was equally striking in an ivory gown with long billowing sleeves slit down the middle and a long silvery braid falling over one shoulder—reached back, and the queens clasped hands across the short distance between them, holding tight.

"Hello," I said, dipping into my deepest and most graceful curtsy, just the way Silvanus had taught me. I held my rib behind my back. "My name is Gemma Belle. I'm looking for your son, the prince. Do you know where I might find him?"

Nothing. I sank even lower into my curtsy and tried again. "Hello, I'm Gemma Belle. Your son might have mentioned me? Would you be able to help me find him, please? It's really very important."

I waited, but still there was no reply. I raised my head and peeked at the queen but she wasn't even looking at me. Her eyes were on the party. Eventually I straightened from my curtsy, my stomach twisting. I stumbled away from the fairy queens, biting my lip so hard I cracked the skin.

The song ended then, and the dance along with it. Still on the dais, I turned toward the ballroom floor and saw the same waiters as before, again distributing pink champagne in sparkling flutes to every fairy in the crowd. As one, the revelers raised their glasses and cried, "To the prince, slayer of the Hunting Beast!" and then tossed back their drinks. "Silvanus, Silvanus, Silvanus!" they chorused, amid laughter and cheers, and their empty flutes shattered when they threw them to the floor and the shards became bubbles, spinning wildly up through the air. The waiter bearing the beast's head on a tray coasted to the center of the crowd, where the revelers jeered and stomped their feet. After the parading of the dead beast, the waiter disappeared and the music began. It was the same song as before, but again slightly altered. A faster tempo this time, and more percussion—a quickstep instead of a waltz. As the revelers returned to formation, I allowed myself to think the thought I had not wanted to think before.

Something here is terribly wrong.

16

Virginia

I T BEGAN WITH MY FEET, ROOTS GROWING OUT OF MY heels and twining into the earth. Then it crawled up my shins, my skin hardening into bark as my knees fused together, my thighs into one. The tiniest branches sprouted from my hips, jutting out of my bones, and flowers bloomed from my wrists as my arms twisted up toward the sun. My heart stopped; it hurt. The enchantment reached my neck and tore away my breath and I tried to scream but without air I couldn't, and the last thing to go was my eyes, my ears, and my mouth, the world going still and dark, no sense of sight or smell or sound.

I woke with my hands at my throat. I gasped, my fingers digging into the flesh, trying to let the air in. I kicked the covers off and sat up, my heartbeat falling heavily in my ears, and just the simple fact of my pulse was enough to reassure myself that it hadn't been real. Almost enough. I touched the bottom of my feet, my knees; I checked my hips and my chest, felt the smoothness of my skin, and only then could I breathe properly again, certain that I wasn't turning into a tree.

It was the third night in a row that I'd had this dream.

Somewhere after midnight but well before dawn, I stood and paced around my room, not knowing what else to do; sleep was now impossible. The floorboards creaked with each step, but I couldn't stop, couldn't stop scratching an itch on my wrists where the flowers had unfurled in the dream. I wanted Ash, but the night was clear. He wasn't here and he wouldn't come, and I would spend the following day as I had the last and the one before that: hoping for clouds and praying for rain, ceaselessly searching the horizon for a sign of storms.

It was a kind of madness, this yearning, this restless turning of my heart. It was horrible to feel so helpless, to have to wait and wait and wait. So I slept and I dreamed and I paced, and the days passed in this manner, then weeks. It was just like my longing to return to the woods, to the fairyland of my child-hood, but a thousand times stronger. The warmth I felt when he was near was like the warmth of magic surrounding me on all sides, but so much brighter. Ash had visited me three more times since the first, and still it was not enough.

I needed a glass of water. Or rather, I needed to go get a glass of water. It was the going that mattered, the getting. I couldn't stay in my room, which felt both smaller and emptier for the lack of Ash; the kitchen was the safest retreat. But when I stepped into the hallway I was drawn in the other direction, toward my mother's room and the utter silence beyond her cracked door. I had the sudden ridiculous longing to climb into bed with her like children did in stories after they'd had a night-mare, even though I was far too old for such things and I had never done anything like that before. I was not welcome in her space, and in turn she had always respected mine, rarely ven-turing past the threshold to my room, only standing in the doorway if she needed to speak to me urgently. Still, I drifted toward her door, and when I reached it, I pushed it wide. Hold-ing my breath, I stepped inside.

The curtains were shut tight and the room was so dark I couldn't see my own hands. I blinked and waited for my eyes to adjust before creeping carefully toward the window, to the wide bed where my mother slept. I sank to my knees near the nightstand and leaned my head against the side of the mattress, my shoulder pressed uncomfortably into the bed frame. After a long moment my mother stirred, sensing my presence.

"Ma?" I whispered, my voice shaking. "Ma, are you awake?"

"Hmm, what is it?"

"I can't sleep."

The bed groaned as she rolled toward me. "Mmm?"

My feet were cold; I'd forgotten my slippers. "Ma, what if we're wrong about the woods?"

A deep sigh. "What?"

"What if there was . . . a protector?" I asked, tucking my knees to my chest. My heart was so loud in the quiet, and I was sure she could hear it, hear the word that it said over and over again: *Ash, Ash, Ash.* "Someone good who could lead me through the woods unharmed? Someone who could keep me safe? If there was someone like that, would you let me go into the woods?"

The bed groaned again, and my mother sat up. She was more awake now, but not fully alert. If she had been, I think she might have told me to go back to bed. Instead she reached for the glass of water she kept on her nightstand. I heard her swallow, and then set it down with a delicate clink. "It was very hard for me to get pregnant with you. Have I told you that? It took almost a year. Months and months of disappointment. I began to think it would never happen."

A jolt down my spine, an electric shock. No, she had never mentioned it, this time in her life that had everything and nothing at all to do with me.

I had not known I was wanted so desperately.

"During that time, I often heard a baby crying in the night. Quiet, at first, but sometimes it was loud, screaming. It would wake me from even the deepest sleep. A couple of times I even ran outside, thinking that a baby had been left on our doorstep, thinking that it was *mine,* but of course there was nothing. No one."

I began to shiver and couldn't stop.

"It was the woods, Gigi. It was something in the woods, calling to me. There is no one—*no one*—in the woods you can trust. Especially the ones you think you love the most."

First one revelation and now another. *Especially the ones you think you love?* I didn't know what to say. What to *feel.* I loved her and I was so mad at her, and the love and the rage were all wrapped up together so that I could barely tell which was which anymore. I was so cold, and not just my feet but everywhere, a layer of ice under my skin.

Several minutes passed, and finally my mother settled back onto the pillows, tugging the sheet up to her chin. When she spoke again, her voice was thick with sleep, almost slurred.

"Sometimes it calls to me still . . ."

I stayed there on the floor beside my mother's bed, unwilling to move until dawn, until the moon disappeared in the warm morning light and I felt similarly hidden, and safe.

"I DON'T UNDERSTAND it. I can't find her anywhere. It's like she just . . . vanished."

Ash paced through the rows of antiques behind me as I flipped the *open* sign to *closed* and locked the front door. It was raining, a light but relentless drizzle, and the front windows were fogged. My mother was away for the weekend—she'd gone to Chicago to attend an auction—and had left me in charge of the shop. I had dreaded being alone, but when the sky began to gray I knew I wouldn't be lonesome for long.

"Maybe she retired." I went to Ash and wrapped my arms around him, holding him in place. He returned the embrace, sighing into it, his chin resting on top of my head. "Even enchantresses deserve a break."

He sighed, and his breath ruffled my hair. I squeezed him tighter, my cheek pressed to his shoulder. "No one can remember exactly the last time they saw her. And I don't know what to do if I can't find her."

"I suppose you could ask your mother." With his hands on my waist, Ash pulled away so he could look at my face. I smiled, but it was thin. "Kidding."

Ash shook his head, amused, then leaned down and pressed his forehead to mine. I would never get tired of this, these little acts of tenderness. Ash closed his eyes but I didn't close mine, my gaze on his mouth as he spoke.

"I have one more lead to follow, but if it's a dead end . . ."

"We'll think of something," I said. He brought his hands to my face, his palms cool.

"You're right. No use worrying about it now. *Oh*." Ash released me, and the sudden loss of contact left me dizzy. He crouched down and rummaged through the pack he'd deposited on the floor. "I almost forgot. I brought you something."

It was a flower. He held it up to me, still on his knees, and I took it from him reverently, as if it might shatter at my touch. It was not so strange a precaution, as the petals looked like glass: thick and translucent with bloody red veins, and a black stem with little knots where the thorns had been clipped off. I touched the petals carefully—they were soft and pliant, surprising me, as delicate as new skin. And its scent, when I raised it to my face, was unlike anything I'd known before: spicy rather than sweet, similar to cinnamon but also not like cinnamon at all. I pressed the flower to my lips and breathed deeply, desiring more. As I inhaled I felt my heart begin to slow, a tingling sense of calm that made me feel as though I were floating. Dreaming while awake.

"It's called a sore flower," Ash said, and his voice snapped me back to clarity. "If you put it under your pillow, it will help you sleep. You said you were having bad dreams."

"I am."

Dreams of creatures with wings too heavy to fly; dreams of walking in a labyrinth of high hedges, blood dripping from my fingertips. Dreams of Ash, of smiles and secrets. Dreams of Ash dissolving in the sunlight, nothing left of him for me to hold. Dreams of strange plants growing from the cracks in my bones.

I trailed the flower along my jaw, tickling my skin.

"Thank you," I said, feeling suddenly as if I might cry. "It's beautiful."

Ash smiled, and I turned my face away so he wouldn't see the bright sheen of my eyes. He stood, and I reached for his hand.

"I have something for you too," I said, barely more than a whisper. I felt shy and bit my lip so hard I thought my teeth would leave a bruise. "It's, um, in my room."

Ash squeezed my hand. "Lead the way."

I had been alone with Ash in my room before, of course, but it felt different this time and I wasn't sure why. There was something growing between us, something unspoken taking up space. I hurried to the nightstand where I had set aside the thing that made me think of him, the world's tiniest music box. It was smaller than the palm of my hand, a round locket on a silver chain that opened to reveal the mechanism inside: a gold wheel with little spokes that clinked the notes as it turned. The song was one I'd never heard before, tinny and light. Like flying, but not too high; like falling, but not too fast. I held it out to him wordlessly, and he took it as if amazed. He opened the locket and wound the crank in the back so that it played. It flooded the space between us, beautiful and a little ghostly.

He looked at me, sort of strangely, like maybe he had a question. Like maybe *I* was the answer.

"I found it in the shop. It reminded me of you." I clasped my hands behind my back so he wouldn't see their trembling.

"It did?"

I nodded. "The music. It sounds to me like magic. Like you."

The locket played the same refrain on an endless loop. There were only so many spokes, after all, so many notes. Ash set it carefully on the nightstand and then he reached for me, his lips already parting. I met him halfway.

It was a kiss that lingered, and lasted, and left its mark. Ash held on to me just a little too tightly, pressed against me a little too fiercely. I didn't mind it, though; I wanted him close. I think we both knew, but didn't want to say, that anything could happen now. That we could be together forever if things worked in our favor, or else never see each other again if they didn't. Would the woods claim him, or would I be allowed to keep him?

Are you mine? I wanted to whisper, but I wasn't quite brave enough to say it.

His hand slid under my shirt, splayed against the small of my back. "Is this all right?" he said, and I nodded. This was nothing we hadn't done before on his previous visits, but we both wanted more and I knew that *that* was what he was asking about. We pulled each other down onto my bed, conversing through touch, through kiss and caress. Little whispers, a dance of breath.

"*I've never . . .*"

"*Me either.*"

"*Do you want to?*"

"*Yes.*"

Our clothes were in a pile on the floor, the rain beating at the window. Skin and sweat, our shadows indivisible, more tangled than our limbs. I was not prepared for the intensity of such intimacy, the way he could see all of me, the way there was nowhere to hide. I buried my face in his chest and lost myself there, his heartbeat a song that only I could hear. Afterward, we curled into each other, unwilling to be the first to let go.

"Virginia," Ash whispered, stroking my hair. "I'm afraid."

I sighed. My head fit so comfortably on the cradle of his shoulder, like it was made for me. "I am too."

Ash's skin was warm. "If I don't come back—"

"You will."

He paused with his hand on the back of my head, holding me. "You don't know that."

It was true; I didn't. The Slit Witch could get him, or the smoke-demon, or some other horror I had no name for. And what would the witch do if she caught him? Lock him in a tower and erase all his memories from the past few weeks? Cast a curse on him, turn him into a frog? I knew nothing of witches but what I'd read in storybooks, and I wasn't sure what one might do to punish her own son. There were a thousand ways that things could go wrong, and only one way that they could go right.

"Ash, what are you going to do?" Panic licked up my throat, but I swallowed it down. "I mean, after you break the spell and get your memories back?"

"I'm going to find my mother. My *real* mother. Once I remember, the witch can't keep me from her."

What if she still doesn't want you? I thought but didn't say. What if it was true that Ash's mother had abandoned him to the Slit Witch? What would it do to him to be rejected again?

My mind went to my own mother, how beautiful I'd always thought her, with her shiny hair and thin hands, and how terribly bright her eyes had been when she told me that I didn't have to return to school if I chose not to, but that I couldn't stay here. Couldn't stay with *her*.

She had wanted me once—she had said as much—so why was she so willing to send me away at the cost of creating such a huge rift between us? She said she wanted greater things for me, but why couldn't I be great *here*?

I lifted my head so I could see Ash better, so I could see his face. His cheeks were flushed, his hair a mess of tangled curls. I loved him like this, and I smiled despite the fear that had surged through me only a moment ago. Fear had no place here. Later, maybe, but not now.

"Can I come with you?" I said, and then held my breath, waiting for his answer. Maybe his own mother had wanted great things for him too, and had misunderstood how to help him, same as mine. Maybe finding his real mother was a most noble quest and undertaking it would set everything right. For both of us.

See, Ma? I'm perfectly capable of making my own decisions. I'm capable of battling monsters, of finding my way through the dark of the woods to someplace better, someplace brighter.

"You would want to?" Ash whispered.

I nodded against his chest.

"I'd like that very much." A pause, a breath. "And after that, when the quest is done?"

"I'll follow you anywhere," I said, just as quietly. "Will you follow me too?"

Lithe as a cat, Ash rolled so that he hovered over me, his knees on either side of my hips, holding himself up on his hands, hair hanging forward. He smiled, and it was all I could see. "Yes, Virginia. Always," he said, and then he leaned down and kissed me.

I could see it already, Ash and me building a life together, living by a lake in a little cottage with sore flowers growing in pots along the windowsills, baking bread in a brick oven and hanging strings of fairy lights in the backyard, dancing together on the back patio beneath the stars. It was a pretty picture, highly idealistic, but as soon as I thought of it, I could not let it go. I had never wanted this before I'd met him—never wanted domestic bliss, never wanted wide skies or dancing or bees buzzing in a garden—but now it was all I could think about: a safe space for just the two of us, protecting each other from monsters. We didn't even have to live in or near the woods at all; we could move anywhere, go anywhere together. I was beginning to think that maybe I didn't need fairyland anymore. Maybe I just needed him.

Ash stayed longer than perhaps he should have, neither of us ready to give the other up. At some point I fell asleep and awoke later to Ash saying my name and shaking me gently.

"Virginia, I have to go."

"No." I reached for him but the room was one thick shadow and I couldn't find him; he was already gone. No, not gone but going, leaving me here alone. I shivered and curled into a ball, wanting to cry but I was too sleepy. Already my eyes were closing. What time was it?

A kiss on my temple, warm and light. "I'll be back soon."

I reached for him again but caught only air. "Promise?"

An exhale. "I do."

"Good." My eyes were shut, too heavy to force open. "Bye, Ash . . ."

I should have fought harder to keep him there, and our mothers be damned. I should have insisted he take me away—*right now, let's go right now*—insisted that we stay together no matter what. But the sore flower was under my pillow, its piquant scent pulling me under, carrying me to a hazy place of soft-cushioned dreams where the woods couldn't warn me of what was to come, even if it tried.

17

Gemma

THE GLASS STAIRWAY WAS GONE. I CIRCLED THE dance floor as the fairies spun around me and the river rushed beneath my feet, trying to find a new way out. Another bottle of champagne appeared, followed by the Beast's head. Laughter rose like smoke from a fire, hisses and jeers. The fairies' faces had grown red, swollen, and sweaty, but the party dragged on.

Was there no way out? I circled once, twice, before deciding to shove a path back to the queen and her consort, desperate for air. I thought maybe I'd locate an exit up there that I couldn't see from down here—a hot-air balloon waiting for takeoff, a pool slide into the river, a rickety rope bridge guarded by a troll. Anything would suffice. But halfway there a fairy bumped into me, hard enough to send me stumbling into another fairy, whose flailing elbow caught me in the chin—a crushing hit to my jaw that rattled my teeth and made me see stars. Neither of those fairies noticed me, and no one paid any attention when eventually I fell to the ground, dizzy beyond belief. They simply stepped around me, over me, sometimes even *on* me, pinning my clothes and my hair beneath their stamping feet. I curled into a ball the way they taught us to in school in the event of a tornado, on my knees with my head tucked down, my hands over my neck to shield the top of my spinal cord from falling debris (or falling fairies). A few tripped over me, but somehow they never lost their balance. They didn't stop moving until the music ceased, and the head of the Beast was paraded through the crowd on that same silver platter, a twisted trophy awarded to all. They cheered and hollered as if they hadn't just seen it five minutes ago, jumping and whooping in place. Quickly I stood, jaw aching, shaking all over, and nearly fell down again.

I wasn't going to make it to the dais. I knew it as surely as I knew Mama loved me, was waiting for me, and that I was about to let her down. *Please, please let me out!* The dance resumed, more raucous than ever, a blur of slanted smiles and shiny faces, a mad light in their eyes. They closed in around me, breath hot and sour, and I pushed against them with all my might. I shouted and scratched, clawing at skin, at faces, but it didn't snap them out of it; it didn't make any difference. It was like we were trapped in a music box and someone kept winding it up. Frightened, alone, I stood in the center of the revel and cried, *"Enough!"*

I put my whole soul into it, igniting every nerve as I released that word—both a warning and a plea. And I felt something unlock in me, and I knew at once that I had used—was using— the Touch.

It was force and motion, energy and light—not like the sun itself, but like the act of it rising. The world awoke to it—my will, bright and shining—and though the revel didn't stop entirely, the dancers slowed and the mirth became muted. The chatter dulled, and all but the most garish of colors drained from the fairies' faces, from their dresses and masks. Skirts floated on the air as the dancers twirled at a torpid pace; the fireflies swayed drunkenly above them, and the music was only a murmur. Time had come to a crawl around me, and in the almost-silence and the almost-stillness, I closed my eyes and breathed.

Hush.

Almost at once, footsteps cut through the quiet, echoing and assured. A song began to play, louder than the one in the background, and this one was plucky and light, flutes and drums and tambourines. The mysterious footsteps grew louder as they drew closer, and perhaps I would have been alarmed if the music wasn't so joyous—so *right*. I had this feeling like it was playing for *me*, specifically. And the sense of rightness only deepened as a tall, lanky figure emerged from between the slowly spinning fairies, dressed in a burgundy velvet tunic and with a sword at his hip like a knight. Dark curls framed a face half concealed by a glittering gold mask with little devil's horns attached. He said not a word, but his eyes were large and bright, fixed on me intently as he stopped and bowed, quite properly.

I curtsied in return, feeling rather shabby in my dirty sweater and leggings. But at this thought of my grubbiness, the Touch surged through me and my outfit *transformed*. Suddenly, I wore a gown of pale blue that rippled to the floor; my pack had shrunk and was tucked away safely in my pocket, and my rib had become a bracelet of bone wrapped three times around my wrist. My curls were clean and had been pulled into a coil at the nape of my neck, and my jeweled tears had become a diamond necklace. The boy smiled at me, and my heart twisted. He took a step closer and he smelled like . . . like . . .

Spring.

We didn't speak. There was no need. He simply held out his hand to me.

I took it.

Somehow I knew precisely what to do, and I knew too that we danced in the high fairy fashion of old. Not face-to-face but shoulder to shoulder, our palms pressed together as we flipped from one side to another, hands coming apart and meeting again as we turned and stepped and circled each other. And whether by the power of his magic or mine—perhaps both combined—we began, steadily, to rise.

Up and up, we floated on air, repeating the pattern we had set, in and around, forward and back. The fairy boy smiled and his canine teeth were sharp and long, but I wasn't afraid of him; I wasn't afraid of anything. As we rose to the height of the tree-tops, leaving the almost-frozen revelers behind, the stars above us sparkled like crushed pieces of crystal scattered across the whole of the sky. And there beneath it I felt as if I didn't have edges, as if I were endless. As if my heart and its beat were just for show, because I wasn't going to die and I wasn't going to age; I wasn't ever going to do anything that I didn't want to do. Some moments last forever, it's true.

But most of them end too soon.

"Silvanus?" I whispered, and saying his name was like breaking a spell. We stopped mid-step, mid-air, and our hands clasped as the song wound on without us, as we began to descend so incrementally that I hardly noticed. "Is it you?"

"Wait," he said, and there was hurt in his voice. "Don't you know me?"

Yes, I wanted to say—*Yes!*—but I bit my cheek and held my tongue. I knew it was him, that this was the fairy prince, but there was so much more that I didn't remember, that I *couldn't.* We'd gone into the woods, but why and when? What was he to me, and I to him? I'd thought it would come back to me when I saw his face, but my mind was still mostly blank. He might as well have been a stranger. All I knew was his name.

"I'm sorry." Our toes touched the ground as the music faded out. The revelers were little more than ghosts around us, shadows moving on a wall. "I *want* to remember, I really do. I'm trying so hard, but it's like, like there's a dead space inside of me, or a great dark mouth, and it's eaten parts of me that are gone now. And I'm afraid—I'm afraid I can't ever get them back."

I had started to cry, but this time my tears were just water and they fell like ordinary drops of rain to the ground. Silvanus removed his mask and ran his fingers through his windblown curls; his cheeks were as pink as roses. He tossed the mask aside and pressed his hands to my face, holding me there as he leaned down so that we could be closer, his breath upon my lips.

"Oh, Gemma Belle," he whispered. "Nothing lost is ever really gone. And this time—*I promise*—you will not forget."

Then Prince Silvanus kissed me, and in the kiss there was memory. His face, less lean, a few years younger than it was now; his hand, so small and slim, reaching for my own. The woods and its hidden spaces, the forbidden places where darkness pooled like water, where shadows cut from the ones who had cast them had been abandoned to the wild and the rot. Silvanus and I, dancing and laughing and eating strange fruit that made us quite drunk, chasing bubbles that popped with a sound like the cracking of bone.

Climbing trees and splashing through streams, crawling through a perfectly round tunnel made of twigs. Meeting a white stag on the other side that bled out of the corners of its eyes, the two of us watching as the entirety of its thin, shriveled body seized in a retch, as it opened its mouth and its still-beating heart fell out, wriggling in a wet bed of leaves. Silvanus had wanted to eat it but I had told him to leave it, sickened at the thought even as my mouth watered and my stomach screamed in hunger. Running back through the woods to my house and the shop where Silvanus bade me farewell and kissed the back of my hand. *Tomorrow then.*

And finally, a wishing well with a surface concealed in steam, the last of the woods' wonders that Silvanus had shown me before the Slit Witch took Mama away and everything changed. Before Mother came and blocked me from the forest, severing my connection to Silvanus.

So many memories recovered at last! I even remembered where I had seen the woman who'd been trapped in the tree. It was in that strange and pulsing garden I'd stumbled upon when I'd heard someone—the woman—weeping. (And a whistle, high and sharp. *My handler,* she'd said, before bolting into the woods. From whom had she been hiding? The person who would put her in a tree?) All this I remembered, and more besides, but I still could not think why I had forgotten in the first place. Had Mother cast a spell on me? Had the Slit Witch? But no, these memories were from longer ago, before the monster named Ash took Mama into the woods and my whole world fell apart. Was it possible that Mama . . . ? *No!* Mama was not a witch. She had no magic, and besides, why would she do such a terrible thing? To erase what rightly belonged to me?

A puzzle, a very harrowing one, but I found I couldn't dwell on it too closely because Silvanus was still kissing me and the thrill of it went all the way to my fingertips. I felt like I was made of stars, and all the stars were *shooting* stars—a sky filled with streaks and stripes of light.

Silvanus pulled away, smiling and looking quite pleased with himself.

"I daresay that that was the most perfect kiss of any kiss that ever was or ever will be," he declared, thrusting his chin in the air. "Until the next one, of course."

"I like kissing," I said, my cheeks pulsing with heat. "Does kissing mean we're all grown up?"

Silvanus's expression darkened at once, and his hand went to the hilt of his sword. "Not grown up enough."

"Oh." I looked around and remembered where we were with a jolt: in the midst of a fairy revel. A revel in celebration of *him*. "But, Sil— You slayed the Hunting Beast! You're a warrior now. A hero!"

Silvanus turned from me abruptly, half his face cloaked in shadow. The fairies around us began to dance a little faster than before—just a smidge—and staccato notes of laughter broke through the dim.

"You *are* a hero." I felt the magic retreating in me, and when I looked down I was wearing my old clothes again, with my pack on my shoulder and my rib in my hand. "Aren't you?"

"I *will* be," he said with grave vehemence, and when he faced me once more his mouth was a thin, grim line. "Gemma Belle, I . . ."

"What is it?" I said and touched his cheek with my fingertips so that he would not be afraid. He closed his eyes, and his shoulders fell in a sigh.

"I told a lie."

He paused, glancing at me with a look of guarded anticipation, as if bracing himself for an explosive reaction. But I only felt lost. Lying could cause problems, of course, but surely there had to be more to it than that? Silvanus pinched the bridge of his nose, shaking his head in a rather dramatic fashion.

"I see not all of your memory has returned, or maybe you've truly forgotten. Fairies do not tell lies, Gemma Belle. There are grave consequences for a liar. It is worse than anything to lie, even than murder."

Oh. I listened, rapt, as he explained further. It was a limitation of their powers—part of the bargain the fairies had made with magic itself when the world was young, though no one alive now knows why. (A jolt in the back of my mind, the image of Silvanus and me sitting side by side behind a tree carved with curling patterns, ancient runes of some kind, and him teasing me, saying: *A fairy can't lie, but that doesn't mean we're always honest.*)

"But I thought, perhaps, that I would be spared. I am a *prince*, after all." Silvanus gestured at the revelers all around us. They danced even quicker than before, nearly back to normal. "I lied to my mothers, and to all the others of the high fairy court. And now . . . they are stuck."

Stuck. Yes, that was a good word for it, this repetition without end. Destined to dance themselves not to death but near to it, as near as they could get.

"What did you tell them?" I asked, as lightly as I could manage. I had a suspicion, but I didn't want to assume.

Silvanus bowed his head. "That I slayed the Hunting Beast. That I killed it, and now it is dead."

This was more or less what I had guessed. It was a big lie, to be sure, but was it really so bad? I smiled softly, but he would not meet my eye. "It's all right, Sil. You don't have to use a sword to be a hero. There are other ways to save ourselves from monsters."

"But I nearly had him!" he cried, barely listening to me. He threw up his arms and pressed his fists to his eyes as he stomped in restless circles. "I was *so close.* I cut the Beast, right across the gut, and his blood was the color of moonlight on a cold night, so pale and thin and *wrong.* But before I could deal the mortal blow, he swiped me with his claws like knives. See here—" Silvanus lifted his shirt to reveal three thick scarlet gashes on his left side, below the ribs. "And they must have been tipped with poison, or some other manner of drug, for I became dizzy and fainted dead away."

He was breathless. His chest heaved, and his cheeks were flushed, no longer from kissing. "He did not kill me, the Beast. He did not kill me when he could have so easily. I have no idea why. He left me there in the mud for my hunting party to find."

I stood still and watched him pace. I thought of how the head on the platter had vaguely reminded me of the monster named Ash, but that Ash was not—*could* not—be the Hunting Beast, not if Mama trusted him. And how this monster that Silvanus had described didn't seem like the Hunting Beast either. Why would the real Hunting Beast leave Silvanus alive? Who had Silvanus really battled? *Could* it have been Ash, mistaken for the Hunting Beast?

"I shot a boar instead, and glamoured it to look like the Beast's head." His voice was so quiet I could barely hear it. "When we returned to the palace I presented it to my mothers, and the hall erupted with cheers. They hosted this revel the very same evening. A celebration, it was supposed to be, but as soon as they beheld the false head a curse came upon them— a terrible doom which prevents them from moving either forward in time or back. And me, outside of it all, unable to do anything but bear witness to the endless repetition. This is my punishment."

With great gentleness, he reached for my hand and pressed it to his chest. Beneath my palm the beat of his heart was steady but swift.

"I do not know which is worse, Gemma Belle. That I told a lie, or that they believed it."

It was all very strange and I told him so; I shivered with the chill of it, with this magic like a shadow that could be seen and felt but never quite held.

"You must think me a coward," he said, his gaze downcast. "A failure, and worse."

I shook my head. "No, I don't think that."

I was relieved that the Beast wasn't slain—*murdered*—in case it wasn't the real Beast that he had fought, and I understood why he'd lied. He wanted to prove himself so badly, to be worthy of his title and birthright. I believed that it was his kindness that made him worthy, but sometimes the stories we grow up with give us certain ideas about what it means to be a hero—and what it means to be a monster too.

"I think you're very brave," I said honestly, "and that your heart is true."

Silvanus exhaled; he'd been holding his breath.

"Thank you. It is more than I deserve." Suddenly he squeezed my hand, almost painfully tight. "But what of you? How came you here? And wherefore? How rude I am, to spill my woes like a cloud full of rain when I have asked nothing of your present health and happiness! But wait—"

A bit bewildered by the suddenness and ferocity of this speech, I stumbled as he tugged my hands and led me through the crowd of dancing fairies. They whirled faster and faster, the music louder and more manic than ever before.

"Not here, I think. Your magic is strong, Gemma Belle, but it cannot hold. Come, I know a safe place where we can go."

We climbed a new glass staircase that Silvanus summoned with his Touch and reached the top of the ravine just as the song ended and the cheering began. I caught a glimpse of the glamoured severed head on a platter right before Silvanus pulled me into the cover of the trees, and we left the cursed revel far behind.

"IT BEGAN ONE night when Mama took a mirror to the edge of the trees and showed it to a monster there. I don't know why, except, well—I think the monster is under a spell." I paused, tucking a strand of hair behind my ear. "In fact, the monster as I remember him looks a bit like the false head on the platter at the revel . . . You don't think it was *that* monster you fought, my mama's monster? Could you have mistaken him for the Hunting Beast?"

"No," said Silvanus with such firm conviction that I didn't doubt him, and even felt a little foolish for asking. "I fought the Hunting Beast, not some human in disguise. But do go on, Gemma Belle. Your tale has begun on a fascinating note."

In a warm, cozy cave about a mile from the ravine, with some kind of moss glowing silver-blue-green all around us, I told Silvanus everything. About the Slit Witch and Mother— how I'd chopped off her head—and the monster named Ash and the mirror that shows one's true self that I had not been able to find, for the world was wide and I was only a fifteen-year-old girl (almost), and how I had decided to take my chances in the woods and start by rescuing Mama, even if there were flesh-eating monsters afoot. I told him of the guardian of the forest and the ax I'd turned into a sword; I told him of the tree-woman and the removal of my rib. My shadow; the wall; the fairy village, empty and cold. The revel, and how I'd realized that something was wrong. I told him how frightened I was, how I had shouted, just the one word—*Enough!*—and how the fairies had come to an almost-halt at the behest of my Touch. And how, just when I'd despaired of ever seeing him again, he'd appeared.

Silvanus listened and did not interrupt, and he fetched me a cup of water from a crystalline stream when my throat became too dry to speak. It took me an hour to disclose the whole story, and when it was done my voice was a raspy whisper. My chest was sore and I was tired, but for the first time in quite a while— since even before I stepped foot in the woods—I felt like everything might be all right. I wasn't alone anymore, and even though I was still afraid, I knew I could do whatever I had to in order to get Mama back. *Pretend-brave.*

"Well, I guess that's the end," I said in conclusion. I stretched my legs long in front of me, my knees cramped from keeping them folded to my chest. "I couldn't find the magic mirror, so I decided to break the spell myself, you see. Only, I have no idea where to find Mama or the Slit Witch, or even the monster named Ash. If I just knew where to look . . ."

Suddenly, my head snapped up. An idea had taken shape as I spoke, and now I was so excited I could barely get the words out. "Sil! It's a *quest*. You couldn't complete yours, but you can help me complete mine, and maybe rescuing Mama will help you free your people from the curse. A noble deed to counteract your lie."

"*Yes*. How very clever you are." Silvanus smiled, and it was like waking after a good long sleep. Energy, and the lingering taste of sweet dreams. "Gemma Belle, I will help you, but first—!"

Silvanus leapt to his feet and offered a hand to pull me to mine. His skin was warm and I felt myself smiling in turn, the light of the cave illuminating his face. I had come so far—so very far—that surely, *surely* there could not be much farther still to go. I could feel it, the path of destiny. All I had to do now was take it.

"First, we shall need wisdom and a blessing," Silvanus said, as we made our way out of the cave hand in hand. "And directions; that would help. There is only one person I know of who can provide all that we seek."

"Who?" I asked eagerly. We emerged from the cave and the clear night air was cool on my face. Night lasted so long here that I couldn't tell how much time had truly passed. But I was becoming fond of the dark.

"You've heard of her, I think." Silvanus breathed deeply, his eyes like pieces of glass. "Now, let's away. The Great Ensorceller of the Hidden Moon awaits."

18

Virginia

M Y MOTHER AND I COOKED TOGETHER IN THE EVE-
nings as July ended and August began, and though we
chatted over the clatter of pots and the slicing of vegetables, we
never really *spoke*. Not about the things that mattered most.
Things like bodies and how to live in one; things like monsters
and why they find us so delicious. Is it our meat that they're
after or our fear?

Ma, I went into the woods.

Ma, I met a boy there.

*Ma, something happened between us, something like swallowing
the moon.*

Instead we discussed the weather—cloudless, hot—and
items in the shop. Her recent acquisition of Royal Lace depres-
sion glass, a complete serving set. Safe topics, so bland that I
wanted to shake her shoulders and make her angry again. At
least in the silence we hadn't felt a need to pretend that everything was fine. At least in the silence there was still a chance
that one or the other of us would reveal our secrets. I had secrets inside of secrets now, hidden like nesting dolls. I was a
stranger to her, even if she didn't know it yet. I was becoming a
stranger even to myself.

The sore flower's scent burned beneath my pillow. At first it served its purpose, softening the edges of my sleep, but as the days passed and Ash failed to return, not even magic could banish the chill that crept across my dreams. It could not keep me from jolting awake at even the softest creak of the house shifting in the wind, or an owl's lonesome call, or the fingerlike branches of the cherry tree outside my window brushing against the glass. It could not stop the percussive pounding of my heart in my ears as I pressed my face into the pillow, or the hitch in my breath, or the ache in my chest. The sore flower had cast a spell, but it only lasted until morning.

I began to dream of blood, but when I awoke there was none. In the dark I stumbled to the bathroom to check, squinting in the too-bright fluorescent light as I scanned for even the slightest stain. But there was nothing, and I went back to bed lamenting that just when I *wished* for blood it refused to come. In the morning I checked again, and about a thousand times throughout the day, but always it was the same. I pressed my fingers into the soft flesh of my belly, dread burning in the deep of me.

Ash, please come back. I need to tell you something . . .

I went for walks along the edge of the woods. I shivered in the sunlight, feet bare in the grass, drops of dew glistening on my ankles as I followed the curve of the trees. When I grew tired of walking I sat at the base of the old oak in the far corner of the yard with my spine curled against its bark, watching the birds flit through the branches. I folded my legs to my chest and waited for someone who clearly wasn't coming. I pressed my cheek to my knee and hummed the song from the miniature music box I had given Ash, wondering if he knew and was humming it too. I stayed only until the light began to fade. Every day now was shorter than the last.

My mother watched me out of the corner of her eye. In the kitchen, in the shop, from the window as I paced the backyard.

I was certain that she attributed my distress to the looming deadline of school starting soon (if *only* it were that), and I knew she would never ask, not wanting to pry. In the past, her strict notions of privacy annoyed me to the point of tears—

(Why can't you just ask me what's wrong, like a normal mother would?

Because, Gigi, it isn't my place. If you want to share with me, you will, and if you don't you won't, whether I ask about it or not.

But it makes me feel like you don't care. Like you don't want to know.

Of course I care.

You don't.

I do. If you believe nothing else about me, please believe that I care about you.

Well, you have a funny way of showing it.)

—but now it felt like a blessing, knowing I wouldn't have to face her. I wouldn't have to confess until I was absolutely ready to tell the truth. And I *would* have to, eventually. This was not something I could hide forever, or even for very much longer.

I'm not sorry, Ma. I'm not.

THE LAST DAYS of summer passed in stops and starts, too slowly one moment and too quickly the next, and soon it was the end of August, only two weeks before school was set to begin. It was early evening, the clouds above bruised and swollen, and I'd barely eaten anything all day, too nauseated to keep anything down. It had been five weeks since I'd seen Ash, but it felt much longer—a nightmare without pause even to take a breath. My mother had just brewed a pot of after-dinner coffee to go with the coffeecake, and I was halfway through my cup before I realized I probably shouldn't be drinking it. I immediately blanched, my hand tightening around the mug as I drowned slowly in the depths of all the things I didn't know and wasn't prepared for. What was I doing?

My God, what was I *doing*?

"I'm not going to ask because I already know the answer," my mother said suddenly, and I jumped in my seat, spilling a drop of milky coffee onto the table. I wiped it away with my sleeve. "You're not going back to school."

I looked at her and didn't blink. "No."

Heavy dark clouds continued to drag across the sky, smothering the last of the sunlight. "Then what will you do?"

Here it was then, the moment of reckoning. I knew she would judge me harshly and I braced for it, as ready as I would ever be.

But would she forgive me?

Help me?

"I met someone," I said as the room filled with shadows. "We're going to make a life together."

"You met someone," she repeated. "At school?"

"No." The air went still between us. "In the woods."

My mother's eyes were hard and bright. "I told you never to go there."

I laughed. I don't know why, but I did. It was funny, I suppose, in a grim and twisted way. "I remember."

"And yet."

"And *yet*," I said, "I went there anyway. Because I was angry with you, Ma, and because I wanted to see the woods through *my* eyes, not yours. I was so tired of being afraid. You cursed me, in a way. Because I was afraid, I could never be fully part of the woods, and because you had also shown me magic, I could never be fully part of *this* world"—I gestured vaguely around us—"here."

A sharp inhale. I nearly didn't hear it over a sudden roll of thunder, a sound as welcome to me now as my own heartbeat. Thunder meant rain, and rain meant Ash.

"I did want you to be afraid." My mother stared not at me but past me, out the window to where lightning cracked open the sky. She looked so sad. Not angry as I'd expected, or ashamed of me. Only sad and distant. She was somewhere inside herself, somewhere I'd never been and couldn't follow. "I hoped fear would protect you. It was the only way I could think to keep you away from the woods. A child won't believe the stove is hot until they've touched it."

"You hoped fear would *control* me, you mean. Well, I suppose you got your wish. I'm more scared than I've ever been, and I can't ever leave the woods because it's inside of me now. No matter where I go, no matter what I do . . . it's growing in me, full as the moon."

The wind picked up then, and with it came an inhuman shriek. Not of pain, but of triumph and malicious glee. I was already running down the stairs by the time the shrieking stopped, my mother close behind me. The silence after the shriek was worse than the shriek itself and I nearly knocked over a dozen breakable things in the shop as I sprinted through the darkened aisles. My mother swore and I heard a crash, but I didn't look back. The only thought in my head was of Ash as I threw open the door and burst into the gloom, no rain yet but the clouds about to rupture at any second. I started toward the woods, the wind blowing my hair into my eyes so that I did not quite see the dark figure slip from between the trees until he was only a few feet in front of me. And then he was in my arms, and I was in his, holding on so tightly that it would hurt to let go, tangled together like a knot that could not be loosened, only cut.

"What's happened? Are you all right?" I said, but he didn't

hear me over the wind, plus my face was pressed into his chest. I didn't want to relax my grip on him even a little bit, but I couldn't look into his eyes otherwise. I pulled away just slightly, and gasped at the scratches crisscrossing his cheeks, the dripping gouge on the side of his throat, not very deep but enough to make him bleed.

"*Ash*. Ash!" I cried, not knowing what to do or how to help, but he wasn't looking at me. He stared past me, at something—someone—over my shoulder. I turned and saw my mother standing there, only a few yards back, her arms crossed tightly over her chest. The wind tugged her hair out of its coil at the base of her neck as her gaze flicked between the two of us.

"Enchantress, is it you?" said Ash in a voice full of awe. "I've been looking everywhere for you."

Now it was my turn to look between them, feeling small and lost and confused.

"Ma?" I said, but my mother didn't respond. A second later it didn't matter anymore, because a high cackle came from the edge of the woods and out stepped the Slit Witch with her demon beside her, a thick curl of smoke, vaguely human-shaped, with eyes that glowed like tarnished rubies. Was it the demon shrieking and cackling, or was it the witch? The sound echoed off the trees before a deep growl of thunder chased it away. Ash pushed me behind him, shielding me from the intruders, but I didn't want to cower or hide. I took his hand and pressed myself to his side.

The Slit Witch smiled at us. It was a crooked thing, like a painting slipping off a wall. She had changed since the last time I'd seen her; little slits had opened on her arms and across her neck, flaps of flesh dangling like torn fabric. Her face was all angles, her hair dry and thin.

"Oh, hello," she said, and her smoke-demon curled around her shoulders, fell down her back like a billowing cape. Her impossibly dark eyes were fixed on me. "I thought I was going to have to break into your house, little girl, drag you out by your hair, all kicking and screaming. And with your mother begging for mercy, powerless against me. She's become so afraid of me, even though I gave her every reason not to be. It's sad, really, how easily her love turned to fear." She sighed and shook herself, while I tried to figure out what the hell she was talking about. I came up empty. "But here you are, waiting for me! So much easier, but a lot less fun."

"Leave her alone," Ash said in a voice as deep and rumbling as the thunder over our heads. "I'm the one who wronged you, not her."

"Hmm, no." The Slit Witch crooked a finger and beckoned to me, and I felt my body respond without my consent, taking a step forward before I even realized what was happening. Ash grabbed my arm and pulled me back, his touch disarming whatever spell she'd cast. The witch only laughed. "You, girl. You stole from me. There's a price to be paid for that."

"You can have the brush back," I said at once. "I'll just go get—"

"No, no, no. I don't care about *that*." The Slit Witch took a step closer. Just one step, and she was still yards away, but it felt somehow as if we'd been standing on opposite ends of a bridge over a river, and now we were all on the same side with nothing between us. "You took my son's heart and ate it all up, didn't you, sweetie, without saving even a morsel for me? Such gluttony! Every crumb gone, and now I'm so very hungry."

"No." Ash stepped in front of me again and this time I let him. My heart was beating so fast I imagined it like a blur in my chest. "I gave my heart to her freely. No part of it ever belonged to you anyway."

"Not true." The Slit Witch shook her head slowly. "A child's heart always belongs to the mother first and foremost, longest and last. Wouldn't you say so, Clarice?"

I startled at my mother's name, and turned to find her still behind me, closer than she'd been before. I'd forgotten she was there at all, witnessing every moment of this in silence. And not only that, but the witch knew her name.

But of course—hadn't my mother known this woman, long ago? After the fairy wedding we'd never spoken of her again, but I still remembered how the woman had approached her with familiarity, and had even called her Clary. Why was the witch regarding her as if they had a history?

And Ash had known her too. *Enchantress, is it you?*

"Let's make a bargain," my mother said, coming around me to stand next to Ash. I watched her, as fascinated as I was furious, for it was clear to me now that she had been keeping secrets. *There is no one—no one—in the woods you can trust. Especially the ones you think you love the most.* Apparently that included my own mother. "Anything you want, anything from the shop. Name it and it's yours."

The Slit Witch huffed.

"You think I want your old junk? Some of it came in handy, I'll admit, once I'd put my spells on it. The hairbrush, of course, the one currently in your thieving daughter's possession." The witch took another step. "Oh, but we're beyond the hairbrush now. No item, no *material thing,* is equal to a heart. We can all agree on that, if nothing else. No?"

"I'm telling you," Ash said, yelling now to be heard over the storm, "there is no exchange to be made. What's mine was mine to give. We're done here, Mother. *Leave.*"

"My son, my only one." The Slit Witch smiled slowly. "He's given me a gift, though he doesn't know it. You took his heart, and now I shall take yours and much more besides."

Then—my God, it happened so fast. Earth-tilting, time-warping, space-bending *fast*. The Slit Witch was before us and then she wasn't. She disappeared in a blink and reappeared right behind me, her hand reaching, fingers skimming the back of my neck. I tried to turn, but she had me in her grip, my whole body frozen. In her touch there was magic; somehow, she reached inside me, a careless surgery, excising my secrets.

"Oh, oh! What's this?" Her breath on my ear, warm and whispery. Ash turned at her voice and my mother did too, but it was too late; she had me. "You naughty girl! And still just a child yourself. Have you told him yet? Does he *know*?"

"Let go, *please*." I was crying, quiet tears sliding, because this moment was supposed to be joyous, or I'd hoped it would be. I'd hoped it would be the beginning of my dream, the one with the cottage and Ash and me safe inside it, a little family . . .

"He doesn't, does he?" The Slit Witch's face was so close, her cheek brushed my cheek. Ash didn't move, and I realized that he *couldn't,* that whatever power she'd used on me, she'd used on him too. My mother stood like a shadow on a wall. "Tell him now; I want to watch. It will be so much sweeter if he knows before I cast my spell."

The Slit Witch released me, and I stumbled forward. Ash caught me and held me, with the witch close beside us, hovering. There was no way out of this.

"Ash, I . . . We . . ." I didn't know how to say it, how to tell him with our mothers watching us. "Something's happened. You see . . ."

"What is it?" Ash said softly, stroking my hair. Oh God, I wished we were anywhere but here.

"I . . . I'm . . ."

"*Spirits below,*" the Slit Witch swore, impatient. She moved to Ash's side and rested her chin on his shoulder. If I didn't know better, I would have said it was a loving gesture. "The girl is pregnant, Ash. Your doing, obviously. Aw! See how she's look-ing at you? Like you're the one who places the stars in the sky each night, lighting up the galaxy so that she'll never be lost in the dark? I think she's in love." The witch lowered her voice to a whisper. Ash's eyes never left mine. "I think she doesn't know any better."

"Is this true?" Ash said, and I didn't know what he meant: Was it true I was pregnant, or was it true that I loved him?

"Yes," I said, answering both at once, doing my best to ignore the witch and to focus only on him. "I—I'm sorry."

"What are you sorry for?" He looked at me like I was the only thing in the world keeping him warm. Like without me he'd be ice, he'd be steel, he'd be gone. "Virginia—"

"Oh!" The Slit Witch stepped between us, looking from Ash to me and back again. "You love her too, do you? Well, too bad. There has been a change of plans. I have no use for a pregnant girl, but I can tell that the child will be special. I suppose I can wait. I don't really want to raise another child. Look how un-grateful this one has become! And his magic not nearly as strong as I'd hoped. Sometimes it skips a generation or two."

It was like she was speaking in riddles. I could make no sense of a word she said. But something bad was coming; that much was clear.

"All right," she said with a snap of her fingers, "I'll let you do the childrearing until I'm ready to take over. But a heart has been stolen and someone needs to be punished! Ash, my dear, it will have to be you."

The Slit Witch spoke an incantation and at once a great gust of wind—of magic—ripped Ash and me apart, pushing me with enough force that I fell backward into the grass, landing so hard on my back that the breath was knocked out of my chest, leaving me gasping. My mother rushed to my side, helping me to sit up, and that's when I saw Ash, floating a few feet off the

ground, his body stiff and long, locked in the witch's enchantment. She stood nearby, muttering something in a language I
didn't understand as she swirled her hands as if stirring a pot,
just as the clouds cracked open above us. The rain was cold,
and my mother wrapped her arms around my shoulders as we
watched the witch cast her spell, as Ash's eyes closed and he
began to transform.

First his feet, which lengthened into giant padded paws, and
then his legs, his knees bending backward like a goat's. His
torso stretched, and his arms too, spindly like tree branches,
and from his head sprouted a pair of silver antlers, heavy and
twisting, shining in a sudden lunge of lightning. His mouth
widened, fangs biting into his lower lip, and his skin grew fur
like a deer's, short and brown. When the change was complete
he dropped to the ground on all fours. For a second our eyes
met—his round and enormous, pure black—and then he
sprinted into the trees with an agonized growl from deep within
his chest. He disappeared and I just stood there, shocked to the
core, my beloved now a beast. When the reality of this finally
hit me, I folded to my knees.

"What have you done to him?" I cried, my mother still at my
side, both of us bent in half in the grass. The rain kept coming,
washing away my tears. *What have you done?*"

The Slit Witch only waved a hand, breathless from her nefarious chant. "He'll recover his senses eventually, if that's what
you're worried about. Transformation is a tricky thing. Takes
time to adjust to, naturally."

"Take it back," I said, my fingers digging into the wet grass.
"I'll give you whatever you want, just take it *back*!"

"Mmm, no. This has all worked out so much better than I
imagined." The Slit Witch walked over to me and crouched
down so that we were eye to eye. A new slit had opened in her
skin, a slanted gash above her chest. "Only you can save him,

dear. A task! Nearly impossible, but not quite. No, no, not quite."

The Slit Witch's smoke-demon had retreated to the trees where the rain didn't reach, its eyes glowing crimson.

"What must I do?" I asked.

"Nothing like turning straw to gold, I assure you!" The Slit Witch sighed as if exhausted. The wound on her chest didn't bleed. "There's a mirror, a special mirror, somewhere in the world, and it's this mirror that you must find. A mirror to show one's true reflection, to show the *heart*. It will reveal to him who he was—who he used to be—and he will be human again. Easy?"

"No," I spat, disgusted. "Where am I supposed to find something like that?"

"Well, yes, that's the hard part, my dear. And then, of course, there's this: If you fail to find the mirror to show one's true reflection, then Ash will turn into a beast in truth and eat the heart right out of your chest. *Literally,* not metaphorically, the way you ate his. Beasts eat meat! It's just the way of things, the natural cycle, you understand. He won't be able to help it. He'll remember every minute of the devouring—delicious!—and he'll have to find some way to live with what he's done." The witch stopped, shrugged. "Or not. His fate no longer matters to me. He's yours now—your responsibility."

"You're a *monster*," I said, and I had never meant anything more in my whole life, even the words I had not yet had the chance to say to Ash (*I love you*). This was *hate,* and it was all-consuming.

"Maybe. *Maybe*," the Slit Witch said, unbothered by my loathing. "But at least no one's going to eat *me*. I'm at the top of the food chain, and it's a very nice place to be."

"You won't be. Not forever."

"But I don't need forever." The Slit Witch straightened, and I followed her with my eyes, too sick and tired to stand. I was barely aware of my mother next to me, smoothing my hair back out of my eyes. "I probably should have mentioned the time limit—oopsy! I'll give you until your daughter turns—hmm. Let's say . . . *fifteen*. In fifteen years she'll be all grown up and ripe enough for my purposes. *Yes*. A daughter for a son, is that not a fair trade? I'm nothing if not fair, see? I stake my very reputation on it."

"You will never have her," I said, and though the fire of hate was in me, I knew I couldn't let it touch her. My child, the only little piece of Ash that I had left. The hatred, the *rage*—it *must* not touch her. "I will break your spell long before the fifteen years are up."

"We'll see," she said, and then she was gone, running back into the woods where she belonged.

And I was left with the ruins of myself, a life turned upside down.

I MEANT TO run after him. Ash, the monster; Ash, transformed. I had some mad notion that if I could only reach him and kiss him, he'd turn into a prince again. But I only made it two steps before my mother grabbed my arm and said gently, "No."

That one word stopped me cold. Even with a head full of fury, my feet went numb, my heart heavy and weighing me down. I allowed my mother to lead me out of the woods and into our house, stumbling through the rain. Even once we were past the front door, she steered me around the antiques and up the stairs. I didn't know where we were going until we were there. In the bathroom, she wordlessly helped me undress and climb into the bath as if I were a little girl again. I was so dirty, mud under my nails and wet, tangled hair. I tucked my knees to my chest and stayed still as my mother knelt beside the tub and rinsed the crust of the forest from my skin, her fingers working at the knots in my hair. The water was hot but not enough to burn, steam lingering in the air so long over our heads it became ornamental, lending the scene the mist of a dream. I hadn't cried in front of her since I was small, but I cried as she cleaned me and I didn't bother to hide the sobs. When at last she shut the water off and sat back, the silence thickened and it was hard to breathe.

"Do you hate me?" I said, staring not at her but at the drain, the last of the water swirling away. Strands of dark hair were caught on the plug.

"No." My mother, still kneeling on the bathroom floor, sighed. "Do I wish you hadn't slept with some boy from the woods where I told you never to go? *Yes.* Do I wish you had gone back to school and taken the opportunity never afforded me? *Of course.* But wishing won't change anything now. Wishing isn't magic."

In my mind I again saw his face when the Slit Witch split open my secret, like my gaze on his was the only thing keeping him from turning forever into stone. *You love her too, do you?*

"Maybe you're right." I buried my face in my bent knees. "Still, I wish . . ."

"I know." I felt her fingers on my wet hair, stroking gently, almost brushing. It was so idle a movement I wasn't sure she even knew she was doing it, but I didn't want her to stop. "Sometimes hope is terrible, isn't it? It makes you believe you can have things you can never have, or be someone you can never be. And when a hope fails to come true, it is worse than if you'd never had any hope at all."

I could only nod. For once, we agreed. My mother fetched a towel from the closet and draped it over my shoulders. She left so I could have privacy drying off and getting dressed, but for a long time I simply stood there, dripping and shivering as the steam dissipated and the heat of the bath faded. I rested a hand on my flat abdomen and had a hard time believing there was really anyone in there, no matter how infinitesimal at the moment. I had wanted to live with Ash and our baby in a house far away, but that dream had surrendered to a nightmare. Was the baby part of the nightmare now too, or the last shard of a shattered future? And if I clung to it, this jagged piece of a lost dream, how deeply would it cut me?

After I had changed into my pajamas, and twisted my hair into a damp plait, I found my mother in the kitchen, preparing to boil water for tea. I sat down at the table, across from the stove, watching her slow, sure movements as the storm quieted outside.

"Ma," I said, and though she nodded over her shoulder to show that she was listening, she didn't turn around. "We don't have to talk about magic mirrors or monsters ever again if you'd prefer. I can handle all that myself. But tell me now: Why did Ash call you an enchantress? And how did you come to know the Slit Witch?"

The questions rested heavily between us. After what had happened that night, all I wanted was honesty, some truth I could stand upon solidly. My mother looked me in the eye.

"Gigi," she said in a voice I'd never heard before. It was high, almost girlish. I realized that this was a confession, and that she was afraid. How strange to know my stony, inflexible mother was afraid. "It's my fault that the woods are here. The magic, the monsters, the witch—everything. They came for me. They came *because* of me."

My heart sank. "What do you mean?"

She rolled her shoulders back, tilted her head so that her neck cracked. "I married young—too young—and to a man I didn't love, because it was expected, and because I thought settling down would make me feel . . . normal. And then when that wasn't enough, I prayed for a baby, in the hopes that being a mother would fill the ache inside of me. But I was still dissatisfied. Not that you didn't bring me joy," she hastened to add, as my heart sank deeper. "You did, and still do—but it was unfair of me to expect you to solve all my problems. What a terrible burden to place on another! You are your own person, Gigi—sometimes I still forget that. In some ways, I'm still trying to learn how to love you as you are, and not as an extension of myself."

I nodded, trying hard to understand but not quite grasping it. She loved me, but I wasn't enough? Or . . . or I *was* enough, but it's like how a heart has four chambers and it needs all of them to beat? There was something missing. But that didn't mean I wasn't still a vital part of the whole.

"Why didn't you feel normal?" I asked, and thought quietly, *What is normal even supposed to feel like?*

My mother didn't look at me. She began slowly. "Gigi, when I was around your age, I realized I had . . . certain . . . desires that aren't openly accepted by our society. I . . ." She sighed. "I'm not attracted to men. I never have been. My first love—though unrequited—was a woman."

Oh. My breath left me in a rush, and a flush crept up my neck. Not because my mother was attracted to women—that part surprised me, though I wasn't upset—but because it was embarrassing to think about my mother having desires at all. For us to be sitting here talking about them, especially now that she knew that I had desires too. That I'd acted on them. That I would soon be a mother. That I was truly a child no longer.

"Did my father find out?" My voice was hoarse. I cleared my throat and tried again. "Is that why he left?"

My mother raised her eyes to mine. "Yes."

"I'm sorry." None of this was what I'd expected. I wanted to still be angry with her, and with the witch, and with the world, because it was easier. Because sorrow was so heavy, but anger was strong enough to lift it and make it feel lighter. "I'm sorry that all these years you couldn't be yourself."

"Oh, Gigi, that's not for you to worry about." My mother reached out, touched my cheek. Just as quickly, she dropped her hand. "I only want you to understand. Do you see now? My longing to live the way I wanted to—my dissatisfaction with the world I was forced to inhabit—was what called the woods to us. One day the woods were just trees, and then, like magic . . . it was more."

"The fairy queen," I said suddenly, remembering. "She married a woman, didn't she?"

My mother smiled. Short-lived, but genuine. "It's what drew me to them. At first the woods were all I had hoped for, until I looked deeper. Until . . ."

Nausea, bile, a burning behind my eyes. "Your first love," I said uneasily. "The unrequited one."

My mother looked at me and I knew. *Nicasia.* It felt like a curse to say her name aloud, so we didn't.

"She was beautiful once," my mother said, and lifted her chin, her mask sliding back into place. I wanted to tell her I wasn't judging her, wasn't placing blame, not after all she'd confessed, but she pressed on, giving me no chance to chime in. "Beautiful before her magic ripped her apart. She was kind, and enchanting—and the things she could do amazed me. Her poise, her *freedom*—I wasn't sure if I wanted her, or just wanted to *be* her. She was—*is*—fearless, and I both envied and admired her that. But fearlessness—literal, *true* fearlessness—just isn't *human.* And it took me longer than perhaps it should have to realize that she wasn't, despite her human face and her human touch. She's very good at pretending; I'll give her that. She's lived so long that she's had plenty of time to practice. She's learned how to be exactly what someone needs in order to get close: a friend, a sister, a mentor. A lover. Even when I started to see the cracks in her character—*literally*—she knew exactly what to say and do to keep me coming around. I was lonely and she knew it. It wasn't easy for me to let go."

A phantom touch on my forehead, a memory of cold. I shivered, and once I'd started, I couldn't stop.

"But how did you figure it out?" I said. "That she was only pretending?"

"I wandered where I shouldn't have. In her cellar I found dozens of glass jars, each containing a human heart. The very strangest thing was that they were still beating—some slowly and some racing. Enchanted, somehow, and for what purpose I still don't know."

I was colder than ever now, my throat so tight I couldn't speak.

"I fear for that boy of yours, Gigi. And for you too."

My mother stood abruptly, her face in shadow as she looked down at me. Her confession was finished; a curtain had fallen between us.

It's an old story, isn't it?

"The witch has killed before," she said. "I doubt that she'll hesitate to do it again."

19

Gemma

IT HAD BEEN A FEW YEARS SINCE I'D LAST HAD GROW-
ing pains—that strange, stretchy ache in my legs, and especially my shins. But I felt it again, for the first time in so long,
as I followed the fairy prince quietly through the village that
was a little bit asleep and a little bit dead, magic like wind drifting over our heads. I felt the ache not in my limbs, but in my
head—twin aches on either side of my skull, several inches
above my ears. With both hands I reached up to touch the
spots, and beneath my fingers felt a protuberance as hard as
bone, spiraled ridges along the edge, not terribly thick around
but raised too high from the scalp to be considered a mere
bump. I clutched the knots, my hair neatly parted around them,
and tried to picture myself with horns—not like a devil, a monster or beast, but like an animal, majestic and strong.

An *animal,* yes—I could be an animal. I despaired of turning
into a monster, but an animal would be all right; an animal
would be easy. Weren't humans just animals that could do
math? I'd never excelled at math anyway. I'd hardly miss it, especially geometry with its radians and matrices.

You'll be fine, Gemma Belle, I said in my head. *As long as you
get Mama back, there's nothing you can't handle. Even turning into
an animal. You'll be fine.*

I hoped that this was true. I didn't like to lie to myself.

"Hey, Sil?" I said, as we reached the piazza with the fountain at its center. Funny how the way back felt so much shorter than it had going forward. "Do I look, um . . . different to you?"

Silvanus turned without breaking his stride, loping backward to get a good look at me. He considered. After a moment he delivered the verdict.

"No," he said and, with a slight shake of his head, flipped around again. We had nearly reached the fountain; it seemed, peculiarly, to be our destination.

I stared at him, at the back of his head. Did he really not see the forest in me?

"Although," he added, "you *do* look more like you than you used to. Now that you mention it."

Huh, I thought, completely thrown. *I look* more *like myself? Not less?* Jogging along beside him, I touched my inchoate horns again. *Hmm.*

Silvanus strode right to the fountain and hopped onto its stone lip. With a little wink at me, he took the lady's hand, leaned forward, and kissed her cheek.

The glowing eyes went dark, and though the statue didn't move, there came a deep sigh like the grinding of rough stones. Some enchantment had been activated, and I watched with eager eyes as the opaque pink water drained from the fountain's basin to reveal a marble staircase that spiraled into blackness. Without a word, Silvanus reached for my hand, and because I trusted him, I let him lead me down and around, even when it felt like my head was being squeezed between invisible hands so tightly I nearly couldn't breathe. But just when I thought I would collapse from the pressure, the staircase ended and we emerged into a garden of wildflowers. We should have been underground, but somehow the world had turned upside down and there was sky above us. It was dawn.

"Silvanus, where are we going? Silvanus, what is this place?"

Rich golden light fell so thickly on the garden that I tasted it on my tongue as sweet as honey. I couldn't see the sun, or where the light was coming from; it shone in my eyes from every angle so that I walked with my head down.

"This is where we keep our secrets," said the fairy prince to me. I gripped his hand as we walked through the garden on a path of loose dirt, the flowers around us swaying gently even though there was no hint of a breeze. "You must promise not to tell."

The request was innocent enough, but it made me want to cry. Besides Silvanus, the only other person I would tell was Mama. And Mama was still gone.

"What do you miss most about her?" Silvanus said, as if he could hear my thoughts like noisy chewing, the worries chomping, chomping, chomping the same old dried-up bone. "Your mother. The real one."

It was a struggle to think with all that light in my eyes. I tried to shield my face with my arm across my forehead, but it was no use. I kept my chin bowed as we wound on through the garden, the flowers growing taller and taller still: First they came to my knees, then halfway up my thighs, and then my waist. At last we came to a long stone tunnel, and we rested a minute beneath it, the shade a great relief.

"She was sad, most of the time," I said, remembering all the plants she would buy for our house but then neglect to water; the half-read books she kept in a stack by her bed—too tired to finish, she said. The way she would stand in the Glass Room looking at the mirrors as if she couldn't see herself in any of them. In the warm light of sunrise, she often looked ancient, gnarled hands and bruises beneath her eyes. But as night approached, in the rose glow of the gloaming, she seemed to me as ageless as the sky, very few clouds and little stars in the upturned corners of her mouth. "But when she wasn't sad, she was . . . well, not happy, exactly, but *warm*. I miss her kisses on the top of my head."

Silvanus nodded encouragement. "What else?"

"We played a lot of board games, like Scrabble and Clue. There was this game called Princess where we had to work together to stop the darkness from taking over the princess's castle." I paused, turning my rib over and over in my hands. "Every evening before bed she used to brush my hair. I didn't really like it, the brushing, but—I liked that she was near."

I swallowed around a knot of grief in my throat.

"One hundred strokes exactly—no more and no less—and when it was done my head went sort of fuzzy; it made me think that that was what love felt like. That soft, slippery nothingness right before you fall asleep."

"Hmm," said the fairy prince, crossing his arms over his chest. "Would that I could see the hairbrush."

"Oh!" I reached into my pack. The brush with the yellow bristles had fallen all the way to the bottom. I brandished it with a flourish of triumph. "Here it is."

Silvanus seized it eagerly, flipping it this way and that with his long deft fingers, weighing it on his palms, and closing one eye as he held it up toward the light. I watched in fascination. It was a fine piece—I knew that much from living in an antiques shop all my life—but perhaps there was more to it than my untrained eyes could perceive. I waited patiently for his appraisal.

"Just as I'd thought," he said, passing the brush back to me. A rabbit with gold fur leapt suddenly over my feet, and I saw a flash of violet eyes, a long mouth curved up into what I can only describe as a smile. "That is an enchanted object."

"What?" For some reason, this was not what I had expected. I thought he'd say, *Oh, yes, of course, this is from France, made*

*approximately in the year of our Lord 1798 by the great Pierre de
Tartuffe of Lyons, a renowned hairbrush maker who was also secretly a fairy, my thrice-removed great-uncle and a dastardly rogue,*
or something of the sort. I had not thought my little old hairbrush itself might be *magic*.

"Oh, yes. I can tell by the weight of it—much too heavy to
have been Touched by a fairy. Certainly it's under a witch's spell,
by which I mean smoke-magic. *Illusory*." He said this last with
a heap of derision, his chin in the air as if turning away from a
bad smell. "Your hairbrush has been altered to steal memories."

My chest became hollow, my heartbeat an echo. Suddenly
the brush was like a knife in my hand—dangerous. I thought
of all those days with Silvanus in the woods, erased. All those
nights on the stool in my room, sitting quietly while Mama
brushed and brushed and brushed my hair. *Go to bed now, love.
Hush, hush.* Each day wondering anew at what a monster was,
wondering why I was not allowed to go into the woods. *Are you
a fairy prince? Always you ask me this!* Doomed to learn the same
lessons over and over. The hairbrush had stolen my memories.

My *mother* had stolen my memories.

Why would Mama do that to me?

"Maybe . . . she didn't know," I said, my voice like a tiptoe
down a dark hall. "Maybe Mama didn't know about the spell?"

Silvanus leaned over and kissed my cheek. "Surely not. Your
mother is not a witch."

"No." The silver handle of the brush was cold, like ice and
winter, like snow. "I mean, I don't think so . . ."

Very gently, Silvanus took the brush from my hand and put
it back in my pack. We continued through the tunnel and
emerged into the sunlight on the other side.

It was not so much a garden as a jungle. A grove of black
trees, with vines and wild hedges, leaves the color of blood.

Almost too consumed by foliage to view it properly was a great stone wishing well, as wide as a swimming pool with water like old rain in a puddle. Several lily pads floated on its murky surface, and a brown toad watched us with a bright yellow gaze as we leaned over the well and peered inside. I couldn't tell how deep it was—if there was only a foot of water or if it went on and on forever.

"O, powerful and wily Ensorceller, mighty heiress to the benevolent secrets of the Hidden Moon," Silvanus chanted, leaning so far down that his chin nearly skimmed the water, "arise and bless us with your majestic presence, that we might ask a favor of you. You, who owe the fairies a great debt and have only served but two years of your eternal sentence."

The shape of a woman rose from the gloom. She lay on her back, her eyes closed, her arms crossed in an X over her chest. Her legs were long and her feet were bare; she wore only a pale, thin gown, which clung to her in wet folds of fabric. Curls of silvery hair spread out in the water around her head like a halo, and her lips were as blue as if she'd been kissed by a demon of frost. When her face at last surfaced fully, a torrent of dark water poured from her nose and mouth. She floated serenely on the surface, taking her first breath in what might have been years. Her eyes opened slowly.

"Yes?" she said, her gaze fixed straight up at the sky. It was still very bright, and I blinked against it, my heart falling like a bird shot out of the air. "Prince of the Forest Fey, what must you ask of me?"

It took me a moment to fully comprehend just what—just *who*—I was seeing. Silvanus was speaking to the woman in that same reverent but commanding tone, but I heard not a word, the world around me growing muted and dim as a storm began churning in the place where my heart should have been. Considering the shocks and scares, the wonders and horrors, the trials and bargains I'd yet experienced in the woods, this was the greatest—*the worst one*—of all.

"Clarice?" I breathed, and at last her dark eyes swiveled. They were like a mirror, reflecting my own confusion and awe and deep dread back to me. Silvanus ceased talking abruptly. I gripped the rough stone lip of the well so hard that it cut into my palms. *"Grandmother,"* I said. "Is it really you?"

I THOUGHT SHE might wade out of the well, rush to me, and wrap me up in a hug. Something she'd never actually done before, though surely the situation warranted it now. But my grandmother didn't move, only sighed.

"Gemma," she said. "I wish you hadn't come."

There was a bleak note in her voice, and I shivered as the light above us turned to gray, the day already at an end.

"You know the Great Ensorceller of the Hidden Moon?" Silvanus said, taken aback. I threw down my pack and my rib, and climbed onto the well's edge.

"She's not an ensorceller. She's my grandma!" I held out a hand, straining to reach her, and at once an arm wrapped around my waist and pulled me back.

"Stop," cried Silvanus, holding me against him as I struggled for release. "If you touch the water, you will be imprisoned along with her."

"Why is she imprisoned? Let her out!"

"I cannot. Only my mothers hold the key."

I cast a disdainful glance at him over my shoulder. He still held me, my spine pressed to his chest. "You don't need a *key*! It's a *well*."

"On the contrary," he said gently. "This well is locked up tight."

"He's right." At my grandmother's words, I finally went limp, sagging quite heavily against the fairy prince. "I'm sorry I never arrived to help you, Gemma. I thought to ask the fairies for help in getting your mother back from the Slit Witch, but they arrested me instead. They entombed me here—without a trial, I might add."

"But why?"

"An imagined slight," she said with bitterness. "I used to bargain with the fairies, when your mother was still a child. They were fascinated by ordinary objects—clocks, music boxes, even dolls with weighted eyelids. Things the fairies didn't have and couldn't make. They were convinced the antiques were magic—and, by extension, that *I* was magic—and they would not have it when I explained otherwise. I went into the woods once a month, so they began to associate me with the new moon. That is how I built my reputation, and I clung to it. It's easier to protect yourself if they are even a little bit afraid. I never thought they'd do something like this, not to me."

I wasn't sure I liked this story, but I knew it was important to hear it. Beside me Silvanus listened too, equally enraptured.

"In my travels through the woods, I met a woman named Nicasia; she lived in a beautiful cottage and invited me in for tea. She knew I had no magic, though she had plenty. Oh, the things she could do—the things she could *create*. She perused my wares that very first day and we soon became friends. She had a young son, around the same age as Gigi—your mother—and I even thought about bringing her with me, to let the children play. He seemed so terribly lonely, the little boy, and Gigi was shy—she'd just started preschool, and she wasn't making any friends."

We kept our captivated silence as my grandmother went on, telling us about Nicasia, how they had fallen in love—or, rather, how my grandmother had thought she was in love. But she didn't know everything about that woman, and soon she discovered a secret: hearts in the cellar, still beating.

"And with the discovery of the hearts, I saw Nicasia for the first time as she really was: a murderer."

Murderess, hissed that long-ago voice that sounded so eerily like my own, and I shook my head to clear it.

No, I thought sternly. I wasn't like Nicasia at all. I wasn't a murderess. I wasn't a *witch.*

"I ended our relationship," my grandmother continued, "though I did see Nicasia one more time, at the queens' wedding. I sold her a sterling silver hairbrush in exchange for a promise that she would leave Virginia and me alone. She enchanted it right in front of me. She desired to steal her son's memories. Perhaps he had found the hearts in the cellar too."

I glanced quickly at my pack, where my old hairbrush was tucked out of sight. Could it be one and the same? It *had* to be.

"I was so afraid. Afraid of her, and afraid for your mother most of all, whose heart could have easily ended up in one of those jars. Afraid for her son too, but what could I do? There were no lawmen in the woods, no child protective services to call. And more than that—I was consumed with guilt. Magic could be dazzling, yes, but I didn't truly understand it, its depths and dark crevices. It could be made to bring forth miracles, but just as easily take them away. I didn't want my antiques to be used for such purposes, so I decided to stop my visits to the woods altogether. But evidently, the fairies had taken my abandonment personally, which I hadn't known until I sought their help. They seized me and left me here to rot."

"You won't rot," said Silvanus at once, though he had a faraway look on his face. "Those waters are preservative. In there, you will live forever."

My grandmother rolled her eyes. "Even better."

"What does not make sense to me," Silvanus said, almost

vehemently, coming out of his daze, "is that you blessed my sword. When I was little—don't you remember? You came to the village and I asked you to bless my sword with your magic that I might someday slay the Hunting Beast. Was it all a lie?"

"Naturally. I told your mothers time and again that I was no sorceress. But because the fairies cannot lie without consequence, they believe that others not of their kind are always out to deceive. They took my dissent as an attempt to conceal the extent of my power. Eventually I grew weary of arguing and let them believe what they would."

Silvanus touched the hilt of his sword as if he'd never seen it before.

"Isn't there any way to release her?" I asked him, but he only shook his head, distracted.

"Don't worry about me, Gemma," my grandmother said, the water framing her face like a veil. "You must rescue your mother, first and foremost. Now, come here—and listen closely."

In the cool grip of dusk in that place where secrets are held like hard candies melting between tooth and tongue, I grasped my fairy boy's hand and listened to my grandmother, the false ensorceller, as she told us exactly where to go and what we must do to find my lost mother. I listened, and a hole opened in my belly as big as the moon as she told us how difficult it would be, and how perilous, to bring her home again.

HUSH, I TOLD my heart. *Hush, hush,* I told my breath. *It is only a little magic,* I told my quivering bones. *You have done magic before.*

Yes . . . but not like this.

"It is not really the blood that they want," Silvanus said as he unsheathed a small dagger from his belt. "It is the pain."

"Sil," I said, glancing from the shiny tip of his dagger to the

dark, churning surface of the river below. We stood on a sloping bank, green moss clinging to the stones, a silvery fish flop-
ping in the current. The wind surged, carrying cold moonlight
on its breath, and I shivered. "Sil, that's *worse*."

We had found this place easily enough; that wasn't the tough
part, Clarice had made clear. It was what we'd encounter *after*
that was to fear—after we jumped into the river, a narrow black
ribbon caught between the trees, and through the portal to the
Woods Below. Our blood was an offering to the sirens that
dwelled in those twisting dark waters: creatures of moonlight
and rot, red-eyed and toothless, tails sharpened to a point.
Once they were human, but now they were not, hapless wan-
derers whose bodies had gotten separated from their souls by
the Eater—a monster of legends that possessed the ability to
step on one's shadow, to pin a person in place with its feet, no
need to touch flesh as it held its prey captive and devoured
one's soul. I wasn't sure how it had eaten the soul, and I wouldn't
let Silvanus tell me, especially because it didn't matter anyway.
The Eater was gone now—or so it was said—devoured in turn
by the Hunting Beast. All that remained was the Eater's victims,
whose hollow bodies had then stumbled into the river, its cold,
inescapable embrace a peculiar kind of mercy. Its magic had
granted them a second life—or second death, depending on
how you looked at it—guarding the entrance to the Woods
Below.

"I didn't like that story," I'd said when Silvanus had finished.
Silvanus led the way toward the river, hacking with his sword
at the worst of the trees' tangles, the roots and thorny bushes.
A new blister had formed on my heel in the time since the tree-
woman's magic rain had healed me, and it made me so angry,
that tiny blaze of metallic hot pain, that I kicked a stone in my
path, launched it into the shadows and didn't bother to put it
back. Stupid, stupid—why were blisters even a thing that hap-

pened? What use was skin if it couldn't protect me from my own shoes? I wanted to rip it off, discard it like a coat, run without the burden of keeping myself together. Let my muscles and my bones untangle. *I'm tired and I want my mama back!* To Silvanus I said, "Tell me another, please. A happy story."

But either he didn't hear me or he didn't have a tale that was not all horror and loss and grim; he was silent the rest of the way to the river, his shoulders tense as he sliced and huffed and sweated. Perhaps he was angry too. Or just impatient.

It was almost *too* easy, actually; we'd reached our destination without impediment. We were deep in the woods, though there was little indication of that besides Silvanus telling me so. The trees looked the same here as they had everywhere else, and the sky was still the color of a bruise, black with a violet sheen. The woods were endless and ageless and didn't care whether we lived or died. And right now, it seemed more and more likely that we would die.

Silvanus held out his hand and I silently placed mine on top of it, palm up. His skin was reassuringly warm, and I relaxed—but only a bit. I didn't know why I should be so afraid of a little bloodshed when I had already given up an entire rib, except that now there was a *knife* involved. It winked, catching the starlight and throwing it in my eyes. My head hurt. I swallowed hard as Silvanus brought the tip of the dagger to my palm and held it against my skin. The blade was the coldest thing I'd ever felt—colder than ice, colder than the deep, colder than death and endless sleep. I clenched my jaw and nodded, as if to say, *Okay, I'm ready.*

But I wasn't ready, not really, and panic flared bright in my chest. How many more pieces of myself would the woods demand? Blood; blood and bones; blood and bones and skin. There were leaves in my hair that had *grown* there, dangling from my scalp, tangling with my dark strands; the veins in my arms were still thick and green beneath my skin, and the green had begun to creep over my shoulders, up my neck, as inexorable as ivy. My horns were still nubs, but when I reached up to touch them I could've sworn they were just a little bit taller than before. *What if the woods take and take and take until there's nothing left?*

"Be brave, Gemma Belle," said the fairy prince with a smile that glowed, and I hoped he couldn't tell that my courage was only pretend. With no further ceremony, he pressed the knife into my waiting hand.

I bit the inside of my cheeks to keep from crying out. It was more than pain; it was also the *memory* of pain, every cut and scrape and bruise and welt, all the pain of my life surging to the surface at once. Every skinned knee and torn nail and long, scarlet scratch. Why must there be so much? It came in waves, radiating—hot, it was *hot*—as Silvanus pressed slowly but steadily, as the blood welled around the blade and clung there for a moment before it spread and spilled over the edge. It dripped from my hand and, swept sideways by the wind, fell into the water below.

"No," Silvanus commanded as I closed my eyes against the hurt. "Look at me. *Look.*"

With excruciating reluctance, I opened them and kept my gaze on his. It helped. I stared into his eyes and knew that I was not alone. The dagger pressed deeper, and just when it felt like he meant to poke a hole clean through, he eased off, as slowly as he'd pushed down. But even with the gradual absence of pressure, the wound continued to bleed, and there was no time to clean and wrap it before Silvanus flipped the dagger and held out the hilt to me.

"My turn," he said. "Quickly."

I didn't chance a glance at the river, but I could hear that something was happening: a gurgle, a swirl, the water swelling and opening like a great wet mouth. I took the dagger from Silvanus and pushed it into his palm; it hurt me to do so, the flesh more pliant than I'd expected, like slicing an apple, and again I clamped my jaw shut—this time, though, so that I wouldn't throw up. I didn't look away once, watching as his golden brown eyes filled with tears, as his face flushed pink, then red. His blood and mine entwined, and just when the pain became unbearable, for him and me both, I let go, dropping the dagger and finally releasing the cry that had been blistering in my throat. Silvanus grabbed my hand and held it, open wound to open wound, and I choked on another cry as the sting of the cut shot up my arm to my elbow.

A shout filled the clearing, terrible and endlessly deep. For a second I thought it had somehow come from *me*—not from my throat, necessarily, but from inside my head. Like telepathy.

It wasn't me, though. It was a monster, hurtling toward us through the trees.

Silvanus pushed me behind him, drawing his sword. Not with the bloodied hand, but with the other one. The sword made a sound like a hiss as it left the scabbard, an iron warning. The sound a stout heart might make if it could do anything other than beat. A sound that said, *Have at me! I am not afraid.*

I stepped around Silvanus, brandishing my rib. The monster roared again, its heavy footsteps shaking the ground and the leaves; it was on the opposite side of the river but approaching us quickly, a devilish silhouette tearing through the shadows.

"The Hunting Beast," Silvanus breathed, as he held his sword toward the sky, the moonlight casting a prophetic glint on its sharpened tip. His cloak fluttered behind him; he dug his heels into the dirt. "Go, Gemma Belle—find your mother! I shall slaughter this monster once and for all. And with this act, what once was a lie shall become truth, and through this I will be redeemed."

"No," I said, tugging his arm. My heart was a ringing alarm. "I'm not going down there alone."

"You must." The Hunting Beast was closer now, only thirty, twenty feet beyond the river. "It is your destiny, as this is mine!"

At the precise moment Silvanus said *mine,* the Hunting Beast bounded into full view. It crouched, preparing to spring over the water, and I had just one split second to look at him and determine—just as I'd suspected at the fairy revel before Silvanus talked me out of the idea—that this wasn't the Hunting Beast at all.

It was the monster named Ash.

True it was dark, and true that I'd only seen him once before, but I had not forgotten him, not any little detail: the spindly limbs, the hoofed feet like a faun's; the broad shoulders, thin through the waist, the double bend in the legs. Tangle of antlers, lightning white; the green eyes that were soft, that were human, that were . . . kind of like mine. Not the color—my eyes were brown—but the shape of them. Or the intensity, the *luminousness.* Something about them was like looking in a mirror. We locked gazes, the monster and me, and I saw something there I didn't expect to see: *pain*—and fear. I watched as he leapt across the river; he soared over our heads and landed just behind us, trapping us between him and the water.

"She's coming," said the monster named Ash, his voice ragged and low, chest heaving from the sprint. There was a gash across his belly, not fresh and bleeding but brown and crusty. *I cut the Beast, right across the gut.* Yet more confirmation that it *had* been Ash that Silvanus fought! "Gemma, the Slit Witch is coming."

What a relief: Ash hadn't come to eat us—only to warn us (because, as I still firmly believed, he was *not* the real Hunting Beast, despite what Silvanus thought). The Slit Witch was coming, and what would she do to him for helping us? What had he already endured? And how much time did we have left before the curse took effect? Days? Hours? *Minutes?* I felt sad for him, and sad for Mama, and sad for myself. This wasn't the way it was supposed to end.

Another voice broke through my thoughts.

"Hunting Beast, we meet again."

Beside me, Silvanus twirled his sword, adjusting his grip, and the monster growled—a natural enough response when faced with a weapon meant to kill. Below us, the surface of the river had formed a whirlpool, red with our blood, the hollow center of it descending into dark and unknown depths. The Slit Witch was coming. We had to go *now*.

"Don't hurt him!" I shouted, imploring both Silvanus *and* Ash, but neither of them acknowledged my plea. A bright flash of foresight gripped me, a premonition so vivid that I knew it would come true if I did not act soon: Ash, lying prone at the river's edge, a sword skewered straight through his heart; and Silvanus, collapsed on his side with a gash so deep across his throat that the bone glowed white in the starlight. Each the destruction of the other, empty death and dull vengeance—not glorious but piteous and pointless. *Do something, Gemma! Now!*

"I'm sorry, Sil," I said, and then, already leaning most of my weight over the riverbank, I grabbed his arm—*hard*—and jumped.

Well, more like *tumbled*—a clumsy descent, arms and legs flailing before we hit the surface, leaving the monster named Ash behind. And just before the water folded around me like fingers lacing, the last thing I heard was laughter.

Laughter? Yes. High and shrill, a laugh like a crow screaming at the moon, like a wolf choking on a bone. It scraped over me, familiar and wrong, and I shivered, thinking how close to falling into the Slit Witch's grasp I'd come.

* * *

BLOOD IN MY mouth. My own blood, watered down and sharpened with salt. Why didn't I keep my mouth shut? My lips parted to breathe or to scream or to—I don't know what. At least I kept my eyes closed. The water wasn't cold but it wasn't warm either, a great tepid nothingness, and even when my limbs went numb, the edges of myself becoming a blur, I still felt the rib in my hands, a true anchor. I squeezed and squeezed as we sank and sank, as the water pressed against my chest until I thought I would drown. But just when I was on the precipice of death—I like that word, *precipice,* the rise and fall and rise of it—a hand wrapped around my ankle and tugged me down to the deep.

PART THREE

20

Virginia

I SIT ON THE STOOL IN FRONT OF THE MIRROR, MY BACK very straight and my shoulders square, and I brush and brush and brush my hair.

Night blooms at the window; wisps of clouds and cool air. It's summer, I think, or nearly summer, or just past summer—at least, no part of winter touches me. How long have I been here? I have a heartbeat—of course I do—but it's soft, a whisper, when I want it to scream. The brush is sterling silver, cold in my hand, the bristles yellowy, thick, old. My arm aches, my palm cramps, but still I brush my hair smooth, even as my mind wanders, as I slip in and out of dreams. The sound of the brush along my scalp and dragging through the strands is like *shhh, shhh, shhh.*

Hush.

I watch the mirror like a television, and it's as though I'm having a dream within a dream. In it I walk backward into the woods. The first step is silent, and it is the hardest step of the journey—*to begin*—but only until the second: *to keep going.* My feet are clad in the thinnest of slippers, and I take nothing with me into the dark temple of the trees but the slip of a nightgown I wear as I have every night for years, my hair in a long black braid down my spine. Beneath me a twig snaps, as easily as a bone, and above me the sky is tinted glass, the stars trapped under a bell jar like the ancient curiosities they are. I want to be a star; I want to be the wind. Even a girl again. I'm thirty-five, my girlishness gone but not forgotten.

Hush.

I walk backward into the woods with a slight swell in my belly where a secret made flesh is growing steadily in the dark of me. Only nineteen years old, and I have become a home to someone I don't yet know, and though she is still months away from emerging, I'm not sure I'll ever be ready to live alone inside my body again. *Don't leave me, little one. Stay here where it is safe.* She is safe—*for now*—and I am as well, as long as I keep going.

Where am I even going?

Hush.

I walk backward through the woods, and my belly grows, just a little bit. It pokes at the loose fabric of my nightgown, visible now, and undeniable. All around me the trees are still and silvered in moonlight—almost, they glow. The air here is warm, but barely—only the suggestion of summer, a blank between seasons. A rabbit watches me from the shadows of the foliage, eyes the color of honey, golden warm and sticky. I have two heartbeats now, mirrors of each other. One is grown and the other growing, splinters of dreams wedged in each. One in shadow, and the other in light.

Hush.

I walk backward through the woods, and my feet swell, my ankles become bloated and sore, and an ache spreads through my lower back. The first hint that, though this process is natural, it may not be pleasant. My footsteps slow, but I'm not tired. The trees open around me and soon I come upon a little glade. There's a house in the glade, a stone cottage with a braid of smoke curling from the chimney, a soft light radiating from beyond a half-closed curtain. The light calls to me just as surely as if it has spoken my own name, and I hesitate, slowing not to a stop but to a hover, my heart crashing in my chest like a bird against glass. The cottage seems familiar, though I'm certain I've never seen it. Yet the pattern of the shadows of the trees beckons me as if I've traced them before in my dreams. A dream, yes. It is like a dream, but I know this is not one. It's more like a story that hasn't been told. A story that sits on the tip of my tongue.

Hush.

I walk forward through the glade; I step off the path. A mistake that may cost me, but a mistake I must make. I walk right up to the window with its golden glow, the bump in my middle feeling heavy in a way that it hadn't before. The glass is clean and clear, and through the curtains I see them, two strangers, one of whom has my name. She lies on the couch with her head in a man's lap, her belly as distended as mine. He is thin but broad through the shoulders, with messy black hair and strong hands, and his gaze is downcast so that I can't see his eyes (*I wish I could see his eyes*). He smiles as he strokes her hair away from her face, as she tilts her chin toward him and says: *What do you think our baby will be like?*

Her voice is my voice, low and a little timid. She has stolen it from me. I cling to the windowsill, and when I try to cry out, to tell her to be quiet, nothing comes from my throat but a pathetic puff of air.

Charming like her father, comes the reply, a smile lighting his lips like dawn on the horizon. *Intelligent like her mother.* He lifts her hand to his mouth and kisses her palm. My own palm begins to burn, the skin blistering, and I back away from the window, one step and then another. *And very, very loved.*

I heave into a bush nearby. The color of what comes out of me isn't quite right: green and blue and violet, as thick as paste.

My body curves around the little creature growing inside me as I am so violently sick I fear I'll break apart bone by bone. So sick I'm convinced there will never be an end to it, but the end comes eventually, as the end always does. There is only so much grief a body can hold. I wipe my lips with the back of my hand, and then, my throat seared, I walk backward away from the cottage, from the memory I will never make.

Hush.

I walk backward through the woods, and I cut my heel on a sharp twig. It hurts and I wince, biting my lip; it throbs as I leave a trail of blood in my wake. A fox creeps from between the trees, bows his neck to lap at my unwilling offering, his glowing eyes never leaving mine as the tongue darts in and out of his blood-darkening mouth. He follows me for a while, licking at every little pool, and I grow hungry just watching him. A deep ache for the loveliest, most impossible things. I crave wind and sky, clouds and stars. I crave whole rivers of water, and the rocks at the bottom, and the fish, gutted and fried. I crave ice and fire, daylight and midnight, whole centuries, history, the Renaissance crunching between my teeth. Every song ever sung, every book ever written; every painting, every carving, every old thing that has been passed through human hearts and human hands. I grew up surrounded by old things—clocks to mark the hour, dolls to fill the arms of a child, mirrors to show what cannot be spoken—and I am surrounded still. The trees and the dirt beneath me are old things too, the oldest of all. The fox, satiated, soon slips back into the shadows, and I envy him. I will never be full.

Hush.

Faster now. My mother told me never to go into the woods and the wild, to turn my face away from the chill and the shadows, but I defied her and now I can never leave, not really. I defied her and met my monster, all on the very same day. Did I meet my monster *because* I defied her, or do monsters have a way of finding us anyway? I walk backward without rest—I don't need it, not here and not now—and my belly swells so that I can't see my own feet without bending forward, without actively seeking them out. My throat closes with the first flush of panic, of dread: The bigger I get, the closer I come to the end. *Please, I'm not ready!* I cry into the sky and the wind, but there's no one to hear me. Only a few tiny birds in the branches, and what do they care? On dark, silent wings they take to the air, moonlight caught in their feathers, eyes like black pearls. I envy them too, for their weightlessness. It is difficult, in my current form, to imagine rising even a foot from the ground.

Hush.

I don't recognize the shape of myself anymore. Surely, my belly's not meant to be this large. But still it grows, and still it grows, and each step costs me, exhausts me, and for the first time I feel afraid, truly afraid. Who am I, *what* am I, that my body can do this—(*oh, my God, I can't do this*)—that my muscles can stretch, that my skin can expand, that I can open wide enough to expel a whole tiny human? I think something is wrong. I've seen pregnant people before and they didn't look like this. *Did they?* In the abstract I'd known that this would happen, but it was easier in the beginning when I was smaller, lighter, more like myself. When I look down now all I see is an enormous bulge, no longer quite cute but strange and taut and so perfectly round. I lift the straining fabric of my nightgown, and I can see little limbs moving beneath the flesh, rippling. Alien. The baby kicks, once, and the strength of it surprises me; it feels almost . . . angry.

I'm sorry, I say, or try to say—it's hard to speak with all this old blood in my mouth, cotton of dreams to stanch the flow—but I don't know what I'm sorry for. I haven't done anything wrong. Not yet. I wrap my arms around my middle as if to comfort her, my daughter, but I don't know if she feels it, if she knows me. I didn't choose this—I'd chosen Ash, and though I'd known in some distant part of me that this baby was always a possibility, I'd never imagined it would happen to us. To me. Why should I? I'm only nineteen, and in love for the very first time.

Hush.

A boy at the edge of the woods. No, not a boy—a monster. No, not a monster—a *creature*. You can't love a monster, can you?

Hush.

The dark of the woods closes around me. I trip on a rock and fall backward, landing so hard that pain lances through my tail-bone, up my spine, and the pain doesn't stop. It seizes my belly, the little creature rolling within me. The tiny limbs press, push against me, and they don't look like arms and legs anymore, not like hands. No, more like the curve of a horn, the hook of a claw, a hoof instead of a foot. *Ash, oh, Ash—what is it that we've made?*

Hush.

Oh, God—it *hurts*. The mirror goes blank and the stool rocks beneath me. I bring a hand to my belly, to the pain, but it's mostly flat there now, only a layer of fat to protect my organs. Still I feel it: the loss of her, the hollowing out. Where is she now, where is she? Inside me she was safe, as safe as I could make her; in the wild she has no protection, no weapons but wishes and dreams. Flimsy things. *I did not even tell her what a monster is! Only that it would eat her, only not to stray in its path.* The brush catches on a tangle of hair, pulling my focus away from the pain in my belly to the pain in my head. It's an old story, isn't it? The sins of the mother, repeated, because the daughter tricks herself into believing that she can save her own daughter from the ache of regret. *Don't look behind that door. I did, and it cost me. If you do, it will cost you too.* And the daughter looks anyway, because she has to know. When you are young, there's not a price high enough you won't be willing to pay. *Invincibility.* Decay, seemingly, is a long way off, and consequences don't have meaning yet. But they will.

They will.

Hush.

21

Gemma

DOWN BECAME UP. LIKE WITH THE FAIRY FOUNTAIN that led to the garden where my grandmother was imprisoned—imprisoned!—I wasn't sure how or when the world tilted and tilted again. There was water in my mouth, and I tried to spit it out, but more water came rushing in. It left a lingering taste of salt, of iron and rust. Of blood, my blood, still swirling around me. At last I broke the surface of the water, and took a deep, spluttering, greedy breath.

"My name is Gemma Ashley Cassata. Also Gemma Belle," I said into the darkness of—well, wherever I was. A cavern? It was so dark that I couldn't see much beyond wavering impressions of rock and roots hanging from above. My voice echoed like the fading instrumentals at the end of a song. "I'm looking for my mother, Virginia Cassata."

The well—or pool, or lake, I couldn't be sure how big it was, only that the water was at a standstill, not rushing like the river had been—was deep, at least deeper than I was tall, and I had to keep kicking my feet to stay afloat. I repeated my mantra twice more, stating my name and my purpose in coming to the Woods Below, precisely as Clarice had instructed.

You must make it clear who you are and why you're there, Cla-

rice had said, *else you will lose yourself, as I suspect your mother did. It's not her fault; she was unprepared.*

I tightened my grip around the rib still in my hand and I swam, uncertain of where I was going but knowing that I couldn't stay in the water much longer without drowning—for real this time, my limbs growing heavy and tired. As my vision adjusted to the darkness, I spotted two rows of tiny twinkly lights bobbing just above the surface of the water. No, not lights—*eyes*. The eyes of the Eater's unfortunate victims, the guardians of the Woods Below. They floated in place, only the upper halves of their faces visible above the water, forming an illuminated pathway toward the shore. I paddled, a stitch in my side jabbing painfully with each breath, and soon my toes touched silt, slimy with seaweed, a gradual incline. The moment I reached dry land, half-collapsing on the hard sand, the eyes blinked in tandem and the guardians sank, leaving me in near darkness again.

"Hello?" I whisper-called, shivering in my wet clothes. My legs were still too shaky to stand. "Sil, are you here?"

A muffled response, a whimper or a sniffle. So quiet and quick a sound that I couldn't be sure it had been there at all. The silence pressed in on me from all sides.

"Please, please answer me. I can't see anything."

Nothing again. Only my heart, swelling like a sprain, taking up too much space in my chest and in my ears. The old, familiar flush of heat rolled through my body, from my face to my feet, and I felt simultaneously as heavy as a stone and as intangible as a shadow. Laying my rib across my lap, I tugged my pack off my back and rummaged around inside it; my hands needed something to do. I took stock of my belongings: five granola bar wrappers, crinkling between my fingers (I hadn't wanted to litter); two desiccated apple cores; a giant empty water bottle, plastic bent out of shape; the hairbrush that was enchanted to steal one's memories—I pushed that aside quickly—and there, at the very bottom, a handful of my tears that had hardened into diamonds.

I clamped my hand around one of these strange jewels. *Eat it,* said a little voice in the back of my head that was both my voice and not mine, as if I were speaking across a dream or from the future or through a roaring fall of water. And so, trusting it—trusting *myself*—I shoved the tear onto my tongue, cracked it between my back molars—not like a diamond at all, actually, more like sugar candy—and swallowed.

How many mistakes had I made on this journey? I'd been tricked by a tree into biting my own hand, traded a rib—a *rib*! A bone that was supposed to stay safely inside of me at least until I was dead!—to an old woman in exchange for absolutely nothing, and stumbled upon a cursed fairy revel. Not to mention eating all my food and drinking all my water within the first two hours. It was mostly luck and timing that had sustained me so far—somehow I'd met possibly the *one* wolf that didn't mean to eat me—and just a dash of cleverness. So many mistakes, and I knew, before I rescued Mama and defeated the Slit Witch, I would probably make a million more.

But this—consuming a salty drop of liquid that had leaked out of my eye and mysteriously become a glittering gem before it had even hit the ground—wasn't one of them.

It filled me with light.

A not quite unpleasant tingling sensation spread outward from my middle, and with it came the light—a soft but steady brilliance shining from my skin. My hands burned the brightest, and though it wasn't enough to irradiate the whole of my environment, I could now see at least several feet in every direction. The water behind me, its surface gone as still as death;

the cavern's domed ceiling above me, not quite so high as I imagined it but sweeping nonetheless; and a tunnel leading away from the cavern, a tangle of thick white roots dangling down through the dirt from the Woods Above. That was where I needed to go, but first—where was my fairy prince?

"Sil? Are you here?"

My heart had not stopped pounding, even as the flush of panic had faded, leaving me wobbly and brittle. I snatched up my rib and stood, and turned in a slow circle, letting my light brighten the area around me. I walked away from the water, scanning the wide shoreline, and called out to him again. "Sil . . . ?"

"No, no, no." A low moaning came from somewhere nearby, like the whimper from before but louder and more full of despair. I followed the sound and found him just to the side of the mouth of the tunnel, hunched on the ground with his knees pulled to his chest and his head in his hands, his eyes squeezed shut. *"Nooo . . ."*

"Sil?" I whispered as I dropped to my knees beside him, but he didn't acknowledge me in any way. "Sil, did you state your name and purpose? Did you do it, Sil? Remember what Clarice said, that if we failed to do so we might lose ourselves. Do you remember, Sil? Sil? *Silvanus?*"

Ever so slowly, I reached out and touched his shoulder. He jerked wildly, and for a moment I was terrified I'd electrocuted him with my light. But then he leapt to his feet, towering over me. I scrambled to stand, holding my rib with both hands, his hot, heavy breath blasting over me in waves. His eyes were red—not the whites, like he'd been crying, but the irises, bloody rings around the pupils.

"You," he growled, drawing out the *u* so that it stretched long and accusatory between us. I flinched, stepping back. "I almost

had him, but *you*—you stopped me. Why did you stop me? *You shouldn't have stopped me!*"

"That wasn't the Hunting Beast!" I said, watching in horror as his hand went to the hilt of his sword. "Silvanus, listen to me! You would have killed each other. And that wasn't the Hunting Beast anyway! It was my—"

Father.

The trueness, the *rightness* of this, shocked me like icy water. Hadn't I once suspected that Mama was hiding something in the woods from me?

A mean thought flashed in my head, there and gone just as quickly again: *Why should I even rescue Mama? She didn't tell me anything!*

"Better to die than to live with the shame." Silvanus unsheathed his sword, the steel scrape of it ringing around the cavern. I backed away until I came to the edge of the water.

But Silvanus won't hurt you, I thought frantically. *Silvanus loves you, he—*

He raised his sword and charged at me.

I didn't have time to think, only to react. He crossed the space between us in three seconds flat, almost flying, toes just skimming the ground, and I did the only thing I could: I raised my rib to block the attack.

It held. The rib actually *held.* Was it a miracle, or was it magic? Maybe it was both. I'd expected it to snap easily beneath his strength and the pressure of the blow, but it didn't even fracture. Sword met bone with a clang like blade against blade, loud and metallic, and I pushed back, my arms trembling from the effort. Silvanus stared at me through our crossed weapons— well, his was a weapon, mine more like a shield—and a little of the red drained from his eyes. But then he spun away from me, positioning for another swing, and I was not at all versed in dueling. All I could do was keep blocking him.

"You. Should. Not. Have. Stopped. Me," Silvanus grunted between clashes. He struck and I parried, and soon I began to sweat from the strain. How long could I go on like this? At last he knocked the rib from my grip, rendering me defenseless. As he readied to lunge for a final time, I closed my eyes and reached for the Touch. I felt a stirring in my chest, like a warm summer wind picking up.

I hoped it would be enough.

"I wish that Silvanus won't harm me!" I cried, just as he thrust his sword at my heart.

I PREPARED TO be slain. I hoped it would be painless, and I hoped it would be quick. I waited for the cold bite of metal; the bone-split and the muscle-unravel, the severance of my poor heart. I was quite fond of my heart, even if it raced when I wanted it to rest and whispered when I wanted it to scream. It was a good heart, a true heart, and in that moment between life and death I mourned myself: the loss of my dreams, the end of my whims and wildest fancies. I even mourned for my panic, my anxiety, my fear—I wouldn't miss any of that, naturally, but it was still a part of me. Once upon a time I had thought of panic as a monster that could be killed, then a monster that could be lived with. But really it was a *human* experience, and there was no reason to think that even if I panicked, even if I was afraid and didn't know what I was afraid *of,* I wouldn't also be absolutely okay. Panic is temporary; it ebbs and it flows. But *I* am forever, my heart steady through it all. Even after I die, I think, my heart will continue to beat in my soul.

I waited, tense through every nerve, but the fatal blow didn't come.

I was still hit—I couldn't prevent that entirely—but instead of a hilt in Silvanus's hand, he held a flower by the stem. A daisy, my favorite. Its open face smacked my chest and crumpled a bit, but aside from a few bent white petals the flower was fine.

And so was I.

For a moment we stood frozen, Silvanus in the act of stabbing, the daisy smashed against my heart—my *heart*! Still beating!—and then . . .

I laughed—a high, hysterical sound of relief, of triumph, of magic zapping through me. It echoed around the cavern like a thousand birds taking flight. Silvanus's fingers went limp and he dropped his arm as I plucked the flower that was once a sword from him and tucked it behind my ear. I took his face in both of my hands and tilted his head down so that he had no choice but to look at me.

"Who are you?" I commanded, watching as the red drained from his eyes, leaving them the familiar warm gold of a raw honeycomb. "Who. Are. You?"

"S-Silvanus," he gasped. His skin was icy cold beneath my palms, and so pale he was almost gray. "Prince of the Forest Fey. Heir apparent to the Throne of Thorn and Holly."

"*Again.*"

"I am Silvanus, prince of the Forest Fey." His voice was getting stronger. But I wanted to be certain.

"*Again.* Who are you?"

"I am Silvanus! Prince of the Forest Fey!"

"And why are you here?"

"To—to help my dear Gemma Belle find her mother." He blinked, breathing hard. "To find some way of releasing my mothers from the wretched woe I brought upon them."

"Good," I said and kissed him, lightly, on the mouth. He exhaled and wrapped his arms around me, holding me tightly as if he intended never to let go. I leaned into him, and only now began to tremble all over, thinking how very narrowly I had avoided certain death.

"Forgive me, forgive me," Silvanus said. "I lost myself. I was . . . gone."

"Luckily you had me to bring you back." Gently, I pried myself from his embrace and rummaged through my pack until I'd closed my fist around one of my remaining magic teardrops; I only had six of them left. "Here, swallow this," I said, and when he'd done as he was told, the light that had filled me filling him as well, I scoured the cavern floor until I found my rib. It was perfectly intact, not even a scratch, and I began to consider the possibility that bargaining with the tree-woman hadn't been a mistake, after all. I snatched it up and smiled my wolf-smile over my shoulder at the glimmering fairy prince.

"No more delays," I said, and started toward the tunnel, the roots of the trees forming a dense, tangled wilderness, a snarl of darkness and secrets. "I'm coming, Mama. I'm coming."

22

Virginia

THE WINDOW BEHIND ME IS OPEN; I CAN SEE IT IN the mirror. The sky is pink and I think I could sleep, if only I weren't so tired. My arm aches, my hand cramps, my wrist is locked and sore. How long have I been brushing my hair?

The house creaks and settles around me while I sit on my stool, alone. Oh, but where has my mother gone? It's been ages since I've seen her, or since I've seen anyone. A pain in my chest throbs each time I try to remember, so I let myself forget and breathe much easier for it. See? Forgetting is easy. A little brown bird lands on the windowsill and trills a song I'm not really in the mood for, but I grit my jaw and listen politely until it wings away. I wish I could do that—*fly*. I don't even fly in my dreams anymore, and I used to all the time.

Hush.

Hours pass—I *think*—and the sky is still pink, and all the clocks downstairs begin chiming at once, slightly out of sync. I count thirteen chimes, each higher pitched than the last, until it is less like chiming and more like shrieking. Finally they all fall silent, but the silence is worse. It's worse because it has teeth, and the mouth full of teeth speaks without ever making a sound. It says: *If you fail to find the mirror to show one's true reflection, then—then—then he will turn into a beast in truth and eat the heart right out of your chest.* Yes, remember? A *curse,* a curse upon my head! The beast will be here soon, and when he arrives, all slobbering and starving, he'll go straight for my heart; he'll tear it from me with no more care than plucking an apple from a tree. I must finish brushing my hair by then.

But how will I know when I'm finished?

Hush.

There's a creature at the edge of the woods. I've waited three months to see him again, anxiously tearing myself to pieces just to have something to do with my hands while I wonder where he's been. He growls at me as I run toward him, so I stop—it's so hard to make myself stop—and wait for him to come to me. He does, slowly, and I want so badly to touch him, but I force my arms to stay at my sides, my nightgown sticking to the backs of my thighs. His pupils quiver rapidly as he stares at my face; as he drinks me in, his eyes rove downward, over my mouth and my chin to my neck, to my chest, and finally to the swell of my belly, where his gaze comes to rest. He lifts his hand—his knuckles knotted, bent in a way that appears painful—carefully toward the bump, with a look of fascinated concentration as he tilts his head. Just before his fingers make contact he stops, his hand hovering in the air.

I say his name quietly—in the dream, memory, whatever this is, I still remember it—and his eyes snap to mine. I nod, managing a small smile. *It's okay. Go on.*

His fingers begin to tremble, but instead of touching me he backs away, shaking his head. He looks at his hand as if he doesn't recognize it, the claws and bulging veins. A whimper escapes him, so full of anguish, and then he scuttles back toward the trees. I chase after him, a sob in my chest, stumbling in the boots I hadn't bothered to lace. He is too fast; I can't reach him.

Hush.

The hairbrush feels hollow in my hand. Why am I doing this? The sky is pink, verging on red. *I'm not safe here,* I think, and at the same time the thought appears, a knock comes from somewhere downstairs. My heart tries to take flight like that bird on the windowsill, but there's just nowhere for it to go. I set the brush down and turn slowly, careful not to make a sound.

Shhhh. Someone is in the house.

IT TAKES TIME, and several more meetings as my belly continues to grow, but soon the creature knows me, remembers me. Sometimes, he even holds me close. He's strong in the way a tree is strong, able to withstand any storm, and I promise him again and again that I will find the mirror to break the spell. *I will, I will.* I don't know if he believes me, though.

I don't want her to know me like this, he says, placing one hand tentatively in the precise spot where I feel a tiny kick. *I don't want her to know any of this.*

He means the woods, and everything in it.

How can I possibly keep her from it? I too mean the woods, and everything in it. My mother told me to stay away, and despite the fear she'd instilled in me, in the end I didn't. Why should I expect any different of my daughter?

He looks at me, and it is like being seen by the sun. *Do what you must.*

Hush.

I creep from my room, scalp tingling now that the brushing is done, and wait in the doorway, listening. Voices—or one voice and its echo—come from among—no, *beyond*—the antiques. Someone is banging at the front door. Curses and muttering, heavy footsteps and heavier breathing. I tiptoe into the shadows, down the hallway and out of sight of the stairs. I know this place better than anyone. No one will find me if I don't want to be found.

Shhhh.

At last, the monster has come for my heart.

23

Gemma

MY HORNS WERE GROWING. BEFORE, THEY'D BEEN only as tall as the length of my thumb, but now they were at least as long as my hand. And the tips had begun to taper, as if they meant to sharpen to a point. I no longer noticed the growing pain; it had become dull enough to ignore. Who knew that total transformation would feel so ordinary? Like digestion, or little cuts healing, it was a thing I knew was happening but that I didn't have to think about actively. My veins were still rich green under the skin, and the leaves in my hair dangled down to my chin. If I stood before a mirror now, would I even recognize myself?

"By the Hidden Moon, does this tunnel go on forever?" Silvanus swore. He went a little ahead of me, using a small dagger he kept in his boot to hack at the branching radicles in our path. Though it would have been easier to clear the way with his sword, I thought it prudent to hold on to his weapon-turned-flower a little longer, at least until we found Mama. It wasn't that I didn't trust him; I just didn't trust the Woods Below. Didn't trust us—*either* one of us—not to lose ourselves. "We've been walking for ages and found nothing but more roots, more dirt, more darkness. Ah!"

"It's only been about fifteen minutes," I said, though of course I couldn't be sure because I didn't wear a watch. It was merely a guess, but I thought it was a good one. We'd each had to swallow another of my enchanted tears to reinvigorate the light within us when it began to dim, but even still we hadn't been there long at all. Not long at all, although . . . I reached up, touched the horns on my head. Had they grown again? "We just have to keep going. If we stop, we'll—"

Suddenly we came upon a thick drape of ivy and vines. Silvanus pushed it aside, revealing a solid dirt wall.

A dead end.

"Well," he said with a sigh, sounding almost relieved. He knocked on the wall, and the sound bounced back at us like a reprimand. *None shall pass.* "Nothing to do but turn around and leave the way we came. Shall we?"

I glared at the wall, and then turned my glare on him.

"No," I said, and it echoed like thunder around us.

"No? Gemma Belle, there is nowhere else to go."

"We're not going back," I said, pushing past him and placing my hand on the wall. I felt a tiny, rhythmic tremor, almost like a pulse. "This is merely a test."

Silvanus groaned, rubbing a hand over his face, and I remembered a story Mother once told me about a half-man, half-bull beast that lived in an endless labyrinth. Every year, seven youths from the town were selected as martyrs to satiate the bull-man's hunger so that he would not break loose and consume the entire population. *Sometimes it is necessary to sacrifice a few to protect the whole,* she'd explained. *Not everyone can be saved.*

What about the bull-man? Why didn't they just kill him? I'd asked, even though I didn't like to think that anyone should be killed, even monsters. (Even Mothers, though sometimes it was a *necessary sacrifice;* she'd told me so herself.)

Oh, I'm sure someone did, eventually, she'd said with a shrug. *There are always heroes waiting in the shadows for something heroic to do.*

My shoulders had slumped.

How sad, I'd said, *to be a monster in a world with a hero lurking in every shadow.*

Mother laughed, and it was so like Mama's laugh—light on water, splash and sparkle—that I flinched from her, and went rigid as she pressed a quick kiss on my forehead. She looked just like Mama, and talked like her too, and there were times I'd wondered if she believed she really *was* Mama, if she liked being Virginia Cassata so much better than being a smoke-demon bound to the Slit Watch that she had made the choice to forget that she was ever anyone else. But I must not forget that she was anything other than what she was.

Quite right, she'd said. *Heroes are a plague.*

I'd flushed at her praise, realizing too late that I'd gotten it all wrong. Heroes were to be *revered;* only a monster would scorn a hero. Mother was a monster. I was not.

But now I looked at Silvanus, the fairy prince of the forest with his stupid little dagger and the disdainful frown on his too beautiful face, and I'll admit I felt rather angry. *Irate,* in fact. It was like wind trapped beneath my skin, blowing down branches and power lines, a steady stream of electric shocks to my heart. Only an hour ago, Silvanus had desired to slay my *father* without bothering to ask himself first if someone deserved to be slain merely because they *looked* like a monster. I looked like a monster now, or half a monster at least. Would he try to murder me at some point as well?

But wait—he *had* tried to kill me, and would have succeeded if I had not called upon the Touch. Certainly he had been out of his mind at the time, but did that truly exonerate him? *Maybe.* But that didn't mean I had to forgive him.

"You're bored, aren't you?" I kept my tone measured, even as the anger crackled below the surface. I'd never shouted at anyone before, not even at Mother when she dug her fingernails into my shoulder as she steered me away from the woods every time I'd tried to enter. "You're bored because there's no one around for you to stab with your sword. You think killing makes you a hero, but really it makes you a killer, nothing more. You think you'll be satisfied once you've slayed the Hunting Beast, but you'll only start looking for someone else to slay, and someone else after that, on and on forever because killing is empty and it will never be enough."

For a moment Silvanus simply stared at me, and I thought maybe he'd apologize. But instead he inhaled loudly as he squared his shoulders, every inch a haughty prince.

"Monsters aren't people," he said, his knuckles white around the hilt of his dagger. "They don't deserve to live."

I lost it then. I couldn't hold back any longer.

"Then go—kill all the monsters!" My voice reverberated in the narrow space so that it sounded as if a hundred Gemmas were shouting. I plucked the flower from my ear and threw it at his chest. He caught it out of the air. "Perhaps one of them will kill *you*."

I didn't mean that. I didn't want Silvanus to be killed—of *course* I didn't. But I wanted to land a blow, and I did. His eyes widened and he stumbled backward. He recovered quickly, though, gazing down at me with a shrug.

"You surprise me, Gemma Belle," he said coolly, and slid the dagger back into his boot. He held the daisy as if it were once more a sword. "I had thought us on the same side."

"Yeah," I said, breathing so hard it felt as if my remaining ribs might snap apart. "Me too."

Without another word, the fairy prince turned and left me alone.

* * *

NO, NOT ALONE.

Mama.

She was just on the other side of the wall. I could feel her presence like heat.

"All right, Gemma girl," I said to myself as soon as Silvanus's receding footsteps had faded away. "You have dealt with far worse obstacles than this. Think of a way through that wall. Not around, not over—*through*."

My legs were tired, so I sat in front of the wall covered in ivy and vines, my rib in my lap. It was a puzzle before me, and as I thought about it I found that I quite enjoyed the challenge of it. A wall? A wall the Woods Below had put in my path to test the strength of my will? That was easy. Almost too easy—but then, didn't I deserve a break after the trials and travails the Woods Above had put me through? Silvanus had taken one look at this wall and given up. He didn't want to battle a wall; he wanted to fight a monster. His heart wasn't in it, but mine was, and the answer came to me as if written on a neon sign flickering in front of me.

There is no wall.

I stood and did a few stretches; flexed my feet and rolled my neck. I really was very tired and sore. Then, with the confidence of a famous magician performing her favorite trick, I squared my shoulders and walked right through the wall that was not there.

It wasn't magic, only illusion. When I'd believed the wall to exist, then it did; but when I stopped believing, it ceased to be. The wall wasn't there and so I walked through it—*easy*—and came out the other side, smiling triumphantly. *Ta-da!* I'd executed the trick to perfection, but there was no audience to gasp and applaud. That was a good thing, though; I didn't feel so victorious half a second later when I realized where I was.

Home.

I was *home*—except, not quite.

It was a fun-house version of the shop, the grandfather clocks twice as tall as they'd normally be, and also twice as skinny. Cedar chests so wide I couldn't see around them, the knobs on the drawers as round as those on a door. Dolls so big they'd become life-size. Lampshades like umbrellas, ceramic cookware large enough for me to step inside and roast myself over a witch-tended fire. Giant, floating flakes of dust— ubiquitous dust!—clouds of it swirling overhead.

And through the windows the light was wrong, slanted and bloody. I took one step forward into the menace and gloom. The floorboards made no sound, so I took another, and another, and stopped.

"*Mama?*" I whispered, because I really didn't want to go any farther. I could barely breathe and the dolls . . . the dolls were watching me. "Mama . . . I know you're here."

No answer but the wind, pushing against the walls of the house. (No, not the house; I was still in the Woods Below, and this was another illusion. I must remember that. *Remember, Gemma.*) A skitter, a patter, a footstep—*Someone is coming down the stairs.* I waited another moment, my heart turning circles, but there was no further indication that I was anything other than alone.

No, I'm not alone. Mama is here.

All right, Gemma Belle. Time to be brave. Real-brave, not pretend-brave, which I was beginning to suspect was actually the same thing.

With my rib clutched to my chest, I walked through the rows of antiques, feeling as if I had stumbled into someone else's dream. Creeping through those odd slants of light, navigating through chess pieces as high as my knee, vintage poster-size postcards with illustrations of faraway places I'd never been and likely would never be. Up ahead I spotted a streak of movement between the slats of a Japanese screen, and I broke into a run, careless now of the noise, my shoes slapping the floor *clickety-clack*.

"Mama!" I cried softly, rounding the screen only to find nothing. "Mama, where—?"

Another flutter—a lock of hair or a sleeve—just beyond the next bend, around a massive armoire with a dent in its doors. I hurried, but again there was no one. My scalp began to prickle, and I felt as if I had a thousand eyes on me, a thousand enemies that I couldn't see.

"Mama, why are you hiding from me?"

"Monster," came a hissed reply, and it was Mama's voice, but distorted. As if we were deep underwater. *"The monster has come for my heart."*

I froze.

"Monster?" I said, transfixed by an image unbidden of a long-clawed hand reaching for the back of my neck. "There's a monster here?"

I did not know what a monster was. Or what made a monster different from a hero if both wanted to kill the other. Perhaps it had to do with *intention*? But the results were the same—death, destruction. I did not want to die and I did not want to kill, so I did the only thing I could think of to do: run and hide.

Mama, please help me. I tiptoe-ran as fast as I could, careful not to bump into anything as I zigzagged through the antiques toward the Glass Room. But the shop had been stretched into a dizzying labyrinth, and even after a full minute of running I had not reached my destination. Great thumping steps fell behind me, but I couldn't tell if they were real or imaginary. Tooth-flash, jaw-snap, skin peeling from bone. *We'll hide from the monster together, and then figure out what to do.*

At last I came to the Glass Room, and the doors were closed but not locked. I slipped inside but gasped when I saw the wreckage: glass like an abandoned mosaic on the floor, splinters and shards, every mirror destroyed. A terrible mess, made all the more awful for the strange wounded light from outside refracting off the pieces and turning the walls red.

The Glass Room suffered from the same distortion as the rest of the shop. The mirrors—what was left of them—stretched from floor to ceiling, and the smallest of the shattered slivers was at least as long as my forearm. The room was still round, but there was an inner wall that curved in both directions. I followed it, and soon realized I was on the outermost ring of a tightening coil. Shoes crunching over broken glass, I kept going, round and round, the passage gradually narrowing, and wondered what I would find at the center. Mama?

Or the monster?

Around one last bend and there it was: the end. End of the journey, end of the world. Only, it was not what I'd expected at all. A lone mirror was propped against the wall, long and rectangular, its glass still whole. I approached it slowly. Was this the mirror to break the spell? A simple frame, the glass perfectly clean. But other than that, the only thing remarkable about it was *me*.

I stared at my reflection—my *new* reflection—for a very long time.

"*Monster.*" A murmur behind me. Mama's face appeared in the mirror over my shoulder, but I didn't turn around. I couldn't, somehow. "Monster, we meet again."

She was right; I did look like a monster. The curving horns, the mossy veins, the hair entwined with sprigs and foliage. My lips were as pink as fresh petals, fuller than before; my teeth, when I smiled, were straighter, whiter, not quite pointy but sharp. My collarbones stood out like spindly branches, and my arms were a little longer and thinner, but strong. My knees bulged like tree knobs, but my legs too were strong. They would carry me fast and carry me far—and, in fact, they already had. I waited for the horror to set in—the gut-twist and recoil—but revulsion never came and remorse didn't either. Prince Silvanus of the Forest Fey had spoken true: I looked more like me than I ever used to.

"I am not a monster," I said, and turned to face my long-lost mama. Oh, how I had missed her! How I had missed *me* when I was with her. "I am your daughter."

"Daughter?" she echoed, and touched the place on her abdomen where I was missing a rib. She looked exactly the same as the last time I'd seen her, down to the short-sleeved dress with the tiny floral pattern. Her hair loose, as black as a charm; skin pale but rosy-cheeked, her neck thin and long. She was so young—I'd never realized before—and she reminded me of a lost little girl, as if we'd switched places in the night, and now it was I who would take care of her the way for so long she'd taken care of me. "No, my daughter is . . . is . . ."

"I am *not* a monster," I said firmly, and reached into my pack, digging for the hairbrush at the bottom. "And I *am* your daughter. Look."

I proffered the enchanted brush and Mama took it; snatched it, more like, as if I had stolen it. She ran her fingertips over the bristles, plucked loose the dark hairs—my hairs—stuck in the soft spines, and dropped the tangled clumps of it to the floor.

"A baby," she said softly. "My daughter is still a baby. Not even born yet."

And then Mama's eyes rolled sideways and she fell.

24

Virginia

I AM NOT A MONSTER. AND I AM YOUR DAUGHTER. LOOK.

The dream was dying before my eyes, the false façade of the shop peeling away, leaving only hard earth and emptiness in its place. But I didn't want to wake up, so I clenched my eyes shut. If I woke I'd remember, and if I remembered it would hurt. It would hurt everywhere, not just in my heart.

Why isn't the monster eating my heart?

"Hush," I said, aloud to myself, but that wouldn't work now. Like a magic word, it wouldn't take me away to somewhere else. I was stuck on my knees with a hairbrush—*the* hairbrush, not one born of delirium—in my hands and the monster that was not a monster but my daughter crouched beside me, looking concerned. Her wide brown eyes, her face the same shape it always had been, long through the chin but round in the cheeks. But those horns were like nothing I'd ever seen before, and the green veins slithering beneath the pale skin, ropes of strong muscle through her arms and legs. Certainly not a baby any longer.

"*Gemma.*" I reached for her, my daughter—not a monster—and touched my fingertips to her temple. Her skin was hot, as if she'd been lying in the sun for hours. "Oh, my girl, what has she done to you?"

"She?" Gemma tilted her head and scrunched her lips in confusion. Light seemed to shine not around her, but *from* her, and in the gentle illumination I saw that the house and its antiques had disappeared entirely now. In its absence, I realized I didn't know where we were. Hell, perhaps? Or somewhere worse? The walls were close and made of dirt. Above us, a mass of tangled roots. "Who?"

"The Slit Witch," I said, before I remembered that I never told her about the Slit Witch. I never told her anything. I shook my head, feeling fuzzy, the lines blurring between illusion and reality. Gemma, just born, swaddled and cradled in my arms; Gemma toddling around and touching everything in the shop. Meeting Ash—*Ash*—at the edge of the woods with yet another mirror, another disappointment. Ash carrying me to a thin dark river. *I will hide you where she cannot get to you, down in the Woods Below.* Memory after memory, as palpable as if they were happening all over again.

"Surely, you're under some kind of curse? You're halfway to looking like your—" I stopped, running tremulous fingers through my hair. *Just say it.* It was long past time she knew. "Your father."

I waited and braced myself as best I could. Would she weep? Would she yell? Would she tell me she hated me? For various reasons throughout my adolescence—and as an adult—I had felt all of these things and more toward my own mother: rage and bitterness, hurt and quiet madness, but always I'd kept it inside.

I didn't want that for Gemma, I realized. I didn't want her to feel like she had to keep herself contorted into a recognizable shape just to appease me. *Let it out,* I urged silently, searching her face for a clue of what was to come. I could handle it. I hoped.

But my girl surprised me, as she so often did.

"Oh, I know," she said, completely calm. "I just saw him. He looked different than before, though. *Angrier.*"

"Before?" I pressed my palms to my cheeks. My hands were so cold it helped me to focus. "You've seen him before?"

"Yes, the night he carried you away."

Of course Gemma had seen us that night. She was always right where she shouldn't have been. I had tried so hard to make her forget, to snatch any scrap of feeling she had toward the woods, good or bad. I hadn't wanted to be like my own mother, who steered me away from the woods by making me afraid. I'd thought I could save Gemma from fear and let her keep her childhood.

But it didn't work that way. It never has, and it never would.

"You should have told me about the monsters, Mama. About my father, and about fairies and witches and wolves. And magic. I have *magic*! And I don't really know how it works or what to do about it—only that it's changing me."

"Telling you about monsters would only have scared you. I didn't want you to be afraid." There was a knot in my throat, beating in time with my heart. "Not you."

At the time I'd believed that what I was doing was right. (Villainesses always do, don't they?) But as I said it now, I was struck by the full force of how terrible it was, how futile and how cruel. Besides taking her memories—a hideous violation—I had never let her form her own fears. I'd only clung to and passed on to her my own.

It's an old story, isn't it? Given new life each time it is told.

Gemma sucked in her cheeks. "A little fear is good, I think. Too much can make us . . ."

"Monsters," I finished very quietly.

"Yes, though the problem is not the fear itself. It's what we do with it." Gemma nodded once, firmly, to herself. "Not enough fear can make a monster too."

"I'm sorry," I said, and it wasn't enough. But was it, at least, a start?

Gemma sighed, huge and sweeping, and then she crawled into my lap as she used to do when she was small. I was both surprised and pleased to find that even though she'd grown, even though she'd *changed,* she still fit within me perfectly, a warm and snug embrace. Working around her horns, I pressed a kiss to her crown, her spine to my chest. Could she feel my heart beating? I could feel hers, a wild little bird.

"Mama, I didn't find the mirror," she said. "I don't know how to break the curse."

"That's all right, Gem." I tightened my arms around her. She smelled like the forest, moss and damp. "It's not your responsibility. You've done more than enough."

She was quiet a moment. Then, "Mama, is my father the Hunting Beast?"

I leaned to the side to look at her, to see if she was serious. She was, her eyes huge and clear and imploring. And why wouldn't she be? Wasn't he the monster I had imagined the Hunting Beast to be?

"No," I said, tucking her head beneath my chin. "He is not the Hunting Beast."

"Oh, good." She relaxed, her body slumping against mine. But a second later she went tense again. "I'm not sure there's much time left until the curse takes effect. I went into the woods a week before my fifteenth birthday, and then I lost track of the days. It's got to be close, though. Maybe even tonight."

I had figured the deadline was close from how much Gemma had grown, but to find we had only *hours* left stole my breath. Gemma twisted her neck around to look at me.

"What are we going to do?"

That was the question, wasn't it? I was her mother—wasn't I supposed to have answers? But I still didn't know where we were, and if I couldn't surmise that, then how would I know what to do next? I didn't know where Ash was and what he was doing. Or the Slit Witch, or Clarice. All I knew was that Gemma and I were together, and we were safe. For now.

"I don't know." Oh God, I was going to cry. I didn't want her to see, but I couldn't help it. Thankfully the tears came silently, and when I spoke, my voice barely shook. "Why don't you start by telling me everything that's happened to you?"

"Okay," she said, and began.

25

Gemma

I TOLD HER EVERYTHING, EVEN THE BITS ABOUT SILVA-
nus and me kissing. About Mother and the ax I'd used to kill
her, about the wolf-guardian and the tree-woman and the rib
that had saved me from certain death. About the Hunting Beast,
and the fairy prince's determination to slay him. About the
Great Ensorceller of the Hidden Moon (it turned out Mama already knew this), and her imprisonment by the Forest Fey (this
part Mama did *not* know), and how she'd told me to rescue
Mama from the Woods Below.

I told her how much I had missed her, and how sorry I was
that I didn't crack the curse. And when that was done, I picked
up the hairbrush from where it had fallen and held it up for her
to see.

I was nervous about this part—even more so than admitting
I kissed a boy and that I was technically, sort of, a murderer. I
was angry in a way I never had been before, not even when I'd
banished Silvanus from the Woods Below. It blazed up my
throat and pushed behind my eyes, so that for a moment I
thought I wouldn't be able to get the words out. *You are brave,
Gemma,* I said to myself. *Go on.*

"Mama, this brush is enchanted to steal memories." I shook
all over; I couldn't stop it. "Did you know? Did you know and

did you use it on me anyway, so that I would forget the woods?"

I didn't have to turn around to know that Mama was crying. The tremors wrenched through her whole body, shuddering around me. I felt a little sorry for her, but more sorry for myself, for all the lost memories that Silvanus's kiss had helped me recover, though I suspected that there might be more I was missing—stolen glimpses of my father, the monster at the edge of the woods.

I waited.

"I'm so sorry, Gem," she said, and I slid out of her lap so I could look at her fully. Her eyes were red, her face ghost-pale.

I tilted my head, watching her. I didn't think my heart had ever hurt so much as it did then. "Why did you do it?"

"Because the forest and everything in it is cursed. I didn't want that for you. I didn't know what else to do." She wrapped her arms around her middle. "I'm your mother, and I always will be, but you don't owe me anything, Gem. I won't ask you to forgive me."

I sat very still, even closed my eyes. Examined my depths. Did I want to forgive her? Certainly I didn't want to *not* forgive her, but that wasn't the same thing. I felt a pulse in my fingertips, on the side of my neck, but it was slightly different from my regular pulse—a metaphorical one, I guess, an electric current that would always be present even when I wasn't actively thinking about it. A new, permanent part of me—another thread in the tapestry, another wire in the machinery. Perhaps someday I'd cut it loose, but not now. Not anytime soon.

"I love you," I said, and opened my eyes. "I really do. But I'll always be a little bit mad at you."

Mama nodded, and I could see that she was trying to be brave. She was hurt, but it wasn't my job to soothe her. She'd work through it on her own; she had to.

"That's fair," she said, her voice a raspy whisper. "More than fair."

Her fingers went to the strange split that went through skin and bone, just visible over the collar of her dress. I'd never thought about it much before—it had simply always been there—but now it reminded me of something. Of *someone*.

The Slit Witch.

"What is that on your chest?" I asked. "Is that—is that because you used magic?"

"Yes." She dropped her hand. "There's always a price to pay for selfish magic. I thought it was worth it—though now I can't really remember why."

"Weren't you afraid of becoming like her?"

Mama shook her head. "I never really thought it would go on this long. I thought I'd break the spell on Ash long ago and we'd be free from all of this."

"Well, we're free from *part* of it. This is over now." I curled my hand around the hairbrush, calling the Touch within me. I squeezed, and the hairbrush cracked; I squeezed harder and it crumbled to dust, the bristles floating to the ground before those too dissolved and were gone.

"Ash's memories were in there," Mama whispered, staring at the place where the dust had been. "I suppose he'll have to find another way to remember, like you."

Ash—that was my father, the one I was named after. *Gemma Ashley*. But was I truly Gemma Ashley, or was I Gemma Belle? Was it possible to be both? Gemma Ashley Belle? And what of Mama, what of her in my name? Could I be Gemma Gigi Ashley Belle? Maybe the more people I loved, the longer my name would become.

I was okay with that.

Anyway, my hunch about Ash being my father had been correct, but I didn't blame Mama for not telling me about him sooner. He was, after all, a monster. Or rather, a man who *looked* like a monster.

My heart jolted forward as I thought about him. What was he really like beneath the talons and teeth? Was he kind? Was he funny? Did he think of me often? Did he love me? I wondered too what I should call him when I finally met him properly. Dad? Daddy? Papa? Pops?

And did he, like me, have the Touch?

I breathed deeply of the damp underground air and recognized something I hadn't before: I had always been part of the woods, the same as the trees and the rocks and the rabbits and, yes, even the Slit Witch. The woods were in me since I was born, because they were in my dad and in Mama too, and even in Clarice. Maybe Mama and Clarice didn't have the Touch, but that didn't mean they weren't part of this place as surely as the fairies or the tree-woman or the noble guardian of the forest's edge. No one could possibly live that close to the woods for so long without inhaling a tiny bit of its darkness, without letting it into your heart and your imagination. I belonged here; the woods were mine too.

"What are we going to do?" I asked her again. She was my mother; I wanted her to have answers. I wanted her to know everything and to tell me so that I would know everything too. "How will we save him without the mirror?"

Mama hung her head in her hands. "I'm beginning to think there is no mirror. That it was all just a ruse."

A *ruse,* yes—like so much of the woods, both above and below, most things here were not as they first appeared. Even monsters. Even mirrors.

"What was it the Slit Witch had said the day she took you away?" I said, thinking aloud. "Something like, 'You should have listened more closely to your daughter's stories before you made them disappear.'" It was so strange that I still remembered it, though of course at the time I had no idea what it meant. *Your daughter's stories.*

I stood, feeling jittery all over, and paced the width of the tunnel. "What stories did I tell you before you used the hairbrush on me?"

Mama flinched at the mention of the hairbrush, but she would just have to get used to that. "Often you spoke of the fairy prince. Of the places in the woods that he had shown you."

I nodded, bouncing frantically on my heels. *Come on, Gemma, use your brain!* "And it must have been a place that he had shown me earlier that day, or why else would the Slit Witch have come?"

I flipped through my memories as if paging through a book: Silvanus's hand in mine as we flew through the fairy village and then over a wall. A hill and then a clearing, where there was a still pool of water. He had peered into it and seen—himself. His reflection.

Just as if he'd looked in a mirror.

"It was a wishing well." My heart tipped as if over a precipice. I could feel my every nerve prickling. "Silvanus peered into it and we saw a great fairy revel, a triumphant celebration of his heroic deeds. He thought that the pool revealed your greatest wish. But . . . what if . . . ?"

A mirror to show one's true reflection.

Suddenly Mama lifted her chin. Her eyes were bright, and when she spoke she was as breathless as if she'd been running.

"Do you think you could find it again?" she asked, so full of tentative hope that I could give no other answer than *yes.* I didn't know where the pool was exactly, but I did have some idea—through the fairy village and over the wall. *Easy.* A place where the darkness was as sharp as thorns, steam rising off the water's surface in elegant curls. We would find it, even if I had to use every last ounce of the Touch I possessed.

In the dark and the stillness of the long, silent tunnel, Mama and I looked at each other. And then, slowly, we smiled.

26

Virginia

THE MOON WAS HIGH AND FULL AS WE EMERGED from the Woods Below. Dirty and drenched in sweat, we climbed through a root-concealed cavity in the tunnel's ceiling, the dangling vines knotted to form a sturdy ladder. The way had been narrow and tight, but at last we breached the surface and crawled through a gap at the base of a tree into the open air. A silent sob of relief shuddered through me as we knelt in a pile of crisp fallen leaves and waited for our vision to acclimate to the dim after so long underground. I had thought I'd known dark before, but now I saw that the night was bright in its own way. The night was *alive*. It breathed, and it beat, and it danced. The pulse pounded on the side of my neck, and it was the woods' pulse too, the pulse of every living thing.

I am not alone, I realized as I sat up and rubbed my eyes. *Nor have I ever been.*

"I think we're safe," Gemma said, standing and brushing the dirt off her legs. "For now, at least."

We could not exit the Woods Below the same way we had come, Gemma had explained, and memories I'd long forgotten fought their way to the surface: A lovely, painful, sharp, and bloody kiss; sinking into heavy black water and waiting to drown. A hand on my ankle pulling me down. But now the

Slit Witch was there, prowling the land surrounding the river's mouth.

"She'll catch us as soon as we leave," Gemma had said, with the confidence of one who had, against all odds, become comfortable traversing the strange and perilous woods. "We have to find a new way out—and if we can't find one, we'll forge our own."

"But how will we get Ash to the pool? If Ash is with the Slit Witch, and the Slit Witch is by the entrance?"

"Even if we use a different route, I'm sure they'll find us eventually. We just need a head start. Then we can lead them to the pool, and—and somehow get Ash there without the Slit Witch getting us first?"

She chewed her bottom lip. I wondered too how exactly this was going to work. Maybe we would simply have to wing it? I had never "winged" anything in my life, but what other choice did we have?

After a moment Gemma shook herself, and I did too. "Well," she said. "We can't do anything trapped down here. Let's go."

I trusted Gemma more than anyone, but as I followed her through the endless, sinuous tunnels, something old and familiar puffed up and prickled inside me. Wasn't I the mother here? Shouldn't I be taking the lead? I had known all along that I could not protect her from monsters forever, but surely, *surely* my shelter should have extended longer than this? She was only fifteen. A child, even if she didn't see herself that way. But I stamped down my pride and trailed my daughter as we searched for—and eventually found—a way out.

"Which way to the pool?" I said, and used a knob in the tree to help me climb to my feet. My knees were weak, my hands trembled, my heart skipped. How long before the curse took effect? How long before Ash tackled me and lowered his lips to my chest to rip me apart? How long before he clamped his teeth around my still-beating heart? There were worse ways to die, I supposed, though I couldn't really think of any at the moment. A little laugh bubbled up my throat, but I swallowed it. The woods were so quiet that every errant sound was like a beacon leading straight to our location. We had to be careful and quick.

Gemma turned in a circle and scanned the trees. Suddenly she stopped and tilted her head. "This way," she said, pointing with her rib—I still couldn't quite believe that that thing was *really* her rib—and together we moved through the woods, stepping softly.

"Mama?" Gemma whispered, and slipped her hand into mine. She had a much easier time running over the brambles, nimble and nearly silent, while I kept tripping and stubbing my toes on jutting rocks. "Let me help you," she said, and sizzling warmth spread from her palm to mine. A slightly unpleasant prickling coursed up my arm and filled my body until I was hyperaware of every nerve. Soon I knew just where to step so that I wouldn't stumble, and didn't have to think too hard about it.

"What did you do?" I said, confused but not upset.

"I used the Touch. I just wish really, really hard for things and usually they happen—though sometimes they don't. I wished for you to have speed and stealth," she added, flashing me a quick, glorious smile. "Like a beautiful deer that no hunter can touch."

"Thank you," I said, in awe of her. "I hope it's not much farther."

"Not *much* . . ." Gemma said, but I could tell it was a lie by the way her eyes slid to the side. A gentle lie for my benefit, but it pierced me all the same. Cold panic rushed through me, replacing the tingling warmth of a moment before. *We aren't going to make it.*

No, not we, I corrected, and derived some comfort from this. *Just me. I am not going to make it.*

Still, we pressed on. A quiet dash between bushes, ducking under low branches and swerving to avoid fallen logs. Sweat gathered under my arms and dripped into my eyes; my chest heaved and my throat grew dry. Every tree looked identical to me; every thorn pricked the same. I couldn't be sure we weren't running in circles, but maybe it didn't matter. Maybe this had always been an unwinnable game.

Around us, the woods began to whisper. Crickets, wind, the leaves rubbing together like hands. *Tshh, tshh, tshh.* Tiny creatures scurrying, birds pecking and hopping from tree to tree. Flies humming, bees buzzing, a concentrated symphony. It rose all around me, and I stumbled for the first time since Gemma's spell. My foot caught on a root, and I fell.

Hush now. It will all be over soon.

Gemma tugged at my arm, hauling me upright. "Come on, we're almost to the fairy village. See through the trees, that wall? From there the way is easy. I promise, Mama, we just have to—"

But whatever sentiment she was about to express was lost in a laugh like birds screaming as they're being eaten alive. *The Slit Witch.* Could she sense it, that we'd found the secret to the mirror at last? I barely had time to step in front of Gemma to shield her with my body before a figure emerged from the trees, coming straight at us. But it was not the Slit Witch, whose laughter echoed still, growing nearer as she steadily closed in.

It was Ash.

He looked exactly the same as last I'd seen him, though perhaps a bit more hunched with exhaustion. There was a half-healed cut across his belly, and his eyes were wild—sweeping back and forth, never settling—but they were still his eyes, unclouded. I started toward him, but he raised a hand, already backing away.

"The curse—our time is about to run out. I'll lead her away from you, for as long as I can," he said, and then he was gone again. I started to run after him, but Gemma placed a hand on my arm. Had that really just happened? Had he really been here?

"We're not going to make it," I said, voicing my fears aloud. "Ash will—" I stopped, choking on the words. On the *reality* of them. "Ash will—he'll turn soon, and we can't outrun her. Not with this wall in our way."

Gemma tugged on my arm.

"No," she said, and then—inexplicably—she *grinned*. "But I bet we can out-jump her."

I followed her gaze as it darted toward the not-so-distant wall. That must be the fairy village she had spoken of, and I wondered what we might find there. Safety, sanctuary? Or would it only buy us a little more time before the inevitable?

I breathed deeply and reached for Gemma's hand. It was worth a try. Besides, I didn't want her last memory of me to be colored by defeat. For her, I could be strong.

"Don't let go," she said, and then we were running, skimming, *flying,* our toes barely touching the earth, waves of heat and electric energy rolling through her and into me. Nausea swept up my throat, but I held on to Gemma and did not let go. We approached the wall at a dizzying speed, and just when I thought we were about to smash right into it, Gemma jumped, pulling me with her.

We left the ground completely, and in the air, I looked back. Just a quick glance, but it was enough to catch a glimpse of them, Ash and the Slit Witch close behind, even closer than I'd thought.

And then they were gone—or, more accurately, *we* were gone—falling back to the earth on the other side of the wall, and I almost hoped that the impact would shatter me into a thousand pieces, an instant and painless death. So that when Ash finally swallowed my heart, he wouldn't have to live forever with the guilt of killing me. So that at least one of us could continue on in this world without regrets.

I DID NOT shatter into a thousand pieces. Not even into two. Our feet touched the ground as lightly as if we'd hopped over a puddle. Gemma and I were both whole and alive, and, despite my cavalier thoughts of dying from only a moment before, I was grateful. Maybe we would make it to the pool, after all.

Maybe.

My hand and Gemma's still firmly clasped, we nodded at each other once before breaking into a run again, finding a slightly smoother path over the cobbled street than the prickly one through the woods. I didn't have time or the mental clarity to take in my surroundings, though from the buildings blurring past it looked exactly as Gemma had described it: the winding alleys and empty market stalls, the gondolas bobbing on the river, a fountain with a statue of a woman that seemed alive somehow, as if there were a soul trapped beneath the marble. The air glittered—magic, she'd said—and there was the faintest scent of spices and sweets, of rich charring meat. And music, quiet at first, but growing louder the farther we ran. Beautiful but strange, I was drawn toward the sound for reasons I couldn't quite explain, but Gemma kept steady, tugging me back on course each time I began to stray.

"Don't let it in," she said. "Focus on your breathing, or your heartbeat instead."

Oh, yes, my heart. I wasn't ready to lose it, even if it felt too much at once or else nothing at all. But as I pushed the music from my mind and focused on the rush of blood in my ears, something else pushed through the noise, another kind of rhythmic drumming. A growl, a laugh, quick footsteps on stone. *She's coming.* I'm sure Ash did his best, but he couldn't quite keep her from us.

"Almost there!" Gemma cried, half-triumphant, half-terrified, and though I didn't think we could possibly move any faster, somehow we did. An all-out sprint, and a squeeze of the hand from Gemma was the only warning I had before she yanked me into the air with her again, not so gracefully as before. My legs cycled as if I were riding a bicycle, and the breath left my chest; another wall, this one not quite so tall as the last, and on the other side was the woods once more. My ankle twisted under me on the landing, a bright shock of pain. I tumbled to the dirt, letting go of Gemma's hand.

"I can't," I said as she tried in vain to yank me back to my feet. I started to cry and couldn't help it now if she saw. "My God, it *hurts.*"

"It's just through there," Gemma said, pointing. But she could have pointed up to the moon for all that it mattered; I couldn't walk. "Please, Mama, just a few more steps."

She slid an arm around me and forcefully hauled me to standing. Leaning on her heavily, I was able to walk forward with her into the trees and up a steep hill, biting my lip so hard that blood welled and drizzled down my chin. Oddly, the lesser pain steadied me, and we had not gone far when I spotted curls of steam in the distance. *The mirror to show one's true reflection.* If I looked into it, what would it show me? A mother? A monster? A girl still filled with wonder for all the ways the world could be?

Or something else entirely?

We didn't make it. Was I surprised? No, but still disappointed. At the top of the hill, I glanced over my shoulder at the precise moment the Slit Witch stepped *through* the wall, as if it were no more substantial than mist. Ash followed, swaying a little on his feet, and the Slit Witch put a hand on his shoulder with a smile that chilled me to the core.

"Midnight," she said, her voice carrying on the wind. "In three, two, one—"

The light went out of Ash's eyes as if a wire had been cut. He dropped to all fours, his bones popping, the muscles of his back expanding, his shoulder blades sharp and protruding almost like little wings. He groaned, long and low, and when he lifted his head we locked eyes; his green gaze was as cold as I'd ever seen it. Was there anything at all of the man inside the beast? Did he know it was me, or did he see only prey, the promise of a feast?

"Gemma . . ." I whispered as the monster that was Ash lowered on his haunches, preparing to spring. "Run, Gemma. As far and as fast as you can."

"No. I won't leave you!" she said, just as the monster broke into a sprint.

"*Go,*" I commanded, and pushed Gemma out of the way. I heard her go down heavily, stumbling on the side of the hill, but I knew she'd be all right. She had to be. I turned and ran, leading him away from her. Leading him, still, toward the mirror, even though it was too late.

God, but how that moment stretched and contorted, making it feel longer than it truly was. Only half a minute, but as I limp-ran toward the pool, shoving aside the pain in my ankle, Ash crashed into me, knocking us both to the earth right at the pool's edge, the wind our bodies made in the fall dispelling the steam. He brought his face very close to mine, his front claws digging into my shoulders. From his neck dangled the locket music box I'd given him so long ago. I searched him for some sign of recognition, and found none. He didn't know me; he'd only remember after it was done. And I couldn't decide if it was better this way, or worse. If I told him I loved him, would he understand how much I meant it? I lay very still, and kept my gaze firmly on his, even as he tensed and bared his teeth to strike.

I remembered the long-ago story my mother had told me, about a prince who had loved his power more than his own child and ate it out of fear. And when that was not enough, he ate his wife and all the others of his kind so that there could be no beings more powerful than he. Was a monster that which consumed more than its share? One that ate and ate and ate, leaving great holes in the world, gaps the rest of us could never hope to fill? I hadn't believed this particular monster was real, but I suppose every monster is real for someone, somewhere. Why would we bother to tell fairy tales if no part of them was to be believed at all?

Hush now.

Hush.

How quiet the world was as Ash bent over me. How quiet the sky and the trees as Ash bit down and opened me to the night.

27

Gemma

I WATCHED MY DAD EAT MAMA'S HEART.
It didn't seem real. Like a dream, or a movie, or—or a story someone was telling me. *And then the monster ate the woman's heart. And there was blood and there were teeth and it only lasted a moment but that moment lasted forever.* She didn't even scream. That was maybe the worst thing. It was all so silent, so hushed.

When it was done, my dad sat back on his haunches, licking his lips with a long, rough tongue. Slowly, he looked around, the light back on in his eyes, as if he didn't know where he was—or what he had done. I saw it the instant his gaze snagged on Mama's body lying prone and torn before him: His back went rigid, every muscle tensed and still. He reached one trembling, claw-tipped hand toward her, touching her face, and then he let out a wail so powerful it rattled the vegetation around us. It changed the direction of the wind from west to east. He slid his arms gently beneath Mama and cradled her to his chest. Over his shoulder, her half-lidded dead eyes stared back at me.

It wasn't real. It couldn't be! This was all just a horrible, twisted, poison-filled dream. Any minute now I would wake, safe in my bed. Mama would have brushed my hair, taking all my cares away, and when I woke I would be happy, never know-ing what a monster was. Any minute now. Any—

"Hello there," said the Slit Witch pleasantly as she stepped up close behind me and put a hand on my shoulder. She smelled so rotten, like raw, rancid meat, and I gagged—almost vomited.

I shook her hand off, and then I covered my face with my hands and screamed, *"I wish the Slit Witch was dead!"*

No luck, though. Either I didn't wish hard enough, or the Touch couldn't be used to kill. And I was glad of it, really, be-cause I didn't actually want to murder her. I just wanted her gone, and for this to all be over. But she was still there, standing calmly as the beast that was Ash cried and cried into the lonely, unhearing night.

And then a peculiar thing happened—a thing I probably should have expected: Silvanus burst from the shadows with a determined war cry, his sword a sword once more and not a flower. It was pointed straight at my dad as the red-faced fairy prince rushed forward.

"No!" I cried, but Silvanus didn't slow. My dad saw him coming, though, turning just in time to knock the sword from Silvanus's grip as if it were just a toy. Still, Silvanus crashed into him, and the two went rolling, a blur of boy-limbs and monster-claws and mutual hissing and snapping. Mama lay still—slain or murdered, what was the difference now? None of it was glo-rious, all of it was wrong—and I moved toward her. Could I magic her a new heart? Could I wish and wish and *wish* for one? But the Slit Witch raised a hand and said simply, *"Stop."*

The scene froze around us: Mama slumped in the dirt, a hor-rible gaping hole in her breast; Silvanus sitting on Ash's chest, caught in the act of reaching for the dagger in his boot. Ash's mouth opened wide, mid-thrash as he tried to buck Silvanus off, as he meant to rend and tear the courageous, stupid fairy prince into pulpy little bits. Even the tree branches ceased swaying and the stars stopped sparkling, the colors and the sounds of the world muted to a gray whisper. There was the shadow of a familiar figure among the trees that I had not noticed before, watching the scene, and the shadow had frozen too. *The tree-woman.* What was she doing here? Only the Slit Witch and I were left untouched, her smile stretching so wide it didn't seem confined to the boundaries of her face.

"Ah," she sighed, and I took a good long look at her, the bloodless cuts all over her body, the way her skin sagged over her shoulders like a dress that was slightly too big. Her eyes glowed pinkish-red in the long oval of her face. "Finally, no more distractions. Just you and me, Gemma. Just you and me."

Very suddenly, I missed the sun. The warmth of it, the overwhelming bright. I hadn't seen it in hours or days—I didn't know anymore. How old was I now? Still fifteen, or fifteen plus something else? Fifteen and half a night sky, fifteen and three quarters of a wolf's howl, fifteen and two refrains of a lullaby sung by a bird lost in the dark? I wasn't the same as I was before. Still scared, but I didn't push the fear away. Like my shadow, it would always be with me.

"I *hate* you," I said, and my voice didn't tremble, not even a little. "You did this—all of it. You cursed Ash and *you* killed Mama!"

The witch was completely calm. I almost wanted her to be angry back at me. I wanted to feed off it.

"It *is* unfortunate," she said without a trace of apology, "but it had to be this way. As you can see, I've worn out this body. I require a new one, and hers is the one I've been waiting for, despite what she's done to it. It's only a little crack, and as you see, I've endured much worse." The witch tilted her head, considering. "Unless you'd like to give me yours? A bit young for my taste, but you're strong, aren't you? You're healthy. It's harder to wrestle a living soul from the flesh, but not impossible. No, not impossible at all."

A sickening realization; it turned my stomach inside out. "You've done this before. Stolen a body. Used it all up."

"Of course. I would've done it to your grandmother, in time, if she'd stuck around long enough. It helps when they trust you, when they feel warmly toward you. The body is less likely to rebel if the soul still harbors some affection for the soul slithering its way inside."

The sky was so dark above us. I wished I could crawl into it and disappear. "The hearts she found in your cellar . . ."

"Oh, yes, my collection. I can't bring myself to throw them away. Though in your mother's case, I won't have to." The Slit Witch reached between her ribs and stroked the slick, pulsing meat sack hanging there. "Always, my heart has been my own. It stays."

I recoiled, my own heart pressed against my spine as if to get as far away from her as possible. "You can't have my body. And you can't have Mama's either!"

"And why not? She's got no use for it anymore." The Slit Witch came toward me, and as much as I wanted to hold my ground, I took half a step back for every one of her steps forward. Down the slope of the hill, closer to the scene frozen behind us: Mama lying limp and Silvanus pinning my dad to the ground. "I'm going to take your mother either way. Either her body will rot where it lies, and the foxes will come to nibble on her flesh and the weeds and the dirt will reclaim her bones, or I shall wear her body for a few years more. It will serve me, the same way it would serve the worms."

"You don't deserve her," I said, and stopped abruptly at the bottom of the hill, ending our little dance. She was so much more terrible up close, little more than muscle and bone; all the parts of her that we're never meant to see were exposed. "Let the worms have her."

The Slit Witch shook her head. We were so close that if she reached out her arm, her fingertips would have just grazed my jaw. "Oh, Gemma. Sweet, naïve, fearful little Gemma. Haven't you figured it out? Are you listening? Hmm?"

I took one more step back and I tripped over something—a rock or a root or my own unsteady feet, I don't know—and I fell hard, pain radiating through my tailbone. The witch crouched down, pressing her knuckles to the dirt for balance. She loomed over me; she was all I could see.

"I *am* the worms, and the weeds, and the dirt," she said. "I am the *woods* made flesh. I am the woods given breath, able to roam as the trees cannot, able to bleed as the rivers cannot, able to speak as the stones cannot. The woods formed itself into a human shape—into me—so that I might best the great Hunting Beast. I was made for this purpose, and this purpose alone. But I realized quickly that, once the purpose was fulfilled, the woods would unmake me. And I *liked* being human; I liked the power it gave me. So I turned my back on my purpose and imprisoned the Hunting Beast where no one will ever find her and slay her and render my purpose complete. Oh, I let her out from time to time—a little terror now and then is good for the creatures of the woods, keeps them vigilant—but I've made certain that no one will touch her. That decision cost me, cursed me, marked the beginning of my unraveling—but I wouldn't have it any other way."

"*Her?*" I said, suddenly so dizzy even though I was already on the ground. If I were standing I would have had to sit, to recalibrate everything I thought I knew about the Hunting Beast, about monsters, about the woods. "The Hunting Beast is . . . a woman?"

But Nicasia wasn't listening to me, too lost in her own madness. Her cheeks—what was left of the skin—had flushed red, and her eyes had grown huge and dark, black holes threatening to swallow me whole.

"I was there at the beginning of all things," she said, "and I will be there at the end. I am in you, and in your mother, and in that silly fairy boy who puts the pink in your cheeks. Every shadow wears my face; every bird sings the rhythm of my footsteps. You cannot escape me. The woods are in you, and I am the woods."

Despair opened up in my chest like a wound. If the Slit Witch was the woods manifesting itself as human—or something that *looked* human—then how could I win against her? What could I do? I forced myself to take a deep breath.

"What do you want with me?" I asked, and there was no masking the fear in my voice. It overwhelmed me. "The night you took Mama away, you said I'd be ripe for your purposes at fifteen. What does that mean?"

The Witch's whole demeanor changed. Her eyes brightened, and her shoulders straightened, and she smiled—but it was different from her previous smiles, not so much like a leer. There was genuine joy in it.

"I'm so glad you asked, Gemma mine." She stood and held out her skeletal hand, the skin completely shed from fingers and palm. I declined the offer, using both my hands to lift myself to my feet. My knees were still weak, but I felt perversely steady.

"I'll be honest with you, Gemma. When I first cast my curse over your hapless parents, I had a mind to take your magic from you, compound it with my own. I could feel the Touch in you even then, when you were still in your mother's womb, and it excited me. I've never tried to steal magic—indeed, as powerful as I am with the spirit of the whole woods in my veins, the thought had never occurred to me. But in you I felt something special. Something that sang to me in a way no other magic had before. I knew I would have to wait, though, for magic only begins to ripen at puberty, and in the meantime I could at least entertain myself with the curse, yes? I could still set up your mother to fail, and your father to eat her heart. Killing two birds with one stone, see? In the end I would have magic *and* a body."

I couldn't speak. I curled my fingers into fists.

"But then I got to know you, Gemma. As Mother, I saw you. I— Oh, yes, did you not know?" she said when my mouth fell open. I had thought of Mother as a totally separate being, but of course—of course!—she was the Slit Witch all along. "My smoke-demon gave Mother her shape, but *I* was the heart of her. She was my ears and my eyes. And wasn't I so much nicer than your own mother? I never stole your memories. Didn't need to with my demon so vigilant in keeping you away from the woods."

That was true—Mother never used the brush's magic on me. But I'd still take Mama and lost memories over Mother and Nicasia, a thousand times over.

"In spending all that time together, I must say that I've grown rather fond of you, Gemma. Especially when you chopped off Mother's head! In that moment, I knew you were mine. And so I've decided not to take your magic. I've decided I will *teach* you magic instead. I will take you on as my apprentice."

I stared at her, stunned. She was smiling at me almost benevolently, holding her palms out in offering. Did she expect me to feel grateful? Was I supposed to thank her for her oh so generous decision to not steal what was mine and instead teach me to be just like her?

I would've laughed if I weren't also still terrified.

"Isn't that a lovely word, *apprentice*? Someone with all the secrets of the world yet to discover—a learner, a *seeker*," she said, and I shivered. "I thought I would never take on another after the failure that was your father, that son of a water sprite who was more interested in finding out the truth of his history than in the power he could wield. But you're different, Gemma. You *want* to learn; you want to take advantage of all the gifts the woods have granted you. I simply can't wait to share with you everything I know, everything I—" She cut herself off abruptly, her eyes going dark. Flakes of skin fell off her arms and floated to the ground. *Dust.* Always more dust.

"It's really rather lonely being one of a kind. One of a kind, and so brilliant besides. So I thought, well, what if there were two? No more, no less, just two, for companionship. Me and . . . *another* me. A vessel through which to experience it all again, fresh. And someday the apprentice will become a partner, and—oh! You and I will do great things, great things. Not good, you understand, but *great*."

I felt her enthusiasm; it rolled off her like sour perfume. And it was really a shame that she was so evil, because she was absolutely right about me: I really wanted a teacher. Now that I knew about the Touch, I couldn't go back to my old life and pretend it wasn't there, twitching just under my skin. I wanted to learn; I wanted to know *everything*. Starting with the depth and breadth of what, exactly, magic could do, and eventually working up to ethics and philosophy. Just because you *could* do something with magic didn't necessarily mean you *should*. And what was the purpose, the meaning? Like the Slit Witch said, this was a whole new world of discovery for me, but I didn't know how or where to start. I *needed* someone to guide me.

Just not her.

"You're still using wishes, aren't you?" she said, as if she could sense my longing to explore. "That's baby magic, Gemma. Small-time stuff. True magic is about *belief*." She bent to the ground and picked up a leaf. Held it up for me to see. "I could wish this leaf into a mouse, and it would probably work. But wishes are weak. They don't last—especially once the feeling of fulfillment has passed. Now, if I *believed* this leaf was a mouse"—as she said this, the leaf contorted, the point becoming a pink nose, the stem transforming into a tail, growing and changing until there was nothing of the leaf left and a tiny gray mouse blinked once—"then it will become so, forever and always, or at least until I believe differently, because my faith is as strong as the muscles in my jaw."

She went on, but I wasn't listening. I watched the mouse that was previously a leaf leap off her palm and scurry into the trees, a thought forming in the back of my mind. I wasn't sure if the idea was my own, or if the woods were whispering it to me— maybe both—but as it solidified, I felt something that was more than hope. I felt, deep down in the gritty marrow of my bones, that everything was going to be okay. At least where the Slit Witch was concerned.

I found my voice at last. It seemed to come from very deep within me. I reached into my pack and grabbed my rib, holding it behind my back.

"No." I looked at her with my feet firmly planted and my back very straight. Pretend-brave or real-brave, it didn't matter anymore. "I won't be your apprentice. I'd rather you take my magic."

The witch blinked slowly, like a cat. "You'd rather be powerless than my apprentice?"

"I won't be powerless," I said. "I just won't have magic. That's not the same thing."

The woods were very quiet, and the witch's voice, when she spoke, was quiet too. "At least tell me why."

"Haven't you figured it out? Are you listening? *Hmm?*" I knew it was cruel to throw her own words back at her, but I was beyond angry. I was *furious*—and it felt good in that moment to be bad. It felt *great*. But she didn't so much as flinch, watching me with her round dark eyes, too big in the skull of her face. "You killed Mama, and now you plan to take her body. You cursed my dad, and now he'll be a beast for all eternity. So why would I want to be your apprentice? You're a monster, Nicasia. You're monstrous."

The woods were so silent that it was like we were trapped under a bell jar, just her and me. I tightened my grip on my rib.

"Am I?" Her tone was curious, as if she genuinely wanted to know. As if she'd never considered it before. She took one step toward me, and I didn't step back. "What is a monster, truly? A murderer? A cheat, a liar, a thing that hides in the dark, or one that moves freely in the light, all the more terrifying for blending in, for being difficult to spot? What does a monster look like? Do claws and fangs alone make a monster? A cat has both, and we call it cute. What is a monster then? Ask one hundred people and you will get one hundred answers." She was breathing so heavily, spit slick on her lips. "With so many possibilities, is a monster not simply a mirror, a glass to gaze into and see our own dread, our own fear, reflected back?"

Closer. I needed her to come just a little bit closer.

The Slit Witch licked her lips with a pointed white tongue. "As a monster, allow me to remind you: Heroics cannot save you. Your youth cannot save you. Your intelligence, your beauty, your courage, your kindness—none of those will save you. Not even your anger, your boiling rage. You are doomed. You will not last. Your loved ones will not last. You cannot save them. They are not yours. They never were."

She's wrong. *She's wrong, she's wrong, she's wrong*. I thought it over and over again, like a chant. If I didn't, I would break.

"Only magic can save you," she said, and for the first time, she sounded sad. Sad and lonely and—and *hurt*. I had done that. I had hurt her, and it made me feel small. "Magic can make it so that you never die. Magic can take away your fear, your pain, your panic and uncertainty. But you've rejected it, Gemma. Rejected *me*." She inched forward, her rotten breath on my cheek. "I could've helped you. I could've saved you. Remember that this is the choice *you* made."

It happened very quickly, her movement a blur: The Slit Witch pressed her thumb to my forehead, right between my eyes. Her touch was cold—icy numbing cold that made it difficult to think or to breathe. It was painful, and yet it was also the absence of pain. A blank void, a deadened space that spread through my skull, down my cheeks and past my jaw. I could feel her reaching inside me, rooting around, sifting through quick flashes of random memories and replaying my favorite dreams. Down my neck to my chest, and when the cold seized my heart, I gasped. That was where my magic lived, and I felt her grip close around it. Her grip severed me from my daze, granting me a moment of clarity. Though my fingertips were tingling, I still sensed my rib in my hand—smooth, cool bone, an object of sacrifice and bargaining. *The forest is in you now, in your flesh. Be sure it doesn't spread.* I laughed without a sound as I brought the rib around and plunged it through a gap in the Slit Witch's chest, very near her heart.

I wish the Slit Witch would turn back into the woods! I cried, both aloud and in my mind. The witch's eyes widened, and her thumb fell away from my forehead. *No! I believe the Slit Witch is the woods. I believe that she is not made of flesh, that she is not given breath. That she is unable to roam, just as the trees cannot. That she is unable to bleed, just as the rivers cannot. That she is unable to speak, just as the stones cannot. That she was there at the beginning of all things, and she will be there at the end,* in this spot!

I pulled my hand out of her chest, leaving my rib—my precious, beloved rib!—behind. Leaving it inside her, both as an offering and as a conduit for my spell. The Slit Witch screamed—a sound like a thousand ravens drowning; I clapped my hands over my ears, but there was no blocking it out—and clawed at the place where the rib had entered her, trying desperately to remove it. But it was already too late. A layer of craggy, bone-colored skin had grown over her chest and sealed together, patching the hole that was there only a second ago. The bone-skin continued to grow, filling her in, and she wailed as her feet elongated into roots that spiraled down into the dirt. At this I scrambled back; she tried to chase after me, but she had sunk into the ground up to her calves, her legs now entirely made of that same strange rigid material that was not quite skin and not quite bone. More like bark and like stone. She bent forward slightly as her torso stiffened and her arms froze in front of her, reaching for me. The last thing to transform was her face, the bone-skin, stone-bark creeping slowly up her neck, as if politely letting her get her last words in.

But I was not so polite; if there were to be last words, then they would be mine. They would be the last words she'd ever hear.

"Remember when Mother—when you—told me the story about the half-man, half-bull stuck in an endless labyrinth, and how every year seven children were sacrificed to the monster's appetite to appease it? You said something like, 'Sometimes we have to sacrifice a few people to protect the whole.' You said, 'Not everyone can be saved.'"

The Slit Witch was panting, taking her last breaths before her jaw hardened. But she could still hear me; she could still listen.

"You were right, Mother," I said, and a tear slid from the corner of my eye. "Maybe I can't save everyone I love from death, or pain, or even fear, but we can still save *each other*. From loneliness, from hatred, from sorrow like a hand wrapped around our throats. We save each other with love and with patience." I wiped away the tear, rubbing it between my fingers until it evaporated. The Slit Witch's eyes closed as the skin-not-skin overtook them, as it crested over her forehead. I leaned very close to her ear. "But I can't save you. I'm sorry."

And with that she went completely still—a statue or a strange sort of tree; I don't know. In time maybe she would grow toward the sky, branches sprouting from her chest, and little buds would burst from them with flowers the color of blood. All I knew was that she would be here until the end. And maybe—it was *possible*—I was wrong. Maybe, in a way, I *had* saved her. After all, she wasn't dead or gone—only transformed. She was still part of the woods. Even the most powerful magic couldn't change that. And I wouldn't want it to.

I collapsed. Not unconscious, only tired. So, so tired. And I missed my rib. I felt its absence acutely, an ache above my belly, to the left.

But I didn't have time to rest. With the Slit Witch quieted, the world became unstuck. Several things happened at once: Ash roared; Silvanus closed his fist around the hilt of his dagger. Then another howl joined the melee, and the wolf I had met a lifetime ago at the woods' edge emerged from the trees. I jumped to my feet, a sudden surge of adrenaline pulsing through me. I reached around to my pack for my rib, only to remember all over again that it wasn't there.

What have I done? I thought as I charged toward where Mama lay in the midst of it, her chest still torn in a cruel parody of the witch's own, ripped open right along the crack that had been there before. *And what am I going to do now?*

28

Virginia

THERE IS NO ROOM IN THE WORLD FOR ANYTHING BUT *pain. No sky, no earth, nothing above me or below me. No future, no past, just this moment, enduring. I feel every scrape of Ash's teeth as they tear through bone, muscle, tendon, vein. I feel my heart leave my body.*

And the venom that replaces it.

I ROSE ABOVE my body.

As weightless as the wind, as intangible as a shadow, I rose into the air and hovered there, and though I had no eyes with which to see, I saw; though I had no ears with which to hear, I heard. I watched as Ash bent over my limp form, his cries of misery shaking the earth so that the surface of the pool rippled and clouded. I watched as the Slit Witch caught Gemma in a time-stopped bubble, as she told my daughter how she planned to steal my body—*Oh, Ash,* I thought, though I did not have a mind to think, *I know what must have happened to your mother*—as Gemma rejected the witch's offer to teach her magic, as Gemma used her rib to return the witch to the woods. I watched as Prince Silvanus of the Forest Fey—for that could only be him, in his pantaloons and cape—rushed at Ash, and as they tumbled together. As the most enormous wolf I'd ever seen flew from beyond the hill, his long, terrible teeth bared. I watched as Silvanus turned his attention on the wolf, as the wolf nipped and clawed in self-defense as Silvanus swung his sword. I watched as Gemma ran back to my body, and as Ash joined her there.

"Do something," Gemma pleaded, staring at her father as if he were a savior, not a monster at all—is it possible to be both at once?—but Ash only hung his head. *"Do something,"* Gemma pleaded, but it was already done. Something was growing inside me, and slowly my consciousness was spooled back into my body. Into the cold, and into the dark.

IT'S THE VENOM, said my mother on that long-ago day when she'd brought me to that place of rot and rebirth where the Hunting Beast had buried his—*her?*—victims. Where I learned not necessarily what a monster is but what a monster *does.* How it can change you, how encountering a monster can remind you of what you fear. How a monster can force you to confront the truths that you know. Truths like: *Childhood is over and I can't ever go back* and *someday I will die and everyone I love will die and there is nothing,* absolutely nothing, *I can do about it.* Ever since, I had been terrified.

But isn't there something freeing in it too? In facing what you fear the most, in looking at it and saying: *Yes, I see you.* There will always be life after death, with the flesh feeding the dirt and the flowers that sprout, and the flowers feeding the rabbits and the rabbits feeding the wolves. It's magical and mundane and all things between, and it is a cycle that will repeat until the end of time. *I* am both magical and mundane, and I too will go on until the end and the end isn't now. The Slit Witch had cursed Ash into the image of the Hunting Beast from my most frightful imaginings, and that meant a monster with claws and teeth, with rough skin and piercing thorns, and venom too. The venom above all.

The Beast's venom keeps them alive.

If I had breath in my lungs to laugh, I would have. Raucous, joyous laughter, an offering to the woods in exchange for this magic. This wonderful, weird, terrifying magic. A seed took hold in the open mess of my chest, and I felt it as the seed split into two, then three and four. A painful severing, but cathartic too. The seeds grew, and when each was about the size of one quarter of my fist, they began to beat, blood rushing through the four chambers of my new heart. Though they pulsed in sync, each chamber was separate, one in each corner of my chest. Nothing could be as it was before, not even this. My strange new heart pounded, and my lungs filled with air, and I opened my eyes.

I was alive.

"Mama?" said Gemma, her face filling my vision. "Mama! Are you . . . ?"

I couldn't speak, not yet. I sat up slowly, and pressed my hands to my chest, feeling the skin that had closed over my four little hearts, the crack that still ran down the center and always would, because I could not erase or excuse what I had done. Gemma crawled back to give me space, uncertain if I was real or a ghost. I turned and peered over the edge of the pool into the still water, ready to see my true self at last. The steam cleared, licking my cheeks and curling the ends of my hair.

A scene unfamiliar to me played over the surface, colorless but clear: a little family outside of a thatched cottage in a sunlit glade, a man with thick hair and a pale crescent scar on his jaw—it had been so long that I'd forgotten about the scar on his jaw—the woman beside him gazing up at him with a smile. Between them a dark-haired child, one hand in each of theirs as they swing her back and forth, her feet leaving the ground as her mouth opens in soundless laughter, as she turns her face to the cloudless sky.

I watched until the scene dissolved, replaced by another, equally unfamiliar but unmistakably mine: the little family picking berries, juice running down their chins. And one from earlier, the man lying with his head on the woman's lap as she asks, *What do you think our baby will be like?* They flashed past me, more and more rapidly, until I sat back on my heels, my breath coming in ragged gasps. This wasn't my true self. It was a self that could have been but never was. And these weren't memories or even dreams. They were *wishes.*

This *was* a wishing well.

Gemma was crouched at my side, watching with me. She looked at me, a question in her eyes, but I only shook my head, still unable—or unwilling—to speak. Silvanus had been right about this pool, but I think we were still right about it too; this was also the mirror the Slit Witch had intended to break the spell. That was why she'd come to me two and a half years early, why she had said we were getting close. Because Silvanus had shown Gemma the pool, and if I had only told Gemma about the curse, she might have recognized it for what it was. Wishes came from the heart, from the true self, didn't they? This pool would have revealed Ash as he was beneath his monstrous visage, what he wished to be again: *human.*

A growl split the silence behind me. I swiveled round to find him several feet away, tensed to spring. The light was gone from his eyes again, replaced by pure hunger. It was as if he'd never lamented my death, all despondency erased. And I realized that it would always be like this between us, that he would eat my heart as long as I had a heart to eat, and I would grow a new one, on and on and on.

"*No,*" I tried to say, but my voice had rusted with despair. The wishing well wouldn't break the spell because the deadline had passed and his only wish now was to devour me. "Please . . ."

But there was no stopping it: Just like the last time, he leapt onto me, pinning me at the pool's edge. He bared his teeth, a terrible pause before he ripped into me, the anticipation building. I looked into his eyes, utterly blank, and I thought of the curse, and what the Slit Witch had said to Gemma before Gemma transformed her.

Is a monster not simply a mirror, a glass to gaze into and see our own dread, our own fear, reflected back?

Looking at Ash, at what he had become, I knew that her words were true. The Slit Witch had been right about so many things, and what did it mean that one so wicked could also be wise? I wanted to reject her wholeheartedly, but I couldn't. She was right, and I could use it. I could twist this truth to my purpose, and save Ash once and for all.

Using every last bit of strength I possessed, I grabbed on to him—my monster, my mirror. I placed my hands on his shoulders, wrapped my legs around his waist, and rolled with him into the water.

No splash, no sound. The water was scalding like a newly filled bath; I clung to him as we sank. And I wondered if it was better to be eaten or to drown.

To drown, I decided, even as my lungs burned and begged for air. Ash thrashed and flailed, still hungry for my heart, but I held on to him stubbornly. We were in this together, or not at all.

How deep did the water go? It must have connected to the river somehow. When I closed my eyes, I was back in a memory-place. Only it wasn't a memory but a dream. A dream that was really happening. Hard to explain, like our spirits had fled our bodies, and we could meet in a place beyond flesh and bone, beyond light and dark. I was in the woods, and I'd been walking for so long that I'd almost forgotten where I was going. Walking away or walking toward? I was afraid to stop, but I knew I must. I couldn't feel my feet anymore, and there was blood in my mouth from biting the inside of my cheek so hard.

I went still, catching my breath, and in the darkness there was a song: one that was familiar but that I hadn't heard in so long. Tinny and light, the music grew louder, and when I felt I'd had enough rest, I turned around completely, facing boldly the direction I'd been traveling all this time.

I walked forward through the woods, and each step became easier than the last, until soon I was running, following the music that called to me as clearly as a voice saying my name. *Virginia, this way!* I ran through the woods, and above me the stars brightened, the moon widened, crescent to full glowing orb. The entire length of my body was sore, but I didn't slow; someone was waiting for me in the shadows with his arms outstretched. I ran right into them and held him tight, closing my eyes.

This is goodbye, he said, the vibrations of his voice rumbling through me. *I am sorry, Virginia, for all the hurt I've caused you.*

He tried to push me away gently, but I held on. *No,* I said.

You must let me go. One knobby hand stroked my hair, the locket around his neck falling very close to my ear as I pressed my cheek to his chest, listening to his heart and the music that had called me here. *Let go, and swim to the surface. I am only holding you down, Virginia. Some curses cannot be broken.*

The Slit Witch never said that he would remain a beast *forever,* only that he would turn into a beast in truth to eat my heart. He'd done that once, and once was enough. Besides, the Slit Witch was gone, or as good as gone anyway; surely, her magic couldn't hold. Not against me. Not against *us.*

I won't. I squeezed him harder, crushing the air from his lungs and mine. I could feel him trying to slip from my grasp, but true to my word I would not let him go. I would not let it end. Not like this.

Why not? he said, in a voice so soft and genuinely perplexed that I laughed just a little, breathless. Did he really not know? All these years, and I'd never said the words aloud.

Because I love you, I said, for the first time and possibly the last. *Isn't that enough?*

Ash shuddered and sighed, and leaned into me, holding on to me as I held on to him.

Come back, I whispered, pulling back just far enough that I could look into his eyes, and he could look into mine. If a monster was a mirror, then couldn't a loved one be a mirror too? A mother, a daughter, a partner, a friend? When he looked at me, he would see *love* reflected back at him; he would see his dreams and his hopes, his past and his future. He would see himself as he truly was, loved and accepted. I didn't care if he would always possess the guise of a monster, if his hugs would always hurt, his kisses always excoriate. All I needed was for him to know me again. To know his true self, the one that didn't hunger for my heart because it was already his. I'd given it to him long ago.

Ash gazed into me and I gazed into him. I said, *It's time to come back from the dark.*

THE FIRST THING I saw upon breaking the surface of the pool was Ash's face—his human face—very close to mine. He looked just a bit different than I remembered; he was older, with only a trace of boyishness left in the brightness of his eyes below the thick brows. His cheeks were lean, almost sallow, but his hair was still dark with only a touch of gray near the temples and in the stubble on his chin. We floated in the warm water, gasping but alive. And for all the firmness of my hold on him in that in-between dream, I touched him tentatively now, pressing my fingers to his cheek and tracing along his jaw. He smiled a smile like pure golden light.

We reached for each other and met in the middle, our first kiss in fifteen and a half years. Well, minus the bloody, desperate one on the bank of the river when he hid me as best as he could from the monster chasing us into the night. Long and slow, a kiss like getting to know someone you've only met before in a dream. But this wasn't a dream, and I wouldn't wake to find myself alone again. I could pull away knowing that there would be more kisses, so many I might get sick of them, except I never would. There were tears in my eyes and there was laughter in my throat; my heart hurt from feeling too much at once. Ash rested his forehead against mine, and we stayed that way awhile, oblivious to everything around us.

"Virginia," he said, and it had been so long since I'd heard his voice without the gravelly roughness of a monster's mouth that I began to cry in earnest. He stroked my soaking hair and kissed my damp cheeks. "You didn't let go."

"Of course not," I said, and kissed him again. "We still have a whole life to live."

I began to shiver despite the warmth of the water, the warmth of his embrace, the warmth of *I love you* whispered in my ear, and then Gemma was there, pulling us onto dry land. I reached for her, hugging her close, but I knew I couldn't keep her all to myself. When at last I released her, she glanced from me to Ash and back again. He watched her all the while, looking at her like he meant to memorize every feature. I smiled, wiping the tears that had come to my eyes with the back of my hand.

"Ash," I said, "this is our girl. This is Gemma. And, Gemma, this is your father."

A moment of silence while they took each other in, and then Ash hung his head, tears dripping from his chin.

"Gemma," he said gently, "I'm sorry I haven't been there for you. I'm so sorry, I—"

His voice cracked; I reached for his hand and gripped it tight. Of course this wasn't going to be easy, but what part of this journey had been? He started to speak again, still tremulous, but Gemma laid a hand on his arm. His gaze rose to hers and she smiled.

"I'm sad we lost so much time together," she said. "But I'm really happy you're here now."

"Me too," Ash said, and I squeezed his hand. The three of us, linked.

"Just don't get yourself turned into a monster again," Gemma said, and Ash laughed—a deep, rasping sound that echoed through the night.

"I promise, I won't."

Curiously, Ash said nothing about Gemma's strange appearance, about her horns and thick veins, as if the woods were growing not just around her but inside of her too. So I didn't say anything either, because I knew what that felt like even if I didn't show it on the outside. We had all been altered, and in ways we might not yet understand. Maybe the signs would disappear in time, or maybe they wouldn't. I was tired, and the pain of my ankle was beginning to cut through the armor of adrenaline; we'd figure it out later.

"Can we go home now?" I said, but nobody answered so I asked it again. "Can we go home?"

Ash and Gemma had turned their attention to the shadows, fixated on a point beyond the trees that I couldn't see, listening to something that I couldn't hear. Silence, to my ears, split suddenly by a yelp, as of a great animal struck down. *The wolf.* Silence again, and then someone cutting swiftly through the dark.

"Hunting Beast!" cried Prince Silvanus as he burst into the clearing. "We're not finished yet."

29

Gemma

"AH, SO YOU'VE TURNED BACK INTO THE SPURNED prince of legend, I see," Silvanus said, pointing his sword at my dad, at *me*. His features were so red and contorted with rage he was nearly beyond recognition, his voice coarse and low. "But you cannot fool me, wretch. I see through your disguise! Your days of hunger and terror are at an end."

"Sil!" I said, leaping to my feet. I had known since I met him that he desired to slay the beast and be made a hero, but I never expected this . . . *desperation*. He had lost himself in the pursuit of glory—a word I was distinctly beginning to dislike—and I hoped he hadn't fallen so far that he couldn't climb back out. "I told you already. This is *not* the Hunting Beast!"

"Gemma Belle," he said, laying a hand over his heart as if to protect it. "You defend this monster? This *thing*?"

I stamped my foot—childish, I know, but I couldn't help it—and the ground quivered beneath us, rolling like water. I noticed again the shadowy figure of the woman lurking in the trees, watching us. *The Hunting Beast . . . is a woman?* Something clicked in my brain then, but I didn't have time to dwell on it. "His name is Ash and he's my dad."

Silvanus scoffed, his hair stuck to his forehead with sweat.

His eyes were burning gold, and his crown of laurel and berries lay crooked and limp.

"Delusions and nonsense!" he said, twirling his sword. "The woods have warped you, Gemma Belle. They have turned you inside out! But have no fear, for I will save you, and all the fairies put under a spell!"

"By *you*," I spat, entirely fed up with this. I remembered how it had felt to kiss him, soft and sort of glittery, a furious flutter in my belly. Why couldn't we go back to that? Why did we have to fight? "The fairies are under a spell because you *lied*, not because you failed to murder the Hunting Beast."

The fairy prince drew himself up and widened his stance. His back foot swiveled, grinding into the dirt, and he lowered his chin, setting his eyes on his target.

"And so I shall murder him," he said, "and it will no longer be a lie."

I wish I knew how to fight! I thought, calling upon the Touch as Silvanus advanced. Longing for my rib, I reached for a twig on the ground, hoping—no, *believing*—it would work just as well. I raised my twig, and watched as it lengthened, as tendrils like vines wove together into a hilt, as the tip of the twig sharpened into a point. I planted my feet and inhaled deep. *I believe I can fight.*

Our weapons clashed, metal on wood, and he was so close I could feel the heat from his body, see the sweat dripping down his forehead, the strain of the tendons in his neck. He spun and brought his sword down on me again, but though his iron blade hacked a huge splinter out of my wooden one, it wasn't like the last time we'd fought. He wasn't trying to hurt me, only to push me aside. Still, it was hard, and the Touch could only do so much. I gave myself over to it, letting the magic guide me as we struggled with each other, forward and back. It was like a dance, a deadly one, and soon my breath was coming in quick little hiccups.

"Let me through, Gemma Belle," Silvanus said, pushing against my enchanted twig with so much force my legs nearly buckled beneath me. If not for the magic providing a boost, I might have collapsed. The blade of my makeshift weapon was perilously close to snapping, the wood whittled halfway through where his sword pressed against it. "I must do this! It is my destiny."

"No. It's. Not." I was leaning so far back my spine was nearly parallel to the ground. Thinking fast, I raised my leg and kicked him, as hard as I could, in the chest.

The fairy prince did not expect that; he lost his balance and fell ungracefully to the ground, limbs flailing as he landed hard on his rump. I stood, my shadow falling over him like a net, and he looked up at me with wild eyes and gritted teeth. He reached for his sword, but I stepped on the blade. At my touch it turned once again into a daisy, its long stem caught beneath my foot. He scowled at me but didn't try to get up.

"Tell the truth, Silvanus," I said. "It's time to tell the truth now."

Silvanus said nothing, and it was like the world had narrowed to include only him and me. I was unaware of Mama and Dad behind me, unaware of the sky beginning to lighten on the distant horizon. Unaware of the wind tugging at the tangles in my hair, of the steam from the pool dissipating, of the birdsong and call of the crickets, the beetles in the underbrush.

"All right," I said, and lowered myself to sit in front of him. "I'll go first."

His breath and mine, a matched set.

"I killed Mother with an ax. A smoke-demon; she dissolved into nothing but a dark, ashy mark. No blood, even. And I'm not sorry. I would do it again if it meant saving Mama and Dad.

Maybe that makes me a monster, but maybe I'm okay with that."

I shuddered, a deep, full-body shiver like the release after a good long cry. I was letting go.

"Sometimes I'm afraid and I don't know what I'm afraid *of*— sometimes a shadow, and sometimes a shadow I imagined. But even if the shadow *is* imaginary, my fear is real. Fear is powerful, but it's temporary. It will pass. It will always pass. Like the moon: Sometimes it's full, and sometimes you can't see it at all. My fear belongs to me. But I don't belong to *it*."

My heart had steadied, too quiet now to hear it.

"I transformed the Slit Witch back into her true form: the woods, made dirt and tree and stone again. I did it so that she wouldn't hurt anyone anymore. Noble, right? But it didn't feel noble. It just felt sad. Not *wrong,* but sad."

Almost done now. Almost there.

"I don't know what this magic will do to me. I think if I use it only in service of myself, it will eat me all up like it did to the witch when she turned her back on her purpose. But if I use it in service of others, and the woods—if I remember to give back just as much as I take—I think I'll be okay. More than okay; I'll thrive. Isn't that a wonderful word, *thrive*? Like *alive,* but with a little hum to it. It vibrates in the throat."

Slowly, Silvanus pushed himself up from his half-sprawled crouch, crossing his legs so that our knees almost touched. He kept his eyes on mine, clearer now and bright.

"I did not slay the Hunting Beast," he said, but he'd said it too softly, and the woods didn't hear him. He tipped his head back, opened his throat, and cried, *"I did not slay the Hunting Beast!"*

I felt it at once, the undoing of the spell, even as far away as we were from the cursed fairy revel. Not a simple *snap!* and all was well, but a methodical untangling of the knotted strings of fate. The magic of it ran through the ground, through the trees and the sky, through Silvanus and me. It felt like a cramped muscle unclenching. In tandem we sighed, and I reached for his hand, but he wouldn't look at me.

"I may have slayed the giant wolf," he said in a more normal tone of voice. He coughed, cleared his throat. "The guardian of the forest's edge. I left him grievously wounded."

I was on my feet in an instant. "Where?"

Silvanus pointed. Still by the pool, Mama and Dad were looking at me with an odd expression, not fearful but wondering and a little bewildered. I suppose it is not every day that your daughter fights a fairy prince using her magic and a random twig as a defense. I turned without waiting to see if they would follow, and ran in the direction Silvanus had indicated, hoping I wasn't too late.

I WAS.

Too late—I saw that at once. The wolf lay on his side, still breathing, but there was a slit in his belly, and blood soaked the ground around him. I dropped to my knees near the wolf's head and put my hand on his muzzle, wondering if there was a way to use the Touch to heal. But I was drained from my fight with Silvanus, and I couldn't conjure the belief that the wound was minor. He opened his golden eyes at my touch.

"Gemma Belle, guardian of antiques," he said, his voice much gentler than I remembered. "Do not weep for me. My flesh will return to the woods soon, and my soul will move quietly on. It is the way of all things."

I was weeping; I hadn't even realized. For the wolf, for myself, for this terrible, beautiful adventure I'd been set on. How could it end like this? But this wasn't the end, as the wolf said. I believed that. I did.

"You must take my place," said the wolf, in a way that left no room for doubt. "You, Gemma Belle, will become a guardian of this great forest."

I felt the truth, the *rightness* of it, in my bones. I was the daughter of the son of a water sprite; the daughter of a woman who walked into the woods and never really left; the grand-daughter of the Great Ensorceller of the Hidden Moon, no matter that the title meant little in the way of actual magic. The woods were my home; I would not abandon it.

"Yes," I said to the wolf as he closed his eyes for the very last time. "I will guard and protect."

My parents were behind me, Mama with her hand on my shoulder and Dad gathering stones. Mama and I watched as Dad placed the stones around the wolf in a circle, each no more than six inches apart. He hummed under his breath as he went along.

Silvanus was there too, standing apart, and when our eyes locked he hung his head, the only apology for the wolf's death I was likely to receive from him. He was proud; maybe he'd always be so. *Where did a hero end and a monster begin?*

Soon Dad laid the last stone, and with the circle complete the stones began to glow. Between them roots climbed out of the ground like grasping hands, growing up and around the wolf as they weaved into a cage. The ground cracked and groaned, and then the stones brightened and the root-made casket sank as easily as if the earth were water, swallowed by the dirt until every last trace of root and stone and wolf were gone. The silence left behind was reverent.

Well, not *every* last trace was gone—something hard and white poked through the earth like buried treasure rising to the surface of the sea. I bent down and grasped it, thinking it a stone, only to pull an entire bone from the dirt. A *rib,* slightly longer than mine had been and perfectly curved. I gripped it tight, holding it close to my heart.

"Can we go home now?" Mama said, her voice like a tiptoe, and I wished I could say yes. But the fairies still had Clarice, and now that the spell was broken, we had to ask for her release.

"Soon," I said. I glanced to the trees where the woman had stood while I fought Silvanus. She was gone. "But not yet."

I CURTSIED BEFORE the fairy queen and her consort, just as Silvanus had shown me. He stood by my side, laying a fist over his heart. The queen gazed down at us implacably from her throne.

"Son, you have broken the curse, but do not expect gratitude. We know it was you who brought it upon us."

"Indeed, it was I." He drew himself up to his full height, one hand going to the hilt of his sword before he remembered that the sword was not there. "I expect no word of thanks, and would not accept it if it were offered. I have failed you, and I promise never to do so again."

The fairy queen stared at her son for a long moment, the jewels in her crown glittering. Then, she smiled. "Very good. Your destiny awaits you still." She turned her eyes on me. "And you, Guardian of the Forest's Edge, why have you come before us?"

"I would beg the release of a prisoner who has wronged you unintentionally," I said, choosing my words with care. "My grandmother, Clarice. Known to you as the Great Ensorceller of the Hidden Moon. It is my understanding that she disappeared abruptly from your village after you had gotten used to purchasing her wares, but she did not mean to slight you. She did it for protection, to keep her home and her daughter safe from the one they call the Slit Witch and her unpredictable machinations. Please, allow me to extend my sincerest apologies on her behalf."

I finished, out of breath but quite pleased with myself. Even Silvanus shot me a sliver of a smile, impressed.

I did not smile back.

The fairy queen was silent while she contemplated. "We accept your apology and will release the prisoner on one condition: that she reopen her trade with us."

"I'm not certain she'll be open to that," I said, thinking of how eager she was to turn away from the woods after severing ties with Nicasia. It was reasonable that she'd be doubly inclined to have nothing to do with the fairies after they'd imprisoned her for so long.

The fairy queen frowned. "She gave her word."

"There must be something—" I began, but suddenly Mama was there at my side.

"I'll do it," she said, and my head whipped toward her. *Mama* wanted to take over as the Great Ensorceller of the Hidden Moon? I had thought that, after today, she would never step foot in the woods again. "I will assume my mother's place if you will release her from her bonds and her bargain."

I wanted very suddenly to throw my arms around her and squeeze and squeeze forever, but I didn't think it would be an appropriate gesture in the middle of a fairy negotiation, so I restrained myself. But barely.

After a long tense moment, the fairy queen nodded. "Agreed. A new deal is done. Vulcan," she said, turning to one of her nearby fairy guards. "Fetch the Great Ensorceller and bring her here. Tell her that her family has successfully negotiated the terms of her release."

While we waited for Clarice to come, Silvanus and I drifted away from the throne, away from Mama and Dad who watched warily from the edge of the open-air ballroom, so that we could speak privately. We sat together on a low stone wall as dawn's first light spread across the sky.

"I will not rest until the Hunting Beast is dead," Silvanus said, again putting his hand on his sword hilt, only the hilt was not there. I felt a tiny bit bad about that, but then, I was certain he'd be able to acquire another one. A sword that hadn't been blessed by a false enchantress.

I knotted my fingers in my lap, remembering the Slit Witch's words. *So I turned my back on my purpose and imprisoned the Hunting Beast where no one will ever find her and slay her and render my purpose complete.*

Her. Where no one will ever find *her.* There was something we were missing, and had been all along.

"What if the stories are wrong?" I said slowly, careful not to give away too much. Maybe it would be better if Silvanus didn't know. Better for him to keep chasing a fake Hunting Beast rather than a real one. "What if the Hunting Beast is not what you think?"

"He is *exactly* what I think. A child-eater, a monster, and I *will* find him, Gemma Belle, even if I must spend my whole life searching." A flush lit his cheeks, heat from within. "I will hunt him as he has hunted so many others, and the people of the woods will sing my praises for generations to come."

I was quiet. Why did Silvanus insist on the approval of many when the adoration of just one or a few would suffice? I liked him very much as he was, and his mothers loved him too. Why was that not enough?

"If you insist on this path," I said, "I'll do what I can to stop you."

Silvanus glanced at me sharply. "You would protect a monster such as him?"

"No." I shook my head vigorously, trying to convey how much I meant this. "I would protect *you* from an act that you cannot take back. One that might not fulfill you the way you think it will."

Silvanus turned and cupped my chin with his hand. My heart began to race. From fear or lingering affection, I wasn't sure.

"Then we shall be enemies," he said. "Henceforth and evermore."

"I suppose so." I looked into his eyes, lost in the gold of them, and I knew I *was* trying to save the Hunting Beast from Silvanus as much as I wanted to save Silvanus from being consumed by his own hunger. I couldn't save the Slit Witch, but maybe I could save everyone else in the woods—even the most terrible monster. Maybe there didn't have to be any more stories with unhappy endings.

I kissed Silvanus on the cheek—both a promise and a farewell—just as the fairy guard led Clarice into the ballroom. I pulled away and left him sitting there alone, the fairy prince who was my first crush and my first heartbreak too. Maybe heroes weren't quite a *plague,* as Mother had once said, but I couldn't put my faith in them anymore. What if one day Silvanus decided *I* was too monstrous to live, and that he needed to slay me too?

In the meantime, I would put my faith elsewhere—in friendship and in family, in love and even in fear, because having a little fear is good. We *should* be afraid of the stove because it is hot and will burn us. We *should* be afraid of the dark woods because there are wolves that might eat us (not *all* wolves, but some). That doesn't mean we shouldn't use the stove or explore the woods in the daylight. It means we should be cautious. Our fear just might save us.

Clarice and Mama and Dad were still talking to the fairies— I could hear the queen inviting them to a feast—and so I slipped away quietly. There was one more thing I had to do, and it was, possibly, the most dangerous thing of all.

I'll be right back, I thought, and wished with the Touch that my family wouldn't notice that I was gone.

* * *

I FOUND THE tree-woman in the eerie garden of roots that looked like fingers—that *were* fingers, I realized—the sun just beginning to peek over the horizon. Thin trees with pink mouths open to the sky, roses that crawled on spider's legs, a deer that chewed on a leaf leaking blood. She knelt in the center of it, her white hair shining with a bluish tint in the rising light. I walked through the zigzagging rows of mushrooms and plants and bodies until I was right in front of her. I folded to my knees too, forgetting how very tall she was, how she towered above me even when sitting. She was plucking the petals off a remarkably normal-looking daisy, except that every petal transformed into a slug-like creature as it hit the ground and slithered away. She didn't look up at me when I spoke.

"I don't want to hurt you, but I can't let you keep eating people."

I held my breath, waiting for her response. Both afraid that I was wrong and afraid that I was right.

With the tip of her tongue she licked her lips, and plucked until every last petal was gone. At last, she lifted her head. "Why not?"

I exhaled, and almost laughed. How could she ask that in so reasonable a tone? I liked her, despite myself. Despite who she was. "Because it's wrong."

She twirled the empty daisy stem between her fingers, and then tossed it over her shoulder. "What if I only eat the bad ones? The people no one will miss?"

"Sorry, but no."

She leaned very close to me—so close I could feel her hot, rancid breath on my face—and I clutched my wolf-rib in my hand and steeled myself against the urge to cringe away. I would not show weakness. Not in front of the Hunting Beast.

"Then what are you going to do?" she said, her eyes as shiny as jewels, and in them was a challenge. She was curious, I think. As fascinated by me as I was by her. I was confident she wasn't about to eat me.

Mostly.

I did lean back then, but only to position my legs in front of me. Settling in for a story. "Why don't you tell me?"

That surprised her. She sucked in a breath, the air whistling over her wet lips. She tilted her chin to the sky and she smiled, a little one. Faint, but there.

"You've heard the story, I suppose, about the nightshade prince who ate his children so that none might surpass him in greatness and strength? How distorted history has become! Nicasia was clever. It was *she* who first spread the lie that the Hunting Beast was a man so that others would be less likely to identify and kill me, rendering her purpose complete. The lie caught on. Even that she-devil knew that a greedy prince is more palatable than a woman who simply wants to be left alone. I'm too monstrous even to be a monster in my own story."

She paused and lowered her eyes to mine.

"I never wanted to be a mother. But it was expected of me, being married to the nightshade king. I never wanted to marry him, and I never wanted children. But, again, it was expected of me—not only to *be* a wife and mother, but to *desire* these things as well—and when my first was born I did not feel anything but exhaustion. I did not see my face in hers; I did not recognize the creature in my arms. She cried and cried, and I didn't know how to make it stop. I was so tired, and I'd never *wanted* this. So I unhinged my jaw and shoved the weeping creature down my throat, to my belly where she was finally quiet, and I felt at peace."

She stopped and swallowed, as if remembering that very day. She brought a hand to her throat, and trailed her fingertips down to her belly, where once she had gobbled her baby.

"I told my husband that the child had passed in the night— some do, suddenly and without seeming cause. We grieved together, and my grief was true despite the circumstance, and I hoped that would be the end of it. But he would not stop until he had made a mother of me once more. A king requires an heir, and a childless woman is a thing that arouses suspicion and distrust. So I ate each child as it came, and each time I mourned but prayed for an end to it. My body was stretched and strange—I no longer felt like myself. I no longer felt like a *person*. I was only a vessel for someone else's desires."

I felt very cold all of a sudden. I wanted to tell her I understood, but I didn't dare to speak just yet. Of course I had never had a baby, or been forced to have one that I didn't want, but I too knew what it was to feel disconnected from my body when my memories were stolen from me. Or even when she herself took my rib, which was now no longer part of me and never would be again.

I had not expected to empathize with the Hunting Beast.

"They found me out—my husband, his kingdom—and they condemned me. They said I was a villain. *How could you? How could you reject motherhood, the greatest gift of all?*" Her voice went high in imitation of the accusations. She shook her head, giving a grim, low laugh. "They said little of my cannibalism, though of course they were appalled. They didn't care so much about the children I'd devoured; they were more outraged by the motivation behind it. It is a depraved and immoral thing, they said, to reject what your body was made for. What *you* were made for, the only thing. A monster, they called me. So a monster I became.

"I ate them—all those terrible nightshades, and some of the fairies too, starting with my husband. I didn't stop, and my hunger has become such that I *won't* stop. How can I? I'm so angry, and the anger doesn't stop. I only ever wanted a *choice*."

She sighed with a full-body shudder and brought her hands to the dirt.

"This is my garden. Here the soil is sweet and imbued with ancient secrets. See these trees all around us? They were the first; this is the birthplace of the woods. Here I bury the bodies of those who forced others into roles they didn't desire, into lives they didn't want, in the same way I was forced into motherhood. You wanted me to be a mother? Well, look what I have created. *Look at my children, look how they grow*." She grinned, and it was crooked and sad and full of hunger, full of rage. "They made me a monster and my venom is more than poison—it corrupts. It gives them a second life—a terrible, strange second life, twisting them into grotesqueries, punished for eternity."

The Hunting Beast went silent, and I was silent too. Thinking, thinking, and feeling like I might cry. I didn't want to transform her as I had Nicasia, and I certainly didn't want to kill her. But I couldn't allow her to keep eating people—even if those people were not exactly innocent. I wouldn't exert my will or my wishes over her, or my control. The cycle must be broken now.

An idea had begun to form as she spoke, but I was hesitant. Once I offered, I couldn't take it back.

"Give your hunger to me," I said. I knew it was right, but that didn't mean it would be easy. I had changed so much already.

She blinked, her eyes as silvery-blue as the lightening sky. "My *hunger*?"

"Yes," I said firmly. No going back. "I will bear the burden for you. I will carry your anger with me, and honor it, but I won't appease it. I won't eat people—I promise."

She looked at me for a very long time.

"You will try," she said at last. "But I think you'll find my appetite is strong."

"I think you'll find my will is even stronger." Even as I said it, I wasn't really sure. But I would have to be—no more people would be eaten. I could handle it.

I hoped.

The Hunting Beast straightened, her hands on her knees. "And what will you give me in return, my sweet?"

"No," I said, shaking my head. "This is a gift, not an exchange. And giving it will set you free."

"I knew from the first that you were a clever one," she said, and I couldn't help it; I glowed at the compliment. "I believe you mean what you say."

"I do."

"Not all true things stay true forever, sweet. Remember that." The Hunting Beast stood, rising to her full height, and I stood too, looking up at her and into the sunlight. Setting my wolf-rib gently on the ground, I held out my hands to her, palms up. She seized them, her skin as soft as tissue paper. "All right then. Here is my hunger."

I held her stare over our clasped hands, and soon my fingertips began to grow hot enough to burn. The heat slashed through me, up my wrists and arms, an electric current narrowly missing my heart as it crested my shoulders and shot down through my torso, where it settled. Eventually the burning cooled to embers and then to nothing, and I was left with a little beast in my belly—stretching, yawning. It groaned, and we both heard the rumble but only I felt it, her hunger making itself known in me. The Hunting Beast dropped my hands and smiled ruefully, as if to say *good luck with that*.

"My name is Norah," she said, closing her eyes and breathing deeply. Already she looked older, creases around her eyes that had not been there before, her hair more gray than brilliant white. I wondered how long she would live now that her curse, such as it was, was lifted. Fairies lived a very long time, but the

Hunting Beast—Norah—must have been ancient. "And thank you for what you've done for me. If you ever need me . . . well, please don't try to find me. I'm grateful, but I really don't ever want to see you again." She leaned down and kissed my cheek. "Farewell, my sweet."

I remained there for a few minutes after she had disappeared into the mist of the morning, the sun bathing the garden in a warm pinkish glow. There was such intense suffering here, but gardens were meant to be tended, no? I vowed to return, to do what I could to turn terror into beauty. The little beast in me growled again, and I told it to hush. *You will never get what you want.* But I would feed it other things, like love and family. *Belonging.* With my little beast inside me, and my wolf-rib tight in my hand, I fled the garden of sorrow and hope, and ran all the back to the fairy village.

MY PARENTS WERE just promising the fairies that, yes, we would see them the following evening for the Hidden Moon's feast, and yes, we'd also attend the anniversary celebration of the fairy queen's three-hundred-year reign next month. For the first time since entering the woods I felt—truly *felt*—the heat of the sun on my face, comforting and calming, warming me all the way to my bones. It was morning, a new day full of possibility, and maybe there was a monster lurking in every shadow, but the idea of facing the hissing things hiding in the shadows didn't frighten me quite so badly now that we were together.

Together.

My favorite word of all.

30

≱⨠

Virginia

IT WAS A QUIET WALK BACK THROUGH THE WOODS. There was so much to say that none of us knew where to start. Ash supported me against his body so that I wasn't putting too much weight on my twisted ankle, while Gemma raced ahead and my mother trod silently behind. I was so tired, and yet my heart was bursting in my chest in a last push of adrenaline. Or simply a surge of relief.

I could just see our house through the empty patches between the branches and leaves when we finally caught up to Gemma. She was completely still, her entire body tense as she glanced at us over her shoulder.

"What's wrong?" I said, and my voice sounded like it came from very far away, even to my own ears. Just a few more steps and we'd be there, into the safety of the open lawn. My heart beat even faster, and Ash squeezed my hand reassuringly.

Gemma tilted her head. "I'm the guardian of the forest's edge."

I felt so cold all of a sudden, and the cold came from inside me. I had heard her fiercely whispered promise to the wolf as it lay dying, and I knew she would not break it. I could forbid her, but what was a mother's word against a daughter's destiny? And what kind of mother would I be to keep her from it? My fear was my own; no longer would I let it touch her, intentionally or not. I remembered the way she had taken the hairbrush and crushed it, how she had looked at me and said, *This is over now.* I had done it for my sake more than for hers, but she had paid the price.

"Yes," I said, and some of the tension left her shoulders. "But you're a teenage girl too, aren't you? A teenage girl who is still in school and will *not* be skipping out, who will need to learn how to glamour herself, as I'm not sure horns are allowed. And teenage girls need to sleep, and to eat, and maybe watch a little TV, no?"

She grinned, looking more fey than ever before. The horns suited her, and that green, mossy tint below her skin. "I suppose I *would* miss my Game Boy if I only slept and ate in the woods."

"What's a Game Boy?" Ash said, but Gemma was already too far ahead to answer, racing toward home.

"Come on," I said, laughing, and led him out of the woods at last.

I SHOWED ASH Gemma's Game Boy, as well as the Glass Room, and Gemma's school artwork on the fridge, and all the other mundane and magical things he'd missed. I had tried not to spend too much time imagining what our life would look like after the curse, in case it was never to be. But now—despite the fluttery joy and rightness of having him here—I felt uncertain and shy, as if we were getting to know each other all over again. Which, in a way, we *were*. We hadn't become strangers, never that, but he was a different man than the one who had taken my hand in the woods sixteen years ago, and I was different too. His smile came easily, bright as ever, but it cast a longer shadow than it used to, dark crescents beneath his eyes that wouldn't go away anytime soon. Physically, he was still adjusting to his body, sometimes smacking into doorjambs or dropping things because his hands didn't always obey his commands. It was difficult for him to make a fist, to find his grip on the slippery wood floors, to linger too long in the sun. Sometimes I would wake in the early morning to find him gone, and I would kick off the covers and rush outside before my panic could swallow me whole, and there he would be, pacing by the edge of the woods. I would slip my hand into his and walk with him, for as long as he needed, right there beside him.

Always.

The day after the curse was broken, I told Ash my theory about what had happened to his mother: that Nicasia had stolen his mother's body as she had intended to steal mine. Together we went to the witch's cottage and found her grotesque collection of still-beating hearts in the cellar. Ash found the heart that was hers—using the Touch he could *hear* it, understand its pulse as if it were speaking in words—and I rubbed his back in slow circles as he sat hunched over the jar, holding it in both hands as the truth of his mother was revealed at last.

As the heart spoke in its strange staccato language, Ash recounted it all to me: His mother *had* met a human in the woods, just as Nicasia had said, and she *had* made a bargain to exchange her baby for a spell to become human. But after Ash was born, the water sprite changed her mind. The human who had abandoned her had long since faded from her heart, and Ash had filled that space instead. When the sprite went back to Nicasia to cancel the deal, the witch was surprisingly gracious about the whole thing. In fact, Nicasia was so accepting of the spoiled contract that the two remained close friends. But Nicasia's body—her *stolen* body, far from the original—began again to deteriorate, and one day when the sprite came for a visit, the witch tore the heart right out of her chest, stepping into the body and adopting Ash as her own. After the bargain fell through, it had probably been Nicasia's plan all along to steal the sprite's body and take the child as an apprentice, her good-will toward the sprite only a ruse to get what she wanted. I shuddered, thinking how the same thing might have happened to my own mother in time.

The story finished, we watched as the heart in the jar ceased to beat. Finally at rest; finally, some peace. Ash took the heart back with us through the woods and we placed it in a carved silver urn.

"Thank you," Ash said, as we stepped back and gazed to-gether at the urn on the windowsill in the kitchen, the silver sparkling in the late afternoon light. He took my hand in his, brought it to his lips and kissed the center of my palm. "Thank you for helping me, Virginia. I promise there will be no more looking back now. Only forward."

I smiled, the center of my palm tingling.

I had pictured us living on the fantastical *other* side of the woods, where there was plenty of light but not a single shadow, but that was impossible now. (Plus, we were not sure it even existed.) Gemma was a guardian of the forest, and I was the heir of the Great Ensorceller of the Hidden Moon. A title that meant little to her or to me, but a deal had been made and I had vowed to keep it.

"I CAN'T STAY."

These were the first words my mother said since the fairies had released her from whatever strange cage they'd kept her in, and the sound of her voice startled me more than the words themselves. It was the morning after the curse was broken—the rest of time would be measured by how much time had passed since the curse, I reckoned—and the three of us sat in the kitchen sipping the peppermint tea I'd made. (Gemma was already out in the woods, wolf-rib in hand, guarding the forest's edge.) Ash and I both jumped, setting down our teacups with a clatter.

"What?" I said, relieved she had finally broken her silence. I'd begun to worry, though I wasn't sure what to do.

"I've had just about enough of the woods and the fairies and whatever other monsters live there," she said, and I realized with some shock that she was on the verge of tears. Her eyes watered, but, ever restrained, she didn't let the tears drop. "I'm done, Gigi. I'm done."

I nodded, sensing, as she must have too, that the woods were ready at last to let her go. When I was young and wondered why we simply didn't move away, she had explained to me that the woods were only here *because* of her. Because of her desire for a place where she could be free. The woods would have followed her wherever she went.

But something had changed. *She* had changed—we all had—and it was just as much to do with her letting go of the woods as the woods letting go of her. She didn't need them anymore.

"I understand," I said, and she glanced up at me sharply. Her cheeks had grown so thin.

I remembered the story she'd told me once, about how she'd heard a baby crying in the woods, about how hard it had been to get pregnant with me. I was wanted, I was loved, even if she didn't love me the way I wanted her to. Displays of affection didn't come easily, so used was she to disappointment, afraid to let anyone get close, and she was stubborn when it came to what she thought was best. She wasn't a *bad* mother, though certainly a difficult one. *I love you,* I wanted to say, but didn't. Maybe I was a difficult daughter too.

"Where will you go now?" I said instead. In trying so hard to keep me away from all of it, she'd ensured I'd be tied to the woods forever. But *she* didn't have to be. She was free.

She released my hand and tucked hers in her lap. "Oh, I don't know. I've been traveling so much trying to find that mirror of yours"—here, she eyed Ash, not disdainfully, but not fondly either—"and now I have contacts all over the world. In Paris I—I met someone. About two and a half years ago. She restores antique furniture, the most beautiful craftsmanship I've ever seen. I told her she didn't have to wait for me, but . . . Well, I hope she did. I haven't called her yet."

More things I hadn't known about my mother, that she had someone waiting for her. I found I didn't resent her for keeping it from me—maybe I would have, when I was younger, when she still insisted I return to college and live a life I didn't want—but not now. Now I was just happy for her, though I could admit that part of it was because I was happy myself.

"Ma, what are you waiting for? Go call her right now."

My mother shrugged, and dropped a spoonful of sugar into her tea, stirring it round and round. After a minute of stirring without drinking it, she gave another tiny shrug and left the table; I heard her footsteps on the stairs. And then her voice, muffled through the floor, as she used the phone in my office—previously *her* office—to make a long-distance call. Ash put his arm around me and pulled me close.

"You won't have to do it alone," he said, and I felt the truth of it in my bones.

"I know." The glare of the light through the window was so bright that I couldn't see much beyond the glass, but just because I couldn't see the woods didn't mean that they weren't there. They'd always be there, a part of him and a part of me too. "I know."

* * *

GEMMA SAT ON the stool in front of the mirror while I brushed her hair. She'd asked me to do it, not long after our return home. We'd quickly fallen back into our old routine, one hundred strokes before bed—well, bed for me—but it was different now, as it should be. Nothing was stolen or lost, nothing taken by force. It was simply a quiet moment of togetherness. The *shhh, shhh, shhh* of the bristles along her scalp was magical in itself, a lullaby gently reminding us of how far we had come. *Hush now. It's all right. We made it through. And we'll make it through the next stretch of the labyrinth too.*

I was so concentrated on my task, working carefully around her horns, that it took me a while to notice that Gemma had her eyes on me in the mirror, unblinking as she tracked my movements with the precision of a practiced huntress. When our gazes met she smiled, showing just how pointy her canine teeth had become.

"I think I understand now why Dad wanted to eat your heart."

In my surprise, I yanked the brush through her hair and it snagged on a tangle, her head jerking back. An accident truly, but she didn't cry out or complain. She simply lowered her chin again, keeping her eyes on me the whole time.

"I can hear them now, all four of your hearts," she said thoughtfully, tilting her head like she was listening. Listening closely. *Hush.* "Thump-*thump,* thump-*thump,* thump-*thump.* Like rabbits running through a field. A drove of delicious, juicy rabbits."

Silence, a stalled breath. Then Gemma laughed, and I stood with the brush hovering over her hair, my mind empty but for the sound.

"Don't worry, Mama," she said, and hopped off the stool. She leaned over—no need even to rise on tiptoe anymore, so much had she grown in the two years we'd been apart—and kissed my cheek. "I would never let anyone eat your heart. Even me."

Her kiss tingled on my skin. I knew she meant what she'd said, which only made it that much more unsettling that she felt the need to promise such a thing. I watched her skip from the room, wolf-rib ever in hand, knowing that she would not sleep at all tonight. It had only taken a month to transform herself into a nocturnal creature, staying out until dawn before crashing hard in the early morning, and only then for a few hours, awake and energized in time to go to school. I didn't know how long I'd stood there after she had gone, raking my palm over the coarse bristles of the brush, remarkably similar to the one she'd crushed. She'd found it in the basement, or so she'd said; I wasn't entirely sure it wasn't without a slight Touch of Magic. A spell to calm her, maybe, in preparation for the long night. Eventually, a sigh in the doorway made me look up.

It was Ash, leaning against the frame, his dark bangs falling into his eyes. My heart spun at the sight of him and I set the brush down. Wordlessly he held out a hand to me, and normally I shook my head, a gentle refusal; this was part of the routine now too, after the brushing was done. He'd follow Gemma into the dark, running beneath the clot of branches above, forgetting for a little while who and what he was. He'd return sometime after midnight, sweaty and smelling of moss, and when he crawled into bed I would bury my face in his chest. Secretly I waited for him, unable to sleep until he was back safely beside me. Until he was mine again.

But tonight I looked at him, and I could still hear Gemma's laughter in my ears. The echo of an echo, rolling endlessly. I crossed the room and took his hand.

I just had time to catch the edge of his grin before he turned, tugging me with him down the stairs and through the quiet shop, down a row of antiques towering in the dim. Soon we were out the door and into the open, running across the lawn. I stumbled, just a little, but he didn't let me fall; a surge of what could only have been magic passed from his palm to mine. I felt electrified; truly awake in a way I had not felt in a long time. The air was pleasantly cool, the moon a bright sliver; the trees loomed ahead, and curiously I felt my four little hearts race out ahead of me, eager for the coming night. If there were monsters, well, so what? Maybe I still didn't know exactly what a monster was, but I knew how to love them, *my* monsters, and sometimes that was enough.

Hand in hand, Ash and I followed the glitter of our daughter's laughter into the dark, into the woods.

Acknowledgments

I began the earliest draft of this book in late 2019, and through some combination of pandemic anxiety, distraction, and low confidence, I almost didn't finish writing it. It exists now due to Penelope Burns, my awesome agent and number-one champion. Thank you for your encouragement and guidance. As always, I could not have done any of this without you.

Thank you to my editor, Anne Groell, who took all my fuzzy ideas for this story and sharpened them to a point. I'm so grateful to you. Working with you is truly a dream.

Thank you to the entire team at Del Rey: Tori Henson, Hope Heathcock, Ashleigh Heaton, Emily Isayeff, Sabrina Shen, David Moench, Keith Clayton, Scott Shannon, Jordan Pace, Adaobi Maduko, Tricia Narwani, Alex Larned, Cassie Gonzales, Regina Flath, and Ayesha Shibli. You are the best team a writer could ask for.

Thank you to everyone in my life who keeps me going, from my longtime besties to my friends at CLPL. I'm so lucky to know so many wonderful and supportive people.

I would be lost without my family. Dad, Mama, Kara, and J.D., you're a bunch of absolute weirdos and I love you.

Frank, you are my favorite person. Thank you for keeping me going and for believing in me always.

About the Author

ALYSSA WEES is the acclaimed author of *The Waking Forest* and *Nocturne*. She grew up writing stories about her Beanie Babies in between ballet lessons. She earned a BA in English from Creighton University and an MFA in fiction writing from Columbia College Chicago. Currently she works as an assistant librarian in youth services at an awesome public library. She lives in the Chicagoland area with her husband and their two cats.

alyssawees.com
Instagram: @alyssa_wees

About the Type

This book was set in Berkeley, a typeface designed by Tony Stan (1917–88) in the early 1980s. It was inspired by, and is a variation on, University of California Old Style, created in the late 1930s by Frederic William Goudy (1865–1947) for the exclusive use of the University of California at Berkeley. The present face, in fact, bears influences of a number of Goudy's fonts, including Kennerley, Goudy Old Style, and Deepdene. Berkeley is notable for both its legibility and its lightness.